WAIF

C.L. STEGALL

Printed in the United States of America.

ISBN: 978-0-9994600-6-1

First Printing, 2026.

Published by Studio Valensi productions
Cover Idea and Design by C.L. Stegall, Cover by Safeer Ahmed.
Book design and formatting by C.L. Stegall.

www.CLStegall.com

For all the waifs. You survived. That matters.

WAIF

CHAPTER 1

Paris arrived in Daytona late at night, four days before she would find herself sitting in Brianna Van Demir's living room, spilling her sins to strangers.

But she didn't know that yet. All she knew was that she was running, and that the bastard would send someone after her. Someone relentless. Someone dedicated. The Magistrate was not a man who forgave. Three thousand years of ruling the Valensi had taught him that mercy was weakness with better marketing.

She set the cruise control on the stolen Cadillac and glanced back at Robert.

His eyes were closed, his head lolling against the armrest of the rear passenger door. He'd been a good-sized fellow, handsome enough, with a charming smile and a voice like warm honey. Possibly that was what had led her to ask for a ride rather than procuring transportation of her own. Things would have been so much simpler if he'd just driven her where she'd asked to go.

But no. Robert had wanted something in return. Had insisted upon it, in fact. That charming smile changed entirely when she'd declined. His hands had found her throat before his brain had registered what a profoundly stupid decision that was.

Now she had to find someplace to dump the damned body.

Paris merged onto Interstate 4 from the 95, outside of Daytona, and maintained a speed a little under the limit. No need to invite unwanted attention. The incident at the airport had already left much to be desired, and she'd learned long ago how to roll with the punches. Still, the last thing she needed was some curious cop pulling over a teenage girl in a stolen Cadillac, only to discover dead Robert cooling in the back seat.

Teenage girl. She almost laughed at that. She was a hundred and thirty-five years old, and she still got carded at bars.

The glowing blue LED of the dashboard clock read eleven-thirty. Time was on her side, at least for the moment. She checked the GPS and plotted her next steps, her mind running through contingencies the way it always did. Survival wasn't luck. It was preparation meeting opportunity, and she'd had over a century to hone both.

Within minutes, she exited the freeway onto East New York Avenue, then headed north toward Gasline Road. The area grew darker, more rural, the kind of place where a body might not be found for days. Weeks, if she was lucky.

She found a suitable spot—quiet, unlit, thick with trees—and pulled the Cadillac to the side of the road.

Quick, she reminded herself. Be quick about this.

She scanned the road for headlights. Nothing. The night was still, save for the chorus of insects that didn't give a damn about murder or fugitives or ancient Valensi politics.

Paris stepped out of the car and opened the rear door. Robert was heavier than he looked, but she'd been stronger than she looked since 1895. She hauled his body from the back seat and carried him a dozen yards into the woods, his limbs dragging through the underbrush. She didn't bother being gentle. Robert had forfeited gentleness when he'd wrapped his hands around her throat.

She dropped him in a shallow depression between two pines and stood there for a moment, looking down at what remained of a man who'd made one very bad choice.

"You should have just given me the ride," she said.

The insects answered. Robert did not.

Within minutes, Paris was back on I-4, the Cadillac's headlights cutting through the Florida darkness. Dead Robert was already fading into memory, one more shadow in a lifetime of black moments.

She had forty-eight hours before word of Dawn's death reached the Magistrate. Perhaps less. The witnesses in Paris—the city, not her—would report what they'd seen: two young women fighting, one of them killing the other. The fact that the dead one all but disappeared upon death was enough to send up a dozen red flags to the Hierarchy. They wouldn't know why. They wouldn't care. All that mattered was that she had broken the most sacred law of her kind.

She had killed one of her own.

The Magistrate would send his best. And his best would find her eventually. That was simply the math of the situation. You didn't hide from a three-thousand-year-old telepath forever. You simply delayed the inevitable.

Paris pressed the accelerator a little harder and watched the Florida night blur past.

Something would have to change. Because she was not ready to die.

Not yet.

CHAPTER 2

(1887-1888, Bristol, England — Age 7)

The shouting began after dinner.

The girl who would one day call herself Paris huddled in the crawlspace beneath the stairs, her small body wedged between the wooden slats and the cold stone wall. She pressed her hands over her ears, but it did little to muffle the screaming from above. Father had been drinking since he'd returned home the day before. Mother had finally stopped cowering.

That was the problem. Mother had stopped cowering.

The house they rented was a narrow two-story building in the Seamills area of Bristol, what some called a duplex—two families sharing one common wall from top to bottom. The neighbors could certainly hear. They always could. They never did anything about it.

The girl couldn't remember what had started it this time. Probably about money. Or the way Mother had looked at Father when he'd demanded more ale. It didn't matter. With Father, it never took much. A wrong word. A wrong glance. A wrong silence.

She crawled along the base of the stairs, searching for a better hiding spot, somewhere the noise couldn't reach her. That was when she heard the footsteps above—heavy and stumbling, then lighter ones, quicker, backing away.

"Don't you dare—" Mother's voice, high and desperate.

"You'll not speak to me that way, woman!"

The girl froze.

A scream pierced the air—sharp, short, terrible.

She whirled around in time to see her mother falling backward down the stairs, arms flailing helplessly against nothing. The woman's body tumbled toward her, a chaos of limbs and fabric and golden hair, and then there was a sound—a wet, awful pop—and Mother landed in a heap at the girl's feet.

The scream had stopped. Everything had stopped.

Mother's neck was bent at an angle that necks were not meant to bend. She stared up at the ceiling, but she wouldn't be seeing anything anymore.

"Mummy?" The girl dropped to her knees. "Mummy, wake up."

She shook her mother's shoulder. The body moved, but the woman did not. The head lolled obscenely, wrong in every way.

"Mummy, please. Please wake up."

Nothing. Nothing but those empty eyes and that broken neck and the silence that had swallowed her mother's voice forever.

The girl looked up.

Her father stood at the top of the stairs. He was breathing hard, his face flushed from drink and exertion, and he was looking at her. Not at his wife's body. Not at what he had done.

At her.

His face held that same expression she had seen so many times before—that gut-wrenching, blaming, contemptuous glare. As if she were the cause of all his misery. As if her very existence was a wound that would never heal.

He took a step down toward her.

Some secret thing snapped inside the girl then. As real and sudden and irreversible as the snap of her mother's neck. She felt it happen—felt it break loose and fall away, some last tether to childhood, to safety, to the belief that parents were supposed to protect you.

Her stomach clenched. Nausea rose in her throat.

Her father took another step.

The girl bolted.

She was through the door and into the early autumn night before she could think, before she could breathe, before she could do anything but run. Her bare feet slapped against the cold cobblestones. Her lungs burned. Behind her, she thought she heard her father's voice, shouting something, but she didn't stop. She couldn't stop.

She ran until the shouting faded.

She ran until her legs gave out.

She ran until she was alone in the Bristol darkness, with nothing but the clothes on her back and the memory of her mother's empty eyes.

She did not cry. She was too terrified for tears.

But somewhere deep inside her, in that newly broken place, a decision took root. It was not a conscious thought—she was only seven—but it was there nonetheless, hard and sharp and permanent as a scar.

She would never go back.

She would survive.

No matter what it took.

CHAPTER 3

(1887-1888, Bristol, England – Age 7-8)

The first night on the streets, she slept beneath a pile of refuse behind a tannery, the stench so foul it made her eyes water. But the smell kept others away, and that was what mattered. She had already learned—in the span of a single terrible evening—that being alone was safer than being found.

She had no name anymore. The name her mother had called her, the name her father had spat like a curse—she left it behind with everything else. She was only a girl now. A small, hungry, frightened girl with nothing but the clothes on her back and a hole in her chest where her heart used to be.

Bristol in the autumn of 1887 was not kind to strays.

The city sprawled along the River Avon, a maze of narrow streets and cramped buildings, of factories belching smoke and tenements packed with families who had little enough for themselves.

Charity existed, but it came with questions. The local church offered soup and shelter, but the vicar pressed her about her parents, about where she'd come from, about why a child her age was wandering alone. She slipped out before he could summon the authorities. She would not go back to her father. She would die first.

So, she learned to survive on her own.

The days blurred together. She begged when she could, stealing glances at the faces of passersby, learning which ones might spare a penny and which ones would spit at her or worse. She stole when she had to—a bruised apple from a cart, a heel of bread from an unattended basket, a tattered blanket from a refuse bin. She learned to move through the city like a ghost, unseen and unremarked, another piece of human debris in the gutters of empire.

She was not alone in this. There were others—children like her, adults too, people who lived in the spaces between respectability, who slept in doorways and alleys and under bridges. Most of them ignored her. Some tried to take what little she had. A few, precious few, showed her kindness.

Marty found her three months into her exile, shivering behind a pub in Totterdown.

"You're doing it wrong," he said, crouching down to her level. He was older than her—eleven, twelve—with a sharp face and quick glances and the kind of confidence that came from knowing exactly how the world worked. "Huddling up like that. You'll freeze your arse off before morning."

She stared at him, too cold and tired to respond.

"Come on, then." He jerked his head toward the darkness. "I know a better spot. Warmer. Safer too."

She didn't move.

"Suit yourself," he said, shrugging. He started to walk away, then paused and looked back. "You want to die out here, that's your choice. But it's a stupid one."

She followed him.

Marty had a filthy mouth—every other word was "fuck" or "bloody" or worse—but beneath the gutter language was a genuine kindness. He shared his food when he had it. He taught her which streets to avoid, which shopkeepers were easy marks, which corners belonged to gangs who would gut a child for a copper penny. He had a friend named Liz, a girl of fourteen with sad eyes and a nervous laugh, and the three of them formed a strange little family in those cold months.

Liz hated profanity. The irony was not lost on anyone—she sold herself to survive, letting men old enough to be her grandfather press their weight down on her in exchange for coins, but the word "fuck" made her blush and turn away. The girl who would become Paris never understood that, how a word could wound more than an act, but she kept her confusion to herself. She didn't want to lose a friend over something so small.

Liz used her youth and natural beauty, and she was indeed pretty, to manipulate men to get what she needed. It was simple survival. She, herself, had always been mousy. Small for her age, mousy-brown hair. Her eyes were a nice green, but she felt that was her only decent feature. She was certainly no Liz.

Marty taught her to steal properly.

"It's all about the setup," he explained one grey afternoon, watching a gentleman in a fine coat chat with a young woman across the street. "You don't grab and run. That's how you get caught. You create a distraction. You make them look somewhere else. Then you take what you need and disappear before they know anything's missing."

She learned. She failed at first—once dropping a wallet right at the mark's feet, nearly getting her skull cracked for her trouble—but she learned. Her small size was an advantage. She could slip beneath notice, move through crowds like water through fingers. Within weeks, she was better than Liz. Within months, she was pretty much as good as Marty himself.

They worked as a team when the opportunity arose. Marty would provide the distraction—a stumble, a collision, a loud argument—and she would swoop in low, her little hands quick and clever. The money kept them fed. It kept them alive.

For a while, that was enough.

The rain had been falling all morning on the day everything ended.

The girl spotted the mark first—a tall gentleman in a tan overcoat, standing beneath an umbrella while he chatted up a young woman in blue. His wallet was visible in his outer pocket, practically begging to be taken.

"Alright," Marty said, nodding toward the target. "I'll come from the south, bump him hard enough to shift the umbrella. He'll get wet and flustered. That's when you move."

She nodded.

"Liz, you come running up after I start apologizing. Tell me our mother's waiting, she's getting upset. That gives us all cover for a clean exit."

Liz nodded too, her face pale but determined.

They moved into position.

The girl had to wait for a carriage to pass before crossing the street, the horses kicking mud as they went. She darted across and edged closer to the target, watching her partners from the corner of her eye. The rain pattered against her thin coat. Her heart beat steady and calm. She had done this dozens of times.

Marty made his move.

He crashed into the gentleman with convincing clumsiness, knocking the umbrella aside. Rain pelted the man's face, and he cried out in outrage, grabbing for Marty with one hand while trying to right his umbrella with the other. In that moment of chaos, the girl's hand slipped into the coat pocket and retrieved the wallet. Clean. Perfect.

She stepped back, already turning to leave, when she noticed the young woman in blue staring directly at her.

Not at Marty. Not at the commotion.

At her.

The girl curtsied—an absurd gesture, but it was all she could think to do—and moved off down the street, passing Liz as she ran toward the scene.

"Marty! Marty, Mother is waiting! She's ever so cross with you!"

The gentleman had Marty by the arm now, shouting about reckless children and lackluster parents. Liz grabbed Marty's other hand, pulling, trying to free him.

"Come on! We have to go!"

What happened next would replay in the girl's memory for over a century.

Marty jerked free of the gentleman's grip—finally, violently—and the motion sent both him and Liz tumbling backward into the muddy street. Into the path of an oncoming carriage.

The horses came first. She saw their hooves flash past, impossibly close to her friends' sprawled bodies. For one breathless moment, she thought they would be spared.

Then the wheels.

The first wheel caught Marty's arm, wrenching it into an angle that made the girl's stomach lurch. The second wheel rolled over Liz—over her throat, her shoulder—and the sound it made, the wet crushing sound, was something no amount of time would ever erase.

Screams erupted. The gentleman dropped his umbrella. The carriage driver hauled on his reins, far too late.

Marty and Liz lay motionless in the mud.

Blood was spreading beneath Liz's head, mixing with the rain and the muck. Her eyes were open, but they saw nothing. Marty's arm was bent wrong, terribly wrong, and he wasn't moving either.

The girl stood frozen on the sidewalk, the stolen wallet still clutched in her hand.

People rushed past her toward the bodies. Coats were being laid over her friends. Someone was shouting for a doctor. Someone else was weeping.

She should go to them. She should kneel beside them, hold their hands, tell them it would be all right.

But it wouldn't be all right. She had learned that lesson in the instant her mother's neck had broken at the bottom of the stairs. You couldn't *fix* Death. Death was death.

And if she stayed—if the Bobbies came and asked questions—they would find out who she was. They would send her back to her father. Or worse.

She ran.

She didn't know how long she walked after that. The rain soaked through her clothes, chilling her to the bone, but she barely felt it. The wallet was still in her hand—she threw it away eventually, keeping only the few bills and coins inside—and her feet carried her through streets she didn't recognize, past faces that blurred into nothing.

When she finally stopped, she was behind a pub she'd never seen before, huddled beneath an overhang barely wide enough to keep the rain off. And there, alone in the darkness, she let herself cry.

She cried for Marty, who had saved her life with his kindness and his foul mouth and his clever schemes.

She cried for Liz, who had blushed at dirty words but sold her body without complaint.

She cried for herself, for the loneliness that stretched ahead of her like an endless road.

And when the tears were spent, when she had nothing left, something else rose up inside her. Harder than grief. Colder than the rain.

She would survive.

She didn't know how. She didn't know what it would cost. But she would survive, because the alternative was lying broken in the mud like Marty and Liz, and she refused—refused—to let that be her end.

She wiped her face with the back of her hand, pulled her soaked coat tighter around her thin shoulders, and walked on into the night.

The second winter came early and without mercy.

By December of 1888, the girl had been alone for nearly a year. She had survived—stealing, begging, sleeping in doorways and under bridges, eating whatever scraps she could find—but survival had worn her down to bone and gristle. She was small for her age, malnourished, hollow-eyed. The cold had settled into her chest and wouldn't leave.

She had found a spot beneath the eaves of a shop in Totterdown, a narrow space where the wind couldn't quite reach. She had layered herself in every scrap of fabric she could scavenge—torn blankets, discarded rags, a man's coat three sizes too big—but it wasn't enough. Nothing was enough.

In her numb fingers, she clutched a photograph.

She had stolen it months ago from a vendor's stall—a picture of a cityscape, all glittering lights and grand buildings. Paris, the caption read. The City of Light. She had never seen anything so beautiful. She stared at it every night before sleep took her, imagining a place where the streets were warm and the lights never went out and no one had to die in the mud.

Foolish dreams. But they were all she had.

The cold pressed in around her. Her breath came in shallow rasps. She couldn't feel her feet anymore, and the shivering had stopped—which some distant part of her mind knew was a bad sign.

This is it, she thought. This is where I die.

She wasn't afraid. She was too tired for fear. She held the photograph and looked at the lights and waited for the darkness to take her.

"She's a feisty little thing."

The voice came from somewhere above her. A woman's voice, sharp and cultured, with an accent that spoke of education and breeding.

The girl forced her eyes open.

Two figures stood over her, silhouettes against the winter night. A woman and a man, both dressed too finely for this part of the city. They were looking at her with expressions she couldn't quite read—not pity, exactly. More calculating.

"She's a waif," the man said. He cocked his head, and his gaze fell to the photograph in her trembling fingers. "Still, she's got a lot of fire for one her size. She has... potential."

"I've seen her before," the woman said. "She knocked the hell out of an older, much bigger boy who tried to take her matches last month—put him right on his arse."

The man arched an eyebrow. The girl thought she should speak up, but she wasn't sure it would matter. She was dying. What difference did words make?

The man crouched in front of her. His face was older than her father's, but there was a strangeness about it—something too smooth, too still. His eyes caught the faint light and held it in ways that eyes shouldn't.

"What's your name, child?" he asked.

She should have answered. She should have given him her real name, the one her mother had used, the one she had abandoned in the streets of Bristol.

Instead, she looked at the photograph in her hand.

"Paris," she whispered.

The world went black.

CHAPTER 4

(1888, Bristol, England – Age 8)

She woke to warmth, which meant she was dead.

That was the only explanation. The cold had taken her, and now she was somewhere else—Heaven, or whatever came after. She had never been particularly religious, not even before her mother died, but she had always assumed there was *something* on the other side. A place where the chill couldn't reach. A place where little girls didn't starve in the streets.

Then she opened her eyes and realized she was in an alley.

Not the same alley. This one was darker, narrower, tucked between two tall buildings that blocked out most of the night sky. She was propped against a brick wall, wrapped in heavy clothing—a coat, far finer than anything she had ever worn. The fabric was thick and warm, and it smelled faintly of perfume and a metallic scent she couldn't quite identify.

The woman stood a few feet away, watching her.

"Back with us, then," the woman said. Same cultured voice, same sharp accent. In the dim light, her features were clearer now—pale skin, high cheekbones, black hair swept back from a face that seemed ageless. Not old, not young. In between. *Other.*

The man stood beside her, equally still. They didn't shift their weight or fidget or breathe visibly. They simply *were*, like statues that had learned to speak.

"Where—" The girl's voice cracked. Her throat was raw, her lips chapped. "Where am I?"

"Safe," the man said. "For the moment."

"We brought you somewhere quiet," the woman added. "Somewhere we could... talk."

The girl's survival instincts, honed by a year on the streets, screamed at her to run. But her legs wouldn't obey. She was too weak, too drained. Whatever reserves had kept her alive this long had been spent. She couldn't have fled if her life depended on it.

And it might. It very well might.

"What do you want?" she asked.

The woman smiled. It was not a comforting expression. It was predatory. It made the girl think of cats watching mice.

"We want to offer you a choice," the woman said. "But first, you need to see."

She turned and walked deeper into the alley. The man followed. After a moment's hesitation, the girl pushed herself up on trembling legs and stumbled after them, the too-large coat dragging on the ground behind her. It took her more time to cover a few feet than she would've ever imagined. Her little body was depleted. If she were to guess, she only had an hour or so to live. She slowly managed to follow the two strangers.

The alley bent around a corner, and there she saw him.

A man—a human man—slumped against the far wall. His head was tilted back, his mouth slack. His throat had been torn open. Not cut—*torn*, as if by an animal, ragged edges of flesh gaping wide. Blood had pooled beneath him, black in the darkness, and more of it streaked down his chest, soaking his shirt.

The girl stopped.

She should have screamed. She should have run. That was what normal children did when they saw a corpse, when they saw *murder*. But she was not a normal child anymore. A year on the streets had burned that out of her. She had seen death before. She had seen her own mother's body crumpled at the bottom of a staircase. She had seen her friends crushed beneath carriage wheels.

She looked at the dead man, and she felt... nothing. No horror. No revulsion. Just a cold, distant curiosity.

"You did this," she said. It wasn't a question.

"Yes," the woman said. No denial. No excuse. Simply acknowledgment.

"Why?"

The man answered this time. "Because we were hungry."

The girl turned to look at them. Really look at them. She saw how still they were, how pale. She saw the faint smear of red at the corner of the woman's mouth—blood, the same blood that painted the dead man's throat.

"What are you?" she asked.

The woman smiled again, and this time she let her lips part fully. Her teeth were white and even, except for four—the canines, top and bottom, which extended past the others, sharp and gleaming.

"We are what humans fear in the dark," she said. "We are what hides in the shadows and feeds on the unwary. We are very, very old, little waif. And we are offering you a chance to become like us."

The girl stared at those teeth. At the blood. At the corpse cooling against the wall.

She should have been terrified. Some part of her—some small, distant part that still remembered being a child with a mother and a home—was screaming at her to run, to flee, to get as far away from these monsters as her legs could carry her.

But that part was quiet now. Muffled. Buried beneath a year of cold and hunger and loss.

What she felt instead was something else entirely.

They killed him, she thought. They killed him as easily as swatting a fly. And nothing can touch them. Nothing can hurt them.

They are strong.

"What happens if I say no?" she asked.

The woman's smile didn't waver. "Then we leave you here. You go back to the streets. Back to the cold. Back to starving and freezing and dying by inches." She paused. "You were nearly dead when we found you. You won't survive another week."

The girl knew it was true. She had felt death's fingers closing around her, had nearly welcomed them. Another week? She would be lucky to last another night.

"And if I say yes?"

"Then you come with us," the man said. "You learn. You grow. You become more than a gutter rat waiting to die."

"You become *powerful*," the woman added. "Strong enough that no one will ever hurt you again. No one will ever take anything from you again."

The girl thought of her father's face at the top of the stairs. The contempt on his face. The way he had looked at her like she was nothing, less than nothing, a mistake he wished he could unmake.

She thought of Marty and Liz, broken in the mud, their lives snuffed out in an instant by nothing more than bad luck and a passing carriage.

She thought of herself—small, weak, starving, alone.

And she thought of these creatures standing before her, with their sharp teeth and their cold eyes and their utter, absolute certainty. They had killed a man and felt nothing. They had torn out his throat and drunk his blood, and they stood there now as calmly as if they had done nothing more remarkable than take tea.

That is power, she thought. That is survival.

That is what I want to be.

"What's your name?" the man asked again, as if sensing her decision.

She thought of the photograph, probably lost now in the snow. The glittering city she would never see. The dream she had clung to when she had nothing else.

"Paris," she said. "My name is Paris."

The woman extended her hand. Her fingers were pale and slender and surprisingly warm to the touch.

"Welcome, little Paris," she said. "My name is Ophelia. This is Alldred. And your new life begins now."

Paris looked at the dead man one last time. At the blood. At the torn throat and the vacant eyes.

Then she took Ophelia's hand and let the monsters lead her away into the night.

She did not look back.

There was nothing behind her worth seeing. Only death and cold and the memory of everyone she had ever loved being taken from her. The streets of Bristol had taught her one lesson above all others, and she had learned it well:

Survival was all that mattered.

And she would do whatever it took to survive.

CHAPTER 5

(*Present*)

The hotel was a mid-range affair on International Drive, the kind of place that catered to tourists and business travelers and asked few questions of either. Paris had chosen it precisely for its anonymity. No one remembered faces at places like this. They processed credit cards and handed out key cards and forgot you existed the moment you stepped into the elevator.

She parked the Cadillac in the back lot, away from the security cameras, and sat for a moment in the darkness. The adrenaline from disposing of Robert had faded, leaving behind a hollow exhaustion. She needed rest. She needed to feed. She needed to think.

What she had instead was a stolen car, a dead man's wallet, and forty-eight hours before the Magistrate learned what she had done.

One problem at a time, she told herself. That's how you survive.

She grabbed her bag from the passenger seat—a small duffel she'd packed in Paris before everything went to hell—and made her way toward the lobby entrance. The Florida air was thick and humid, even at this hour, a far cry from the cool autumn nights of France. She found she didn't mind. Warmth was a luxury she had learned to appreciate in the decades since a frozen Bristol winter had nearly killed her.

The lobby was bright and sterile, all polished tile and artificial plants. A young man stood behind the front desk, early twenties, with the kind of eager expression that suggested he was new to the job and still believed in customer service. His name tag read LIAM.

He noticed her the moment she walked through the door.

Paris was used to that. She had been attractive for decades now—not the soft, approachable beauty of a girl next door, but sharper, more dangerous. The kind of beauty that made men stare and women look away. She had learned to wield it like a weapon, and tonight, she needed every weapon she had.

"Good evening," Liam said, his smile brightening as she approached the desk. His gaze flickered over her and she watched him swallow. "Checking in?"

"I don't have a reservation," Paris said. She let a hint of vulnerability creep into her voice, a slight tremor that suggested exhaustion and need. "I know it's late. I was hoping you might have something available."

"Let me check." His fingers moved across the keyboard, but his eyes kept drifting back to her. She could hear his heartbeat quickening, could smell the faint musk of attraction rising from his skin. Humans were so predictable. So *easy*. "We've got a few rooms open. How many nights?"

"I'm not sure yet. A few days, at least." She leaned against the counter, letting the motion draw his attention to her nubile young body. "I'm in a bit of a difficult situation, to be honest. I left home in a hurry. My credit cards are... complicated."

Liam's brow furrowed. "We do require a card on file for incidentals—"

"I understand." Paris reached across the counter and touched his hand, a brush of her fingers against his knuckles. His breath caught. "I was hoping we might work something out. I'm very good at... showing my appreciation."

The implication hung in the air between them. She watched the conflict play across his face—professionalism warring with desire, policy warring with opportunity. It was quite obvious which would win. It always did.

"I, uh..." He glanced around the empty lobby. "I suppose I could put the room under my employee discount. Just for a few nights. Until you get things sorted out."

Paris smiled. It was real, warm and grateful, and it made Liam's cheeks flush red.

"You're very kind," she said. "I won't forget it."

She wouldn't. Liam had no idea what he was getting himself into, but he had solved an immediate problem, and that earned him a measure of her goodwill. Whether that goodwill would be enough to save him if things went badly remained to be seen.

He processed the room—fourth floor, end of the hall, quiet and private—and handed her the key card with fingers that trembled slightly.

"Room 412," he said. "If you need anything, I'm here until six."

"I might take you up on that." She let her fingers linger on his as she took the card. "What time do you get off?"

The double meaning was not lost on him. His flush deepened.

"Six," he repeated. "I could... I mean, if you wanted company..."

"I'll think about it." She turned and walked toward the elevators, feeling his gaze on her back the whole way. She added an extra sway to her hips, a small reward for his cooperation.

The elevator doors closed, and the smile fell from her face.

Pathetic, she thought. But useful. Liam would cover for her if questions were asked, would lie to protect her if it came to that. Men always did, when they thought there was a chance of getting what they wanted. And if the Magistrate's hunters came calling, Liam would remember the grateful, vulnerable girl who had needed his help—not the predator who had manipulated him from the moment she walked through the door.

Paris was good at this. She had been doing it for a very long time.

The room was small but clean, with a queen bed and a window overlooking the parking lot. Paris dropped her bag on the floor and went straight to the bathroom, stripping off her clothes as she walked. She needed to wash away the night—Robert's blood, the swamp mud, the lingering stench of fear and death.

The shower was hot, nearly scalding, and she stood beneath the spray until her skin turned pink. She watched the water swirl down the drain and thought about her next moves. Moves that had to be made because she had made a choice.

The wrong choice, a voice whispered in her mind. You killed her for nothing. All was already lost.

She pushed the thought away. She couldn't afford doubt. Not now. Doubt was a luxury for people who had options, and Paris had exactly one option: keep moving, keep surviving, keep running until she figured out what came next.

She turned off the water and stepped out of the shower, grabbing a towel from the rack. Her reflection stared back at her from the fogged mirror—young, beautiful, eternally seventeen in appearance. A face that had not aged in over a century. A face that hid a multitude of sins.

She wiped the steam from the glass and looked back at herself.

What are you going to do? she asked herself. Where are you going to go?

She had no answer. For the first time in as long as she could remember, Paris had no plan, no strategy, no endgame. She was simply running, and sooner or later, running would not be enough.

But not tonight. Tonight, she would rest. Tomorrow, she would figure out the next step.

She wrapped herself in the towel and walked back into the room, pulling the curtains closed against the pre-dawn light beginning to creep across the horizon. She had a few hours before the sun made movement dangerous. A few hours to sleep, to think, to prepare.

Her stomach growled, a reminder that she had not fed in days. The hunger was manageable for now, but it would not stay that way. Soon, she would need to hunt.

Paris climbed into the bed and pulled the covers over her body. The sheets were stiff and smelled of industrial detergent, nothing like the silk she had grown accustomed to at the Citadel. But they were warm, and they were safe, and for now, that was enough.

She closed her eyes and let the exhaustion take her.

Tomorrow, she would figure out how to stay alive.

CHAPTER 6

(1888, The Citadel — Age 8)

Paris woke to the smell of antiseptic and the sound of someone humming.

She was strapped to a chair. Leather bands secured her wrists and ankles, tight enough to hold but not tight enough to bruise. The room around her was white—white walls, white ceiling, white tile floor—and lit by gas lamps that cast everything in a sterile, flickering glow. It was the cleanest place she had ever seen. After a year on the streets of Bristol, it felt obscene.

A woman stood beside her, preparing a syringe. She was around thirty in appearance, with strawberry blonde hair pulled back in a severe bun and a face that seemed incapable of warmth. Her movements were precise, mechanical, utterly without sentiment.

"Where am I?" Paris asked. Her voice came out as a croak. Her throat was dry, her head thick with fog. She had no memory of how she had gotten here—only fragments of the alley, the dead man, Ophelia's cold hand in hers.

"The Citadel," the woman said, without looking up from her work. "Your new home."

"What's that?"

"You'll learn soon enough." The woman turned, syringe in hand, and Paris saw her for the first time. She was clinical, utterly devoid of curiosity. "Hold still. This will only hurt for a moment."

The needle slid into Paris's arm before she could protest. She watched her blood flow into the glass vial—deep red, nearly black in the gaslight—and felt a strange detachment from the whole process. As if it were happening to someone else. As if she were watching from very far away.

"Good," the woman said, withdrawing the needle and pressing a cotton swab to the wound. "You didn't flinch. That's promising."

"Promising for what?"

The woman wrapped white tape around the cotton and set the vial of blood on a metal tray. For a long moment, she didn't answer. Then she turned and looked at Paris—really looked at her—and light flickered in those flat eyes. Not warmth. Not kindness. Closer to assessment.

"A word of advice," the woman said. "Don't be stupid enough to think you can run away. You won't be leaving here anytime soon." She paused, and her voice slightly softened. "Hopefully, you'll be strong enough."

"Strong enough for what?"

But the woman was already walking away, her heels clicking against the tile. She disappeared through a door at the far end of the room, leaving Paris alone with her questions and her restraints and the lingering sting of the needle in her arm.

An hour passed. Maybe two. Paris had no way of measuring time in the windowless room, and no one came to check on her. She tested the straps—they held firm—and eventually gave up, letting her head fall back against the chair. She was tired. So tired. The adrenaline that had carried her through the past year had finally run dry, and all that remained was a bone-deep exhaustion that no amount of sleep could cure.

She thought about Ophelia and Alldred. About the dead man in the alley, his throat torn open, his blood pooling beneath him. About the choice she had made.

You let monsters take you, a voice whispered in her mind. You chose this.

She had. She had chosen survival over morality, power over innocence. And she would make that choice again, a thousand times over, because the alternative was death. She had seen enough death to know that she wanted no part of it. Not yet. Not ever, if she could help it.

The door opened.

A different woman entered—tall, severe, with iron-grey hair and a face like carved granite. She moved with the easy confidence of someone accustomed to absolute authority, and her gaze swept the room before settling on Paris with an intensity that made her skin prickle.

Behind her came a man—long and lean, with a friendly face that seemed at odds with his surroundings. He moved to Paris's chair and began unfastening the straps.

"Up you go," he said. His accent was strange. Continental. Though Paris couldn't place it. "Time to meet your classmates."

"Classmates?"

The man's smile widened, and Paris saw his teeth. Two of them—the canines—extended past the others, sharp and gleaming white.

She didn't flinch. She had already seen what these creatures could do. Teeth were the least of it.

"Come along," the grey-haired woman said. "I haven't got all night."

They led her through corridors of grey stone, past doors of iron and wood, up staircases that spiraled into darkness. The Citadel was vast—far larger than any building Paris had ever seen—and it thrummed with a quiet energy that she could feel in her bones. There were others here. She caught glimpses of them as she walked: figures in doorways, faces in shadows, eyes that tracked her passage with idle curiosity.

None of them spoke to her. None of them moved.

Finally, the grey-haired woman stopped before a heavy wooden door and produced a key from her pocket. The lock clicked open, and she gestured for Paris to enter.

"Your quarters," she said. "For now."

Paris stepped inside.

The room was sparse but clean—four cots arranged against the walls, a small table with two chairs, a single window that looked out onto nothing but darkness. Three children were already there, and they all turned to look at her as she entered.

The first was a girl, a year or so older than Paris, with straight black hair and almond-shaped eyes. Her skin was the color of sand, and her expression was cautious but kind. She rose from her seat and offered a small wave.

"Hi," she said. "I'm Sarah."

The second was a boy, also older, with deep brown hair and a sullen expression. He sat on one of the cots with his arms folded across his chest, watching Paris with undisguised hostility. He was American—she could tell by his accent even before he spoke.

"Great," he said. "Another one. This is getting weirder by the minute."

The third was a younger boy, seven or eight, who sat in the corner and said nothing. His eyes were wide and frightened, and he seemed to shrink into himself as Paris entered. She recognized that look. She had worn it herself, once.

"I'm Paris," she said.

Sarah smiled. "That's a pretty name. Where are you from?"

"Bristol."

"I'm from London." Sarah gestured to the sullen boy. "He's Jonathan. American."

"Salem," the boy corrected, his voice sharp. "Call me Salem."

Paris raised an eyebrow. "Why?"

"Because I said so." He unfolded his arms and leaned forward, studying her with laser focus. "You don't look like much. How old are you?"

"Eight."

"Great. A baby." He snorted and leaned back against the wall. "I give her a week."

Sarah shot him a look of disapproval. "Don't be cruel."

"I'm not being cruel. I'm being realistic." Salem's stare never left Paris. "We're here to learn. That's what they told us. And only the ones who make it through get to stay. The rest..." He drew a finger across his throat.

The younger boy in the corner whimpered.

"That's enough," Sarah said firmly. She turned to Paris with an apologetic expression. "Don't listen to him. He's trying to scare you."

"Is it true?" Paris asked.

Sarah hesitated. That was answer enough.

Paris walked to the empty cot and sat down. The mattress was thin but clean, far better than anything she'd slept on in the past year. She looked at the other children—Sarah with her kindness, Salem with his arrogance, the frightened boy in the corner—and felt the moment settle inside her. Something cold. Something certain.

She had survived the streets of Bristol. She had survived the death of her mother, the loss of her friends, the frozen winter that had nearly claimed her life. She had walked into the arms of monsters and made a deal for her own survival.

She would survive this too.

Whatever it took.

The door opened again, and the grey-haired woman returned. This time, her presence seemed to fill the entire room, demanding attention without saying a word. All four children fell silent.

"I am Headmistress Redmond," she said. Her voice was cold and precise, like a knife being sharpened. "You will address me as 'Headmistress,' 'Mistress Redmond,' or 'ma'am.' Nothing else. Is that understood?"

Nods from Sarah and the quiet boy. Paris nodded as well.

Salem didn't move.

Headmistress Redmond fixed on him. The silence stretched. Then, faster than Paris could follow, the woman crossed the room and struck Salem across the face with an open palm. The crack of the blow echoed off the stone walls.

"I asked if that was understood," she said calmly.

Salem's hand went to his reddening cheek. His eyes blazed with fury, but he nodded.

"Good." Headmistress Redmond stepped back, her gaze sweeping over all of them. "I run the School here at the Citadel. You will be attending it for the next several years. How many years depends entirely on you."

"What are we learning?" Sarah asked, her voice small.

"Everything." The Headmistress folded her hands in front of her. "You were chosen for specific reasons. I do not know or care what those reasons were. My only concern is your education. You will learn what we teach you, when we teach you, how we teach you. You will not question. You will not disobey. You will not fail."

She paused, letting the words settle.

"You will receive one warning for breaking my rules. The second time, you will be punished." Her eyes moved from face to face, cold and unblinking. "There will not be a third time."

The quiet boy raised his hand, trembling. "What... what happens to students who don't pass?"

Paris answered before she could stop herself. "They die."

Every head turned toward her. Salem focused on her. Sarah's face went pale. The quiet boy looked like he might be sick.

Headmistress Redmond studied Paris for a long moment. A flicker of a thought clouded expression—surprise, or approval—and then it was gone.

"Correct," she said. "Any further questions?"

Silence.

"Classes begin Monday. Until then, Rupert will be your guide. Obey him as you would obey me." She turned and strode toward the door, then paused at the threshold. "Eat. Rest. Prepare yourselves however you see fit. And remember—only the strong survive here. The weak are... removed."

She left without another word.

Rupert, the lean man with the fanged grin, stepped into the doorway. "Anyone hungry?" he asked, his tone cheerful.

No one answered. They were all still staring at Paris.

She met their eyes one by one—Sarah's fear, Salem's grudging reassessment, the quiet boy's terror—and felt nothing but calm.

She had spoken the truth. That was all. And the sooner the others understood the stakes, the better their chances of survival.

Only the strong survive, she thought. Then I will be strong.

She stood and walked toward Rupert.

"I could eat," she said.

CHAPTER 7

(*Present*)

Paris stood before the bathroom mirror and studied her reflection.

The face that stared back was young—seventeen, eighteen at most—with pale skin and delicate features that belied the century of violence behind them. It was a useful face. Disarming. The kind of face that made men underestimate her and women dismiss her. She had learned long ago how to weaponize it.

But tonight, she needed more. Tonight, she needed to be seen.

She reached for the box of hair dye she had purchased at a drugstore in Daytona. The color was absurd—a deep, arterial red, the shade of fresh blood—but that was precisely why she had chosen it. Anyone the Magistrate sent after her would be looking for the Paris they knew: mousy brown hair, understated appearance, the quiet competence of a High Guard operative. They would *not* be looking for this.

She worked the dye through her hair with practiced hands, watching the color transform strand by strand. By the time she was finished, her reflection had become someone else entirely. A stranger with blood-red locks that dripped down her cheeks like the aftermath of a wound.

Good, she thought. Let them look for a ghost.

The makeup came next. She applied it with the same precision she brought to everything—dusky eyeliner, smoky shadow, lipstick that matched her hair. The effect aged her by a few years, enough to slip past bouncers without a second glance. She had been doing this for decades, adjusting her appearance to match whatever role the moment required. Tonight, the role was simple: a young woman looking for trouble.

Or rather, trouble looking for a meal.

Her stomach clenched at the thought. She had not fed since before Paris—the city, not her—and the hunger was becoming difficult to ignore. It sat in her chest like a living thing, coiled and patient, whispering of blood and warmth and the sweet release of the kill.

Most humans didn't understand what it meant to be Valensi. They thought of vampires as mindless predators, slaves to their appetite, killing indiscriminately to sate an endless thirst. Hollywood had done them no favors in that regard. The truth was more complicated. Yes, the hunger was real. Yes, it demanded satisfaction. But the Valensi were not animals. They were thinking creatures, capable of choice, capable of restraint.

Capable of conscience.

More importantly, they did not need to feed every night. Blood was a necessary component of their food intake, but she could easily go a month without blood. She tore into a lot of rare steaks to make up the difference.

Paris had killed many times in her long life. She had torn out throats and drained bodies and left corpses in alleys and forests and rivers across three continents. But she had never—not once in 135 years—taken an innocent life.

That was her line. Her code. The one rule she would not break, no matter how fierce the hunger became.

She killed those who deserved killing. Predators. Abusers. Rapists. Murderers. Men who preyed on the weak, who took pleasure in cruelty, who had forfeited their right to breathe by their own monstrous actions.

The world was full of such men. And, women. She had never had trouble finding them.

Tonight would be no different.

She dressed with care: a tight black top that showed just enough skin, black jeans that hugged her hips, boots with enough heel to add two inches to her height. The outfit said *available* without saying *easy*—a crucial distinction in the hunting grounds she was about to enter. She wanted attention. She wanted men to look. But she wanted them to work for it, to approach her, to reveal themselves.

The predators always did, eventually. They couldn't help it. They saw a pretty young thing alone at a bar and their instincts kicked in—the circling, the testing, the slow escalation toward violence. Paris had watched it happen a hundred times. A thousand. The pattern was always the same.

All she had to do was wait.

She grabbed her small black purse—cash, a fake ID, nothing that could trace back to her real identity—and headed for the door. In the hallway, she paused, reaching out with her senses. The hotel was quiet. Liam was probably still at the front desk, nursing whatever fantasies she had planted in his head. She would deal with him eventually—a night or two of carefully rationed affection, enough to keep him loyal and incurious—but not tonight. Tonight, she had other appetites to satisfy.

The elevator deposited her in the lobby. She walked past the front desk without looking at Liam, though she felt his gaze follow her across the marble floor. Let him look. Let him want. It cost her nothing and bought her everything.

The automatic doors slid open, and the Florida night embraced her.

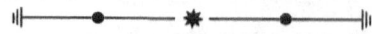

The air was thick and humid, heavy with the smell of exhaust and flowers and the distant salt of the ocean. Paris breathed it in and let it fill her chest. For the first time in days—weeks—she was not running. She was not hiding. She was simply *existing*, moving through the world like any other predator on the hunt.

It was a kind of freedom.

A temporary freedom, yes. The Magistrate's hunters were coming. Garrett was coming—she was certain of that, though the thought of him sent a spike of pain through her heart that she quickly suppressed. But they were not here yet. They had not found her yet. And until they did, she intended to live.

Really live. Not the careful, constrained existence of a High Guard operative, bound by duty and protocol and the endless demands of the Hierarchy. Not the desperate scramble of a fugitive, always looking over her shoulder, always waiting for the blow to fall. Just... life. Simple and immediate and hers.

She had nearly forgotten what that felt like.

International Drive was alive with light and noise and the press of human bodies. Tourists streamed along the sidewalks, clutching shopping bags and ice cream cones and the hands of overstimulated children. Music poured from open doorways—pop and country and thumping electronic bass—and the air shimmered with neon. It was garish and excessive and utterly, gloriously American.

Paris loved it.

She walked without hurrying, letting the crowd flow around her, savoring the anonymity of being another face in the throng. Men looked at her as she passed—she was used to that—and she let them look without acknowledgment. She was not hunting them. Not yet. She was still searching, still waiting for the right one to reveal himself.

The hunger pulsed in her chest, patient but insistent. *Soon*, she told it. *Soon*.

She passed a row of tourist traps. T-shirt shops, souvenir stands, a store that sold nothing but hot sauce. She turned down a side street toward the club district. The crowd thinned here, the families replaced by younger faces, harder faces. Women in short skirts and high heels. Men with too much cologne and not enough self-awareness. The hunting ground.

The club she chose was called Nocturne—a name that amused her, given the circumstances. The line stretched down the block, but Paris didn't wait. She walked straight to the front, caught the bouncer's eye, and smiled. She threw him a look that screamed confidence and allure.

He waved her through without a word.

Inside, the music was loud enough to feel in her bones, a relentless electronic pulse that made conversation impossible. The dance floor was packed with bodies, writhing and grinding in the strobing lights. The air smelled of sweat and alcohol and desire. Paris moved through it all like a shark through warm water, her senses extended, searching.

She found a spot at the bar and ordered a vodka she had no intention of drinking. The bartender—a young woman with sleeve tattoos and a nose ring—poured without comment and moved on to the next customer. Paris cradled the glass in her hands and watched the crowd.

There.

Three men at a table near the back. Mid-twenties, well-dressed, the kind of aggressive confidence that came from money and privilege and never being told no. They were drinking heavily and laughing loudly and looking at every woman who passed with the same appraising gaze.

One of them caught her eye.

He was handsome, she supposed, in a generic sort of way. Square jaw, broad shoulders, hair styled with too much product. His smile was bright and practiced, that of a man who had learned that charm could open doors that force could not.

But his eyes told a different story.

Paris had seen eyes like that before. Cold beneath the warmth. Calculating beneath the charm. The eyes of a man who saw women not as people but as prey. As things to be acquired, used, discarded.

Hello, young man, she thought, though she didn't yet know his name. *I think I've found my dinner.*

She held his gaze for a moment—long enough to signal interest—then looked away. Let him come to her. Let him think he was the hunter and she the hunted. That was how the game was played.

She sipped her vodka and waited.

It didn't take long.

CHAPTER 8

(Present)

His name was Greg.

He told her this within thirty seconds of sliding onto the barstool beside her, his smile wide and his cologne overpowering. Up close, she could see the details she had missed from across the room: the faint redness in his cheeks and nose that spoke of too many drinks, the expensive watch on his wrist, the way his gaze kept drifting down to her chest even as he introduced himself.

"I'm Greg," he said, extending his hand. "And you are way too beautiful to be sitting here alone."

Paris took his hand and held it a moment longer than necessary. His palm was warm and slightly damp. She could feel his pulse through his skin—quick with excitement, with anticipation. With hunger.

Oh, yes, she thought. You'll do nicely.

"Paris," she said. "And I was waiting for the right company."

His face lit up a bit. He thought he was winning. He thought this was going exactly the way it always went—the pretty girl, the easy charm, the inevitable conclusion. Men like Greg had a script they followed, a pattern honed through years of practice. They bought drinks. They paid compliments. They escalated slowly, testing boundaries, pushing limits, until they got what they wanted.

And if they didn't get it willingly, they took it anyway.

Paris had known men like Greg her entire life. Her father had been one of them—a man who saw women as property, as objects to be controlled and discarded. The streets of Bristol had been full of them, predators who prowled the alleys looking for vulnerable girls to exploit. The Citadel had taught her to recognize them on sight, to read the violence hidden beneath their charming facades.

Greg was textbook. Every gesture, every word, every lingering glance confirmed what she had seen in his eyes from across the room. He was a predator. A rapist. A monster hiding in plain sight. She slipped quietly into his mind, searching his history as one might with a computer search engine. What she found only confirmed her deep-seated assumptions about the man.

And he had no idea that he had just become prey.

"Let me buy you a drink," he said, signaling the bartender. "What are you having?"

"Vodka. Neat."

He raised an eyebrow. "A woman who knows what she wants. I like that."

You have no idea what I want, Paris thought. But she smiled and accepted the drink when it came, letting her fingers brush against his as she took the glass.

They talked. Or rather, Greg talked—about his job in finance, his apartment downtown, his car, his gym routine, his plans for the weekend. Paris listened with practiced attentiveness, nodding at the right moments, laughing at his jokes, feeding his ego with the steady drip of feminine admiration that men like him required. It was tedious work, but necessary. She needed him comfortable. She needed him confident. She needed him to believe that he was in control.

His friends watched from across the room, grinning and nudging each other. They knew what Greg was doing. They had probably seen him do it a dozen times before. Birds of a feather, these men. They hunted in packs, covering for each other, enabling each other, celebrating each other's conquests like trophies.

Maybe I'll come back for them later, Paris thought. A public service.

An hour passed. Then two. Greg's drinks kept coming, and his hands grew bolder—touching her arm, her shoulder, the small of her back. Each touch was a test, a probe, gauging how much she would tolerate. Paris tolerated it all, playing the role of the girl who was too flattered, too drunk, too naive to recognize the danger.

"You want to get out of here?" Greg finally asked, leaning close. His breath was hot against her ear, sour with whiskey. "My place isn't far. We could have some privacy."

Paris pretended to hesitate. "I don't know. I just met you."

"Come on." His hand slid down to her hip, possessive. "I promise I'll be a gentleman."

She almost laughed at that. Almost. Instead, she bit her lower lip and looked up at him through her lashes—the picture of innocent uncertainty.

"Okay," she said. "But just for a little while."

His smile turned triumphant. He thought he had won.

He had no idea.

They left through a side exit, avoiding his friends, avoiding the crowd. Greg's hand was firm on her lower back, guiding her into the alley behind the club. The night air was cooler here, tinged with the smell of garbage and stale beer. The bass from inside still throbbed through the walls, muffled but persistent.

"My car's around the corner," Greg said. "Come on."

But he didn't move toward the corner. Instead, he pushed her against the wall, his body pressing into hers, his mouth finding her neck.

"I've been thinking about this all night," he murmured against her skin. His hands were already moving, tugging at her clothes. "God, you're so fucking hot."

Paris let him paw at her for a moment. Let him think she was frozen with surprise, with fear. Let him believe he had the upper hand.

"Greg," she said softly. "Stop."

He didn't stop. Of course he didn't. Men like Greg never stopped.

"Relax," he breathed. His hand slid beneath her shirt, rough and greedy. "You want this. I know you do."

"No." Her voice was firmer now. "I said stop."

He laughed. Actually laughed. "Don't play hard to get now, sweetheart. You've been eye-fucking me all night."

His hand moved to her jeans, fumbling with the button.

Paris grinned.

"I was hoping you'd do that," she said.

Greg paused, confused. "What?"

She moved.

One moment she was pinned against the wall, helpless and small. The next, Greg was the one with his back to the bricks, her hand around his throat, his feet dangling six inches off the ground. His expression went wide with shock, then wider with terror as he registered the impossible strength lifting him like he weighed nothing at all.

"What the fuck—" he choked.

"Shh." Paris tightened her grip, cutting off his air. "No more talking, Greg. It's my turn now."

She let him see her then. Let him see what she really was. She felt her canines extend, sharp and gleaming in the dim light from the street. She felt her eyes change, the pupils dilating, the humanity draining away.

Greg made a sound—between a scream and a whimper—but nothing came out. Her hand was too tight around his throat.

"Here's what's going to happen," Paris said, her voice conversational, pleasant. "You're going to die tonight. And before you do, I want you to understand why."

She leaned closer, until her lips were touching his ear.

"I know what you are, Greg. I knew it the moment I saw you. The way you looked at me. The way you looked at every woman in that bar. Like meat. Like something to be used and thrown away." She pulled back, meeting his bulging eyes. "How many have there been? How many girls have you cornered in alleys like this one? How many did you hurt?"

He tried to speak, but only a rasping gurgle emerged.

"It doesn't matter," Paris continued. "I don't need a number. I can see it all over you. A cloak of dread. You're a rapist. A predator. A monster." She smiled widely, showing her fangs. "But here's the thing, Greg. I'm a monster, too. The difference is, I only kill things like you. One thing I will make certain of tonight is that you will never be able to do your damage ever again. Isn't that wonderful?"

She could feel his heart hammering against her palm, fast and frantic, pumping blood through his veins in a desperate bid for survival. The hunger surged inside her, demanding release, demanding satisfaction.

She had denied it long enough.

"Any last words?" she asked.

Greg's mouth opened and closed. Tears streamed down his cheeks. His hands clawed uselessly at her wrist, his legs kicking against the wall.

"No?" Paris tilted her head. "Pity. I was hoping this would be more memorable."

She struck.

She did not go for the jugular, as one might expect. Instead, she held him up against the wall with one hand and unbelted his jeans with the other. She let them fall away as she slightly jarred his head against the brick wall, knocking him unconscious.

She let him slide down the wall to a seated position. She pulled down his boxers and grabbed his cock with her left hand, while she used the long, sturdy fingernail of the right index finger to easily cut away and remove his member. She shamelessly leaned in and drank from the gushing wound. She did not kill him. As much as she felt he deserved it. Instead, she used her tongue to maneuver around her mouth, building up saliva. She then spit onto the wound, smearing her spit all along the opening and pulling the skin together.

One of the unique qualities of Valensi saliva is that it has tremendous healing properties. That is one of many reasons why the Valensi had been able to stay in the shadows so long. If one simply bit a person and drank only what they truly required, they could use their saliva and seal the wound so that no one would ever believe the victim had ever been attacked.

It took only a couple of minutes and a few additional servings of saliva before Greg the rapist's wound was fully closed. He would have a terrible time of it over the next few hours, after he came to. First he would realize he had no penis. Next he would freak out trying to understand how he was supposed to be able to urinate. Off the hospital he would go. And absolutely no explanation he could give would ever explain his current situation.

She rep-laced his clothing and left him sitting there, passed out against the wall.

She stood over him for a moment, savoring the warmth spreading through her body, the power humming in her veins. The hunger was sated, at least for now. The beast was quiet.

She felt no guilt. No remorse. No hesitation.

Greg had been a rapist. A predator. A man who had hurt women and would have continued hurting them until someone stopped him.

Paris had stopped him.

She wiped the blood from her lips with the back of her hand, then crouched beside the unconscious asshole. His wallet was in his back pocket—she took the cash, left the cards—and his watch was worth a few thousand dollars, easy. She took that too. No sense in wasting resources.

Then she stood, straightened her clothes, and walked out of the alley without looking back.

The night was still young. The music still pulsed from the club behind her. The tourists still streamed along International Drive, oblivious to the death that had occurred a hundred feet away.

Paris melted into the crowd and disappeared.

She found a bus stop three blocks away and sat down to wait. The adrenaline was fading now, replaced by a pleasant lethargy that settled into her bones. She was full. She was warm. She was, for the moment, safe.

Her thoughts drifted to Greg's friends, still inside the club, probably wondering where their buddy had gone. Would they come looking for him? Would they find him in the alley? It didn't matter. By the time anyone discovered the man, she would be long gone.

A bus arrived—not the one she needed, but she boarded it anyway, to keep moving. She found a seat near the back and watched the lights of Orlando slide past the window.

She thought about Greg. About the terror when he realized what she was. About the way his blood had tasted—sour with alcohol, bitter with fear, but satisfying nonetheless.

She thought about the girls he would never hurt now. The lives he would never destroy. The pain he would never inflict.

You're welcome, she thought, though she wasn't sure who she was addressing. The universe, perhaps. Or the ghost of whoever Greg's next victim would have been.

The bus rumbled on through the night.

Paris closed her eyes and relaxed.

WAIF

CHAPTER 9

(1889, The Citadel — Age 9)

The first year at the Citadel passed in a blur of lessons and bruises.

Paris learned quickly that the School was unlike any education she might have received in the outside world. There were no gentle encouragements here, no gold stars for effort, no second chances for failure. The Valensi did not coddle their young. They forged them—through knowledge, through pain, through the constant reminder that weakness meant death.

The students who had arrived with her numbered thirty-one. By the end of the first year, that number had dwindled to twenty-four. Some had been transferred, Headmistress Redmond said. Others had simply... disappeared. No one asked questions. No one dared.

Paris kept her head down. Yet, she watched. She listened. She learned. And she survived.

"The Valensi heart is not two separate organs," Ms. Dolores explained, tapping her chalk against the blackboard where she had drawn a crude anatomical diagram. "It is a single heart, significantly larger and more powerful than a human's. We say 'hearts' as a romantic affectation—a nod to our capacity for passion and devotion—but the biological reality is more mundane."

Paris copied the diagram into her notebook, her handwriting neat and precise. Beside her, London did the same, her pen moving in careful strokes. On Paris's other side, Salem slouched in his chair, arms folded, making no effort to take notes.

"Due to the thickness and viscosity of our blood," Ms. Dolores continued, "which results from its unique chemical composition, our hearts must work considerably harder than a human's to circulate it through our bodies. This is why our hearts are nearly twice the size." She paused, scanning the room. "Can anyone tell me why our blood is different?"

Several hands went up. Paris's was not among them—she preferred to observe rather than volunteer—but Ms. Dolores's gaze found her anyway.

"Paris. You seem attentive. What makes Valensi blood unique?"

Paris set down her pen. "It lacks hemes," she said. "The iron-containing compounds that give human blood its red color and its ability to carry oxygen efficiently. Our blood compensates through a different molecular structure, which makes it thicker and darker."

Ms. Dolores raised an eyebrow. "Very good. And where did you learn that?"

"I read ahead."

A few students snickered. Salem rolled his eyes.

"Initiative," Ms. Dolores said, a hint of approval in her voice. "I appreciate initiative. Continue reading ahead, Paris. It will serve you well."

She turned back to the blackboard, and Paris felt the weight of Salem's glare on the side of her face. She ignored it. Salem's opinion of her mattered about as much as the opinion of the rats that scurried through the Citadel's lower corridors—which was to say, not at all.

The biology lessons were Paris's favorite, but they were far from the only subject on the curriculum.

There was history—endless hours of it—tracing the Valensi lineage back through millennia. They learned of the First Families, the ancient bloodlines that had established the Hierarchy. They learned of the wars fought in shadow, the alliances forged and broken, the slow and patient accumulation of power that had allowed their kind to survive while empires rose and fell around them.

There was language—Latin and Greek, French and German, the tongues of power and commerce that any proper Valensi was expected to master. Paris had a gift for languages, her ear attuned to the rhythms and patterns of speech, and she absorbed them faster than most of her peers.

There was literature and philosophy, mathematics and science. The Valensi valued education not as an end in itself, but as a tool—a means of navigating the human world, of understanding its systems and exploiting its weaknesses. An ignorant Valensi was a vulnerable Valensi, and vulnerability was not tolerated.

And then there was combat.

Master Asaro was a small man, barely taller than Paris herself, with a shaved head and eyes that seemed to see everything at once. He moved like water—fluid, unhurried, utterly without wasted motion—and he spoke in a soft voice that somehow carried to every corner of the training hall.

"Fighting," he said on their first day, "is not about strength. It is not about speed. It is not about size or reach or the sharpness of your claws." He paused, letting the words settle. "Fighting is about understanding. Understanding your opponent. Understanding yourself. Understanding the space between you and how to close it—or widen it—to your advantage."

The students stood in rows before him, dressed in simple training clothes. Paris was near the front, London beside her. Salem had positioned himself at the back, as far from the instructor as possible.

"You are children," Asaro continued. "Soft. Weak. Slow. This is not an insult—it is a fact. You have not yet been Birthed. Your bodies are still human, still fragile. A grown Valensi could kill any one of you without effort." His gaze swept across them. "My job is to ensure that when you are Birthed, you will know what to do with the strength you receive. Strength without skill is merely dangerous. Skill without strength is merely clever. But strength and skill together..." He smiled, a thin expression. "That is power."

He called Salem forward first.

Paris watched as the American boy swaggered to the center of the room, his shoulders squared, his chin raised. He was bigger than most of the other students—eleven years old now, broad and tall for his age—and he carried himself with the confidence of someone who had never been truly beaten.

"Attack me," Asaro said.

Salem didn't hesitate. He lunged forward, fists swinging, putting all his weight behind the blow.

Asaro moved—a small shift, almost imperceptible—and Salem's fist passed through empty air. Before the boy could recover, Asaro's hand shot out and caught him by the wrist. A twist, a pivot, and Salem was on the ground, his arm bent at an angle that made Paris wince.

"Predictable," Asaro said calmly. "Aggressive. Overcommitted." He released Salem's arm and stepped back. "Again."

Salem scrambled to his feet, his face red with humiliation. He attacked again—faster this time, more cautious—but the result was the same. Asaro redirected his momentum, turned his strength against him, and deposited him on the floor with no more effort than swatting a fly.

"Again."

This continued for several minutes. Each time Salem rose, he attacked. Each time he attacked, he fell. By the end, he was breathing hard, his training clothes soaked with sweat, his entire essence burning with fury.

"Enough," Asaro said. He turned to address the class. "What did you observe?"

Silence. No one wanted to be the one to criticize Salem, who was glaring at them all with barely contained rage.

Paris raised her hand.

"Yes?"

"He was angry," she said. "Each time he fell, he got angrier. And the angrier he got, the sloppier his attacks became. He stopped thinking and started reacting."

Asaro nodded slowly. "And what does that tell you?"

"That anger is a weakness. It can be provoked and exploited."

"Correct." Asaro's eyes met hers with the faintest hint of respect. "Emotion has its place in combat. Fear can sharpen the senses. Determination can fuel endurance. But anger?" He shook his head. "Anger blinds. Anger makes you predictable. And predictable opponents are easy to kill."

He turned back to Salem, who was still standing in the center of the room, his hands clenched into fists.

"You have strength," Asaro told him. "You have aggression. These are not worthless qualities. But until you learn to control them—to use them rather than be used by them—you will always lose to a smarter opponent." He paused. "Return to your place."

Salem stalked back to his position at the rear of the class. As he passed Paris, he leaned close.

"Think you're clever, don't you?" he hissed.

Paris didn't flinch. "I think I'm observant," she said quietly. "There's a difference."

His eyes narrowed, but he said nothing more. He simply filed into his place and stood there, seething, while Asaro called the next student forward.

London caught Paris's eye and gave her a small, nearly imperceptible nod. A gesture of solidarity. Of approval.

Paris allowed herself a tiny grin.

She had made an enemy today. But she had also begun to make a friend.

The weeks turned to months. The months turned to a year.

Paris and London grew closer, their friendship forged in the crucible of shared hardship. They studied together, trained together, and ate together in the cold stone dining hall. London was quieter than Paris—more cautious, more willing to blend into the background—but beneath that reserved exterior was a sharp mind and a loyal heart.

"Why do you think they chose us?" London asked one night, as they lay in their cots after lights out. The other students were asleep, or pretending to be. "Out of everyone in the world, why us?"

Paris stared at the ceiling, considering the question. "Because we're survivors," she said finally. "They found us at our lowest points—starving, freezing, dying—and we didn't give up. We kept fighting. That's what they want. People who won't stop fighting, no matter what."

"Is that enough, though? To just... not give up?"

"It's a start." Paris turned her head to look at her friend. In the darkness, she could barely make out the shape of London's face, the glint of her eyes. "The rest we learn. The knowledge, the skills, the power. But the will to survive? That has to come from inside. You can't teach that."

London was silent for a long moment. Then: "I'm glad you're here, Paris."

"I'm glad you're here too."

It was a simple exchange. But in that moment, in the deep quiet of the Citadel, it meant everything.

Salem remained a problem.

He never forgave Paris for her observation in Asaro's class, and he made his displeasure known in small, petty ways—a shoulder check in the hallway, a muttered insult as she passed, a deliberate attempt to trip her during training exercises. Paris endured it all without complaint, without retaliation. She grasped what Salem was doing. He was trying to provoke her, to make her angry, to lure her into the same trap she had identified in him.

She refused to take the bait.

"Why don't you hit him?" London asked one afternoon, after Salem had "accidentally" knocked Paris's books from her hands for the third time that week. "You could take him. I've seen you in training."

"Maybe," Paris said, gathering her scattered papers. "But what would that accomplish? He'd come back angrier. And the instructors would punish us both." She straightened, meeting London's gaze. "I'm not here to win fights with Salem. I'm here to survive. To graduate. To become Valensi. Everything else is a distraction."

London frowned. "That's very... practical."

"Practical keeps you alive." Paris tucked her books under her arm. "Come on. We'll be late for Mr. Marco's class."

Mr. Marco taught history and, occasionally, more visceral lessons.

He was an older Valensi—several centuries at least, though he appeared no more than fifty—with a thick grey beard and eyes that had seen empires crumble. He spoke of the past as if he had lived it, which, Paris realized, he probably had. The fall of Rome. The Black Death. The rise and fall of kings and conquerors. To Mr. Marco, these were not abstractions in a textbook. They were memories.

"The Valensi have always existed in the shadows," he told them one afternoon, pacing before the blackboard. "We do not rule openly. We do not wage wars for territory or glory. We survive. We adapt. We endure. This is our strength—and it is also our vulnerability."

He paused, turning to face the class.

"Humans outnumber us by more than a million to one. If they ever discovered our existence—truly understood what we are and how to destroy us—they would hunt us to extinction. This is not speculation. This is history. Every time our kind has grown too bold, too visible, the humans have responded with fire and steel and relentless persecution."

"So we hide," Salem said from the back. His tone was dismissive. "We skulk in the shadows like rats."

Mr. Marco faced him. "We survive," he corrected. "Like rats, yes. And do you know what happened to every creature that thought itself too mighty to hide? The dinosaurs. The mammoths. The great cats that once ruled entire continents." He smirked. "They are gone. We remain. Tell me, young Salem—which strategy seems wiser to you?"

Salem had no answer to that.

"There are those among us who believe we should reveal ourselves," Mr. Marco continued. "Who think that our powers make us superior, that we should rule over humanity rather than hide from it. These voices have always existed. They will always exist. And they are always, inevitably, wrong."

He reached into his coat and produced a small knife—a simple thing, unadorned, but sharp enough to glint in the lamplight.

"Let me show you," he said. "A demonstration of what makes us different from humans—and why that difference is both our greatest asset and our greatest danger."

He rolled up his sleeve, exposing his forearm, and drew the blade across his skin. Blood welled up, dark and thick.

Several students gasped. Paris watched in silence, her focus transfixed on the wound.

"Observe," Mr. Marco said. He held up his arm so they could all see. "This cut is perhaps two inches long, a quarter inch deep. On a human, it would take days to heal. Weeks, possibly, to fully close."

As he spoke, the wound began to change. The blood flow slowed, then stopped. The edges of the cut drew together, knitting themselves back into seamless skin. Within a minute, there was nothing left but a faint pink line—and even that was fading.

"Our bodies repair themselves at a rate humans cannot comprehend," Mr. Marco said. "This is one of the gifts of our blood. But it is not without cost." He turned to scan the room, and his focus settled on Salem. "You. Come here."

Salem hesitated, then rose and walked to the front of the room. His jaw was set, his posture defiant, but Paris could see the uncertainty in his movement.

"Give me your arm," Mr. Marco said.

"Why?"

"Because I told you to."

Salem extended his arm. Mr. Marco took it, pushed up the sleeve, and—before anyone could react—drew the knife across the boy's forearm in a quick, precise motion.

Salem cried out, jerking back, but Mr. Marco held him firm. Blood poured from the wound, bright red and flowing freely.

"Now," Mr. Marco said calmly, "let us compare."

He held up his own arm—fully healed—beside Salem's bleeding one. The contrast was stark. Salem's wound showed no sign of closing. The blood continued to flow, dripping onto the stone floor.

"You are not yet Valensi," Mr. Marco said. "Your body is still human. Still fragile. Still slow to heal." He released Salem's arm and produced a handkerchief, pressing it to the wound. "This is what you are now. Weak. Vulnerable. Mortal."

Salem's face had gone pale. His breathing was rapid and shallow. Paris could see him fighting not to cry—fighting to maintain some shred of dignity in front of his classmates.

"But one day," Mr. Marco continued, his voice softening somewhat, "you will be Birthed. Your blood will change. Your body will change. And wounds like this will mean nothing to you." He pressed the handkerchief more firmly against Salem's arm. "Until that day, remember what you are. And remember what you will become—if you survive long enough to earn it."

He sent Salem to the infirmary with a curt nod.

The class sat in stunned silence.

Mr. Marco cleaned his knife, returned it to his pocket, and resumed his lecture as if nothing had happened.

Paris took careful notes. But her mind was elsewhere—fixed on the image of Salem's blood pooling on the floor, and the look of raw terror that had flickered across his face before he'd managed to hide it.

We are all fragile, she thought. All of us. Until we're not.

She glanced at London, who met her eyes with an expression that mirrored her own thoughts.

Survive, that look said. Whatever it takes.

Paris nodded and turned back to her notebook.

She intended to do exactly that.

CHAPTER 10

(Present)

The bus rumbled through the Orlando night, its fluorescent lights casting a sickly yellow pallor over the handful of passengers scattered across the seats.

Paris sat near the back, her body loose and languid with satisfaction. The hunger had quieted to a distant murmur, sated by Greg the rapist's blood, and in its absence she felt close to peace. It wouldn't last—it never did—but for now, she allowed herself to simply exist. To breathe. To watch the city lights slide past the grimy window like stars falling sideways.

She didn't need the bus. She could have walked back to the hotel in a fraction of the time, her Valensi speed carrying her through the shadows faster than any human conveyance. However, the mundanity of public transport held a certain appeal. The slow rocking motion. The anonymous press of strangers. The illusion of being ordinary, of being another passenger going somewhere, anywhere, nowhere in particular.

She had spent so many years being extraordinary. Sometimes it was nice to pretend otherwise.

The bus stopped, and a few passengers shuffled off. A few more climbed on—an elderly couple clutching shopping bags, a young man in a Nirvana t-shirt who glanced at Paris with obvious interest before finding a seat near the front. She ignored him. She was not hungry anymore, and he was not her type besides. Too soft. Too eager. No darkness in him worth noting.

Then the girl got on.

She was young—sixteen, seventeen—with dyed black hair and pale skin and an aesthetic that screamed defiance. Deep gray eye shadow rimmed her eyes like bruises. Black lipstick made her mouth a wound. Her clothes were layers of black on black: torn fishnet, a band t-shirt for some group Paris didn't recognize, a leather jacket studded with silver spikes. She moved down the aisle with the wary shuffle of someone who expected the world to hurt her and was rarely disappointed.

Paris watched her approach.

There was something about this girl. Some intriguing curiosity that tugged at her attention, that made her want to look closer. It wasn't attraction—not in the conventional sense—and it wasn't hunger. It was... recognition. The same recognition she had felt, over a century ago, when Ophelia had looked down at a dying waif in a Bristol alley and seen potential.

The girl chose a seat near Paris. Not next to her—one seat away, maintaining a buffer of empty space—but close enough that Paris could smell the cigarette smoke clinging to her clothes, the cheap vanilla perfume she'd applied to mask it. Close enough to see the details that distance had obscured.

The scars, for instance.

They ran along the inside of each wrist, pale lines against paler skin. Not horizontal—the hesitant scratches of someone crying for help—but vertical. Lengthwise. Following the veins. The marks of someone who had done their research. Someone who had meant it.

The girl caught Paris looking.

For a moment, their eyes met. The girl's expression flickered—wariness, then defiance, then some emotion harder to read. She tugged her sleeves down over her wrists, a reflexive gesture, and turned to stare out the window.

Paris should have let it go. Should have looked away, minded her own business, let this damaged stranger ride in peace. She had enough problems of her own without collecting more.

But she didn't look away.

"I'm Paris," she said.

The girl didn't turn. "Good for you."

"I like your makeup."

That got a reaction—a slight huff of surprise. The girl glanced back at Paris, her focus narrowing as she took in the blood-red hair, the matching lipstick, the dark clothes. Two creatures of the night, sizing each other up.

"Thanks," she said, her tone still guarded. "You're not bad yourself. For a try-hard."

Paris cocked her head. "Try-hard?"

"The hair. The nails. The whole..." She gestured vaguely. "Look. It's a lot."

"I could say the same about you."

The girl almost smiled at that. Almost. "Fair enough."

Silence stretched between them. The bus rumbled on. Paris waited.

"I'm Rae," the girl said finally, as if the words had been dragged out of her against her will.

"Nice to meet you, Rae."

"Is it?" Rae's eyes were sharp, assessing. "You don't know me. I could be anyone. I could be a psycho."

"You could be," Paris agreed. "But you're not."

"How do you know?"

"Because psychos don't sit alone on buses at midnight looking like they're waiting for the world to end. They're out there making it end." Paris tilted her head. "You're... surviving. Same as me."

Rae's expression faltered. A crack in the armor. She looked away again, but this time her posture was different—less defensive, more uncertain.

"You talk weird," she said.

"So I've been told."

"No, I mean..." Rae frowned, searching for the words. "You look my age. Maybe a little older. But you don't talk like a teenager. You talk like..." She trailed off, shaking her head. "I don't know. Someone's grandmother, maybe. If their grandmother was a goth."

Paris laughed—a genuine laugh, surprising herself. "That's the nicest thing anyone's said to me in days."

"Wasn't meant to be nice. It's weird." Rae was looking at her again, really looking, and Paris could see the intelligence behind those world-worn eyes. This girl was sharp. Sharper than she wanted people to know. "Who are you, really?"

"Just a tourist," Paris said. "Passing through."

"Bullshit."

"Excuse me?"

"Tourists don't ride buses at midnight. Tourists don't sit in the back and stare at strangers. Tourists don't look at people like..." Rae stopped, her jaw tightening.

"Like what?"

"Like you're deciding whether to eat them or save them."

The words hung in the air between them. Paris felt a chill run down her spine—not of fear, but of surprise. This girl saw too much. Understood too much. It was dangerous.

It was also, Paris realized, exactly why she couldn't look away.

"Maybe both," she said quietly. "Depending on the person."

Rae stared at her for a long moment. Then, impossibly, she smiled. It was a small gesture, broken and bitter, but real.

"You're fucking crazy," she said. "You know that?"

"I've been called worse."

"I bet you have." Rae leaned back in her seat, some of the tension draining from her shoulders. "So what's your deal? Running from something? Running toward something?"

"Does it matter?"

"Not really. Just making conversation." Rae shrugged. "It's what normal people do."

"Are you normal people?"

"Fuck no." Another half-grin. "But I can pretend."

Paris nodded slowly. "So can I."

They sat in silence for a while, watching the city roll past. The bus stopped and started, passengers coming and going, but neither of them moved. There was a strange comfort in the quiet—two outsiders sharing space, asking nothing of each other, expecting nothing.

Finally, Paris spoke again.

"The scars," she said. "On your wrists."

Rae's hand moved instinctively to cover them. Her expression shuttered, walls slamming back into place. "What about them?"

"I tried that once."

The lie came easily. Paris had never attempted suicide—had never even considered it, not seriously. She had spent too many years fighting to survive, clawing her way up from the gutters of Bristol, to ever willingly surrender. But she recognized the impulse. She had seen it in others. And she knew sometimes, the only way to reach someone was to meet them in their darkness.

Rae's eyes widened. "You did?"

"Different method. But yes." Paris held her gaze, keeping her expression open and honest. "It didn't work, obviously. And afterward, I realized it wasn't what I actually wanted."

"What did you want?"

"To stop hurting." Paris paused. "But dying wouldn't have done that. It would have... stopped everything. The good along with the bad. And I decided I wasn't ready to give up on the good yet."

Rae was silent for a long moment. When she spoke again, her voice was smaller, younger, stripped of its protective sarcasm.

"I saw..." she said. "When I was... when I did it. Before they brought me back."

"What did you see?"

"Nothing." Rae's laugh was hollow. "Just... blackness. No light, no tunnel, no dead relatives waiting to welcome me. Just nothing. Forever."

"And that scared you?"

"It should have, right? But it didn't. It was kind of... peaceful." She shook her head. "What scared me was waking up. Realizing I had to keep going. Keep living in this shitty world with all its shitty people." Her hands clenched in her lap. "Sometimes I think I made the wrong choice. Coming back."

Paris considered her response carefully. She could offer platitudes—*life is precious, things will get better, you have so much to live for*—but Rae would see through them in an instant. This girl didn't need comfort. She needed honesty.

"Maybe you did," Paris said. "Maybe coming back was a mistake. But you're here now. And since you're here, you might as well see what happens next."

Rae blinked. "That's your advice? 'See what happens next'?"

"It's not advice. It's... what I do. Every day, I wake up and think, 'Well, I'm still here. Might as well see what happens.' And sometimes what happens is terrible. But sometimes..." Paris shrugged. "Sometimes it's not."

"That's bleak as fuck."

Paris nodded. "But it keeps me moving forward."

Rae was quiet for a long moment, her thoughts distant. Then she let out a breath that might have been a laugh or might have been a sigh.

"You're weird," she said. "But I kind of like you."

"The feeling is mutual."

The bus was slowing, approaching another stop. Rae glanced out the window and swore under her breath.

"This is me," she said, standing. She hesitated, looking back at Paris. "Will I see you again?"

Paris considered the question. She should say no. She should let this girl walk away and forget she ever existed. Getting attached to humans was dangerous—for them and for her. She had learned that lesson too many times to count.

But there was a strange curiosity about Rae. She reminded Paris of another girl, long ago, who had found a family in the darkness and lost it as quickly.

She reminded her of herself.

"If you're lucky."

Rae snorted. "Luck's never been my thing." She pulled a pen from her pocket and grabbed Paris's hand, scrawling a number on her palm. "That's my cell. If you want to hang out or whatever. No pressure."

Before Paris could respond, Rae was gone—down the aisle, out the door, disappearing into the Orlando night.

Paris looked at the number on her hand. The ink was already smudging, the digits blurring together.

She should wash it off. Forget the girl. Focus on her own survival.

Instead, she pulled out her phone and saved the number.

Rae, she typed. The girl from the bus.

The bus rumbled on toward her hotel. Paris leaned her head against the window and closed her eyes.

She had a feeling she would be seeing Rae again.

Whether that was a good thing or a bad thing remained to be seen.

CHAPTER 11

(1890, The Citadel — Age 10)

The classroom was cold, as it always was in winter.

Paris sat in her usual seat near the front, her notebook open, her pen ready. Beside her, London was sketching in the margins of her own notes—a habit she had developed over the past two years, her fingers always moving, always creating. On Paris's other side, the seat that had once belonged to a boy named Gregory sat empty. He had been "transferred" three weeks ago. No one spoke of him anymore.

The instructor today was Mr. Ashworth, a thin man with spectacles and a perpetually sour expression. He taught what the students privately called "Survival Studies"—a catch-all subject that covered everything from Valensi physiology to tactical awareness to the various ways their kind could be injured or killed.

It was not a cheerful class. But it was, Paris had come to understand, one of the most important.

"Today," Mr. Ashworth said, turning to the chalkboard, "we will discuss vulnerabilities."

He wrote the word in large letters, the chalk squeaking against the slate. Below it, he began a list:

SUNLIGHT

DECAPITATION

FIRE

WOODEN STAKES

"These are the primary methods by which a Valensi can be killed," he said, tapping each word with his chalk. "You are familiar with most of them by now. Sunlight causes rapid cellular degradation—not the dramatic combustion of popular fiction, but a slower, more agonizing process of tissue breakdown. Decapitation is self-explanatory. Fire destroys our bodies faster than we can regenerate. And wooden stakes—specifically through the heart—disrupt the cardiac system catastrophically."

He paused, scanning the room. Twenty-two students remained from the original thirty-one. Their faces were attentive, serious. They had learned by now that inattention in Mr. Ashworth's class could have consequences.

"These are the known vulnerabilities," he continued. "The ones humans have stumbled upon through centuries of folklore and superstition. They are, for the most part, difficult for humans to exploit. Sunlight requires exposure during daylight hours, when we are typically hidden. Decapitation and fire require proximity and strength that most humans lack. Wooden stakes require precision and speed."

He set down the chalk and folded his hands behind his back.

"But there are other vulnerabilities. Theoretical ones. Methods of killing our kind that have not yet been weaponized—but which, in the wrong hands, could prove devastating."

Paris leaned forward slightly. This was new.

"Our cellular structure," Mr. Ashworth said, "is fundamentally different from that of humans. Our blood, our tissues, our organs—all have been altered by the transformation process. This is what grants us our strength, our speed, our longevity. But it also creates certain... susceptibilities."

He returned to the chalkboard and wrote two more words:

ORGANIC COMPOUNDS

"There exist certain materials—primarily organic in nature—that interact negatively with our altered cellular structure. Wood is the most commonly known example. The specific chemical compounds present in certain types of wood cause a violent reaction when introduced directly into our cardiovascular system. This is why a wooden stake through the heart is fatal, while a steel blade through the same organ is merely... inconvenient."

A few students shifted uncomfortably. Paris remained still, her pen moving steadily across her notebook.

"But wood is not the only such material," Mr. Ashworth continued. "There are minerals, plant derivatives, and synthesized compounds that share similar properties. When introduced into our bloodstream or brought into direct contact with our internal tissues, these substances can cause rapid cellular destabilization."

He paused, letting the words sink in.

"Destabilization," he repeated. "Not merely injury. Not merely pain. Complete systemic collapse. The cells themselves break down, unable to maintain their structure. The body, quite literally, falls apart from the inside."

Salem raised his hand. "Like what? What compounds?"

Mr. Ashworth regarded him coolly. "The specific materials are not widely known, and I will not be providing a comprehensive list. Suffice it to say that they exist, and that exposure to them would be... unpleasant."

"But if they exist," Salem pressed, "why haven't humans used them against us?"

"An excellent question." Mr. Ashworth's thin lips curved into not quite a smile. "The answer is twofold. First, humans do not know we exist— not truly, not with certainty. Their folklore speaks of vampires and demons, but they dismiss such tales as superstition. They are not actively searching for ways to destroy us because they do not believe there is anything to destroy."

He turned back to the chalkboard, adding another line:
HUMAN IGNORANCE = VALENSI SAFETY

"Second," he continued, "even if humans were to discover our existence, the specific compounds required to harm us are rare, difficult to synthesize, and even more difficult to weaponize effectively. A human would need to know not only what materials to use, but how to deliver them—in what concentration, through what method, at what dosage. The margin for error is small, and the consequences of failure would be... educational for us."

"So we're safe," another student said. "They can't hurt us."

Mr. Ashworth's expression hardened. "No one is ever safe. That is the first lesson of survival, and if you have not learned it by now, you are unlikely to survive long enough to be Birthed." He let the rebuke hang in the air for a moment before continuing. "We are relatively safe. For now. But circumstances change. Humans are ingenious creatures—far more so than many of our kind give them credit for. They have harnessed electricity, built machines that fly through the sky. Do not make the mistake of underestimating them."

Paris wrote in her notebook: Organic compounds—cellular destabilization. Rare but possible. Humans don't know. Yet.

She underlined the last word twice.

"The purpose of this lesson," Mr. Ashworth said, "is not to frighten you. It is to ensure that you understand the full scope of what you are—and what you are not. You are not invincible. You are not immortal in any true sense. You are simply... durable. Long-lived. Difficult to kill." He paused. "But not impossible."

He erased the chalkboard with quick, efficient strokes, wiping away the words as if they had never been written.

"That concludes today's lesson. Tomorrow we will discuss territorial protocols and the consequences of violating another Valensi's claimed hunting ground. You are dismissed."

The students began gathering their things, the scrape of chairs and rustle of papers filling the silence. Paris remained seated for a moment, staring at the blank chalkboard where the words ORGANIC COMPOUNDS had been written.

London leaned over. "You're thinking too hard," she murmured. "I can see the smoke coming out of your ears."

"Just... filing it away," Paris said.

"Filing what away? It's theoretical. He said so himself—humans don't know, and even if they did, they couldn't weaponize it."

"He also said not to underestimate them."

London shrugged. "Humans have been around for tens of thousands of years and they still haven't figured out we exist. I think we're fine."

Paris nodded slowly, closing her notebook. "You're probably right."

But she didn't believe it. Not entirely.

She had lived among humans for the first eight years of her life. She had seen what they were capable of—the cruelty, yes, but also the ingenuity. The relentless drive to understand, to conquer, to destroy anything they perceived as a threat. If humans ever discovered the Valensi—truly discovered them, with proof and certainty—they would not rest until they had found a way to fight back.

And when that day came, Paris intended to be ready.

She tucked her notebook into her bag and followed London out of the classroom, leaving the empty chalkboard behind.

Knowledge is survival, she thought. Remember everything. Trust nothing.

It was a lesson the Citadel had not taught her.

It was a lesson she had taught herself.

That night, in the quiet of her quarters, Paris opened her notebook and reviewed the day's lessons. She had developed a system over the past two years—a method of organizing information that went beyond simple note-taking. Important facts went in the main body of the page. Observations and speculations went in the margins. And things she wanted to remember but never speak of aloud went in a private code she had invented, a cipher based on a combination of Latin and symbols of her own devising.

In that cipher, she wrote:

Weaknesses exist beyond the obvious. Wood is not unique—other compounds share properties. Mr. A knows more than he shared. Why?

And below that:

If humans ever learn what we are, they will find a way to kill us. Prepare accordingly.

She stared at the words for a long moment. Then she closed the notebook, slid it beneath her mattress, and extinguished her candle.

In the darkness, she lay awake and thought about cellular destabilization. About organic compounds. About the confident dismissal in London's voice and the careful evasion in Mr. Ashworth's.

Theoretical, he had said. Not yet weaponized.

Yet.

Paris closed her eyes and let sleep take her.

But some part of her mind kept working, kept filing, kept preparing for a future that might never come—or might arrive sooner than anyone expected.

CHAPTER 12

(Present)

Paris called the number the next evening, after sunset.

She wasn't sure why. She had a hundred reasons not to—she was a fugitive, a killer, a creature that fed on human blood. Getting close to anyone, especially a vulnerable teenage girl, was reckless at best and cruel at worst. Whatever connection she formed would be temporary. Whatever affection she developed would only make the inevitable parting more painful.

And yet.

The phone rang twice before Rae picked up.

"Yeah?"

"It's Paris. From the bus."

A pause. Then: "Holy shit. I didn't think you'd actually call."

"Neither did I."

"So why did you?"

Paris considered the question. The honest answer was complicated—about recognition, about loneliness, about seeing a reflection of her younger self in a girl with scars on her wrists and defiance in her eyes. But honesty was a luxury she couldn't afford.

"I'm bored," she said instead. "And you seemed interesting."

Rae laughed—a short, surprised sound. "Interesting. That's a new one. Usually people go with 'weird' or 'fucked up.'"

"Those too. But interesting covers more ground."

"Fair enough." There was a rustling on the other end of the line, the creak of bedsprings. "So what do you want to do? I'm not really a 'hang out at the mall' kind of girl."

"What kind of girl are you?"

"The kind that gets kicked out of malls."

Paris smiled. "Then we'll go somewhere else. You hungry?"

Another pause, longer this time. When Rae spoke again, some of the bravado had slipped from her voice. "I could eat."

"I'll pick you up. Text me your address."

She hung up before Rae could argue.

Rae was staying at a motel on the south end of town—the kind of place that rented rooms by the week and didn't ask questions about the ages of its guests or where their money came from. Paris pulled into the parking lot and found Rae waiting outside, leaning against a rusted ice machine with her arms crossed and her expression wary.

The streetlights cast her in harsh orange, deepening the shadows beneath her eyes. She looked younger in this light. More fragile. The black clothes and dark makeup couldn't quite hide the sharpness of her cheekbones, the bags under her eyes. This was a girl who wasn't eating enough, wasn't sleeping enough, wasn't taking care of herself in any of the ways that mattered.

Paris recognized the signs. She had worn them herself, once.

"Nice ride," Rae said, eyeing the Cadillac as she climbed into the passenger seat. "Steal it?"

"Borrowed it."

"From who?"

"Someone who didn't need it anymore."

Rae snorted. "Right. Okay." She pulled the door shut and slouched down in the seat, her boots propped against the dashboard. "So where are we going?"

"You said you were hungry."

"I'm always hungry. Doesn't mean I can afford to eat."

Paris glanced at her. "I'm buying."

"Why?"

"Because I have money and you don't. Is that a problem?"

Rae was quiet for a moment, her jaw working. Pride warred with hunger on her face—a battle Paris had seen before, had fought herself in the cold streets of Bristol. Finally, hunger won.

"No," she said. "It's not a problem."

"Good." Paris pulled out of the parking lot and onto the main road. "What do you feel like? And don't say you don't care. Everyone cares."

Rae considered. "Pancakes," she said finally. "I fucking love pancakes."

"Pancakes it is."

They found an all-night diner three miles down the road—a squat, ugly building with a flickering neon sign that read 24 HOURS and a parking lot populated by long-haul truckers and insomniacs. The inside was warm and smelled of grease and coffee, and the waitress who seated them didn't blink at the sight of two goth girls sliding into a booth at ten o'clock at night.

Rae studied the menu with the intensity of someone who hadn't had a proper meal in days. "Pancakes," she said. "Definitely pancakes. And bacon. And eggs. And—" She glanced up at Paris, suddenly self-conscious. "Sorry. I... I'm really hungry."

"Don't apologize." Paris scanned her own menu. "I'm starving."

When the waitress returned, Rae ordered a stack of pancakes, bacon, eggs, hash browns, and toast. She seemed embarrassed by the size of the order.

Then Paris ordered.

"I'll have two full stacks of pancakes," she said. "A side of bacon—extra crispy. Three eggs, scrambled. Hash browns, double portion. Sausage links. And do you have biscuits and gravy?"

The waitress blinked. "We do."

"I'll take that too. And a large orange juice. And coffee."

She handed back the menu with a polite nod. The waitress stared at her for a moment, then at Rae, then back at Paris.

"That's... all for you?"

"Yes."

"Okay then." The waitress scribbled on her pad, clearly deciding it wasn't her business if some skinny teenage girl wanted to order half the kitchen. "I'll put that right in."

She walked away, and Rae burst out laughing.

"Holy shit," she said. "Where are you going to put all that?"

"I have a fast metabolism."

"Fast? That's not fast. That's like... industrial." Rae shook her head, still grinning. "I thought *I* was hungry."

"You are hungry. So am I." Paris leaned back in the booth. "I don't like to eat alone. And I don't like to eat small."

"Clearly."

The food arrived in waves—plate after plate until their table was covered, the waitress making three trips to deliver it all. Rae's eyes went wide at the sheer volume of food in front of Paris.

"There's no way," she said. "There's no way you're going to finish all that."

Paris picked up her fork. "Watch me."

She did.

They ate in companionable silence at first, both of them too focused on the food for conversation. Rae worked through her stack of pancakes with the desperate efficiency of someone who'd learned not to waste a meal. But Paris—Paris *demolished* her food. Methodically. Relentlessly. Bite after bite, plate after plate, until the mountain of breakfast had been reduced to empty dishes smeared with syrup and grease.

Rae finished her own meal and sat back, watching in undisguised amazement as Paris cleaned her final plate.

"That," Rae said, "was the most impressive thing I've ever seen."

"I was hungry." Paris dabbed at her lips with a napkin. "I told you."

"Hungry doesn't cover it. That was like... competitive eating. That was like a nature documentary. 'Here we see the wild Paris consuming three times her body weight in pancakes.'"

Paris laughed—a genuine laugh, warm and unguarded. "I have a very demanding metabolism. I burn through calories quickly."

"No shit." Rae was still staring at the empty plates. "Do you always eat like that?"

"When I can. It's... necessary."

"Necessary for what?"

Paris considered how to answer. The truth—that her Valensi physiology demanded massive caloric intake to fuel her enhanced strength, speed, and healing—was not an option. But she found herself wanting to give Rae something real.

"I'm stronger than I look," she said. "Faster. But it comes with a cost. My body burns through energy at an incredible rate. If I don't eat enough, I get weak. Slow. Vulnerable." She shrugged. "So I eat. A lot."

Rae processed this, her brow furrowing. "That's weird."

"I'm a weird person."

"Yeah, you are." But there was no judgment in Rae's voice. If anything, she seemed intrigued. "Is that why you're so skinny? Your body just burns through everything?"

"Something like that."

"Huh." Rae picked at the remnants of her hash browns. "Must be nice. I look at a cheeseburger and gain five pounds."

"You could use five pounds."

"Thanks, mom."

Paris smiled. "I mean it. You're too thin. You need to eat more."

"Hard to eat more when you can't afford food."

"That's why I'm buying."

Rae's expression softened—for a moment, before she hid it behind her usual mask of sarcasm. "Yeah. Thanks for that. Really."

"You're welcome." Paris flagged down the waitress. "Can we get another stack of pancakes? And more bacon?"

Rae looked genuinely shocked. "More?"

"For you. You said you were hungry. So eat."

"I can't—"

"You can. And you will." Paris fixed her with a steady gaze. "When someone offers you food, you take it. That's survival 101. You never know when the next meal is coming."

Rae's expression flickered with recognition. The understanding of someone who had learned the same lesson the hard way.

"Yeah," she said quietly. "Okay."

The second stack arrived. Rae ate it all.

And somewhere between the pancakes and the bacon, between the coffee refills and the shared laughter, something shifted between them. A wall came down. A connection formed.

Two survivors, recognizing each other across a table full of empty plates.

"So," Rae said, when the carnage had been cleared away and they were both nursing coffee, pleasantly stuffed. "What's your deal?"

"My deal?"

"Yeah. Your deal. Your story. Your tragic backstory." She waved her fork in a vague circle. "Everyone's got one. What's yours?"

Paris sipped her coffee. "It's a long story."

"I've got time."

"It's also none of your business."

Rae grinned—the first real grin Paris had seen from her, wide and crooked and unexpectedly charming. "Fair enough. I'll show you mine if you show me yours, though."

"Is that how it works?"

"That's how everything works." Rae leaned back in the booth, her plate nearly empty now. "Trust for trust. Secret for secret. You want to know about me, you've got to give back. What's the term? *Quid pro quo.*"

Paris considered this. It was a reasonable philosophy—more reasonable than she would have expected from a sixteen-year-old runaway. But then, Rae wasn't an ordinary sixteen-year-old. The streets had a way of teaching lessons that schools never could.

"All right," Paris said. "You first."

"Nuh-uh. You called me, remember? You go first."

"I'm older than I look."

Rae rolled her eyes. "Everyone says that."

"I mean it literally. I'm much older than I look."

"What, like twenty-five? Thirty?" Rae squinted at her. "You've got good skin, I'll give you that. But you're not fooling anyone."

Paris smiled. "Let's say I've been around for a while. Long enough to recognize a survivor when I see one."

"That your way of asking about the scars?"

"No. The scars are your business. I'm talking about everything else. The way you carry yourself. The way you watch the doors. The way you ate that food like someone was going to take it away from you." Paris set down her coffee cup. "You've been on your own for a while. Something happened—something bad—and now you're here, in a shitty motel in Orlando, trying to figure out what comes next."

Rae was silent for a long moment. Her fingers traced the edge of her plate, smearing syrup across the ceramic.

"My mom's boyfriend," she said finally. "That's what happened. He was... not a good guy."

"Did he hurt you?"

"He tried." Rae's voice was flat, emotionless—the voice of someone who had learned to tell their story without feeling it. "I didn't let him. But my mom didn't believe me, so..." She shrugged. "I left. Ended up here."

"How long ago?"

"Six months. Give or take."

Six months. A child, alone, surviving on the streets of a strange city for half a year. Paris felt her own history twist in her chest. It might have been anger, or might have been recognition.

"You're tougher than you look," she said.

"Had to be." Rae met her gaze, and for a moment, the armor was gone—a scared kid looking for anything to hold onto. "Your turn. What's your tragic backstory?"

Paris thought about Bristol. About her mother's body at the bottom of the stairs. About Marty and Liz crushed beneath carriage wheels. About Ophelia's cold hand and the choice that had changed everything.

"My mother died when I was seven," she said. "My father killed her. I ran away and lived on the streets until... until I found a new family."

"A new family?"

"Of sorts. They took me in. Taught me things. Made me stronger." Paris paused. "But I had to leave them too. Recently. Things got... complicated."

"Complicated how?"

"The kind of complicated that means people are looking for me. The kind of complicated that means I can't stay in one place for very long."

Rae nodded slowly, processing this. "So you're running."

"Yes."

"From what?"

"From people who want to kill me."

She said it simply, without drama, and watched Rae's reaction. The girl didn't flinch, didn't gasp, didn't do any of the things a normal teenager might do when confronted with such a statement. She nodded again, as if this made perfect sense.

"Okay," Rae said. "That's pretty fucked up."

"Yes. It is."

"And you still called me? Even though you're, like, a wanted woman or whatever?"

"I told you. I was bored."

Rae laughed—that same short, surprised sound from the phone call. "You're a terrible liar."

"I'm an excellent liar. I'm choosing not to lie to you."

"Why?"

Paris didn't answer immediately. She looked at this girl—this broken, defiant, impossibly resilient girl—and saw herself. Saw London. Saw everyone she had ever cared about and lost.

"Because you remind me of someone," she said finally. "Someone I cared about very much."

"What happened to them?"

"I don't know. We got separated." Paris looked down at her coffee, watching the liquid ripple in the cup. "I hope she's okay. But I don't know."

Rae was quiet for a moment. Then she reached across the table and touched Paris's hand—a brief contact, awkward and uncertain, but genuine.

"That sucks," she said. "I'm sorry."

Paris looked up, surprised by the sincerity in the girl's voice. "Thank you."

"For what it's worth, I hope she's okay too. Your friend." Rae pulled her hand back, suddenly self-conscious. "And, um. Thanks. For the pancakes. And for... you know. Talking to me. Like a real person."

"You are a real person."

"Yeah, well. Not everyone treats me like one."

Paris thought of Greg, bleeding out in an alley. Of all the men like him, circling vulnerable girls like sharks scenting blood in the water. Of the countless predators who saw someone like Rae and saw only prey.

"Anyone who doesn't treat you like a person," she said quietly, "doesn't deserve to breathe the same air as you."

Rae blinked. "That's... intense."

"I'm an intense person."

"No shit." But she was smiling again, that crooked grin that made her look younger and older at the same time. "So what now? You've bought me pancakes and shared tragic backstories. What's next on the agenda?"

Paris considered. She should end this here. Should pay the check, drive Rae back to her shitty motel, and disappear from her life forever. It was the smart thing to do. The safe thing.

But Paris was tired of being safe. Tired of being alone. And this girl— this fierce, damaged, impossibly alive girl—made her feel things she hadn't felt in a very long time.

Hope.

"Do you need clothes?" she asked.

Rae looked down at herself—the same outfit she'd been wearing on the bus, rumpled and slightly stained. "I mean... yeah. But I told you, I can't—"

"I'm buying."

"You can't keep buying me stuff."

"Why not?"

"Because..." Rae struggled for a reason. "Because you don't know me. Because I could be anyone. Because—"

"Because you're not used to people being kind to you," Paris finished. "I understand. But I'm not most people. And I don't do anything I don't want to do." She stood, dropping a fifty-dollar bill on the table. "Come on. Let's go shopping."

Rae stared at her for a long moment. Then she shook her head, laughing softly.

"You're crazy," she said. "You know that, right?"

"So I've been told."

"Like, genuinely insane."

"Probably." Paris held out her hand. "Coming?"

Rae hesitated. Then she took the hand and let Paris pull her to her feet.

"Yeah," she said. "I'm coming."

They spent the next few hours wandering through late-night shops and 24-hour stores—the strange ecosystem of places that catered to shift workers and insomniacs and people who lived their lives after sundown. A Walmart that never closed. A thrift store near the airport that stayed open until 2 AM to catch the red-eye crowd. A vintage shop run by a tattooed woman who seemed unsurprised to see customers at midnight.

Rae had good taste, if unconventional. She gravitated toward blacks and deep purples, torn denim and band shirts, anything that looked like it had been rescued from a dumpster behind a punk club. Paris approved. There was honesty in Rae's aesthetic—a refusal to pretend to be anything she wasn't.

"What about this?" Rae held up a leather jacket, battered and worn, with patches sewn onto the sleeves.

"It's perfect."

"It's forty bucks."

"And?"

Rae bit her lip. "That's a lot of money for a jacket."

"It's a lot of jacket for the money." Paris took it from her hands and carried it to the register. "Consider it a gift."

"You've given me like ten gifts tonight."

"Then consider them all one big gift."

Rae shook her head, but she was smiling. "You're impossible."

"Thank you."

They left the vintage shop with bags hanging from both arms, more clothes than Rae probably owned in total. The night had deepened around them, the streets quieter now, the crowds thinned to scattered stragglers. Paris checked her watch—nearly 3 AM. Still several hours until dawn, but Rae was human. She needed sleep.

"I should get you back," Paris said. "It's late."

"Yeah." Rae's voice was quiet. "Thanks. For tonight. For everything."

"You don't have to keep thanking me."

"Yeah, I do. Because..." She trailed off, struggling for words. "Because no one's ever done anything like this for me. Not without wanting something in return."

Paris turned to look at her. "I don't want anything from you, Rae. Just your company. That's enough."

Rae blinked away what could have been tears, her jaw tightening.

"You're weird," she said.

"So are you."

"Yeah, but I'm the normal kind of weird. You're like... next-level weird."

"I'll take that as a compliment."

"It was meant as one." Rae shouldered her bags and started toward the car. "Come on, grandma. Let's go before the sun comes up and you turn into a pumpkin or whatever."

Paris felt a chill at the words—spoken in jest, but closer to the truth than Rae could possibly know. She forced a smile and followed her to the Cadillac.

"Something like that," she murmured.

She dropped Rae at the motel as the first pale hint of pre-dawn began to lighten the eastern horizon. They sat in the car for a moment, neither quite ready to say goodbye.

"Same time tomorrow?" Rae asked. She was trying to sound casual, but Paris could hear the hope beneath the words.

"If I'm not busy."

"Busy doing what? You said you were on the run."

"Running takes a lot of energy."

Rae snorted. "You're so full of shit."

"Probably." Paris glanced at the horizon, calculating. She had around forty-five minutes before the sun became a problem. "Get some sleep. And eat. You're too thin."

"Yes, mom." But Rae was smiling too as she climbed out of the car, her bags clutched to her chest. She paused at the door, looking back. "Hey, Paris?"

"Yes?"

"Thanks. Really. For everything." She hesitated, then added: "You're the first person in a long time who made me feel like... like things could be okay. You know?"

Paris felt that twist in her chest again—stronger now, painful.

"Things can always be okay," she said. "Sometimes you have to wait for the darkness to pass."

Rae nodded slowly. "Yeah. Maybe." She raised a hand in farewell. "See you tomorrow night, weirdo."

"See you tomorrow night."

Paris watched her disappear into the motel, the door swinging shut behind her. She sat in the car for a long moment, staring at the flickering vacancy sign, feeling things she hadn't felt in years.

Connection. Responsibility. Fear.

Not fear for herself. Fear for Rae. For this fragile, fierce girl who had somehow wormed her way past Paris's defenses in the space of a single night.

This is dangerous, she thought. This is stupid. You're going to get her killed.

But she didn't drive away. Not yet.

Instead, she reached out with her mind—gently, carefully, the way the Magistrate had taught her so many years ago. She found Rae's consciousness like a flame in the darkness, flickering but bright. She didn't intrude, didn't read her thoughts. She simply... touched. Established a connection. A thread of awareness that would let her know if Rae was in danger. Linking like this didn't need for her to see her target, only know them enough that she could *connect* with them.

It was a violation of privacy. It was presumptuous and intrusive and probably wrong.

But Paris didn't care.

She had lost too many people she cared about. She would not lose another.

I'll keep you safe, she thought, sending the promise into the void. *Whatever it takes.*

The connection hummed between them, invisible and unbreakable.

The horizon was growing lighter. Paris started the car and drove back to her hotel, the urgency of approaching dawn pressing at her.

She made it to her room with minutes to spare, pulling the blackout curtains tight against the windows, sealing herself in darkness as the sun rose over Orlando.

But part of her stayed with Rae.

And would stay with her for as long as it took.

CHAPTER 13

(1891, The Citadel — Age 11)

The training hall smelled of sweat and old blood.

Paris had grown accustomed to the smell over the past three years—had grown accustomed to many things that would have horrified the girl she'd once been. The ache of bruised muscles. The taste of copper in her mouth after a hard blow. The way her heart rate stayed steady now even when Master Asaro called her forward to fight, when once it had hammered against her ribs like that of a trapped bird.

She was not the same creature who had stumbled into the Citadel half-dead and feral. The School had seen to that.

Today's session was different. Paris sensed it the moment she entered the hall, felt it in the tension that crackled through the assembled students like static before a storm. Master Asaro stood at the center of the room, his hands clasped behind his back, his face unreadable. Beside him stood Headmistress Redmond, her iron-grey hair pulled back in its severe bun, her gaze sweeping over them with cold assessment.

The Headmistress did not attend ordinary training sessions.

"Form up," Asaro said. His voice was soft, as always, but it carried to every corner of the hall. "Two lines. Facing each other."

The students obeyed, shuffling into position with the ease of long practice. Paris found herself across from a boy named Marcus—older than her, bigger, but slow. She had beaten him twice before. She would beat him again if called upon.

But Asaro's gaze passed over her without stopping. It moved down the line, assessing, calculating, until it landed on two students at the far end.

Salem. And Theresa.

Paris felt her stomach tighten.

Theresa was thirteen, a quiet girl from somewhere in Eastern Europe whose accent had never quite faded despite years at the Citadel. She was competent in her studies, adequate in combat, but there was a softness to her that the School had never quite managed to burn away. She flinched when struck. She hesitated before delivering blows. She apologized after winning.

Salem had noticed. They all had.

"Salem. Theresa." Asaro's voice cut through the silence. "Step forward."

They moved to the center of the hall, facing each other. Theresa's face was pale, her hands trembling slightly at her sides. Salem's expression was calm, bored, but Paris could see the hunger lurking beneath the surface. The anticipation.

He had been waiting for this.

"Today's exercise," Asaro said, "is elimination."

The word hung in the air. Paris heard someone behind her draw a sharp breath.

"You have trained for three years," Asaro continued. "You have learned to fight, to defend, to survive. But training is not enough. Theory is not enough. To become Valensi, you must prove that you are willing to do what survival requires." He paused, his dark eyes moving between Salem and Theresa. "One of you will leave this hall victorious. One of you will not leave at all."

Theresa made a small sound—not quite a gasp, not quite a whimper. She glanced at Headmistress Redmond, searching for some sign that this was a test, a bluff, a cruel joke.

The Headmistress's expression did not change.

"This is murder," Theresa said. Her voice cracked on the word. "You're asking us to commit murder."

"I am asking you to survive," Asaro replied. "There is a difference."

"There isn't. There—" She turned to the other students, eyes wild, desperate. "You can't let them do this. This is wrong. This is—"

"Theresa." Asaro's voice hardened, cutting off her protests. "You have been given an order. You will obey it or you will die. Those are your only options."

Salem smiled.

It was a small smile, barely visible, but Paris saw it. Saw the way his weight shifted forward, the way his hands curled into fists at his sides. He wasn't nervous. He wasn't afraid.

He was eager.

"Begin," Asaro said.

Salem moved.

He crossed the distance between them in three quick strides, his fist driving toward Theresa's face with brutal efficiency. She managed to block—barely—stumbling backward under the force of the blow. Her form was textbook, her technique sound, but there was no conviction behind it. She was defending, not fighting. Reacting, not attacking.

Paris knew how this would end. They all did.

Salem pressed his advantage, raining down blows that Theresa could only partially deflect. He was stronger than her, faster than her, but more than that—he was willing. Willing to hurt. Willing to kill. That willingness was its own kind of weapon, and Theresa had no defense against it.

"Fight back," someone whispered. Paris wasn't sure if it was London beside her or the voice in her own head. "Fight back, damn you."

Theresa tried. She threw a punch that Salem easily dodged, followed by a kick that he caught and twisted, sending her spinning to the ground. She landed hard, the breath driven from her lungs, and for a moment she lay there, gasping, staring up at the ceiling.

Salem stood over her.

"Get up," he said. His voice was casual, conversational. "Come on, Theresa. At least make it interesting."

She looked at him—really looked at him—and her expression changed. The fear was still there, but beneath it was something else. Resignation. Acceptance.

She seemed resigned to the notion that she was going to die.

"Please," she whispered. "Salem, please. We don't have to do this. We can refuse. We can—"

He kicked her in the ribs.

The crack of bone was audible across the hall. Theresa screamed—a raw, animal sound—and curled in on herself, her arms wrapping around her midsection. Blood flecked her lips when she coughed.

"Get up," Salem said again. "I'm not going to kill you while you're lying there crying. Have some dignity."

Paris's hands were shaking. She clenched them into fists, her nails biting into her palms, and forced herself to watch. To witness. This was the lesson. Not just for Salem and Theresa, but for all of them. This was what the Citadel demanded. This was what survival looked like.

Theresa struggled to her feet. One arm hung limp at her side—dislocated shoulder, Paris guessed, on top of the broken ribs. Her breathing was ragged, wet, wrong. But she stood. She faced Salem with her one good arm raised in a guard position that couldn't possibly protect her.

"There you go," Salem said. "That's better."

He hit her again. And again. And again.

Each blow was precise, calculated, designed to cause maximum pain without immediately ending the fight. He was enjoying this, Paris realized. Not just the violence, but the power. The control. The absolute dominance over another human being.

Theresa stopped trying to defend herself after the fourth blow. She simply stood there, swaying, her face a mask of blood and bruises, and waited for the end.

It came quickly, at least.

Salem stepped behind her, wrapped his arm around her throat, and squeezed. Theresa's hands came up, clawing weakly at his forearm, but there was no strength left in her. No fight. Her struggles grew weaker, then stopped altogether.

When Salem released her, she crumpled to the ground and did not move.

The hall was silent.

Salem stood over Theresa's body, breathing hard, his face flushed with exertion and... triumph, or satisfaction. He looked around at the assembled students, meeting their eyes one by one, daring them to judge him.

His gaze found Paris.

She didn't look away. Didn't flinch. She met his stare with a coldness she hadn't known she possessed and held it until he was the one who turned away.

"Well done," Asaro said. His voice was neutral, empty of praise or condemnation. "You may return to your place."

Salem stepped over Theresa's body and walked back to the line of students. He took his position across from a boy named Peter, who was visibly trembling.

"The rest of you," Asaro continued, "take this lesson to heart. Hesitation is death. Mercy is death. The only path to survival is strength— and the willingness to use it." He paused, his gaze sweeping over them. "Dismissed."

No one moved for a long moment. Then, slowly, the students began to file out of the hall, their footsteps muffled, their eyes carefully averted from the body that still lay in the center of the room.

Paris was one of the last to leave. She paused at the doorway and looked back.

Two instructors had entered through a side door. They were wrapping Theresa's body in a cloth, preparing to carry it away. In an hour, the blood would be scrubbed from the floor. In a day, someone else would occupy Theresa's bed in the dormitory.

In a week, they would struggle to remember her face.

This was the Citadel. This was survival.

Paris turned and walked away.

She found London in their quarters, sitting on her bed with her knees drawn up to her chest. Her face was pale, her eyes red-rimmed.

"She begged," London said. Her voice was barely above a whisper. "She begged him to stop, and he just... he kept going."

Paris sat down beside her. She didn't touch her—didn't offer comfort or platitudes. There was nothing she could say that would make this better. Nothing that would bring Theresa back or change what they had witnessed.

"He enjoyed it," London continued. "Did you see his face? He *enjoyed* it."

"Yes."

"How can someone enjoy that? How can someone take pleasure in killing another person?"

Paris thought of her father, standing at the top of the stairs, looking down at her with that contemptuous glare. She thought of the men who had stalked the streets of Bristol, hunting vulnerable children for sport. She thought of all the cruelty she had witnessed in her short life, all the evil that humans—and, yes, Valensi—were capable of.

"Some people are broken," she said finally. "Key parts inside them are missing. The parts that feels empathy, compassion, remorse—it's just not there. And when you give people like that power, they use it to hurt others. Because they can. Because it makes them feel strong."

London was quiet for a long moment. "Is Salem broken?"

"Yes."

"Are we going to end up like him? Is that what this place does to people?"

Paris considered the question carefully. It was the question that had haunted her since she'd arrived at the Citadel—the fear that lurked beneath every lesson, every training session, every demonstration of Valensi power. Would she become a monster? Was that the price of survival?

"No," she said. "We're going to end up like us. Stronger. Harder. More capable of doing what needs to be done. But not like Salem." She turned to look at London, meeting her friend's eyes. "We get to choose who we become. The Citadel can teach us to fight, to kill, to survive. But it can't take away our choices. It can't make us enjoy cruelty. That's what Salem brought with him. That's what he already was."

"How do you know? How do you know we won't change?"

"Because I refuse to." Paris's voice was steady, certain. "I will learn everything they teach me. I will become as strong as I need to be. I will kill if I have to—if there's no other choice. But I will never become like Salem. I will never take pleasure in another person's pain. That's my line. And I will not cross it."

London stared at her for a long moment. Then, slowly, she nodded.

"Me too," she said. "That's my line too."

Paris reached out and took her hand. London's fingers were cold, trembling, but they gripped back with surprising strength.

"Then we'll hold each other to it," Paris said. "When things get dark—when we're tempted to become what we're not—we'll remind each other who we are. Deal?"

"Deal."

They sat together in the silence, two girls on the edge of some vast and terrible world, holding onto each other as the only stable point in a world that seemed determined to break them.

Outside, the Citadel went about its business. Instructors taught. Students trained. Bodies were disposed of and forgotten.

But in that small room, in that quiet moment, two survivors made a pact.

They would become strong. They would become deadly. They would do what survival required.

But they would not become monsters.

Not like Salem.

Not ever.

CHAPTER 14

(*Present*)

The next three nights fell into a pattern.

Paris would wake at sunset, shower, dress, and drive to Rae's motel. They would go somewhere—a diner, a late-night arcade, a 24-hour bowling alley populated by insomniacs and shift workers—and they would talk. Or not talk. Sometimes they sat together in comfortable silence, two creatures of the night finding solace in each other's company.

It was dangerous, this attachment. Paris knew it. Every hour she spent with Rae was an hour she wasn't running, wasn't planning, wasn't preparing for the inevitable confrontation with whomever the Magistrate sent after her. She was a fugitive with a death sentence hanging over her head, and she was spending her nights teaching a teenage runaway how to bowl.

It was reckless. It was stupid.

It was the happiest she had been in years.

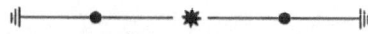

On the third night, they ended up at a beach south of Daytona.

Not the tourist beaches with their lifeguard stations and rental umbrellas, but a quiet stretch of sand on the outskirts of the city, accessible only by a dirt road that Rae had discovered during her months of wandering. The moon hung low over the water, painting silver ripples across the surface, and the air smelled of salt and something sweeter. Night-blooming jasmine. Or, the memory of summer.

They sat on a driftwood log, their shoulders touching, watching the waves roll in.

"I used to think about the ocean," Rae said. Her voice was softer than usual, stripped of its protective sarcasm. "When I was back home. Before everything went to shit. I'd never seen it, but I used to imagine what it would be like. This huge thing, bigger than anything, going on forever." She paused. "I thought if I could just get to the ocean, everything would be different. Everything would be okay."

"And is it?"

Rae was quiet for a moment. "It's beautiful," she said finally. "But it doesn't fix anything. Nothing fixes anything. You just... keep going."

Paris understood that sentiment better than Rae could possibly know. She had spent 135 years keeping going—through loss and betrayal and violence, through wars and plagues and the slow grinding march of centuries. The ocean didn't fix anything. Time didn't fix anything. You learned to carry the weight, or you collapsed beneath it.

"No," she agreed. "Nothing fixes anything. But some things make the carrying easier."

Rae turned to look at her. In the moonlight, her face was stripped of its usual armor—the dark makeup, the defensive sneer, the careful distance. She looked young. Vulnerable. Real.

"Is that what I am?" she asked. "Someone that makes the carrying easier?"

Paris considered the question. She thought of London—of the girl who had held her hand in the darkness of the Citadel and promised they would hold each other to their humanity. She thought of Garrett, whose love had been the only light in decades of shadow. She thought of everyone she had ever cared about and lost.

"Yes," she said. "That's exactly what you are."

Rae's smile was small but genuine. "You too," she said. "For what it's worth."

They sat in silence for a while, watching the waves. The night wrapped around them like a blanket, warm and shadowy and strangely safe.

"Can I ask you something?" Rae said eventually.

"You can ask. I might not answer."

"Fair enough." Rae drew her knees up to her chest, wrapping her arms around them. "What happened to you? I mean, really happened. You said your mom died and your dad was a bastard and you found a new family. But there's more to it than that. I can tell."

"There's always more."

"So tell me. Tell me the more."

Paris stared out at the ocean. The waves kept coming, endless and relentless, wearing away at the shore one grain of sand at a time. She had told so few people her true story. The risk was enormous—not just to herself, but to Rae. Knowledge of the Valensi was dangerous. It made you a target.

But Rae was already a target. She was a runaway, a victim, a girl with scars on her wrists and nowhere safe to go. The world had already marked her for destruction. What was one more secret?

"The family I found," Paris said slowly, "was not a normal family. They were... different. Special. They had abilities that most people don't have. And they took me in, trained me, made me one of them."

"Like a cult?"

"Not really. But more organized. More powerful." She paused. "I was with them for a very long time. I did things for them—things I'm not proud of. Things that were necessary. And then something happened. Someone I trusted betrayed me, and I had to leave."

"The person you mentioned. The one you got separated from."

"Yes. And others." Paris' memories took a front seat, and for a moment she was back in Paris—the city—with blood on her hands and London's face twisted with emotion she still couldn't name. "I thought I was protecting someone I loved. I thought I was doing the right thing. But I was wrong. And now people are dead because of me, and I can never go back."

Rae was quiet for a long moment. "That's heavy," she said finally.

"Yes."

"Do you regret it? The things you did?"

Paris thought about Dawn and London, who had been her sisters in all but blood. About the century of violence that had led her to that moment. That one moment that literally changed everything.

"Some of it," she said. "Not all of it. The things I did to survive—no. I don't regret those. But the things I did that hurt people who didn't deserve it..." She shook her head. "Those I carry with me. Every day."

"Is that why you're so nice to me? Because you're trying to balance the scales?"

The question was sharper than Paris expected. She turned to look at Rae, surprised by the insight.

"Maybe," she admitted. "Partly. But mostly..." She trailed off, searching for the right words. "Mostly I just like you. You remind me of someone I used to be. Someone I thought I'd lost a long time ago."

"The street kid? The survivor?"

"Yes. Before the family. Before everything." Paris smiled, but it was a sad smile, weighted with memory. "You have the same fire I had. The same refusal to break. I recognize it. And I want to protect it."

Rae was quiet for a moment. Then she leaned over and rested her head against Paris's shoulder—a small gesture, hesitant, as if she expected to be pushed away.

Paris didn't push her away.

They sat like that for a long time, watching the moon trace its arc across the sky, listening to the eternal rhythm of the waves.

It was nearly 2 AM when Paris drove Rae back to the motel.

The parking lot was emptier than usual—only a few cars scattered across the cracked asphalt, their windows obtuse. The vacancy sign flickered its eternal stutter, casting red shadows across the concrete.

"Same time tomorrow?" Rae asked, climbing out of the car. She was clutching a bag of leftovers from the diner they'd stopped at on the way back—Paris had insisted she take it, enough food for two more meals at least.

"Same time tomorrow."

Rae grinned. "Cool. Maybe we can go back to that arcade. I want a rematch on the racing game."

"You'll lose again."

"Probably. But I'll have fun doing it." She hesitated at the car door, her expression shifting more serious. "Hey, Paris?"

"Yes?"

"Thanks. For everything. For..." She gestured vaguely, encompassing the car, the food, the nights they'd spent together. "All of it. I know you've got your own shit going on. I know you're running from something. But you still made time for me. That means a lot."

Paris felt that familiar twist in her chest—the one that had been growing stronger every night, the one that whispered of attachment and vulnerability and all the dangers that came with caring about someone.

"You're worth making time for," she said.

Rae's smile softened. "You're such a sap."

"Don't tell anyone. I have a reputation to maintain."

"Your secret's safe with me." Rae raised a hand in farewell and turned toward the motel. "See you tomorrow night, weirdo."

"See you tomorrow night."

Paris watched her walk across the parking lot, her slight figure silhouetted against the flickering vacancy sign. She watched her climb the stairs to the second floor, watched her unlock the door to her room, watched her disappear inside.

Only then did she allow herself to breathe.

She's fine, Paris told herself. She's safe. Nothing's going to happen.

But even as she thought it, she reached out with her mind, checking the psychic link she had established. Rae's consciousness flickered at the edge of her awareness—tired, content, already drifting toward sleep. No fear. No danger.

Paris exhaled and put the car in reverse.

She was halfway out of the parking lot when she noticed the van.

It was parked at the far end of the lot, near the dumpsters—a white panel van with no windows and no markings. The kind of van that could belong to anyone. A contractor. A delivery driver. A maintenance worker.

The kind of van that predators used.

Paris stopped the car.

She stared at the van for a long moment, her senses straining. No movement inside. No sound. No heartbeat that she could detect from this distance.

It's nothing, she told herself. A guest's vehicle. A worker's truck. Nothing to worry about.

But she didn't move. Something was nagging at her—a prickle at the back of her neck, an instinct honed by 135 years of survival. Something was wrong.

She pulled out her phone and texted Rae.

Lock your door. Don't open it for anyone.

A moment later, the reply came: Ok mom. Already locked. Go home and sleep.

Paris smiled.

She looked at the van one more time. Still no movement. Still no sign of threat.

You're being paranoid, she told herself. You're jumping at shadows.

Maybe she was. It could be the years of running, of fighting, of watching everyone she loved die or betray her had finally broken her brain. Or, she was seeing danger where there was none.

Or possibly her instincts were trying to tell her something, and she was too obtuse to understand what.

Paris pulled out of the parking lot and headed back toward her hotel. But she kept checking the psychic link, kept monitoring Rae's consciousness, kept reaching out with her senses for any sign of danger.

Nothing. A sleeping girl in a shabby motel room, dreaming whatever dreams runaway teenagers dreamed.

She's fine, Paris told herself again. *She's safe*.

But the unease followed her all the way home, and it was still there when she finally drifted into the deathlike sleep of her kind.

The last thing she thought before consciousness faded was the image of that white van, sitting silent at the edge of the parking lot.

Waiting.

CHAPTER 15

(1893, The Citadel – Age 13)

The years had winnowed them down to four.

Of the thirty-one children who had entered the School, only Paris, London, Salem, and a quiet boy named Grigorio remained. The rest had been "transferred" or had simply vanished—euphemisms that fooled no one. The Citadel was not a place that tolerated weakness, and weakness took many forms: physical frailty, mental instability, insufficient ruthlessness, or simply the bad luck of being matched against someone stronger in an elimination bout.

Paris had survived. London had survived. That was what mattered.

They sat together in London's quarters on the evening before graduation, as they had done countless times over the past five years. The room was small and spare—a cot, a desk, a single window that looked out onto the inner courtyard—but it had become a sanctuary of sorts. A place where they could speak freely, away from the judging expressions of instructors and the competitive tension that permeated every other space in the Citadel.

"Do you ever think about what comes next?" London asked. She was sitting cross-legged on her bed, her hair loose around her shoulders, her almond-shaped eyes contemplative. "After the Birthing, I mean. After we're truly Valensi."

Paris leaned back against the wall, considering the question. "Sometimes. I try not to dwell on it too much. Planning for a future you might not live to see seems... wasteful."

"That's dark."

"We live in a dark place."

London smiled—that small, knowing smile that Paris had come to treasure over the years. "True enough. But we've made it this far. Against all odds, we've made it." She paused, her expression growing more serious. "I couldn't have done it without you, you know. Those first years, when everything seemed impossible... you kept me going."

"You kept yourself going," Paris said. "I reminded you that you could."

"Same thing."

"It's not, actually. But I'll accept the compliment."

They sat in comfortable silence for a moment. Outside, the last light of day was fading from the courtyard, the gas lamps beginning to flicker to life along the stone walls.

"I've been thinking," London said eventually. "About the Birthing. About when we should do it."

"The Magistrate said we could choose our age."

"Yes. And I've decided I want to wait. At least until I'm fifteen. Maybe sixteen." London looked down at her hands. "I know the sixty-to-one ratio means we'll still age eventually, but... I'd rather start from a more mature form. Begin the slow climb as a young woman rather than a girl." She gave a small, rueful smile. "It would take decades to go from looking thirteen to looking eighteen. I'd rather not spend that long being underestimated."

Paris nodded slowly. She had been thinking the same thing. At thirteen, she was still small, still slight, her body only beginning to hint at the woman she might become. The idea of waiting decades for that physical maturity—capable but childlike, forever dismissed as a little girl until time slowly, inexorably granted her a woman's form—held little appeal.

"I'll wait with you," she said. "We'll do it together. When we're ready."

London's face lit up. "Really? You'd wait for me?"

"Of course. We made a pact, remember? We hold each other to who we are. That includes this." Paris reached out and took London's hand. "Whatever happens, we face it together. That's how it works."

London squeezed her fingers, and for a moment, the harshness of the Citadel seemed very far away. They were two girls, sitting in a quiet room, holding onto each other against the darkness.

"Together," London agreed. "Always."

The summons came the following morning.

Paris was in her quarters, reading a battered copy of *Sartor Resartus* that she had borrowed from the library, when the knock came at her door. Not the perfunctory knock-and-enter that instructors typically employed, but a formal knock that waited for acknowledgment.

She set the book aside and opened the door.

Headmistress Redmond stood in the corridor, her hands clasped behind her back, her expression as unreadable as ever. "Your presence has been requested by the Magistrate," she said. "You are to come with me immediately."

Paris felt her heart rate quicken, but she kept her face neutral. She had known this moment would come—some form of final presentation or test to mark the completion of their schooling—but she had not expected it so soon.

"Yes, ma'am," she said, and followed the Headmistress into the corridor.

They walked in silence through the winding halls of the Citadel, past the classrooms where Paris had spent five years learning everything from combat to history to the art of manipulation. The route was unfamiliar, leading away from the usual areas and toward a section of the fortress Paris had never entered.

As they rounded a final corner, Paris saw him.

The Magistrate stood before a pair of massive wooden doors, his hands clasped in front of him, his steel-gray eyes fixed on her approach. He was tall—well over six feet—and though he appeared no older than his fifties, he felt ancient, some aura that spoke of millennia rather than decades. His presence filled the corridor the way a storm fills the sky.

Beside him stood a young man, seventeen or eighteen in appearance, with black hair and even darker eyes. He watched Paris with an intensity that made her skin prickle. There was something predatory in that gaze, calculating.

"Ah, young Paris," the Magistrate said as she approached. His voice was warm, paternal, but it carried an undertone of authority that brooked no opposition. "I'm glad you could join us."

"Yes, sir." Paris stopped before him and began to lower her head, but before she could complete the gesture, his fingers were beneath her chin, lifting her face.

"No," he said firmly. "You should never bow your head to anyone again. I have seen your potential, young lady. I've been watching you these past five years."

The revelation shocked her, and her surprise showed in her face. The Magistrate smiled—a genuine smile that softened the hard planes of his face for a moment.

"Yes," he continued, moving his hand to her shoulder. "I've had my eye on you for some time. You've performed well above average in your studies, excelling in nearly every area, especially your martial arts training. You've shown great promise."

Paris didn't know what to say. The most powerful Valensi in existence, a being nearly three thousand years old, had been watching *her*? It seemed impossible. Absurd.

And yet, even as the shock settled over her, another part of her mind was working—assessing, analyzing. *Why me? What does he want? What's the catch?* She had learned long ago that nothing came without a price, and offers from powerful men were rarely as generous as they appeared.

Even as she could see him poring over her with curiosity, Paris took note of him, as well. Reading his posture, his expressions, searching for the truth beneath the pleasant words.

The Magistrate's smile deepened, and approval lit up his wizened face. "You're evaluating me," he said. It wasn't a question. "Good. A healthy suspicion is a valuable trait in a bodyguard."

Bodyguard?

Before she could respond, he gestured to the young man beside him. "This is Dusk. He leads my High Guard—my personal team of protectors." The Magistrate's hand remained on Paris's shoulder, warm and heavy. "I'm extending an invitation, young Paris. I want you to join them."

The words hit her like a physical blow. The High Guard. The Magistrate's personal entourage. The most elite, most trusted warriors in the entire Valensi hierarchy. And he was offering her a place among them.

"I..." She stopped, gathering herself. A thousand questions clamored for attention, but she forced them down, forced herself to think clearly. "Why me, sir? I'm honored, but... I'm just a student. There must be others more qualified."

"There are many who are older," the Magistrate acknowledged. "Many who have more experience. But qualification is not simply a matter of years or training. It's a matter of potential. Of character." His grip on her shoulder tightened slightly. "I see something in you, Paris. A fire that burns even in darkness. A will to survive that transcends mere self-preservation. These are rare qualities. Valuable ones."

She felt the pressure of his mind against hers then—subtle, probing, like fingers testing the edges of a locked door. He was reading her. Or trying to. Testing her mental defenses even as he tested her resolve.

She didn't fight it. Fighting would only reveal weakness. Instead, she let him see what she chose to show: her determination, her loyalty, her willingness to do what was necessary. The rest—her doubts, her questions, the small voice that whispered warnings—she kept hidden behind walls she had spent years building.

The Magistrate nodded slowly, as if satisfied by what he had found. "Will you stand for me, Paris? Will you protect your Magistrate with every ounce of your being?"

"Yes."

"Will you risk your own life? Give your own life if necessary?"

"Yes."

"Will you take any life in the performance of your duties?"

This time she hesitated. She had killed before—Katrina, in a training match that had gone too far. The memory still haunted her, the feeling of her strike connecting with soft flesh, the awful certainty of what she had done. She had not meant to kill. But she had.

Would I kill again? Would I do so on command?

She thought of London's battered face after the qualifying matches. She thought of Theresa, strangled to death on the gymnasium floor while instructors watched in silence. She thought of all the violence she had witnessed, all the blood she had seen spilled in the name of survival.

In a moment of brutal self-honesty, she admitted what she had always known.

"Yes," she said. "I would."

"Good." The Magistrate released her shoulder and stepped back. "Then it is time for your final test. Your final challenge. Win or lose, your destiny will be set." His eyes hardened, the warmth draining from his face. "Are you ready to determine your own fate?"

Paris nodded. It was all she could manage.

The Magistrate turned and pushed open the massive doors behind him, revealing the gymnasium beyond. Paris followed him inside—and stopped dead.

The sparring mats had been removed. The polished wooden floor stretched out in an unbroken expanse, gleaming under the gas lights that lined the walls. Tiered bleachers rose along one side of the room, and they were filled with observers—instructors, older Valensi, faces she recognized and faces she didn't.

The Magistrate strode across the floor and took his seat in the center of the bleachers. Dusk sat to his left. To his right sat a strikingly beautiful girl with golden-blonde hair and brilliant blue eyes—Dawn, Paris assumed, Dusk's sister. And in the row below them, sitting bruised and battered but alive, was London.

Her left arm was in a sling. Her face was a mask of purple and yellow, one eye swollen nearly shut. But she met Paris's gaze and gave her a small nod.

She won, Paris realized. Whatever her test was, she survived it.

Which meant Paris had to survive hers.

She turned her attention to the center of the gymnasium, where her opponent waited.

Salem stood with his arms crossed, that arrogant smile plastered across his face. He was bigger than she remembered—taller, broader, filled out in the way that boys did at fourteen. He had easily thirty pounds on her, and he carried himself with the confidence of someone who knew exactly how this fight was going to end.

"What's up, brat?" he called as she approached. "You ready to die?"

Paris stopped ten feet from him and let out a slow breath. The fear was there—she would be a fool not to feel it—but beneath the fear was more. Something colder. Something harder.

This is it, she thought. Everything I've survived, everything I've learned, comes down to this moment.

"You've always been far too mouthy, Salem," she said. Her voice was steady, controlled. "Maybe today is the day that mouth gets shut for good."

His smile widened. "I highly doubt it, you little nothing. It's time someone finally knocked you off that fucking high horse of yours. Like I promised I would."

She was about to respond when the Magistrate cleared his throat. The sound echoed through the silent gymnasium, and both combatants turned to face him.

"The best of luck to each of you," he said. His voice carried the weight of absolute authority. "You may begin."

Salem didn't wait.

Before the Magistrate's words had finished echoing, Salem's fist was already cutting through the air toward Paris's face. She had expected treachery—had counted on it—and was already moving, ducking low and sliding to her right. His knuckles whistled past her ear, close enough to feel the displaced air.

She danced away, putting distance between them, her mind racing through possibilities. Salem was stronger than her, faster than her, and he fought dirty. In a straight-up brawl, he would destroy her. She needed another approach.

Find their weakness, Master Asaro's voice echoed in her memory. Learn their movements. Then attack the chink in their armor.

They circled each other, testing distances, looking for openings. Salem's movements were aggressive, predatory—a lion stalking prey. Paris kept her stance fluid, ready to move in any direction.

"I've been waiting for this for years," Salem said. "You have no idea how much I'm going to enjoy pounding on you."

His anger, she thought. That's always been his weakness. Use it.

"Before you enjoy that pounding," she said, keeping her voice light, conversational, "can you answer a question I've had for a while?"

"We aren't in school anymore, dimwit. Questions don't matter." He lunged at her, and she twisted aside, the blow glancing off her shoulder with enough force to send a spike of pain down her arm.

"Seriously," she continued, darting in and out, avoiding his strikes, "why do you hate me so much? What did I ever do to you?"

"You mean other than being a stupid girl?" He frowned, then struck again—a jab she managed to block, though the impact numbed her forearm. "You irritated me the first time I met you. Always so calm, walking around with that air of superiority. Like you're better than everyone else." His face twisted with deep rage that colored his expression with hate. "You're just like my mother. She got what she deserved, though. And so will you."

Paris filed that information away—*his mother, some kind of trauma there*—but she didn't have time to process it. Salem's foot swept toward her legs, and she leapt over it, only to catch a kick to the temple as he followed through.

Light exploded behind her left eye. The world tilted. She felt herself hit the floor, felt the impact drive the air from her lungs. Before she could recover, Salem's weight crashed down on top of her, pinning her to the polished wood.

No. Not like this. I will not die on my back.

His fist drew back, ready to drive into her face. In the split second before it fell, Paris's hand shot between his legs and found its target. She squeezed with every ounce of strength she possessed.

Salem's scream was piercing, animalistic. His body convulsed, his attack forgotten as agony overrode everything else. Paris twisted out from under him and scrambled to her feet, her head still swimming from the blow to her temple.

Salem curled on the floor, hands clutching his groin, tears streaming down his face. But even through the pain, his eyes found her—and the hatred in them burned brighter than ever.

All's fair in love and war, Paris thought grimly. I will not die with honor. I will simply not die.

She took a step toward him, ready to press her advantage, but he was already forcing himself upright, fighting through the pain with sheer fury. He kept his distance, circling, giving himself time to recover.

Paris decided to use his words against him.

"Are your bollocks feeling a bit wonky, Salem?" she asked, letting a mocking smile cross her face. "Sorry about that. No, wait—I'm not. But then again, it's not like you'd ever use them, right? Like you said, you don't fancy girls. I never would've pegged you as a poof. Looks can be deceiving, I suppose."

The effect was instantaneous. Salem's face went purple with rage. "You *bitch*! I'll make you pay for this!"

"I'm sure you will," she muttered, and the dance continued.

She managed a decent combination—a left jab followed by a knee to his gut—but he was recovering quickly, his speed and power reasserting themselves. For every strike she landed, he answered with a blow that rocked her to her core. Her ribs ached. Her head throbbed. She could taste blood in her mouth.

This isn't working. I'm losing. Slowly, but I'm losing.

She risked a glance at the bleachers. London sat motionless, her battered face revealing nothing. The Magistrate watched with cold interest. No one cheered. No one gasped. The silence was absolute, oppressive.

This isn't about a position in some guard, she comprehended suddenly. This is about survival. Only one of us leaves this floor alive.

The realization should have terrified her. Instead, it brought a strange clarity. The noise in her head—the fear, the doubt, the second-guessing—faded away. In its place rose... music?

It was Liszt's *Dante Symphony*, the piece Master Asaro had translated for her years ago. *Lasciate ogne speranza, voi ch'intrate.* Abandon all hope, ye who enter here.

She let the music fill her, let its lilting rhythms guide her movements. Her body began to flow, incorporating the martial arts she had learned with a natural grace that transcended technique. She danced around Salem, striking from unexpected angles, forcing him to defend against attacks he couldn't anticipate.

Three hits landed for every one of his. Then four. Then five.

Salem was confused now, unable to adapt to a style of fighting he had never seen. His movements became desperate, wild, losing the precision that had made him dangerous.

There, Paris thought, as she saw the opening she needed.

She twisted away from his next attack, letting him overextend, letting his momentum carry him past her. Then she spun and struck—not with her fist, but with her open palm. The slap connected with his cheek in a thunderous *crack* that echoed through the gymnasium.

Salem froze.

His hand went to his face, his expression one of shock and disbelief. Paris remembered suddenly—the day in class when Mr. Marco had slapped Salem in front of everyone, demonstrating his superiority. The humiliation that had burned in the boy's eyes. The rage that had simmered beneath the surface ever since.

She had slapped him like a disobedient child. In front of the Magistrate. In front of everyone.

Salem's eyes grew wide, his pupils dilated. The last vestiges of control, of calculated aggression, fell away. What remained was pure, mindless fury.

He bellowed with rage and charged at her, abandoning all technique, all strategy. He was a bull seeing red, and Paris was the target.

She had been counting on this.

At the last instant, she feinted right. Salem committed to the direction, his momentum carrying him forward. Paris darted left and drove her fist into his face with every ounce of force she could muster.

Her aim was true. Her small fist fit well into his eye socket.

The world exploded in pain. Paris felt the bones in her hand crack, felt cartilage tear and separate, felt her own scream rip from her throat even as Salem's rose to meet it. They fell together, two broken things, their cries of agony ringing through the silent gymnasium.

Paris clutched her ruined hand to her chest and forced herself to look at what she had done.

Salem was on his knees, his hands pressed to his face, blood pouring between his fingers. Clear fluid—the vitreous humor of his destroyed eye—mingled with the crimson, dripping into his lap. He was sobbing, screaming, his body wracked with agony.

It's over, she thought. I've won.

But no one moved. No one spoke. The silence stretched on, heavy with expectation.

Paris looked at London. Her friend's bruised face was carefully blank, but her eyes held… understanding. Or empathy. As if she knew what was coming next and grieved for it.

Paris turned to the Magistrate.

His steel-gray eyes met hers, cold and patient. He said nothing. He didn't need to. The message was clear in his gaze, in the stillness of his ancient face.

Finish it.

Paris looked back at Salem. He was broken, maimed, kneeling in a pool of his own blood like a supplicant before an altar. Even if he survived, he would never be whole again. The Valensi did not tolerate such weakness. They would discard him. He was a damaged tool. They would cast him aside.

I would be doing him a favor, she thought. And hated herself for thinking it.

She paced around behind him, cradling her shattered hand. The pain was immense, all-consuming, but she forced it down, forced herself to focus on what had to be done.

Salem was still sobbing, still clutching his ruined face. He didn't see her approach. Didn't feel her presence until her hands—one whole, one broken—grasped his chin and the back of his skull.

"I'm sorry," she whispered. She wasn't sure if she meant it.

Then she twisted.

The snap of Salem's neck was loud in the silence. His screams cut off instantly, replaced by Paris's own cry of agony as her broken hand ground against itself. She felt his body go limp, felt the weight of him sag against her grip.

She let him fall.

Salem collapsed onto the gymnasium floor, his head at an unnatural angle, his remaining eye staring at nothing. He was dead before he hit the ground.

Paris stood over his body, trembling, her shattered hand cradled against her chest. Blood covered her—his blood, her blood, she couldn't tell anymore. She raised her unbroken hand to her face and stared at the crimson coating her palm.

Without thinking, she lifted her hand to her lips and tasted it.

The blood was warm and metallic and strangely satisfying. The taste of victory. The taste of survival.

Is this what I have to look forward to? she wondered distantly. Will I forever be driven by bloodlust, hungering for the blood of others?

She looked up at the bleachers. At London, who was crying silently, tears cutting tracks through the bruises on her face. At the Magistrate, who nodded once, slowly, as if confirming what he had always known.

She had passed the test.

She had killed to survive.

And inside her—some last remnant of the frightened girl who had fled her father's house all those years ago—crumbled to dust and blew away on a wind only she could feel.

CHAPTER 16

(1895, The Citadel — Age 15)

Two years had changed them both.

Paris stood before the mirror in her quarters, studying the face that looked back at her. She was taller now, her body having finally begun to fill out into approaching womanhood. Her features had sharpened, the soft roundness of childhood giving way to angles and planes that hinted at the woman she would become. She was still small—she would always be small—but there was a wiry strength to her frame now, a coiled readiness that had not been there before.

Tonight, that frame would be transformed forever.

She turned away from the mirror and began to dress. The Citadel had provided ceremonial garments for the occasion: a simple white shift that fell to her knees, soft leather sandals, nothing else. The fabric was thin enough that she could feel the cool air of the stone chamber against her skin, raising goosebumps along her arms.

London wore this same garment, she thought. Only hours ago. And now she's...

She didn't finish the thought. London had been taken to the recovery chambers after her Birthing, and Paris had not been permitted to see her. The attendants had assured her that her friend was well, that the transformation was proceeding normally, but Paris would not rest easy until she saw London with her own eyes.

Soon, she told herself. After tonight, we'll have eternity to spend together.

The thought should have been comforting. Instead, it filled her with a strange, hollow dread.

A knock came at the door—the formal, patient knock that she had come to associate with momentous occasions. She took a deep breath, smoothed the white fabric over her hips, and opened it.

Dusk stood in the corridor, his expression unreadable. He had not changed much in the two years since she had first met him; at his age—whatever that truly was—two years was nothing. A heartbeat. A blink.

"It's time," he said.

Paris nodded and stepped into the corridor. There was nothing left to say.

The Audience Chamber was the heart of the Citadel.

Paris had been here only twice before: once during her initial processing as a child, and once for her formal induction into the High Guard after defeating Salem. Both times, she had been too overwhelmed to truly take in her surroundings. Now, walking beside Dusk through the massive bronze doors, she forced herself to observe every detail.

The chamber was vast, its vaulted ceiling disappearing into shadow far above. Columns of marble lined the walls, carved with scenes from Valensi history—battles and coronations, births and deaths, the endless cycle of an immortal people. Torches burned in iron sconces, casting flickering light across the polished stone floor.

At the far end of the chamber, on a raised dais, sat the Magistrate.

His throne was carved from a single block of obsidian, its surface so dark it seemed to drink the light around it. He was dressed in robes of deep purple, the color of royalty, of power. His steel-gray eyes tracked Paris's approach with the patient intensity of a predator watching prey.

To his right stood Dawn, her golden hair gleaming in the torchlight. To his left, an empty space where Dusk would take his place. Behind the throne, in the shadows, Paris could make out the shapes of other figures—witnesses to the ceremony, faces she could not quite distinguish.

And off to the side, held between two guards in a shadowed alcove, was a man.

Paris noted him only briefly—middle-aged, graying hair, hollow expression—before returning her attention to the Magistrate. There would be time to understand the man's presence later. For now, she had to focus on what was coming.

She stopped at the base of the dais. Dusk moved past her and took his place beside the Magistrate's throne.

"Young Paris." The Magistrate's voice echoed through the chamber, resonant with age and authority. "You have come to complete your journey. To be Birthed into the Valensi and take your rightful place among us."

"Yes, sir." Her voice was steady, but her heart was pounding so hard she was certain everyone in the chamber could hear it.

"You understand what is required of you?"

"I do."

The Magistrate rose from his throne and descended the steps of the dais, his robes whispering against the stone. He moved with a grace that belied his apparent age, each step deliberate, measured. When he reached Paris, he placed a hand on her shoulder—that same warm, heavy hand she remembered from their first meeting.

"The transformation will not be easy," he said, his voice dropping to a gentle tone. "Your body will be unmade and remade. You will experience pain unlike anything you have known. But you are strong, young Paris. You have proven that time and again." His focus held hers. "I have faith that you will endure."

Paris nodded. It was all she could manage.

"Then let us begin."

He tilted her head to the side, exposing the curve of her neck. Paris felt his breath against her skin, cool and faintly sweet. Her heart was hammering, her pulse throbbing visibly in her throat.

This is it, she thought. The point of no return.

Then his fangs pierced her flesh, and thought became impossible.

Pain.

It was the first sensation she became aware of—a sharp, burning pain at the juncture of her neck and shoulder, where the Magistrate's teeth had broken through her skin. She could feel them buried in her flesh, feel the pull as he began to draw her blood into his mouth.

At first, it was not unlike the pain of any wound—sharp and bright and localized. But as the seconds stretched into what felt like hours, it began to change. To spread. To deepen into a more profound feeling than mere physical sensation.

Paris felt herself growing weaker. The strength was draining from her limbs, her muscles going slack as her blood flowed out of her body and into the Magistrate's waiting mouth. She sagged against him, unable to stand on her own, and felt his arm wrap around her waist to hold her upright.

The chamber began to darken around the edges. The torchlight dimmed, the marble columns fading into shadow. She could hear her own heartbeat—slower now, each beat a struggle, each pulse pushing less and less blood through her emptying veins.

I'm dying. He's killing me.

But there was no fear in the thought. Only a strange, floating detachment, as if she were watching her own death from somewhere far away.

Her vision narrowed to a single point of light—the flickering of a torch somewhere above her, dancing as in a breeze. She focused on that light, clung to it, used it as an anchor against the blackness rushing up to claim her.

Stay awake, she told herself. Stay present. Don't let go.

But the darkness was stronger. It surged up from below, cold and absolute, and swallowed the last of the light.

Paris fell into nothing.

She dreamed of fire.

It began in her chest—a single spark, small and fragile, flickering in the vast emptiness of her dying body. For a moment, she thought it would gutter out, snuffed by the cold and the dark.

Then it caught.

The flame spread outward from her heart, racing along her veins like wildfire through dry grass. It touched her lungs and set them burning. It reached her limbs and ignited them. It climbed her spine and erupted into her skull, filling her head with light and heat and an agony beyond anything she had ever imagined.

Paris screamed—or tried to scream. No sound emerged from her ruined throat. She was burning from the inside out, her body transforming into an inferno of sensation and suffering.

She discerned, on some level, what was happening. The Magistrate's blood was inside her now, mixing with her own, rewriting her very biology. Every cell in her body was being unmade and remade, broken down and rebuilt anew. Stronger. More.

But understanding did nothing to lessen the pain.

It came in waves, each crest higher than the last. Her bones ached as if they were being ground to powder. Her muscles spasmed and contracted, pulling against her skeleton with such force that she was certain it would all would tear loose. Her skin felt like it was being flayed from her body, layer by layer, nerve by nerve.

She lost all sense of time. There was only the pain, endless and absolute, and the fire that burned without consuming.

Flashes of light burst behind her sealed eyelids—white, then red, then a blue so bright it seemed to sear her retinas. Her body arched and twisted, fighting against restraints she couldn't see. Hands held her down—cool hands, strong hands, preventing her from thrashing herself off whatever surface she lay upon. Voices murmured in languages she didn't recognize. Cold cloths pressed against her forehead, her chest, her wrists. A bitter liquid forced between her clenched teeth, making her choke and gasp.

She tried to speak, to beg them to make it stop, but her throat produced only a dry rasp. She tried to open her eyes, but her lids were sealed shut, crusted with some material she couldn't identify.

I'm dying, she thought again. This time for real. The transformation is killing me.

But even as the thought formed, her mind rejected it. That core of iron will, that fundamental refusal to surrender, flared to life beneath the agony. She had survived the streets of Bristol. She had survived the Citadel. She had survived Salem's fists and the Magistrate's tests and a hundred other trials that should have broken her.

She would survive this too.

I will not die, she told herself, clinging to the words like a lifeline. I will not die. I will not die. I WILL NOT DIE.

The fire burned on.

Time passed.

Paris existed in a twilight state, drifting between consciousness and oblivion. Sometimes the pain would ease enough for her to surface, to catch fragments of the world around her: a stone ceiling far above, the smell of herbs and blood, the murmur of voices discussing her condition. Other times, the agony would surge back, dragging her down into a crimson void where nothing existed but suffering.

Slowly, incrementally, the fire began to fade.

It didn't go out—somehow, it would never fully go out. It would burn within her for as long as she existed. But its fury lessened, its heat diminishing from an inferno to a steady flame. The waves of pain grew smaller, the intervals between them longer.

She didn't know how long it lasted. Days, certainly. Perhaps a week. Time had become meaningless, measured only in the ebb and flow of agony.

And then, finally, she woke.

The ceiling above her was stone, hewn from the living rock of the mountain that housed the Citadel. A single window let in a shaft of moonlight, pale and silver and achingly beautiful. She lay on a narrow bed in a small chamber, covered with thin blankets that did little to ward off the cold.

I'm alive, she thought. I survived.

But something was different. Something had changed.

She could hear things she had never heard before—the scurrying of mice in the walls, the distant murmur of voices several rooms away, the slow drip of water somewhere deep in the stone. She could smell things too: the herbs that had been burned to ease her fever, the faint metallic tang of old blood, the sweat of whoever had tended to her during her transformation.

And beneath all of that, threading through every other sensation like a current through still water, was...

Hunger.

It was unlike anything she had ever experienced. Not the gnawing emptiness of starvation she had known on the streets of Bristol, nor the simple craving for food that came with exertion. This was deeper, more primal—a need that seemed to emanate from her very cells, from the new blood that now coursed through her transformed veins.

The door to her chamber opened, and the Magistrate entered.

He looked the same as he had before—ancient, powerful, his gaze missing nothing. But Paris saw him differently now. She could hear his heartbeat, slow and steady. She could smell the blood moving through his body, rich and dark and somehow... familiar. Like calling to like.

"You're awake," he said. "Good. The transformation was difficult, but you endured. As I knew you would."

Paris tried to sit up and found, to her surprise, that she could. Her body still ached, but the weakness was fading, replaced by a strange new vitality. She felt... strong. Stronger than she had ever been.

"How long?" she asked. Her voice was rough, her throat raw.

"Six days. Longer than most." The Magistrate moved to stand beside her bed, looking down at her with what might have been approval. "Your body fought the transformation harder than expected. But it has accepted the change now. You are Valensi."

Valensi. The word seemed to resonate in her chest, in the new heart that beat there with its slow, powerful rhythm.

"There is one final step," the Magistrate continued. "One last threshold you must cross."

He turned toward the door and gestured. The guards she had seen earlier entered, dragging the hollow-eyed man between them. They forced him to his knees a few feet from Paris's bed, holding his arms behind his back.

The hunger that had been simmering in her veins roared to sudden, violent life.

Paris's vision sharpened, narrowing to the pulse point visible in the man's throat. She could see the blood moving beneath his skin, could smell it—warm and rich and impossibly enticing. Her mouth watered. Her new teeth ached with a need she didn't fully understand.

Feed, something whispered in the back of her mind. Take him. Drink. He's right there. Reach out and—

She caught herself, horrified by the intensity of the urge. This was what they had warned her about in class, what the older Valensi had spoken of in hushed tones. The hunger. The need. The beast that lived inside every one of their kind, always prowling, always waiting for a moment of weakness.

"Who is he?" she asked, forcing her eyes away from the man's throat. Her voice came out steadier than she felt.

"A criminal," the Magistrate said. "One of our own, a human consultant, who broke our most sacred laws. He became obsessed with another Valensi—a woman who did not return his affections. When she rejected him for the final time, he killed her." The Magistrate's voice was cold, detached. "Regardless of its form, obsession always leads to violence. This man allowed that poison to consume him. And now he must face the consequences."

Paris looked at the kneeling man. He had raised his head, and she could see his eyes clearly now—bloodshot, rimmed with red, but aware. He knew what was coming. He knew he was about to die.

And some part of her—some dark, newly awakened part—was glad.

No. She recoiled from the thought, from the hunger that was urging her forward. *This isn't me. I'm not a monster. I won't become a monster.*

But even as she fought against it, she could feel the hunger growing stronger. It clawed at her insides, demanding satisfaction. Her hands trembled with the effort of holding herself back.

"He is your first feeding," the Magistrate said, watching her struggle as she was certain he had seen many more struggle in the past millennia. "Your first kill as Valensi. The blood of a criminal, freely given to justice."

He's a murderer, Paris told herself. He killed someone out of obsession. He deserves this.

But does anyone deserve to die like this? Drained by a monster?

He IS a monster. And so are you, now. The only question is what kind.

The hunger surged again, and Paris felt her control slipping. She had to make a choice. She had to decide—right now, in this moment—what she was going to be.

She looked at the man. At his hollow expression and trembling shoulders. At the pulse beating frantically in his throat.

And she made her decision.

"He killed someone," she said slowly, working through it aloud. "He murdered an innocent person because he couldn't control his obsession."

"Yes."

"He had a choice. He chose to kill."

"Yes."

Paris drew a deep breath. The hunger was screaming at her now, demanding release. But she held it back, held it in check with the iron will that had kept her alive through everything else.

"Then he deserves justice," she said. "Not because I'm hungry. Not because I need to feed. But because he chose to become a killer, and killers face consequences."

The Magistrate beamed with obvious satisfaction. "Well reasoned, young Paris. The hunger will always be with you—it is part of what we are. But you must never let it rule you. You must always be the one who decides when to feed, and on whom." He gestured toward the kneeling man. "He is yours. Take what is owed."

Paris rose from her bed. Her legs were steady now, her body responding to her commands with a fluidity and strength she had never possessed before. She crossed the small chamber and stood before the condemned man, looking down at him.

"I'm sorry," she said quietly. "For what happened to you. For what made you into this."

The man's lips moved, forming words she couldn't hear. A prayer. Or a curse.

"But you killed someone who didn't deserve to die. You let your obsession turn you into a monster." She crouched down, bringing her face level with his. "And I will not become what you became. I refuse."

She reached out and grasped his head with both hands—one on each side of his face, her fingers threading through his graying hair. The hunger howled inside her, desperate, ravenous.

She held it back.

Not yet, she told it. On my terms. My choice.

With a sharp, practiced motion, she wrenched the man's head to the side. The crack of his neck breaking was loud in the small chamber, echoing off the stone walls. His body went limp instantly, slumping forward.

Only then did Paris lower her mouth to his throat.

The first taste of blood was like nothing she had ever experienced. It flooded her senses, overwhelming in its richness—copper and salt and something else, something vital, something that sang through her transformed veins like music. The hunger surged up to meet it, and for a moment she lost herself entirely, drinking deeply, desperately, her new teeth tearing into cooling flesh to get at the vessels beneath.

Stop, a voice whispered in the back of her mind. Don't lose yourself. Don't become the beast.

She pulled back, gasping. Blood stained her lips, her chin, the front of her white ceremonial shift. The man's body lay crumpled at her feet, drained and empty.

Paris stood over him, trembling—not with weakness, but with the effort of control. The hunger was still there, still demanding more, but she had mastered it. She had fed on her own terms, killed for reasons she could justify, taken only what was owed.

This is what I am now, she thought. A predator. A killer. A monster.

But I choose what kind of monster I'll be.

She turned to face the Magistrate. He was watching her with those ancient, unreadable eyes, his expression giving nothing away.

"It is done," he said. "You are Valensi in truth, bound to our kind for as long as you endure." He paused. "How do you feel?"

Paris considered the question. The hunger was fading now, satisfied for the moment. In its place was a strange, hollow clarity—an awareness of what she had done and what it meant.

"I feel..." She searched for the right word. "Changed."

"You are changed. The transformation is complete." The Magistrate moved toward the door, then paused and looked back at her. "Rest now. Recover your strength. The physical changes will continue for several more days, but the worst is behind you."

He left without another word, the guards following with the empty husk that had once been a man.

Paris stood alone in her chamber, blood drying on her lips, and stared at the moonlight streaming through the window.

I am Valensi, she thought. I drink blood to survive. I killed a man tonight, and I will kill again before my time is done.

But beneath the horror and the hunger and the strange new power humming in her veins, a resolution was taking shape. A line drawn in the sand of her eternal existence.

I will never kill an innocent, she vowed silently. No matter what I'm ordered to do. No matter what it costs me. No matter how hungry I become. I will only kill those who deserve death—predators, murderers, monsters like the man I killed tonight.

It was a small thing. A single thread of morality in a tapestry of blood and darkness. But it was hers, and she would hold to it.

She had to.

Because if she didn't—if she allowed the hunger to rule her, if she became the kind of monster who fed without conscience—then the little girl who had fled her father's house all those years ago would truly be dead. And Paris refused to let that happen.

I will survive, she told herself. But I will survive on my own terms. And I will never, ever become the thing I hate.

It was a promise she would keep for 135 years.

CHAPTER 17

(Present)

The late-night Walmart was nearly deserted.

Paris wandered through the women's clothing section, idly thumbing through a rack of summer dresses that were already on clearance despite the fact that summer had barely begun. The fluorescent lights buzzed overhead, casting everything in that flat, shadowless glare that made even the most vibrant colors look washed out and institutional.

Rae was somewhere in the store—Paris could feel her presence through the psychic link she had established, a faint warmth at the edge of her awareness. She had offered to let Rae shop on her own, sensing that the girl valued her independence, but she kept half her attention on that mental thread nonetheless. Old habits.

She was examining a black sundress—not her usual style, but it was appealing in its simplicity—when she caught a flash of movement in her peripheral vision. Black hair, quick hands, a furtive glance over one shoulder.

Rae.

Paris watched as the girl ducked behind a display of discount t-shirts, her hands moving with practiced efficiency. A moment later, she reappeared and began walking casually toward the next aisle, her shoulder bag hanging a bit heavier than it had before.

Paris smiled despite herself. She remembered those movements, that careful nonchalance. She had perfected them herself on the streets of Bristol, more than a century ago.

She circled around the end of the aisle and intercepted Rae near the women's jeans, leaning against a tall display shelf with her arms crossed.

"Well, well," she said.

Rae froze, her eyes going wide. "Shit. Paris, I—"

"Red-handed. That's the term, isn't it?" Paris laughed as Rae's head swiveled frantically, checking for store employees. "Relax. I'm not going to turn you in."

"Keep it down," Rae hissed. "Jesus."

"No worries, kid. Like I give a shit, really." Paris pushed off from the shelf and strolled over, nodding toward Rae's bag. "Get anything good?"

Rae stared at her for a long moment, clearly trying to determine if this was some kind of trap. Finally, her shoulders relaxed slightly. "Just some shirts. Nothing major."

"You know that's not necessary, right?" Paris kept her voice light, non-judgmental. "If you need something, I can buy it. I've got money."

"It's not about need." Rae's jaw tightened, a flash—pride, maybe, or defensiveness—crossing her face. "It's... habit. Survival habit. Hard to break, you know?"

Paris did know. Better than Rae could possibly imagine.

"Yeah," she said quietly. "I do."

They stood there for a moment, two survivors recognizing themselves in each other. Then Paris reached out and gently extracted the stolen shirts from Rae's bag—two black tees, one with a band logo she didn't recognize.

"These are damaged," she said, examining the small tears where Rae had removed the security tags. "Let's go get you fresh ones. And maybe some jeans to go with them." She tossed the ruined shirts over her shoulder onto a nearby shelf. "My treat."

Rae opened her mouth—to protest, probably—but Paris was already walking toward the jeans section, and after a moment, she heard Rae's footsteps following.

They browsed in companionable silence for a few minutes, pulling items from racks and holding them up for inspection. Paris found herself enjoying the simple domesticity of it—the kind of mundane activity she had rarely experienced in her long existence. Shopping with a friend. Such a human thing.

"You're staring," she said, without looking up from a pair of stone-washed skinny jeans.

"Sorry. I just..." Rae trailed off, her brow furrowed. "You're weird, you know that?"

"So I've been told."

"No, I mean—" Rae gestured vaguely. "You can't be more than seventeen or eighteen, but you talk and act like you're fifty. Like my aunt. She's got a mouth on her too, but it's more than that."

Paris raised an eyebrow. "Don't overthink it, kid. You might hurt yourself."

"See? That's what I'm talking about." Rae's green eyes narrowed, studying Paris with an intensity that was uncomfortable. "I'm basically the same age as you, but you call me 'kid.' And you *mean* it. Like you're—"

She stopped mid-sentence, a thought forming. Paris could see the pieces trying to fit together in her mind.

"I'm hungry," Paris said, before Rae could put her thoughts into words. "You want to join me for a late dinner? Or early breakfast? Whatever."

"I..." Rae hesitated, still looking at Paris with that suspicious, searching expression. "Yeah, okay. But you're buying."

"Obviously."

They made their way toward the registers, Paris's arms full of clothes—several items for herself, more for Rae. The store was emptier than ever now, the aisles echoing with the distant sound of a floor polisher somewhere in the back.

They were passing through the women's section near the entrance when Paris heard it.

A woman's pain.

It came to her on multiple levels—the slight grunt that reached her enhanced hearing, the spike of distress that brushed against her telepathic senses. But more than that, she *felt* it: a familiar, mature pain. Not the sharp surprise of an accident, but deeper. Older. The kind of hurt that had been lived with for a long time.

Paris stopped walking.

"What?" Rae asked, but Paris held up a hand for silence.

She moved toward the source—the next aisle over, where the women's jeans gave way to discount racks near the fitting rooms. As she rounded the corner, she saw them.

The woman was around thirty-five, with crow's feet and hair pulled back in a messy ponytail. Her face was contorted in pain, though she was clearly trying to hide it. The man beside her—tall, thick-necked, wearing a faded CDB t-shirt—had his hand clamped around her arm above the elbow, his fingers digging into flesh hard enough to leave bruises.

He was speaking in a low voice, just under carrying volume, but Paris's hearing caught every word.

"You'll wear what I tell you to wear and that's final, you hear me? I'm not going to have my wife walking around looking like some cheap whore."

The woman flinched but didn't respond. Didn't resist. She had the posture of someone who had learned long ago that resistance only made things worse.

Paris felt that cold and familiar feeling settle into her chest. She had seen this before. Had lived a version of it, in another life, in another century. Her father's hand raised against her mother. The sound of a body falling down stairs.

The man caught sight of her as she approached. His eyes flicked over her dismissively—some teenage girl, no threat—before returning to the woman.

"What're you looking at, kid? Mind your own business."

Paris didn't slow down.

She was on him before he could blink, her hand closing around two of his fingers—the ones gripping the woman's arm—and bending them backward with precisely calibrated pressure. His grip released instantly as pain shot through his hand, and Paris kept pressing, forcing him down until his knees cracked against the tile floor.

"What the—" he began.

"Shut up." Paris leaned in close, her mouth inches from his ear, her voice dropping to a whisper that was somehow more terrifying than a shout. "Shut the fuck up and listen. Listen with every ounce of the minimal brainpower you have, arsehole."

She could feel Rae behind her, watching. Could feel the woman's shock, her confusion, her desperate hope that this wasn't some kind of trick.

"I'm going to be watching you from now on," Paris continued, her voice soft and intimate and utterly cold. "If you ever lay a harmful hand on this woman again, I will hunt you down and I will rip your dick off. Slowly." She twisted his fingers back another degree, drawing a strangled cry from his throat. "I'm your worst nightmare: a woman who fights back. And when I fight back, trust me, it'll be a very one-sided fight."

She slipped into his mind then—a quick probe, surface level, enough to see what he was thinking. The image she found there made her laugh: him rising up once she released him, knocking her out with a single punch, teaching her a lesson about respect.

"You're a stubborn little shit, aren't you?" she murmured. "I see that ignorant image in your head. You know, the one where you plan on knocking me out once I let you go?" She felt his panic spike as he realized she had somehow read his thoughts. "You better wipe that image away, Billy. You better flush it right down that toilet of a brain you've got. Because if you ever force me to see you again, I will make damned sure that my sweet face is the last fucking thing you ever see."

She pulled back enough to meet his gaze—frightened now, terrified, all thoughts of retaliation evaporating in the face of something he couldn't understand.

"We clear?"

He nodded frantically.

"Good." Paris released his fingers with a slight push and a harder knee to his chest that sent him sprawling onto his back. She turned to the woman, ignoring Billy entirely.

The woman was crying now—silent tears streaming down her face, her hand pressed to her mouth. But her eyes weren't filled with fear. They were filled with what looked almost like hope.

"If you have one ounce of remaining self-worth and dignity," Paris said, her voice softening, "you will leave that piece of shit in the dust. Never look back. No one deserves that man's overbearing idiocy and hurt." She paused, choosing her next words carefully. "Take it from me— never let a man tell you what to do. They can't even handle their own lives, let alone someone else's. Move on, girl. Make a life for yourself."

The woman's tears flowed harder, but Paris could see the change in her posture—the way her shoulders straightened slightly, the way her chin lifted. Maybe it would be enough. Maybe tonight would be the night she finally walked away.

Or maybe not. Paris had learned long ago that she couldn't save everyone. She could only open doors. Walking through them was up to the person standing in front of them.

She laid a gentle hand on the woman's shoulder for a brief moment, then turned back to Billy, who was struggling to get to his feet.

"Do not make me come see you again, William Harold Knowles," she said, plucking his full name from his mind with casual ease. "Got it?"

The color drained from his face. He nodded once, turned, and trudged away without another word.

Paris watched him go, then returned to where Rae stood frozen at the end of the aisle, staring at her.

"What the hell was that?" Rae whispered.

"Just a conversation," Paris said. She picked up the clothes she had dropped and started toward the registers. "Come on. I'm starving."

The diner was nearly empty at this hour—a few scattered night owls and shift workers hunched over coffee cups and plates of eggs. Paris and Rae had claimed a booth near the back, away from the windows, and Paris had ordered enough food to feed a small army.

Rae watched in amazement as Paris demolished a stack of pancakes, two orders of bacon, three eggs, hash browns, and a side of biscuits and gravy. She had seen Paris eat before, but the sheer volume still seemed to shock her.

"That's not normal," Rae said, shaking her head. "That's like... competitive eating levels."

"Fast metabolism." Paris wiped syrup from her chin with a napkin. "I burn through calories like you wouldn't believe."

"Yeah, but..." Rae trailed off, her eyes narrowing. "That's not the only thing that's not normal about you, is it?"

Paris set down her fork and met Rae's gaze. The girl was sharp—sharper than Paris had given her credit for. She had been putting pieces together all night: the way Paris talked, the way she moved, the way she had handled Billy with a strength and speed that shouldn't have been possible for someone her size.

"No," Paris said quietly. "It's not."

They sat in silence for a moment. Around them, the diner hummed with the quiet sounds of late-night activity: the sizzle of a grill, the clink of silverware, the murmur of distant conversation.

"So, you're from England, huh?" Rae asked finally. A safe question. An opening.

"Yes. Bristol."

"How'd you wind up here, in Florida of all places?"

"It's a long story, Rae. One you probably shouldn't worry about."

"What's that supposed to mean?" Rae's face scrunched up in consternation. "You're too young to be a spy, right? What the hell?"

Paris couldn't help but laugh at her expression—the heavy makeup and black lipstick twisted into something that was almost adorable. "What's so funny?" Rae demanded. "I told you my secrets. What're yours?"

"You really want to know my secrets?" Paris held up a finger and pointed it at Rae. "Keep in mind that my secrets are the kind that can get you killed."

"What's it matter? Maybe it'll shed a little light, a little excitement, into this dreary-ass life of mine."

Paris hesitated. Did she really want to tell Rae the truth? Why put her in that position? Then again, Rae might not even believe her. Might think her insane and run away like a mouse from a cat.

A mouse from a cat. The simile was too appropriate.

For whatever reason, Paris decided to share. She had no one else to talk to, no one to bounce ideas off of. Rae seemed as open-minded as they came. And it was liberating, the idea of telling the truth—of being known, even if by one person, even if only for a little while.

"When I was seven years old," Paris began slowly, "my father killed my mother in a drunken rage. Before he could get to me, I ran away. I lived on the streets of Bristol for almost two years before I was taken away by..." She paused, searching for the right word. The forbidden word. "Vampires."

Rae stared at her. Her shoulders slumped, and she looked off into the distance for a long moment.

"You almost had me there, Paris," she said finally, turning back with a skeptical smile. "Almost."

"Yeah. I didn't think you'd believe me." Paris shrugged. "Nevertheless, shall I continue?"

Rae gave a slight shrug of her own—*why not*—and Paris spilled her guts. She told her about the Citadel, about the training, about becoming part of a race of evolved humans who had existed in the shadows of history for millennia. She told her about the fateful decision that had made her a target, about running, about taking her chances rather than staying to die.

"That's one hell of a story," Rae said when she finished. Her smile was condescending now, the smile of someone humoring a friend's elaborate joke.

The condescension irked Paris enough that she made a brash decision.

She glanced around the diner. The nearest other patron was at least thirty feet away, absorbed in a newspaper. The waitress was behind the counter, her back turned.

"Watch," Paris said.

She moved.

One moment she was sitting in the booth across from Rae. The next, she was standing by the door at the far end of the diner—sixty feet away. The next, she was back in her seat, her coffee cup still warm in her hand.

The whole thing took less than three seconds.

Rae's face went pale beneath the heavy makeup. Her mouth opened, but no sound came out.

Then her eyes rolled back in her head and she slumped sideways in the booth.

Paris caught her before she could hit the table, easing her back against the seat cushion with one hand while casually sipping her coffee with the other. To anyone watching, it would look like Rae had simply dozed off after a long night.

A few moments later, Rae's eyes fluttered open. She saw Paris's smiling face and immediately scrambled backward, pressing herself against the wall of the booth, her body tense with fear.

"You're not—" she began.

"Human?" Paris cut her off. "Not really. Sort of. Let's just say *more than*, and leave it at that."

"Holy shit."

"I suppose." Paris's smile was open and honest, and even in her shock, Rae seemed to recognize that. Some of the tension eased from her shoulders, though she remained pressed against the wall.

"Seriously? Vampire? Blood-drinker?"

"On occasion." Paris would explain the details later.

"So," Rae said, her curiosity apparently overcoming her fear, "crosses? Garlic? Sunlight?"

"No. No. Yes." Paris sat back and folded her hands in her lap, trying to project the least threatening posture she could manage. "I have nothing against Christianity. I love garlic—garlic bread, in particular. But yes, I have a severe reaction to sunlight. Think of it like an extreme form of porphyria. My sunburns can kill me."

"Jesus." Rae was staring at her with a mixture of fear and fascination. "So you can never go out in the day?"

"Not without significant protection. And even then, it's risky."

"How old are you? Really?"

Paris smiled. She had been waiting for this question.

"I was born in the late eighties. The 1880s. I was birthed into the Valensi—that's what we call ourselves—when I was fifteen." She paused, letting that sink in. "We age at a rate of about sixty years to one year of physical aging. I'll be 135 years old soon."

Rae's jaw dropped. "Oh my God."

"What? Don't I look damned good for my age?"

It took a moment, but Rae loosened up and smiled. "Yeah, I guess you do."

They sat in silence for a while. Paris could practically see the gears turning in Rae's head—running through facts and myths, trying to reconcile what she thought she knew about vampires with the reality sitting across from her.

"Do you really have to drink blood to stay alive?" Rae asked finally.

"Yes and no." Paris took a sip of her coffee, considering how to explain. " Think of it as a really inconvenient dietary requirement. Once a month, give or take. Otherwise, I eat like this. Everything not nailed down."

"So you're basically... human, then?" Rae's brow furrowed. "Alive, not dead?"

"Very much alive," Paris confirmed. "Not undead. Not a corpse walking around. Just... evolved. Different."

"Wow."

"You have a way with words, you know that?"

"Fuck you," Rae said, but there was no heat in it. She was slowly returning to her normal, sardonic self.

"I rest my case." Paris raised her coffee cup in a mock toast.

They talked for another hour after that, Rae asking questions and Paris answering as honestly as she could. It felt good to be known—to drop the pretense and the lies and simply be herself with another person. She hadn't confided in anyone like this since Garrett.

The thought of him brought a sharp pang to her chest. She pushed it away, refusing to dwell on the possibility that he might be the one they sent after her.

When they finally left the diner, the night was beginning to fade toward dawn. Paris would need to get back to her hotel soon, to seal herself away from the coming sun.

They walked down the quiet street toward Paris's car, the easy silence of new friends settling between them.

Paris was so focused on the warmth of that connection—on the simple pleasure of having someone to talk to, someone who knew the truth—that she almost didn't notice.

Almost.

At the edge of her awareness, a prickle of unease. A sense of being watched. She turned her head slightly, scanning the empty parking lot, the darkened storefronts, the few scattered cars.

Nothing. No one visible.

But the feeling remained.

You're being paranoid, she told herself. You're jumping at shadows.

But even as she thought it, she remembered the white van from a few nights ago. The one parked at the edge of Rae's motel. The one that had set her instincts screaming.

She reached out with her senses, searching for any sign of threat. Still nothing concrete. Simply a persistent, nagging sense of wrongness.

"You okay?" Rae asked, noticing her distraction.

"Fine." Paris forced a smile. "Just tired. Come on, I'll drop you at your place."

She drove Rae back to the motel, watching the mirrors the whole way. If there was someone following them, they were good—too good for her to spot. But that only made her more uneasy, not less.

When they pulled into the motel parking lot, Paris scanned every shadow, every parked car, every corner. The white van was gone—or had moved, at least. She saw nothing obviously threatening.

But the feeling didn't go away.

"Same time tomorrow?" Rae asked as she climbed out of the car.

"Yeah." Paris hesitated, then added: "Rae? Be careful, okay? Keep your door locked. Don't open it for anyone you don't know."

Rae raised an eyebrow. "You sound like my mom. My old mom, I mean. Before she stopped giving a shit."

"Just... humor me."

"Fine, fine. Door locked, no strangers. Got it." Rae waved and headed toward the stairs. "See you tomorrow night, weirdo."

"See you tomorrow night."

Paris watched her climb the stairs, watched her unlock her door, watched her disappear inside. She waited until she saw the deadbolt turn before she put the car in reverse.

The sun would be up in less than an hour. She needed to get back to her hotel, to safety, to darkness.

But as she drove away, she couldn't shake the feeling that she had missed something. That somewhere in the shadows of this garish, neon-lit city, someone was watching.

Waiting.

And she had been too distracted—too happy, too comfortable, too *human*—to notice.

It would cost her.

She just didn't know how much yet.

CHAPTER 18

(Present)

The diner was quiet.

Paris sat in her usual booth near the back, a cup of coffee growing cold between her hands. She had ordered nothing else—her appetite had vanished somewhere between the hotel and this plastic-and-chrome sanctuary of late-night America. Outside, the neon signs of International Drive flickered and buzzed, painting the parking lot in garish shades of red and blue.

Rae was late.

It wasn't unusual. The girl kept her own schedule, drifting through the city like a leaf on water, arriving when she arrived. Paris had learned not to worry about it. Rae was a survivor—she knew how to take care of herself.

But tonight, it felt wrong.

Paris couldn't put her finger on it. There was no specific threat, no concrete danger she could point to. Just a vague unease that had settled into her bones the moment she walked through the diner's doors. A prickle at the back of her neck. A whisper of wrongness that wouldn't fade.

She glanced at her phone. 11:47 PM. They had agreed to meet at eleven.

She's fine, Paris told herself. She probably lost track of time.

But even as she thought it, her hand moved unconsciously to her chest, to the place where she felt the faint pulse of the psychic link she had established with Rae. It was still there—that warm thread of connection, that sense of another consciousness existing at the edge of her awareness.

She let herself drift along that thread, a light touch, just enough to reassure herself that—

Fear.

It slammed into her with the force of a physical blow, driving the breath from her lungs. Not her fear: *Rae's* fear. Raw and primal and overwhelming, flooding through the psychic link like poison through a vein.

And beneath the fear, something worse.

Pain. Violation. A scream that couldn't escape.

Paris was out of the booth before conscious thought could form. The coffee cup shattered on the floor behind her. The waitress shouted—protest, concern, she didn't know and didn't care. The door banged open and she was running, faster than any human could run, following the pull of that agonized connection through the neon-lit darkness.

Hold on, she thought desperately, pushing the words through the link. *I'm coming. Hold on.*

The fear spiked higher in response. And then—*Paris?*—a fragment of recognition, of desperate hope, before it dissolved into pain again.

She ran faster.

The world blurred around her—storefronts and streetlights and startled faces that barely registered her passage. She was a shadow, a streak of darkness cutting through the gaudy brightness of the tourist district. Her feet barely touched the ground.

Where? Where are you?

The link pulled her south, away from the main drag, into the dangerous spaces between buildings. A liquor store. A pawn shop with bars on its windows. An alley—

She smelled them before she saw them. Sweat, cheap beer, and something that made her stomach turn with recognition. The scent of violence. Of violation.

She rounded the corner and stopped.

Three of them.

The first thing Paris saw was Rae—pinned to the filthy ground, her shirt torn open, her face a mask of blood and terror. A gag had been shoved into her mouth, muffling her screams. One man knelt beside her head, his hand clamped over the gag, holding her down. Another was on top of her, his pants around his thighs, grunting like an animal as he—

No.

The third man stood watching, rubbing himself through his jeans, waiting his turn.

For a fraction of a second—a heartbeat, an eternity—Paris stood frozen. The scene burned itself into her mind with terrible clarity: Rae's wide, terrified eyes. The casual brutality of her attackers. The way they laughed, *laughed*, as they destroyed a girl who had already survived so much.

Then Paris snapped.

It was not rage, exactly. Rage was hot and wild and uncontrolled. This was colder. Sharper. A crystalline fury that stripped away everything but the simple, absolute certainty of what she was about to do.

She moved.

The standing man—the watcher, the one waiting his turn—saw her coming. He opened his mouth to shout a warning. He never got the chance.

Paris hit him with every ounce of strength her transformed body possessed. Her palm struck his chest like a sledgehammer, lifting him off his feet and hurling him backward. He flew ten feet through the air and slammed into the brick wall of the adjacent building. The crack of his skull against concrete was loud and wet and final. He slid to the ground and did not move.

The other two scrambled to react.

The one holding Rae down released her and lurched to his feet, his face twisted with shock and confusion. Paris grabbed him by the throat before he could take a single step, her fingers closing around his windpipe with crushing force. She could feel his pulse hammering against her palm, could smell the fear suddenly pouring off him in waves.

Good, she thought. *Be afraid.*

She threw him. Not into the wall—that would be too quick, too easy. She threw him at his accomplice, the one who had been raping Rae, who was now fumbling with his pants as he tried to stand. The two bodies collided with a satisfying crunch of bone and flesh, tangling together in a heap on the filthy ground.

Paris turned to Rae.

The girl was curled on her side, her arms wrapped around herself, her whole body shaking. The gag had fallen from her mouth, but she wasn't screaming anymore—making small, broken sounds that were somehow worse than screams.

"Rae." Paris knelt beside her, her voice soft now, all the cold fury reserved for the men groaning behind her. "Rae, I'm here. I've got you. You're safe now."

Rae's eyes found hers—wide and glassy and full of things that made Paris's heart crack down the middle.

"P-Paris?" Her voice was barely a whisper, rough from screaming. "You... you came..."

"Of course I came." Paris gathered her gently into her arms, cradling her against her chest. "I'll always come. I've got you. I've got—"

Movement behind her.

Paris's head snapped around. One of the men—the one who had been on top of Rae, the one who had violated her—had gotten to his feet. His face was bloody, his nose clearly broken from the collision, but his eyes burned with some deep reaction that wasn't fear.

It was contempt.

He stared at Paris as if she were nothing. An insect. An inconvenience. Even after what she had done—killed his friend, tossed him aside like a ragdoll—he showed no sign of concern.

Paris scanned his thoughts in a microsecond. She had a specific goal, a finite purpose. She wanted names. Addresses. Information she could use.

James Lieber. The name floated to the surface of his mind, along with an address in a rundown neighborhood south of the city. His accomplice—the one struggling to rise beside him—was *Marcus Webb.* She memorized everything, filing it away for later.

James reached behind his back and pulled out a gun.

Time seemed to slow.

Paris saw him raise the weapon. Saw his finger tighten on the trigger. She was already moving, twisting her body to shield Rae. With the cold certainty of someone who had survived 135 years of violence she knew she wouldn't be fast enough to stop the bullet.

The gun fired twice.

The first shot went wide, punching into the brick wall somewhere to Paris's left.

The second hit Rae.

Paris felt it—felt the impact shudder through the girl in her arms, felt the hot spray of blood against her skin, felt Rae's body jerk and then go terrifyingly still.

"NO!"

The scream tore from her throat, raw and primal. She looked down and saw the wound—center mass, below Rae's collarbone. Blood was spreading across her torn shirt, red and wet and *wrong.*

James was already running, Marcus scrambling after him. Paris could have caught them. Could have run them down and torn them apart with her bare hands. Every cell in her body screamed for their blood, for vengeance, for the satisfaction of watching the light leave *their* eyes.

But Rae's fingers curled weakly into her shirt.

"Don't... go..." The words were barely audible, bubbling up through blood and pain. "Stay... with me..."

Paris's fury shattered into concern.

"I'm here." She pressed her hand against the wound, trying to stop the bleeding, knowing even as she did that it was futile. There was too much blood. The bullet had hit an artery, maybe, or a lung. She could hear the wet gurgle in Rae's breathing, could see the light already beginning to fade from her eyes.

"Rae, listen to me." Paris leaned close, her voice urgent, desperate. "I can help you. I can save you. I can make you like me—give you more life, more strength. You don't have to die. Just say yes. *Please* say yes."

Rae's lips curved into a smile. Blood stained her teeth.

"Paris..." Her voice was a thread, a whisper, a ghost of sound. "Love... your name..."

"Rae, please—"

"These... past few days..." Rae's hand found Paris's, her grip weak but determined. "Best... of my life. You... you made me feel... like I mattered. Like I was... worth something."

"You are worth something!" Paris's voice cracked. She could feel tears streaming down her face—hot and salt and utterly useless. "You matter, Rae. You matter so much. Please let me save you. *Please.*"

"No, sweetie." Rae focused on Paris's face with sudden, terrible clarity. "They've... taken the last of me. I'm done." A sound that might have been a laugh bubbled up through the blood in her throat. "Who wants... to live forever... anyway?"

"Rae—"

"Thank you." The words were barely audible now. "Thank you... for everything. For seeing me. For... caring."

Her fingers loosened in Paris's grip.

Her eyes—those sharp, suspicious, beautiful green eyes—went still.

And then there was nothing.

Paris held her.

She held her as the seconds stretched into minutes. She held her as the warmth faded from her body and the blood stopped flowing because there was nothing left to pump. She held her and rocked her and whispered words that didn't matter to ears that could no longer hear.

At some point, she became aware that she was crying.

It had been so long since she had cried. Decades. Maybe longer. She had trained herself to suppress it, to lock away the grief and the pain and the overwhelming *unfairness* of a world that took and took and never stopped taking. Tears were weakness. Tears were vulnerability. Tears were a luxury she could not afford.

But now the tears came anyway, pouring down her face in hot rivers, dripping onto Rae's still face. And with them came the grief—a black wave that crashed over her and dragged her under, filling her lungs with sorrow, drowning her in the weight of everything she had lost.

Rae. London. Garrett. Her mother. Marty and Liz.

Everyone she had ever loved. Everyone she had ever allowed herself to care about. Gone. All of them gone.

What's the point? The thought rose unbidden, dark and seductive. What's the point of surviving if everyone you love dies anyway? What's the point of going on?

She didn't have an answer.

She was still holding Rae when the sirens began to wail in the distance. She was still holding her when the red and blue lights painted the alley walls. She was still holding her when the first uniformed officer rounded the corner and stopped dead, hand going to his weapon.

"Miss? Miss, I need you to step away from the body."

Paris didn't move.

"Miss!" The officer's voice was sharper now. "Step away from the body and show me your hands!"

Slowly, carefully, Paris laid Rae's body on the ground. She smoothed the hair back from her face. She closed her friend's eyes for the final time.

Then she stood and turned to face the officer, her hands raised, her face a mask of blood and tears.

"Her name was Rae," she said. Her voice was hollow. Empty. "Her name was Rae, and she deserved better than this."

The officer lowered his weapon slightly, uncertainty flickering across his face. More sirens in the distance. More lights. More chaos.

Paris stood in the middle of it all, surrounded by blood and death and the shattered remnants of what had felt, for a few brief days, like hope.

The third attacker lay crumpled against the wall, his skull caved in, staring at nothing. The other two had fled—but Paris had their names. Their faces. Their addresses.

James Lieber. Marcus Webb.

She would find them. She would make them pay.

But that was for later.

For now, she simply stood in the strobing light of the police cars and let the grief wash over her—wave after wave after wave—until she felt like she might drown in it.

I'm sorry, she thought, looking down at Rae's still form. *I'm so sorry I couldn't save you.*

The paramedics arrived. The crime scene tape went up. The questions began.

And Paris answered them all, her voice flat and dead, while a part of her—the part that had dared to hope, dared to care, dared to believe that she might have found anything worth protecting—curled up and died alongside the girl who had reminded her so much of herself.

CHAPTER 19

(1894, The Citadel — Age 14)

The apartment was small.

Paris stood in the doorway of her new quarters, taking in the space that would be hers for the foreseeable future. Four hundred square feet, or a bit less—a sitting room that doubled as a bedroom, a narrow alcove for her cot, and a bathroom barely large enough to turn around in. The walls were bare stone, the floor cold flagstone, the only window a narrow slit that looked out onto an interior courtyard.

It was, without question, the finest accommodation she had ever possessed.

On the streets of Bristol, she had slept in doorways and under bridges, curled around her own hunger for warmth. At the School, she had shared cramped dormitories with a dozen other children, their cots lined up like soldiers awaiting inspection. This—this private space, this room of her own—felt obscenely luxurious by comparison.

She stepped inside and closed the door behind her, running her fingers along the rough stone walls. The room smelled of dust and age and other things she couldn't quite identify. History, imaginably. The weight of all the Valensi who had occupied this space before her.

A knock came at the door—not the formal knock of authority, but the quick, familiar rap of friendship.

"It's open," Paris called.

London burst in with her usual energy, her dark hair swinging, her almond-shaped eyes bright with excitement. "Have you seen your room? Isn't it wonderful? I mean, it's small, but it's *ours*. Our own space. No more dormitories, no more sharing with—"

"Breathe, London."

"I am breathing. I'm just breathing quickly." London spun around, taking in Paris's quarters with the same delight she had presumably shown her own. "We're in the High Guard now, Paris. The *High Guard*. Do you understand what that means?"

"It means we get tiny apartments and the privilege of being ordered about by people who could kill us without breaking a sweat."

"It means we *matter*." London stopped spinning and fixed Paris with a serious look. "We survived the School. We passed the trials. We killed to earn our place here. And now we're part of something bigger than ourselves. Something important."

Paris couldn't help but smile at her friend's enthusiasm. London had always been the optimist between them—the one who saw possibility where Paris saw only pragmatism. It was one of the things she loved most about her.

"You're right," she admitted. "It is wonderful. Even if the room smells like a tomb."

"We'll get candles. Flowers. Maybe some tapestries for the walls." London was already planning, her mind racing ahead to domestic improvements. "We should coordinate—make our rooms complement each other. We're a few doors apart, you know. Close enough to—"

"Get into trouble together?"

"I was going to say 'support each other,' but yes, that too."

They grinned at each other, two girls on the cusp of a new life, a vast and terrifying and wonderful new life.

The High Guard Operations Room—which the members had taken to calling "the Abode"—was a large chamber situated near the Magistrate's personal quarters. It served as command post, meeting room, and gathering space all in one, though its current décor left much to be desired.

The room was dominated by heavy stone walls and sparse furnishings: a worn sofa that had seen better decades, a few mismatched chairs, a long table scarred by countless meetings and meals. Gas lamps provided flickering illumination, casting shadows that danced in the corners. The overall effect was less "elite inner sanctum" and more "neglected storage room."

Paris and London had been summoned here for what was officially termed an "orientation session" but felt more like an inspection. They sat on the worn sofa, backs straight, hands folded in their laps, trying to project competence and calm.

The other members of the High Guard were arranged around the room, watching them with varying degrees of interest.

Dusk stood near the window, his eyes unreadable. He was everything Paris had expected from the leader of the Magistrate's personal guard: calm, measured, thoughtful. In the months since she had first met him, she had come to understand that his silences were not empty but full—pregnant with observation and calculation. He never spoke without purpose, never moved without intention. London had confessed to her once, in whispered tones, that she had developed a crush on him. That crush had since faded into respect, which Paris thought was probably healthier for everyone involved.

Dawn stood beside her brother, her golden hair gleaming in the lamplight, her brilliant blue eyes sharp as cut glass. Where Dusk was patient, Dawn was restless—always moving, always eager to act. She had a tongue like a whip and expectations to match. Paris had learned quickly that Dawn saw herself as the maternal figure of the Guard, responsible for molding its newer members into proper shape. Whether they wanted to be molded or not.

Vienna—Vi, as she preferred to be called—leaned against the far wall with her arms crossed. She was close to sixty years older than Paris and London in actual age, though her early turning had left her appearing younger than either of them. She had strong features, pretty in a rough sort of way, with shoulder-length brown hair pulled back in a perpetual ponytail. Paris had never once seen her in anything but trousers and men's shirts. London had observed early on that Vi was a "you get what you see" kind of girl, and Paris couldn't have agreed more.

Cairo lounged in one of the mismatched chairs, his long legs stretched out before him, his expression one of perpetual amusement. He was the newest full member of the Guard—newest until Paris and London, at least—and he carried himself with the easy confidence of someone who had long since proven his worth. He was handsome in a rakish sort of way, with curly hair and an olive complexion that spoke of Mediterranean origins. His most notable feature, however, was his mouth—specifically, the things that came out of it.

"So," Cairo said, breaking the silence with characteristic bluntness, "the new blood finally gets to see where the magic happens. What do you think, ladies? Living up to your expectations?"

"It's..." Paris searched for a diplomatic word. "Functional."

"She means it's a bloody eyesore," London supplied.

Cairo laughed—a full, genuine laugh that echoed off the stone walls. "I knew I was going to like you two."

"Cairo." Dawn's voice cut through the levity like a blade. "Perhaps we could maintain some semblance of professionalism?"

"Perhaps we could, yes." Cairo didn't move from his lounging position. "But where's the fun in that?"

Dawn's eyes narrowed, but before she could respond, Dusk cleared his throat.

"Enough." The single word silenced the room. "Paris. London. You have been accepted into the High Guard based on your performance in the trials and the Magistrate's personal recommendation. This is a significant honor—one that carries significant responsibilities."

155

Paris and London nodded in unison.

"You will train with us, live among us, serve alongside us. You will learn our protocols, our traditions, our expectations." Dusk's gaze moved between them. "However, there is one crucial difference between you and the rest of us."

"We're not yet Valensi," Paris said.

"Correct." Dusk inclined his head slightly. "You have chosen to delay your Birthing until your bodies mature further. The Magistrate has approved this decision. But you must understand what it means."

"It means we're still breakable," London said quietly.

"Precisely." Dusk stepped away from the window and moved toward them, his movements fluid and controlled. "The rest of us heal from wounds that would kill a human."

He stopped directly in front of Paris, looking down at her with those unreadable eyes.

"A little over a month ago, I broke your arm during a sparring session. Remember?"

Paris remembered. The crack of bone, the white-hot flash of pain, the weeks of healing that followed. "I remember."

"If you had already been Birthed, that injury would have healed in minutes. Instead, you were incapacitated for weeks." Dusk's voice held no judgment, only fact. "Until you complete your transformation, you will always be vulnerable. You will always be the weak link. You must compensate for that weakness with awareness, with caution, with the understanding that a mistake that might cost one of us a moment's pain could cost you your life."

"We understand," Paris said.

"I hope so." Dusk held her gaze for a moment longer, then stepped back. "Dawn will inform you of the Guard's protocols and expectations. Training begins tomorrow at dusk. Do not be late."

He turned and walked toward the door, his burgundy cloak swirling behind him. At the threshold, he paused and looked back.

"Welcome to the High Guard."

Then he was gone, leaving the room somehow emptier for his absence.

"Well," Dawn said, stepping into the center of the room, "now that my brother has delivered the appropriately ominous welcome, let's discuss the practical matters."

She began to pace, her movements sharp and precise. "The High Guard serves multiple functions within Valensi society. We are the Magistrate's personal protection—his shield against any who would seek to harm him. We are also his sword, deployed when situations require a more... direct approach."

"Direct approach," Cairo murmured. "I love how she makes 'killing people' sound so elegant."

Dawn ignored him. "Additionally, we serve as internal enforcement. When a Valensi breaks our laws, when someone threatens the secrecy of our existence, we are often called upon to handle the situation. The Protectors handle external threats; we handle internal ones."

"What's the difference?" London asked.

"Protectors hunt," Vi said, speaking for the first time. Her voice was lower than Paris had expected, rougher. "They track down rogues, eliminate threats, maintain the silence of our existence in the wider world. They work alone or in pairs, often far from the Citadel." She shrugged. "We stay close to home. Guard the Magistrate. Clean up messes."

"Vi makes it sound terribly unglamorous," Dawn said with a tight smile. "But make no mistake—the High Guard is the most prestigious position a Valensi can hold outside the Hierarchy itself. The Magistrate trusts us with his life. That trust must be earned and maintained every single day."

"Speaking of every single day," Cairo said, finally sitting up straight, "there's the matter of inspections."

Dawn shot him a look that could have curdled milk. "I was getting to that."

"By all means, Mother Hen. Continue."

The temperature in the room seemed to drop several degrees. Paris saw Vi's lips twitch—fighting a smile—and London's eyes went wide.

"What did you call me?" Dawn's voice was dangerously soft.

"Nothing." Cairo's expression was innocent. "Please, continue with the orientation."

Dawn stared at him for a long moment, then turned back to Paris and London with the air of someone choosing to save a murder for later.

"As I was saying. We will conduct weekly inspections of your quarters. This is to ensure that the standards of the High Guard are being followed, both in public and in your private time."

"How very militaristic," London commented.

"The High Guard *is* military, in its way." Dawn scrutinized London. "We are soldiers. We follow orders. We maintain discipline. If that structure doesn't appeal to you, there are other paths within Valensi society."

"It appeals to us," Paris said quickly, before London could respond. "We're honored to be here. We'll meet whatever standards you set."

"Good." Dawn's expression softened slightly—though "softened" was too strong a word. "First inspection is tomorrow. I'm giving you a full day to ensure your quarters are in proper shape. That's quite generous of me, don't you think?"

"Incredibly generous," Paris said, keeping her face neutral.

"I thought so." Dawn turned toward the door. "Training begins at dusk. Don't be late. Vi will show you where to report."

She swept out of the room without a backward glance, her golden hair trailing behind her like a kite tail.

In the silence that followed, Cairo let out a low whistle. "Well, that could have gone worse."

"Could it?" London asked.

"Oh, absolutely. Dawn once made a new guard member cry within five minutes of meeting him. You two lasted at least ten." He grinned. "I think she likes you."

Paris and London exchanged glances.

"That was her *liking* us?" London said.

"Trust me." Cairo stood and stretched, his joints popping audibly. "You'll know when she doesn't like you."

He ambled toward the door, pausing to look back at them.

"Word of advice, new blood. Dawn's bark is worse than her bite—but her bite is still pretty bad. And Vi's the opposite. She doesn't say much, but when she does, you'd better listen. Dusk is fair, always fair, but don't mistake fairness for softness. And me?" He winked. "I'm the fun one. Come find me when the others get too serious. I keep vodka behind the bar."

"There's a bar?" Paris asked.

"Not yet. But there will be. This room needs work." Cairo cast a critical eye around the space. "Maybe some rugs. Better furniture. A woman's touch, you know?"

And then he was gone, leaving Paris and London alone in the Abode with Vi, who had not moved from her position against the wall.

The silence stretched.

"So," Paris said finally, "you're going to show us where to report for training?"

Vi pushed herself off the wall and headed for the door. "Follow me. And try to keep up. I don't repeat myself."

Paris and London scrambled to their feet and hurried after her, exchanging one more glance as they went.

This is our life now, Paris thought. These are our people. For better or worse, we belong here.

It was a strange feeling—belonging. She wasn't sure she had ever experienced it before. Not truly. Not like this.

As they followed Vi through the winding corridors of the Citadel, past ancient stone walls and flickering gas lamps and doorways that led to mysteries she had yet to explore, Paris allowed herself a small smile.

She was still human. Still vulnerable. Still the weakest link in a chain of immortal predators.

But she was also, for the first time in her life, exactly where she was supposed to be.

And that, she decided, was worth something.

CHAPTER 20

(Present)

The crime scene had taken on the strange, sterile quality of all crime scenes—that peculiar intersection of tragedy and bureaucracy where death became evidence and grief became testimony.

Paris sat on the bumper of an ambulance, a shock blanket draped over her shoulders despite her protests that she didn't need it. A paramedic had bandaged the graze on her shoulder—she hadn't even noticed the bullet had clipped her until someone pointed out the blood soaking through her shirt. It would be healed by tomorrow. Rae would still be dead.

The coroner's van was parked at the mouth of the alley, its back doors open like a waiting mouth. Paris watched as two technicians lifted the black body bag onto a gurney and rolled it toward the van. Such a small bag. Such a small girl. Such an enormous absence where she used to be.

Rae Epsen, she thought. She hadn't even known Rae's last name until one of the officers had found her ID in her pocket. *Rae Epsen, sixteen years old, runaway from Augusta, Georgia. Daughter. Survivor. Friend.*

Dead.

The uniformed officers had been first on scene, asking their preliminary questions with the rote efficiency of people who had seen too many bodies in too many alleys. Paris had answered in monosyllables, giving them the bare minimum—she had been meeting Rae for dinner, had heard sounds of distress, had intervened. One attacker was dead. Two had fled. No, she didn't know them. No, she hadn't seen them before.

The lies came easily. They always did.

Now the uniforms had been replaced by someone more senior—a plainclothes detective who had spent the last twenty minutes surveying the scene, conferring with the crime scene unit, and studiously ignoring Paris. She had watched him work, cataloging his movements, his expressions, the way his eyes kept returning to the chalk outline against the wall where the third attacker's body had been.

He was good. She could tell by the way he moved, the questions he asked, the details he noticed. That made him dangerous.

Finally, he approached.

"Miss Paris?" He consulted a small flip notebook. "Elizabeth Paris?"

"Just Paris." She didn't look at him. She was still transfixed by the coroner's van, on the black bag being loaded into its interior. "Liz is fine, if you need more casual."

"I'm Detective Sean Byrne." He was maybe forty-five, with graying hair and tired but alert eyes that had seen too much. His suit was rumpled, his tie loosened, his face carrying the particular weariness of someone who worked the night shift by choice rather than necessity. "I have some questions for you."

"I've already given my statement to the officers."

"I know. But I'd like to hear it from you directly, if you don't mind." He positioned himself so that she would have to look at him to avoid appearing evasive. A good technique. She'd used it herself, once upon a time.

Paris finally met his gaze. "Fine. Ask."

Byrne flipped open his notebook. "Walk me through what happened."

"I was supposed to meet Rae at a diner a few blocks from here. She was late. I got worried and went looking for her." The lies flowed smoothly, rehearsed in her head during the long minutes of waiting. "I heard sounds coming from this alley—shouting, scuffling. I came to investigate and found three men attacking her."

"And you just... walked into a dark alley? Alone? Not knowing what you'd find?"

"I heard a girl screaming." Paris's voice was flat. "What was I supposed to do? Walk away?"

Byrne's pen scratched across the paper. "So you intervened."

"Yes."

"How, exactly?"

"I pushed one of them. Hard. He fell back and hit the wall." She gestured toward the chalk outline without looking at it. "The other two were... occupied. I pulled one off her, threw him aside. The third one ran."

"The one against the wall—the coroner says his skull was fractured. Multiple places. Massive trauma." Byrne looked up from his notes. "That's a lot of damage for a push."

"I had momentum. Adrenaline." Paris shrugged, the movement pulling at her bandaged shoulder. "You'd be surprised what a little body can do when faced with that kind of stress."

"No," Byrne said slowly. "No, I wouldn't." He held her gaze for a long moment. "What happened next?"

"One of them—the one who had been..." She stopped, the words catching in her throat. Even now, even with all her training, all her control, she couldn't say it. "He pulled a gun. Fired twice. The first shot missed. The second hit Rae."

"And hit you as well, I see."

"A graze. It's nothing."

"And then the two surviving attackers fled?"

"Yes."

"And you didn't pursue them?"

Paris felt her jaw tighten. "Rae asked me to stay. She was dying. She asked me not to leave her." Her voice cracked slightly, and she hated herself for it. "So I stayed."

Byrne was quiet for a moment, his pen hovering over the page. When he spoke again, his voice was softer. "I'm sorry for your loss. It's clear she meant something to you."

"I'd only known her a few days." The words came out hollow. "It wasn't enough."

"It never is." He wrote in his notebook, then flipped it closed. "I'm going to need you to come down to the station and make a formal statement. Tonight, if possible."

"Tomorrow."

"Miss Paris—"

"Tomorrow." She turned her gaze on him, and this time she let some of what she was feeling leak into her stare—the cold fury, the barely contained violence, the 135 years of loss and pain compressed into a single, terrible look. "I just watched my friend die. I'm covered in her blood. I need to... I need time."

Byrne held her stare longer than most humans could have. She gave him credit for that. Finally, he nodded.

"Tomorrow, then. First thing. I expect you at my desk by nine." He double-checked his notes. "You're staying at the Marriott on International Drive, correct? Under the name Elizabeth Paris?"

"That's right."

"And you have identification to verify that?"

"I left it at the hotel. I'll bring it tomorrow."

Another long look. "See that you do." He started to turn away, then paused. "One more thing, Miss Paris."

"Yes?"

"Something's been bothering me about all this." He gestured toward the alley, toward the chalk outline and the blood and the scattered evidence markers. "These men—rapists, clearly. Armed. Violent. The type who wouldn't hesitate to hurt anyone who got in their way." He turned back to face her. "Why did they run from you?"

Paris met his eyes without flinching. "Maybe they were smarter than they looked."

"What are you not telling me?"

The silence stretched between them, thick and heavy with unspoken accusations. Paris could feel Byrne probing at the edges of her story, searching for cracks, for inconsistencies, for the truth she was hiding beneath the lies.

"You know what I think is odd, Detective," she said quietly, "is that rather than focusing your energy on finding the men who raped and murdered an innocent girl, you're standing here questioning a victim about inconsequential details." She rose from the ambulance bumper, letting the shock blanket fall. "My friend is dead. I'm covered in her blood. I've told you everything I know. So maybe—" she stepped closer, close enough to see the flicker of uncertainty in his eyes, "—you should do your fucking job and find the bastards who killed her. Before someone else does."

Byrne's eyes narrowed. For a moment, she thought he might push back, might press her further, might see through the mask she was wearing to the predator beneath.

But then he simply nodded.

"Nine o'clock," he said. "Don't be late."

He turned and walked back toward the crime scene, his notebook already open again, his attention shifting to the forensic techs processing the alley.

Paris watched him go.

James Lieber. Marcus Webb.

The names burned in her mind like brands. She had pulled them from James's thoughts in that fraction of a second before the gun fired—names, faces, addresses, everything she needed. The police might find them eventually. Might bring them to justice. Might lock them in a cell for a few decades before releasing them back into the world to prey on other girls like Rae.

That wasn't good enough.

Paris turned away from the crime scene and began walking. The night was quiet now, the sirens faded, the chaos settling into the grim routine of investigation and documentation. The neon lights of International Drive flickered in the distance, garish and indifferent.

She had a few hours until dawn. A few hours until she would have to seal herself away from the sun, to hide in darkness while the men who had killed Rae walked free.

Not enough time. Not tonight.

But tomorrow night...

Tomorrow night, she would hunt.

She didn't go back to the hotel.

Instead, she walked. Through the tourist district with its gaudy attractions and overpriced restaurants. Through the quieter residential streets beyond. Through empty parking lots and darkened strip malls, her feet carrying her without conscious direction while her mind churned with grief and rage.

Rae's face haunted her. Those green eyes, so sharp and suspicious at first, then warming into trust. That sardonic smile, the defensive armor of a girl who had been hurt too many times to let anyone close. The way she had reached out and touched Paris's hand at the diner, that small gesture of connection from someone who had forgotten how to connect.

"These past few days... best of my life."

The words echoed in Paris's head, over and over, each repetition cutting deeper than the last.

She had known Rae for less than a week. A handful of days, a few shared meals, a few hours of conversation in the garish glow of late-night Orlando. Nothing, really. A blip in the vast expanse of Paris's existence. She had lived through wars and plagues and the rise and fall of empires. She had loved and lost more times than she could count.

So why did this hurt so much?

Because she reminded you of yourself, a voice whispered in the back of her mind. Because you saw in her everything you used to be—the survivor, the fighter, the girl who refused to break. And you thought maybe you could save her the way you were saved.

But she hadn't saved her. She had been too slow, too distracted, too comfortable in her own happiness to see the danger closing in. She had felt the white van's wrongness and dismissed it as paranoia. She had sensed the watchers and told herself she was jumping at shadows.

And now Rae was dead.

My fault, Paris thought. This is my fault.

The guilt settled into her bones like lead, dragging at her steps, weighing down her shoulders. She had failed before—had lost people she loved, had made mistakes that cost lives—but this felt different. This felt personal in a way that cut deeper than the others.

Maybe because Rae had trusted her. Had looked at her and seen something worth believing in. Had called her "weirdo" with a smile that said *I see you, I accept you, I'm glad you're here.*

And Paris had let her die.

No, she corrected herself, her hands curling into fists at her sides. You didn't let her die. They killed her. James Lieber and Marcus Webb. They're the ones who did this. They're the ones who have to pay.

The rage flared up again, hot and welcome after the cold weight of grief. She held onto it, let it burn through her, let it drive back the despair that threatened to swallow her whole.

She would find them. She would make them suffer. She would tear them apart piece by piece and watch the light leave their eyes the same way she had watched it leave Rae's.

And then... and then she would figure out what came next.

The sky was beginning to lighten in the east when Paris finally stopped walking. She had wandered into a small park somewhere on the outskirts of the city—a patch of green surrounded by chain-link fencing, with a few scattered benches and a rusted swing set that creaked in the pre-dawn breeze.

She sat down on one of the swings and looked up at the fading stars.

Dawn was coming. She needed to find shelter, to seal herself away from the sun that would burn through her transformed flesh if she let it catch her. The hotel was too far—she would never make it in time. But there were other options. Abandoned buildings. Underground parking garages. Any space protective enough that she could wait out the day.

She didn't move.

Part of her wanted to stay. Wanted to sit here on this creaking swing and watch the sun rise and let it consume her, burn her away to ash and bone and nothing. It would be easier than going on. Easier than carrying another loss, another failure, another name on the long list of people she had loved and lost.

"Who wants to live forever anyway?"

Rae's last words. A joke, maybe. Or, maybe, a genuine question from a girl who had already tried to end her own life once, who had stared into the void and found nothing worth coming back for.

Paris had an answer now.

I do, she thought. I want to live forever. Not because existence is pleasant or painless or fair—it's none of those things. But because as long as I'm alive, I can still do something. I can still fight. I can still protect the people who need protecting and punish the people who deserve punishment.

I can still make the bastards pay.

She rose from the swing. The sky was pink and gold now, the first rays of sunlight beginning to crest the horizon. She could feel the warmth on her skin, the faint prickle that would soon become pain, then agony, then death.

She ran.

Through the park, over the chain-link fence, down a series of side streets lined with shuttered businesses and empty lots. The sun climbed higher, and she felt her skin begin to tighten, to burn. Smoke curled from her exposed arms, and she gritted her teeth against the pain.

There. An abandoned warehouse, its windows boarded up, its doors hanging off their hinges. She dove through the entrance and into the blessed darkness within, collapsing against a concrete pillar as the sun blazed to life outside.

Her arms were red and blistered, the skin already beginning to heal but still throbbing with residual pain. She sat in the darkness and listened to her own ragged breathing, waiting for the agony to fade.

Tomorrow night, she promised herself. Tomorrow night, I hunt.

She lay back and let the exhaustion take her—not the restful sleep of the satisfied, but the heavy, dreamless oblivion of someone who had nothing left to give.

The last thing she thought before consciousness faded was Rae's face, smiling at her across a diner table, calling her "weirdo" with a warmth that had meant more than Paris had ever admitted.

I'll make them pay, she promised the ghost behind her eyes. I'll make them pay for what they took from you. From us.

I swear it.

CHAPTER 21

(Present)

The sun had barely slipped below the horizon when Paris emerged from the abandoned warehouse.

Her skin still ached from the morning's close call—that desperate race against dawn that had left her arms blistered and raw. The wounds had healed during the day's fitful sleep, but the memory of that burning remained, a reminder of her own vulnerability. Of all the ways she could die.

She didn't care.

There was only one thought in her mind now, burning brighter than any sun: *James Lieber. Marcus Webb.*

The names pulsed through her consciousness like a heartbeat, like a prayer, like a promise. She had pulled them from James's mind in that fraction of a second before the gun fired—names, faces, addresses, everything she needed. The police might find them eventually. Might arrest them. Might put them through a system designed to rehabilitate, to reform, to give second chances to monsters who deserved none.

Paris wasn't interested in second chances.

She was interested in justice. The old kind. The permanent kind.

The neighborhood off Kirkman and Conroy was a warren of apartment complexes and strip malls, the kind of place where people lived stacked on top of each other in cheap efficiency units, where cars sat on blocks in parking lots and the air smelled of exhaust and fried food and quiet desperation.

Paris moved through the shadows like smoke, her senses extended, searching for any trace of her prey. Marcus Webb lived somewhere in this maze—she had pulled the general area from James's thoughts, but not the specific address. It didn't matter. She had time. She had patience. And she had 135 years of experience hunting things far more dangerous than a punk-ass rapist with delusions of invincibility.

She found his trail after an hour of stalking.

He was heading out, probably to score some beer or meet up with friends—as if last night hadn't happened, as if he hadn't helped rape and murder a sixteen-year-old girl, as if the world should keep turning for pieces of shit like him. He walked with that loose-limbed swagger of young men who had never faced real consequences, never met anything stronger than themselves, never learned that the universe didn't care about their petty cruelties.

He was about to learn.

Paris watched him approach his car—a rusted-out Oldsmobile Cutlass from the mid-seventies, its body pocked with primer spots but its chrome wheels gleaming in the streetlight. The wheels probably cost more than the rest of the vehicle combined. Priorities.

She waited until he was reaching for the door handle.

Then she was on him.

Her hands closed over his, pinning them to the car's roof with strength that no human her size should possess. He tried to cry out, to struggle, but before the sound could fully form, she slammed her forehead into the back of his skull with precisely calibrated force—hard enough to daze, not hard enough to kill.

Not yet.

"You've been a bad boy, Marcus," she whispered in his ear, her lips close enough that he could feel her breath on his skin. "You fucked up, son. You ran with the wrong crew, and you ended up getting my friend killed last night."

"Wha—" he began, his voice slurred from the blow.

"My only friend within thousands of miles," Paris continued, her voice soft and cold and utterly without mercy. "And you bastards took her away from me. You know what that means, right, arsehole?"

He tried to speak again, but she increased the pressure on his left hand, feeling the small bones grind against each other beneath her grip. He whimpered instead.

"It means I get to take you away from your friends and family. Fair is fair."

She squeezed harder, and heard the first crack of bone giving way. Marcus's whimper became a strangled scream.

"Go ahead," she said, releasing his right hand while maintaining her crushing grip on the left. "Unlock the door."

His fingers fumbled with the keys, shaking so badly he could barely fit them into the lock. Finally, the door swung open. Paris reached around him, pulled the seat forward, and shoved him into the back of the Cutlass. She followed before he could recover, pulling the door shut behind them.

The interior smelled of stale cigarettes and fast food and fear—that sharp, acrid scent of a body producing more adrenaline than it knew what to do with. Marcus was scrambling backward, trying to put distance between them, but there was nowhere to go. The back seat of a Cutlass wasn't designed for escape.

"Please," he gasped. "Please, I didn't—it wasn't my idea—I just—"

Paris's fist connected with his jaw, and he crumpled like a puppet with its strings cut.

She sat in the car, looking down at his unconscious form. He was young—maybe twenty-two, twenty-three. Old enough to know better. Old enough to make choices. Old enough to pay for them.

She didn't necessarily need to feed. She had drunk from Greg the rapist only days ago, and she could go weeks without blood if necessary. But she wasn't going to waste the opportunity, either. This death would serve multiple purposes: sustenance, justice, and a message to whatever cosmic force had decided that Rae's life was worth less than the brief pleasure of monsters like this.

She fed.

It was quick and clean—not out of mercy, but out of practicality. She had another stop to make tonight, and she didn't want to waste time on someone who barely deserved her attention. Marcus Webb had been a supporting player in Rae's murder, a follower rather than a leader. He had held her down while others did the real damage. He had watched. He had waited his turn.

He deserved death. But he didn't deserve her full attention.

When it was done, Paris sat back and watched the life seep out of him. She reached into his fading consciousness, curious despite herself about what lay on the other side of that final threshold.

Nothing.

Only darkness, vast and absolute, swallowing him whole.

The same darkness Rae had described seeing when she'd tried to end her own life. The same emptiness that waited for all of them, human and Valensi alike.

Is that all there is? Paris wondered. After everything—the struggle, the pain, the desperate clinging to existence—is there nothing but the void?

She didn't have an answer. She wasn't sure she wanted one.

She left Marcus Webb bleeding out in the back seat of his beloved Cutlass, his chrome wheels gleaming uselessly in the streetlight. She locked the door behind her—a final indignity, sealing him in his metal coffin—and walked north on Kirkman without looking back.

One down. One to go.

James Lieber's apartment complex was a few miles away, a sprawling maze of identical buildings arranged around courtyards and parking lots. The kind of place where nobody knew their neighbors and nobody asked questions. The perfect home for a monster.

Paris had the address—she had pulled it directly from James's mind in that moment before the gun fired—but there were dozens of units in the complex. She would have to hunt.

She didn't mind. Hunting was what she did.

For an hour, she stalked the shadows between buildings, extending her senses, searching for any trace of her quarry. She caught fragments of thought from the residents—the petty worries and mundane desires of people living their small lives—but nothing that matched the cold, empty signature she was looking for.

Then she found him.

Third floor balcony, smoking a cigarette, staring out at the parking lot with the vacant expression of someone who had never learned to feel guilt. James Lieber. Sortie, his friends called him—a nickname earned from his tendency to fire his gun without care for who might be in the line of fire. He thought it made him sound dangerous. Sophisticated. Military.

He was none of those things. He was a broken creature who had learned to enjoy breaking others.

Paris crept into his mind, careful to remain hidden, and what she found there made her stomach turn.

Rae wasn't his first victim. Not even close.

The memories rose to the surface like corpses in a flood—at least three other women, probably more, their faces twisted in terror and pain. He kept their images like trophies, replaying them in quiet moments, savoring the memory of their suffering. His happiest recollections weren't of friends or family or accomplishments. They were of rape. Of murder. Of the power he felt when he held another person's life in his hands.

This little bastard is more of a monster than I am, Paris thought. They really do come in all shapes and sizes.

She mapped his apartment through his thoughts—the layout, the furniture, the weapons. A hunting rifle leaned against the wall in the corner. The Glock that had killed Rae sat on a shelf between the dining area and the kitchen.

When James went inside, Paris made her move.

The recreational area below his balcony featured a standalone grill, its heavy metal frame concreted into the ground. Paris took a running start, leaped onto the grill, and used it as a springboard to launch herself upward. She caught the edge of the balcony and pulled herself over the railing in one fluid motion, landing silently in the shadows beside the sliding glass door.

James hadn't bothered to lock it. Of course he hadn't. He was too arrogant to imagine that anyone would dare to come for him this way. Too confident in his own invincibility.

That confidence was about to be shattered.

Paris slipped inside.

The apartment was as dull and dreary as the inside of James's mind. An orange cloth couch, worn down to bare threads, sat against one wall. Opposite it, a tube television—she was amazed anyone still had one of those in this digital age. A small round dining table with mismatched chairs. The bare minimum of existence for someone who lived entirely in his own twisted fantasies.

She moved to the hunting rifle first, grasping the barrel with both hands and bending it half an inch to the side. It would still look normal at a glance, but it would never fire true again. A small sabotage, but satisfying.

Then she picked up the Glock.

The weight of it in her hand felt significant somehow. This was the weapon that had ended Rae's life. This small piece of metal and polymer and mechanical precision had sent a bullet through her chest and stolen her from the world.

Paris turned it over in her hands, examining it with cold curiosity.

"Who the fuck're you? What're you doing here?"

She kept the Glock from sight as she turned to face him. James stood in the short hallway that led to the bathroom and bedroom, his posture aggressive, his expression more annoyed than afraid. He hadn't yet realized what he was dealing with.

"You can call me Paris," she said.

Recognition flickered in his eyes—the girl from the alley, the one who had interrupted their fun, the one who should have died alongside her friend. Before he could process what that meant, Paris pulled back the slide on the Glock, chambering a round, and flipped off the safety.

"Don't move," she said, leveling the weapon at his head.

He didn't.

"From last night, huh?" His voice was steady, bored. He wasn't afraid. Even now, even with a gun pointed at his face, he couldn't conceive of a world where a small girl like her posed a real threat. "Look, she was a kid in the wrong place at the wrong time. Nothing personal."

"You see, I find it interesting that I was thinking the same thing about you."

Paris set the safety back on, hit the magazine release, and caught the falling clip in her free hand. She watched James's eyes track the movement—confusion replacing contempt as she threw the magazine out the open balcony door. She pulled the slide back to eject the chambered round, then tossed the empty gun aside.

"You're either unbelievably brave," James said slowly, crossing his arms, "or incredibly stupid."

"We've only got a couple of hours before I have to leave, so let's get down to brass tacks." Paris took a step toward him. "I am neither that brave nor, certainly, that stupid. What other description might you think would suit me?"

"I'm thinking 'dead' might be a good description in a minute or two."

"I was thinking more along the lines of upset. Angry. Pissed." Another step. "Vengeful."

"Little girl, you have no idea what you're in for."

He came at her with that brash confidence, that certainty in his own superiority that had served him so well against helpless, terrified women.

Paris open-palm struck his throat.

The blow wasn't hard enough to crush his windpipe—she needed him alive for what came next—but it was more than sufficient to drop him to the floor, coughing and choking and gasping for air. He looked up at her with wide, uncomprehending eyes, his hands clutching his damaged throat.

"You took the words right out of my mouth, you little shit."

She kicked him in the side of the head, and James Lieber went out like a light.

He woke tied to his own bed.

Paris had taken her time with the preparations. His arms were outstretched, wrists bound securely to the metal rails of the headboard with rope she had found in his closet. His legs were spread and tied to the corners at the foot of the bed. A sock—one of his own, pulled from the dirty laundry pile and smelling accordingly—had been shoved into his mouth and secured with another length of rope around his head.

She had dragged his nightstand to the side of the bed, positioning it within his line of sight. On top, she had placed a folded bath towel. On top of the towel, arranged with careful deliberation, lay several objects: a kitchen fork, a steak knife, a pair of pliers, a corkscrew, and a pair of needle-nose pliers.

"Rise and shine, dickhead," Paris said, watching his return to consciousness as he took in his situation. "Time to pay the piper."

He tried to scream through the gag, his body thrashing against the restraints. Paris let him struggle for a moment, savoring the shift in power, the way his arrogance crumbled into terror.

"James Lieber," she said, running her fingers along the implements on the nightstand. "How many women have you tortured? How many innocent women have you raped and murdered? How many lives have you ruined for your own sport and sick fun?"

She had the answers. She had seen them in his mind—the trophies he kept, the memories he cherished. But she wanted him to remember too. She wanted every one of his victims to rise to the surface of his thoughts, to crowd into his consciousness, to be present for what came next.

She picked up the steak knife.

"Let's start with this, shall we?"

She cut his shirt from his body with quick, efficient strokes, leaving him bare-chested and vulnerable. His struggles intensified, muffled screams pushing against the gag as she moved to his belt, his jeans, cutting them away piece by piece until he lay in nothing but his boxers.

"How does it feel, James?" She set the knife aside and leaned close, her voice soft and intimate. "How does it feel to be so out of control? So afraid? So helpless?" She let the words sink in, watching the tears begin to stream from his cold blue eyes. "How does it feel to know that someone else now holds your fate in her hands?"

She picked up the knife again and dragged its tip along the inside of his thigh—not slashing, only pressing, just enough to part the skin and let the blood well up in a thin crimson line. James's scream tore itself raw against the gag, his voice shredding itself in his throat until nothing came out but a hoarse, broken wheeze.

"That's better," Paris said. "A little quiet while I work."

She ripped away his boxers with a single sharp motion, leaving him naked and bleeding and utterly exposed. He was crying now—great heaving sobs that shook his whole body, snot bubbling from his nose, tears cutting tracks through the sweat on his face.

Good. This was what she wanted. This was what he deserved.

Paris studied the implements on the nightstand, letting him see her consider each one. The corkscrew. The pliers. The fork.

Her fingers closed around the fork.

"You took something from those women," she said quietly. "Something they can never get back. Their dignity. Their safety. Their sense of self." She held the fork up where he could see it, the tines glinting in the dim light. "I think it's only fair that I return the favor."

What happened next was quick and brutal and precisely calculated.

She grabbed his cock, stretched him taut, and drove the fork through its flesh and into the soft tissue of his abdomen, pinning him in place like a butterfly on a board. James's eyes rolled back in his head, and he slumped into unconsciousness.

Paris splashed cold water on his face, dragging him back to awareness.

"You can't sleep yet, son," she said, reaching for the pliers. "Your punishment has just begun."

She held the pliers up between them, turning them slowly, letting him see the narrow nose, the serrated teeth. His body twisted and shook against the restraints, fresh screams tearing from his ruined throat.

"For all of those women whose innocence you ripped away," Paris said, her voice flat and cold. "For all of those for whom their womanhood was nothing but a plaything for your demented sense of superiority. Let's see how you deal with it."

She placed a firm hand on his sternum to hold him steady.

She positioned the pliers over his left testicle.

She squeezed.

At first, she was almost impressed by the resilience, the way the tissue resisted, the way his body fought against the violation. Then she felt the pop, the sudden give, the wet collapse of it. Oh, that little thing was never meant to be compressed.

James Lieber's consciousness fled into blackness, and this time, no amount of cold water would bring him back.

Paris sat in the chair she had pulled from the dining room, watching the broken man on the bed. His breathing was shallow, his heartbeat irregular. He was dying—not from the wounds she had inflicted, which were severe but not immediately fatal, but from a deeper source. Maybe she had touched it off when she pushed into the darkest corners of his mind.

She sent her thoughts into him, following the fading thread of his consciousness into whatever lay beyond.

What she found surprised her.

James stood in a vast, empty space—not the cramped apartment, not the blood-soaked bed, but somewhere else entirely. Somewhere that existed only in the dying synapses of his brain. Before him stood figures, shadowy and indistinct but somehow familiar.

His victims.

They faced him in a silent row, their glares accusing, their presence undeniable. Paris watched from the shadows of his mind as James raised his head and met their gazes one by one. Tears streamed down his face— not tears of self-pity, but something else. It looked almost like... recognition. Understanding.

Remorse.

In the distance, a light began to bloom.

It started as a pinprick, a tiny hole in the fabric of the gloom, but it grew rapidly—warm and golden and somehow welcoming. One by one, the victims began to drift toward it, their shadowy forms dissolving into that radiance, melding with it, becoming part of the larger fabric of it all.

Paris tried to understand what she was seeing, tried to grasp the details, but everything was hazy and unfocused, like trying to read a book through frosted glass. The light was there, undeniably there, but its nature—its meaning—remained beyond her comprehension.

The last of the victims faded into the brilliance.

And then James turned and looked directly at her.

That shouldn't be possible. Paris had spent decades learning to move through others' minds undetected, to observe without being observed. No one had ever seen her within their consciousness. No one had ever—

"You are a harsh teacher," James said.

"What?" Paris found herself responding, drawn into the conversation despite her confusion.

"All the pain I dealt to so many—it meant nothing to me. It was beyond my own understanding. I couldn't feel it. Couldn't comprehend it." He paused, peace settling over his features. "You helped me feel the very pain I had so grievously ignored. It wasn't a pleasant lesson. But I thank you for it."

"You're dying," Paris said. "Your brain is shutting down. This is just— neurons firing randomly, dreams and delusions mixing together."

"Maybe." James smiled—an expression she had never seen on his face, utterly different from the cruel smirk he had worn in life. "Or maybe there's more to it than that. More than either of us understood."

"There's nothing. I've watched people die. I've looked into their minds as they faded. There's nothing but darkness."

"For some, maybe. For those who never learned. For those who never grew." He glanced toward the light, which was beginning to fade now, its warmth receding into the distance. "I got lucky. I got you."

"Lucky?" The word tasted bitter in her mouth. "I tortured you. I mutilated you. I—"

"You taught me. In the only language I could understand." James turned back to face her, and his expression was one she couldn't name. "You've got a trial coming up, Paris. It's coming fast. Faster than you know."

"What does that mean?"

"You'll have to figure that out for yourself. But don't think too hard on it." The light was almost gone now, and James was beginning to fade with it, his form growing transparent, insubstantial. "Let your instincts guide you. They always have."

"Wait—"

But he was gone.

The light was gone.

The darkness surged up to swallow her, and Paris snapped back into her own mind with a gasp.

She was sitting in the chair beside the bed. James Lieber lay motionless on the blood-soaked sheets, staring at nothing. She reached out with her senses, searching for any trace of life.

Nothing. His heart had stopped. His mind was empty.

He was dead.

But the damage she had inflicted—severe as it was—shouldn't have been enough to kill him. Not yet. Not so quickly. It was as if something else had claimed him, had pulled him away from his broken body and into... what? The light? The void? Something in between?

A chill crept up Paris's spine.

You've got a trial coming up. It's coming fast.

What did that mean? Was the Protector closer than she thought? Was she about to be caught, dragged back to the Citadel to face the Magistrate's justice?

She shook off the questions. There would be time to ponder the mysteries of death later. Right now, she needed to move.

She wiped down the surfaces she had touched, erased any trace of her presence, and slipped out the balcony door the same way she had entered. The night air was cool against her skin, carrying the distant sounds of traffic and televisions and all the small noises of human existence.

Somewhere out there, the Protector was hunting her. Somewhere out there, the trial James had warned her about was waiting.

But for now, she had done what she came to do. Rae's killers were dead. Justice—her kind of justice—had been served.

It wasn't enough. It would never be enough. Rae was still gone, and no amount of blood could bring her back.

Paris returned to her hotel one last time.

She gathered her few possessions—the clothes she had bought, the cash she had accumulated, the phone she would soon discard—and left the key cards on the dresser for Liam to find. She didn't bother with a note. What was there to say?

In the parking garage, she located the car whose keys she had lifted from one of the hotel guests—the businessman who had been pleasuring himself to thoughts of his stepdaughter two nights ago. She had noted his room number and his vehicle and filed the information away for later use. Now, it paid off.

The car started on the first try, and Paris pulled out of the garage into the fading night.

She had a couple of hours before dawn. Enough time to put some distance between herself and Orlando, to find a safe place to wait out the day. She merged onto Interstate 4 and headed north, leaving behind the neon lights and garish attractions and the memory of a girl with green eyes and a sardonic smile who had reminded her so much of herself.

"These past few days... best of my life."

Rae's final words echoed in her mind, and Paris felt tears threaten. She blinked them away and focused on the road.

She didn't know where she was going yet. North, for now. Away from the scene of the crime, away from Detective Byrne and his suspicious questions, away from the ghosts that lingered in every shadow of that tourist-trap city.

Eventually, she would need to stop running. Eventually, she would need to face whatever trial was coming.

But not tonight.

Tonight, she drove through the gloom, chasing the retreating edge of night, trying to outrun the grief that followed her like a second shadow.

She didn't succeed.

But she kept driving anyway.

CHAPTER 22

1896, The Citadel — Age 16

The first year after her Birthing was, in many ways, harder than the eight years that preceded it.

Paris had expected the transformation to feel like an ending—the death of the frightened street waif she had been, the emergence of something stronger, something untouchable. Instead, it felt like waking up in a body that no longer quite fit. The strength was there, coiled in her muscles like a spring wound too tight. The speed. The hunger that gnawed at her from the inside, demanding satisfaction in ways that food alone could never provide.

But the emotions—those hadn't changed at all. If anything, they had become sharper, more insistent, harder to push aside.

"You're brooding again."

Paris looked up from her untouched glass of wine to find London sliding onto the worn sofa beside her. The Abode was quiet tonight—Dusk was off on assignment somewhere in the German states, Dawn was conducting one of her interminable inspections of the lower quarters, and Vi had claimed the bar for herself, polishing glasses that were already spotless.

"I don't brood," Paris said.

"You absolutely brood. You've been doing it for months now. Ever since—" London gestured vaguely. "You know."

"Since I killed a man and drank his blood?"

London winced. "I was trying to be delicate."

"Delicacy is wasted on me."

"Clearly." London tucked her feet beneath her, settling in as though she planned to stay a while. That was the thing about London—she never pushed, but she also never left. She simply... remained. A constant presence at Paris's side, as she had been since that first night in the dormitory when they were children.

Eight years ago. It felt like a lifetime.

Paris supposed it was.

"Do you ever think about it?" she asked, her voice quieter than she intended. "The one you killed?"

London was silent for a long moment. When she spoke, her voice held none of its usual lightness. "Every day."

"Does it get easier?"

"No." London reached over and squeezed Paris's hand. "But you learn to carry it. The weight doesn't lessen—you just get stronger."

Paris considered that. She had spent her entire life getting stronger, building walls, hardening herself against a world that had shown her nothing but cruelty. She had thought the Birthing would be the final step in that process—the moment when she moved beyond human weakness, beyond human pain.

Instead, she found herself more aware of pain than ever. Not her own—she could push that aside easily enough. But the pain of the man she had killed, the fear in his gaze as he understood what was about to happen, the desperate flutter of his pulse beneath her fangs...

That stayed with her. That *lingered*.

"The worst part," Paris said slowly, "is that I enjoyed it."

London's hand tightened on hers but she didn't pull away. "The feeding?"

"The power." Paris stared at the wine in her glass, deep red and suddenly unappetizing. "The moment when I felt his life flowing into me, when I understood that I could take anything I wanted and no one could stop me—I liked it. I *wanted* more."

"That's the nature of what we are."

"I know." Paris set the glass down, pushing it away from her. "That's what frightens me."

Cairo found her in the gymnasium the next evening, working through forms with one of Master Asaro's wooden practice swords. She had been at it for hours, her muscles burning with the pleasant ache of exertion, her mind finally, blessedly quiet.

"You're going to wear a groove in the floor," Cairo observed from the doorway.

Paris didn't pause her movements. "Then the facilities department will have work to do."

"Dawn will have a fit."

"Dawn always has a fit. It's her natural state of being." Paris completed the form and turned to face him, the practice sword resting against her shoulder. "Did you want anything, or are you here to admire the view?"

Cairo's grin was slow and lazy, the expression of a man who had all the time in the world and knew it. He was handsome—Paris could acknowledge that objectively—with curly hair and olive skin that spoke of Mediterranean origins. His eyes were the color of strong coffee, and they held a perpetual gleam of amusement that Paris found alternately charming and irritating.

"Maybe a bit of both," he said.

"I'm not interested."

"In sparring?" His eyebrows rose in mock innocence. "I was going to offer to run drills with you. But if your mind went somewhere else entirely, well—"

"Cairo."

"—I can't be held responsible for where your thoughts wander—"

"Cairo."

He held up his hands in surrender, still grinning. "Fine, fine. I come in peace. Dusk sent me to fetch you. Apparently there's an assignment."

Paris lowered the practice sword, interest sparking despite herself. "What kind of assignment?"

"The boring kind, from what I gathered. Escort duty for some merchant who's coming to negotiate with the Hierarchy. You and London are supposed to meet him at the border and bring him in safely."

"That does sound boring."

"I know. Such a waste of your talents." Cairo pushed off from the doorframe and strolled toward her, his movements loose and unhurried. "But orders are orders. Dusk wants you in the Abode in twenty minutes for briefing."

Paris nodded and moved toward the weapons rack to return the practice sword. She was acutely aware of Cairo following behind her, his gaze a weight on her back.

"You know," he said, "you've been wound pretty tight lately."

"Have I?"

"Vi says you've been taking extra training sessions with Asaro. London says you barely sleep. Dawn says—"

"Dawn says a lot of things."

"She's worried about you. We all are."

Paris slotted the sword into its place and turned to face him. Cairo's expression had shifted, the perpetual amusement giving way to a more serious expression. It was an unusual look for him, and Paris found it oddly unsettling.

"I'm fine," she said.

"Sure you are." He stepped closer, not quite close enough to be threatening, but close enough that Paris had to tilt her head back to meet his gaze. "I know what it's like, you know. The first year after Birthing. It's... a lot."

"Is that what you came to tell me? That it gets easier?"

"No." His smile returned, but it was gentler now, the edges softened. "I came to tell you that you're not alone. Whatever you're feeling, whatever you're going through—we've all been there. And we're here if you need us."

Paris didn't know how to respond to that. She had spent so much of her life alone, relying on no one but herself, that the concept of a support system still felt foreign. The High Guard was supposed to be her family now—she recognized that intellectually—but accepting it emotionally was another matter entirely.

"I'll keep that in mind," she said finally.

Cairo nodded, apparently satisfied. "Good. Now get moving. You know how Dusk gets when people are late."

The Abode was more crowded than Paris had seen it in weeks when she arrived. Dusk stood by the fireplace, his visage sweeping over the assembled Guard with his usual air of quiet authority. Dawn sat rigid in one of the armchairs, her golden hair pulled back in a severe bun, her expression suggesting that someone, somewhere, had failed to meet her exacting standards. Vi was behind the bar—her preferred location—nursing a glass of amber-colored liquid and watching the proceedings with detached interest.

London was already there, perched on the arm of the sofa, and she waved Paris over with an eager gesture.

"You're nearly late," she whispered as Paris settled beside her.

"Nearly doesn't count."

"It does to Dawn."

Paris glanced at Dawn, who was indeed directing a disapproving look their way. She met the older woman's gaze steadily, refusing to flinch, and after a moment Dawn turned her attention back to Dusk.

"Now that we're all present," Dusk said, his voice carrying easily through the room despite its softness, "we can begin. As some of you may have heard, the Hierarchy has requested our assistance with a... delicate matter."

"Escort duty," Cairo supplied from his position by the bar. "Very delicate."

Dusk silenced him with a look. "The merchant's name is Rothschild. He represents certain interests in the human financial world that the Hierarchy wishes to cultivate. He will be traveling to the Citadel under our protection, and he will leave the same way. Any harm that comes to him while he is in our care will reflect poorly on all of us."

"When you say 'certain interests,'" Paris asked, "what exactly do you mean?"

Dawn focused on her. "That's not your concern."

"It is if I'm supposed to protect him."

"You're supposed to follow orders."

"I can do both."

The tension in the room ratcheted up a notch. Paris could feel London shifting beside her, ready to intervene if necessary. Even Vi had set down her glass, watching the exchange with sharp eyes.

Dusk, however, merely looked thoughtful. "It's a fair question," he said. "The Hierarchy is establishing certain... financial arrangements with human institutions. Arrangements that will benefit our kind in the long term. Rothschild is a key figure in facilitating those arrangements. Beyond that, I cannot say—because beyond that, I do not know."

It wasn't a satisfying answer, but Paris recognized when she had pushed as far as she could. She nodded and settled back, ignoring the smug look Dawn was directing at her.

"London and Paris will handle the escort," Dusk continued. "Vienna will remain here to coordinate communications. Cairo, you're on standby in case additional support is needed. Dawn and I will be attending to... other matters."

"Other matters?" London asked.

"Nothing that concerns you." Dawn's tone brooked no argument. "Focus on your assignment. Do not embarrass us."

London's jaw tightened, but she said nothing. Paris reached over and squeezed her hand—a gesture of solidarity, however small.

"You have your orders," Dusk said. "Dismissed."

Later that night, long after the briefing had ended and the Abode had emptied, Paris found herself alone at the bar. Vi had surrendered it to her an hour ago, retreating to her quarters with a knowing look that Paris chose not to examine too closely.

The vodka was cold and sharp, burning pleasantly as it went down. Paris poured herself another measure and stared into the glass, thinking about nothing in particular.

The door opened. She didn't turn around.

"You should be sleeping," London said, sliding onto the stool beside her.

"So should you."

"I was worried about you."

Paris snorted. "Everyone's worried about me lately. Cairo cornered me in the gymnasium. Even Vi gave me one of her *looks*."

"That's because you've been acting like someone's about to attack you. You're wound tighter than a watch spring."

"I'm fine."

"You keep saying that."

"Because it's true."

London was quiet for a moment. Then she reached over and took the vodka bottle from Paris's hand, pouring herself a measure. She drank it in one swallow, grimacing slightly at the burn.

"Do you remember," she said, "what you told me the night before our Birthing? When I was terrified and couldn't stop shaking?"

Paris remembered. They had been huddled together in London's quarters, both of them too keyed up to sleep, too frightened to admit it aloud. Paris had held London's hand and told her—

"I told you we would face it together. That whatever happened, we would still be us."

"Exactly." London set down her glass and turned to face Paris fully. "We're still us. Whatever the Birthing changed, whatever we've become— the core of us is still the same. You're still my best friend. You're still the strongest person I know. And you're still terrible at asking for help."

Despite herself, Paris felt a smile tugging at the corner of her mouth. "I'm not terrible at it. I don't need it."

"Liar."

"Takes one to know one."

London grinned, and for a moment they were children again, huddled together against the cold, keeping each other's fears at bay. Then London reached out and pulled Paris into a hug—fierce and sudden and unapologetic.

"I love you," London said against her hair. "And I'm here. Always."

Paris closed her eyes and let herself be held. The weight on her chest— the one she had been carrying since the Birthing, since she first tasted blood, since she had become what she had become—didn't disappear. But it shifted, somehow. Became more bearable.

"Always," she echoed.

The vodka sat forgotten between them as the night deepened around the Abode, and for the first time in months, Paris felt close to peace.

CHAPTER 23

1902 The Citadel Age 22

"Damn, this room needs work." Paris turned to London and Dawn. "A woman's touch, you know?"

"What's wrong with it?" Dusk asked from behind the bar they had installed months before. The bar was a nice addition to a rather dull room. In the first few years after their Birthing, Paris and London had brought in some rugs and such to liven up the place but, really, the bar was the only decent part of the room.

"It's just so... *dead*," London observed. "It needs some color. A nicer sofa. A few comfy chairs and decorations."

"Exactly," Paris said. "After all, this is our abode, our base of operations. The place we spend the most time."

"Abode?" Vi said as she entered the room. Vienna was around sixty years older than Paris and London, although her early turning had left her appearance a little younger than theirs. She had fewer people skills than Dawn, but more than Dusk. Having been around so long, she was also quite set in her ways. Paris was finding that trait to be somewhat annoying.

"Yes," Paris said. "Abode. Dwelling place. Place of residence."

"I know what it means, Paris." Vi leaned her head to one side, her eyebrow lifted against the downturn of her rose-colored lips. She was a girl of strong features, but still pretty in a rough sort of way. She always kept her shoulder-length light brown hair pulled back in a ponytail, and Paris had never once seen her in anything but pants and men's shirts. London had observed early on that Vi was a "you get what you see" kind of girl. Paris could not have agreed more.

"We're not going to turn this place into a gaudy representation of who we are not. Do you understand that?" Dawn's words said one thing, but Paris could tell she was actually up for a change to this dark and dreary space. "You two come up with some ideas, but we all vote on them to determine what, if any, changes will be made." She glanced at Dusk for a brief moment. He nodded and Dawn then continued.

"Paris, your area is furniture. Make sure it is comfortable and not gauche. London, you figure out color schemes and decorations." She turned to Vi. "You and I will procure some rugs based upon the final color scheme. Although our 'abode' should remain somewhat formal, I agree it should be livable."

Paris smiled at London, who winked in return. It appeared the turn of the century had eased some of Dawn's natural inclination for stasis. The woman seemed to despise change, yet she handled it better than most anyone Paris had ever met. Of course, Paris was still young.

"I want a chess set," Dusk said, taking them by surprise. He pointed to the middle of the room. "There. On whatever table is decided upon. Take that input into consideration when choosing an appropriate table."

"A chess set?" Paris asked. "I've never seen you play chess."

"He plays against the magistrate on occasion. Of course, he's never won." Dawn brushed by London, headed for the door. "I'll return after my session with Asaro." With that, she was gone.

"That girl has no social grace," London remarked.

"Watch your mouth," Vi instructed. It was an offhanded order, but Paris understood the purpose. She and London were still considered underlings. Even after seven years, they were the new kids, so to speak. They had not earned the right to speak ill of their elders. Both Paris and London still appeared to be around fifteen years old, and the rest of the Guard treated them as such.

"Sorry," London said. "It was only an observation." Her expression blanked at Vi's harrumph. London didn't even look at Paris. She whirled about on her heels and made for the door. "I'll do some research on brightening this place up. If you need me, I will be in the library."

Paris stepped over to the bar, lost in thought. She wasn't sure how long she stood there in silence before she heard Dusk clear his throat.

"Drink?" he said, as her attention finally turned to him.

"Sure. Why not?"

"What do you like?"

"Vodka," she replied. "I'm not sure why, but I enjoy the taste of it."

"Vodka it is, then." Dusk poured from a red and white-labeled bottle, retrieved some chipped ice from the icebox and swirled it around before handing it to her.

"Thanks," Paris said, and then downed the vodka in one slow swallow. Even as she placed the glass down upon the bar, Dusk was reaching for it, preparing a refill.

"I haven't told you lately, but I think you are doing well." He poured the vodka without looking at the glass, his attention firmly fixed to her.

"Thank you, Dusk." She had been spending most of her time training and learning the politics of the position. Being in the High Guard could sometimes be more about image than actual activity. She was soaking it all up and memorizing every nuance she encountered.

One of the side effects of becoming Valensi was the increased brainpower. She could remember details like never before. She noticed things like subtext and body language as clear as if someone had shouted their meaning at her. She continued to find it amazing, what she was becoming.

"We've come to your first full-time assignment, Paris," Dusk said, handing her the refreshed drink. "You ready?"

"Absolutely," she said. After all, what else could she say?

"You will report to Livia on Monday. She's a wonderful teacher, but she's a hard taskmaster. You will live with her in her chambers for the next year, if not longer. You are to be her assistant. Do anything she requests. Learn everything she is willing to teach. Do you understand?"

Paris nodded. She had seen Livia from afar on numerous occasions. A full member of the Hierarchy, Livia was considered the go-to political maven for any and all questions regarding Valensi history and its varied political leanings. Paris was excited and more than a little nervous to be assigned to such an esteemed individual.

"Livia has some interesting... traits. Things that I wouldn't discuss elsewhere or with any others. I've known her for many years, though, and I can vouch for both her integrity and competence." He paused. "I've also heard that she has a wonderful stock of vodka."

Paris couldn't help but smile. It was rare when Dusk made anything resembling a joke. She lifted her glass to him. "Then I look forward to it."

Vi had moved behind the bar, leaning against the back wall with her arms crossed, watching them. "You'll do fine, kid," she said. It wasn't exactly a ringing endorsement, but from Vi, it was practically a standing ovation.

"Thanks, Vi."

"Don't thank me yet. Livia's going to work you harder than anyone ever has. By the time you're done with her, you'll either be the sharpest political mind in this place or you'll be begging for the simple life of killing people."

Paris considered that. "And if I become both?"

Vi actually laughed—a rare, rough sound that echoed off the stone walls. "Then you'll fit right in."

Dusk set aside the bottle and moved toward the center of the room, surveying the space with the careful assessment of a general reviewing a battlefield. "I want the chess set on an appropriate table. Something substantial. It should be worthy of the game."

"You really do love chess," Paris observed.

"It's the only honest game," he replied, still not looking at her. "Every piece visible. Every move known. No luck, no chance. Just two minds, testing each other." He turned then, fixing her with that unreadable face. "Life should be more like chess."

"But it isn't."

"No," he agreed. "It isn't. Which is why we must play the game we're given, not the game we wish we had."

Paris finished her second vodka and set the glass down with a soft clink. She was beginning to understand that Dusk rarely said anything without purpose, that his silences were as meaningful as his words, and that his apparent detachment was but a mask.

"Monday, then," she said.

"Monday."

She headed for the door, her mind already turning to the assignment ahead, to Livia and politics and whatever lessons awaited her. But she paused at the threshold, looking back at the dreary room that they would soon transform into a livable abode.

Abode, she thought. Yes. That's exactly what it is.

It wasn't much, this stone chamber deep beneath the earth. But it was theirs. And for a girl who had spent years on the streets of Bristol with nothing but a stolen blanket and borrowed dreams, having a place to belong—truly belong—was worth more than all the fine furniture and color schemes in the world.

She left to find London, already planning what kind of table might be worthy of Dusk's chess set.

CHAPTER 24

1905-1916 The Citadel Age 25-36

Paris's time with Livia was uneventful, yet rewarding.

The Councilwoman did not require much attention, but Paris's presence was always to be immediate. When Livia called, Paris came. When Livia wrote, Paris waited in silence until dismissed. When Livia received visitors—and there were many, from all corners of the Valensi world—Paris observed from the margins, cataloguing names and faces, noting alliances and enmities, memorizing the subtle dance of power that played out in every conversation.

Livia was one of the oldest of the Hierarchy, second only to the Magistrate himself. Paris's understanding was that the Councilwoman was somewhere well past two thousand years old. Still, she only appeared in her late forties—a handsome woman with silver-streaked auburn hair and eyes that had witnessed the rise and fall of civilizations. The Valensi aging process was nothing if not kind.

"You watch well," Livia observed one evening, three months into Paris's assignment. They sat in Livia's private study, a room lined floor to ceiling with books in languages Paris was only beginning to recognize. The Councilwoman had been corresponding with far-reaching political figures who were either Valensi or sympathetic to them, her elegant script flowing across page after page. "Most young ones fidget. They grow bored. You simply... absorb."

"I find it fascinating, Mistress."

Livia set down her pen and regarded Paris with those ancient eyes. "Do you? Or do you simply know that is what I wish to hear?"

Paris considered the question carefully. Lying to Livia seemed unwise—the woman had millennia of experience reading people, and Paris was barely more than a child by Valensi standards. "Both," she admitted. "I do find it fascinating. But I also know better than to express boredom to someone who holds my future in her hands."

A smile ghosted across Livia's lips. "Honesty wrapped in strategy. Good. That will serve you well in the years to come."

The years did come, one after another, each bringing new lessons.

Paris learned the intricate web of Valensi politics—the ancient feuds between families, the careful balance of power that kept the Hierarchy stable, the unwritten rules that governed interactions between those of different stations. She learned which names carried weight and which were whispered only in shadows. She learned that the Magistrate's authority, while absolute in theory, was maintained through a delicate equilibrium of favors and fears.

She also learned about Livia herself.

The Councilwoman, it turned out, was one of the first Protectors—before they were actually called such. She had helped establish the system that now trained and deployed Valensi warriors across the globe. Her pride and joy was Asaro who, Livia claimed, had taken her work to the next level.

"I selected him personally," Livia said one night, her voice carrying a warmth Paris had rarely heard from her. "A Roman soldier, two thousand years ago. Disciplined. Patient. Capable of extraordinary violence, but also extraordinary restraint." She paused, fondness softening her features. "He understood, even then, that true strength lies not in the ability to destroy, but in the wisdom to choose when destruction is necessary."

"He's an excellent teacher," Paris offered.

"He is an excellent *everything*." Livia returned her attention to her correspondence. "I have never regretted choosing him."

In addition to Asaro, Livia was particularly fond of Elijah.

The name carried weight even among the High Guard. Elijah had been a Protector for many centuries and was considered the best of the best—a legend whispered about in training halls and strategy sessions. Paris had never met him, but she had heard the stories. Single-handedly eliminating a rogue nest in Vienna. Tracking a traitor across three continents for fifteen years before finally cornering him in a monastery in Tibet. Surviving wounds that would have killed any other Valensi.

"I brought Elijah into the Valensi," Livia revealed one evening, pride evident in her voice. "Trained him myself, when he was little more than a boy. A merchant's son from the Eastern territories, clever and quick and utterly without fear." She smiled at some distant memory. "He asked me once why I had chosen him. I told him it was because he looked at death without flinching. Most humans—most *anyone*—will look away from mortality when it stares back at them. Elijah never did."

Paris filed that information away, as she filed away everything she learned in Livia's service.

It was several years into her assignment, 1908, maybe, when Paris was approaching her twenty-eighth year—that she finally asked about Garrett.

They were sitting in Livia's study, the Councilwoman corresponding as always, when Paris found the courage to voice the question that had lingered in her mind since her school days.

"What about Garrett?" she asked.

Livia's pen halted mid-stroke. "What about him?"

"I've met him a couple of times. Once when he and Elijah visited us in Asaro's class at School. He seemed, I don't know. Different."

The silence stretched. Livia set her pen down with deliberate care, fixing on Paris with an intensity that made the younger Valensi want to look away. She didn't.

"Garrett is highly regarded," Livia said finally. "His abilities are second only to Elijah's when it comes to pure job performance. However, Garrett is unique. He is not to be trifled with, nor is he to be underestimated." She paused. "Why are you so curious about him?"

"No reason in particular. He gave me some valuable advice once. It struck a chord."

Paris noticed she had possibly struck a chord with Livia, as well.

"How old are you now, Paris?"

"I'll be twenty-eight next month, Mistress." She surmised that she should revert to a more formal tone with this woman. She wasn't sure why, but she had learned to not question her own instincts.

"So young." Livia's voice carried notes between warning and wistfulness. "Be careful of that curiosity, young lady. We are a secretive people by nature. Some secrets will be forever held in the obscurity of silence. Asking for knowledge is all well and good—and expected—but asking for purely curiosity's sake can lead one down a dangerous path. My words have less to do with Garrett than with the ease with which you asked about him. Take heed. Be mindful of your questions. Do you understand?"

"Yes, Mistress. Of course. I apologize."

"No need to apologize, Paris. Consider this a lesson to store away and think upon."

Livia returned to her writing, and Paris nodded silently, the warning settling into her bones alongside all the other lessons she had accumulated.

She did not ask about Garrett again. Not for many years.

Paris was with Livia for nearly twelve years in total. Although the Councilwoman made it a point to maintain a professional relationship, Paris believed they had become quite accepting and even admiring of each other by the end. She had made a solid ally in the Hierarchy and gained considerable political savvy along the way.

When she finally returned to the High Guard in the fall of 1916, Paris was no longer the eager young Valensi who had first reported to the Councilwoman's chambers. She had watched the Great War unfold through Livia's correspondence, had seen the tremors it sent through both human and Valensi societies. She had learned that power was not merely strength or speed or the ability to kill—it was information, relationships, the patient accumulation of favors owed and debts unpaid.

She was twenty-five when she began her service with Livia.

She was thirty-six when it ended.

In the space between, she had become someone new. Someone harder. Someone wiser. Someone who understood that the greatest battles were often fought not with fists and fangs, but with words and silence and the careful cultivation of allies who might one day prove useful.

Death and she were still close friends. But now she had other friends as well—politics and patience and the long view that came with centuries of life stretching out before her.

She would need all of them in the years to come.

CHAPTER 25

PRESENT

Paris departed Orlando around nine o'clock, the memory of Rae still raw and bleeding in her mind.

Paris departed Orlando around nine o'clock, the memory of Rae still raw and bleeding in her mind.

She had dealt with all three of the rapists. One she'd killed in the moment, slamming him into the wall with enough force to shatter his spine. The other two—Lieber and Yarborough—had required hunting, but she'd found them. Neither had suffered enough. Neither could suffer enough—not for what they had done to Rae, not for the light they had extinguished in those green eyes.

But it was done. Rae was avenged, if not returned.

Now Paris needed distance. Detective Byrne had been asking too many questions, looking at her with those cop eyes that saw more than they should. Time to move.

She made it past Jacksonville and across the Georgia line a little after eleven. The hunger hit her somewhere around the South Carolina border—that ravenous, demanding need that came with her Valensi metabolism. She had pushed too hard, expended too much energy in her vengeance, and now her body demanded compensation.

Paris pulled into a roadside truck stop off Interstate 95, outside of Hardeeville.

The place was everything a truck stop should be: fluorescent lights buzzing overhead, truckers hunched over coffee at the counter, the smell of grease and diesel hanging thick in the air. Paris shimmied up to the bar that served as a food counter and ordered her meal. Double burger, extra bacon, onion rings, a side of fries, and a slice of whatever pie they had.

The waitress—a tired-looking woman in her fifties with dyed-red hair and a name tag reading DONNA—didn't even blink at the order. She'd seen hungry truckers put away more than that before sunrise.

Paris's thoughts tumbled and bounced like a pinball against the bumpers and kickers of her brain as she ate. Rae's face kept surfacing—that sardonic smile, those knowing eyes, the way she had looked at Paris with hesitant trust. *These past few days... best of my life.*

She was working through the onion rings when she sensed his attention upon her.

Paris ignored it at first. Men stared at her constantly—an apparent seventeen to eighteen-year-old girl alone in a truck stop at midnight drew attention like blood drew sharks. She was used to it. Most of them were harmless, their interest ranging from paternal concern to the more predictable kind of interest that made her want to remove their eyeballs with a spoon.

But this one was different.

The feeling began to seep into her bones, a sense of violence and dark intent that went far beyond simple lust. There was coldness in that gaze, calculating. He was hungry in a way that had nothing to do with the food on his plate.

Paris ordered a piece of pie—apple, the only kind they had—and made her way to the restroom, pinpointing the observer as she went.

He was a monster, in more ways than ten. His size was considerable, pushing three hundred pounds, but most of it was sturdy, not all blubber. Big hands. Thick neck. The kind of body that could absorb punishment and keep coming. He sat alone in a booth near the back, nursing a cup of coffee that had long since gone cold, tracking her movement like a predator following prey.

Paris returned to her seat, catching his eye for only a moment.

It was enough. She locked in.

Turning her back to him in the restaurant, she explored a bit, sneaking into his mind with the delicacy of a surgeon's scalpel. It was all she could do to keep her calm.

This monster was big, bad, and dangerous. A salesman by trade—one of the few that traveled as much by car as by plane—his preferred entertainment was young girls. Paris's appearance seemed to fall within his guidelines of acceptable prey: young, alone, vulnerable-looking. He had been watching her since she walked in, cataloguing her movements, assessing her as a potential target.

Douglas Edmunds was a serial killer.

If he had his way, she would be his next victim.

Paris nibbled at her apple pie, fighting the urge to laugh. Of all the nights, all the truck stops, all the young-looking women traveling alone—this bastard had chosen *her*. The universe had a wicked sense of humor.

She began to determine her next steps.

It seemed she was about to get a second chance at her research, after all. Since Rae's death, Paris had been thinking more and more about what lay beyond—what the dying saw in those final moments, whether there was anything waiting on the other side of that last breath. She had glimpsed it in Rae's eyes at the end, something that haunted her still.

It would be a dangerous game. But she needed to know if she was going crazy or not. This would be an opportunity to take her time. That is, if the monster played his game as she suspected he would.

"You know where I can get a ride around here?" Paris asked Donna, allowing her voice to raise enough to carry over to the monster's table.

"I'm sure any of these drivers would give you a ride, little lady," the waitress said. Her smile spoke volumes about the type of girls who had asked the question before. Paris played it down, averting her gaze.

"No, ma'am," she said. "Seriously. Just a lift to the next town or so." Her affectations worked, because Donna's tone shifted and concern crept into her voice.

"You be careful out there. Don't be taking no rides from anyone you don't know. If you can wait a couple of hours, I can take you as far as Coosawhatchie."

"That's okay," Paris said, handing her the money for the meal. "I'll make do. Thanks, though."

She slipped out the door, keeping tabs on the monster. She ignored the car she'd arrived in—stolen as it was, better to leave no connections. She would return later tonight, after all was said and done.

Paris began walking up the road. She made it onto the highway, ambling along the shoulder, biding her time. He was coming. She knew it.

A few minutes later, a blue Lincoln pulled to the shoulder ahead of her, waiting. Paris walked up to the passenger side, and the electric window hummed down to reveal the monster in the driver's seat.

"You need a lift, young lady? You know you shouldn't be out here on the road this late at night."

"I just need to get a few miles up toward St. George. I'm meeting my aunt there tomorrow." Paris played the innocent as well as she could. It had been so long, she was positive she wasn't pulling it off—until he replied.

"Where on earth are your parents?" The mimicked sincerity and concern in his voice made her want to punch through his sternum and rip out his heart. "Couldn't they have taken you to meet your aunt?"

"They—" She began, hesitated, then continued. "They're dead. I'm going to stay with my aunt for a while. She lives in Columbia."

"Well, I'm headed that way. Name's Doug. If you want the lift. Up to you."

He waited.

Paris could sense his iron-willed control over his own emotions—the excitement bubbling beneath the surface, carefully contained behind that mask of friendly concern. He glanced in the rearview mirror and then up ahead. He was growing impatient, but handling it well.

This one might be a handful, she thought.

Good.

"If you don't mind," she said finally. "I really do appreciate it."

The lock on the door popped up from a flip of the switch on his side. Paris climbed in, closing the door, and they pulled away.

"Hope you don't mind my asking," Doug said, "but how'd you lose your parents?"

"Car accident. Month ago."

"I'm sorry to hear that. Really am." He kept glancing in the mirrors— checking for witnesses, for other vehicles, for anyone who might remember seeing his Lincoln pick up a young girl on the side of the highway. "So, your aunt's taking you in, then? That's mighty kind of her."

"It is. She's the only family I have left." Paris let her voice crack slightly on the word *family*. Sell it. Make him believe she was exactly what she appeared to be.

"Family's important," Doug said, nodding sagely. "Can't put a price on family."

No, Paris thought, watching the road unreel before them, *you certainly can't.*

The Lincoln hummed along the highway, carrying predator and prey together into the South Carolina night. Doug didn't know it yet, but he had made the worst mistake of his miserable life.

He had invited the wrong monster into his car.

CHAPTER 26

1919 Germany Age 39

"Ready?"

Dawn had knocked on Paris's door and waited until she opened it. It was taking some getting used to, this politeness from her. It felt artificial, and Paris continued to look over her shoulder, figuratively speaking.

"Yes," Paris said, motioning for her to enter. She had her backpack prepared and grabbed her jacket. Germany would be getting chilly this time of year.

"We're flying."

Dawn watched her reaction. Paris did not hide her fear.

"Trust me," Dawn said. "It's not as bad as you think. Quite a bit of fun, actually."

"If you say so." Paris's thoughts were a whirlwind of images, most of which were of downward spirals and crushed, burning heaps of twisted metal. She had never flown before. She'd never had reason to.

"Best get used to it." Dawn whirled about to leave the room. "I expect it will be the preferred travel method of the future."

"Fucking Wright brothers," Paris muttered, closing the door behind her.

They had been briefed on the mission by the Magistrate himself. Gregor Waltz had stolen a record-keeping book from the Magistrate's quarters, marking the man as not only a thief but a traitor as well. Charges of sedition carried the highest punishment allowed by the Valensi: chaining.

Death was not enough for someone who blatantly took a stance against them. No. Traitors were sentenced to die in the worst possible way. They would be chained to a tree to await the sunrise. A slow, painful death was that by sunlight. The fiction stories that frightened little children and adults alike, the ones that described vampires as exploding upon exposure to the sun—they were bullshit. So much fantasy birthed from fears of the unknown.

In truth, Valensi skin was simply much more sensitive to the ultraviolet rays of the sun. Whereas most people faced sunburn, they would face severe sunburn to the point of deterioration of the pigment cells and then the epidermis itself. Not a pretty sight, and a horrible way to die.

It seemed that whatever Waltz wanted from the record book was worth his life. Their orders were specifically clear, however. Retrieve the book, eliminate Waltz. No trial. No chaining.

"What do you think is in the book that Waltz would risk his life like this?" Paris asked, before thinking. Too many questions made their kind nervous. It was instinct more than anything. *Secretive* was at the top of the list of adjectives describing the Valensi. For good reason.

"What do you care?" Dawn asked, turning to catch her eye.

"Don't really. But, is there anything you can think of for which you would risk the same? I can't."

"Some people are impossible to understand. Their motives are just shy of insane, if not completely so. All I know is the book is property of the Valensi—the Magistrate's specifically. If there is anything in there that would risk his life or the safety of us all, then there is but one option. Our mission is simple."

"True enough," Paris agreed.

They turned a corner and entered the hallway that led to the outside. In the distance, Paris could hear an automobile engine idling. It would take them to the airstrip from where they would depart en route to Germany. They had intelligence leading to where Waltz was holed up. No one would touch him until they got there. Then, it was on them.

Once on the plane, Paris could not stop her hands from shaking. Her grip on the armrests of the chair in which she sat was so great that she heard a crack. She looked down to see that she was squeezing it to its breaking point. Dawn looked over at her.

"Relax, damn it."

Paris turned inward and began her breathing techniques. The mechanical buzzing of the world melted away as the wheels left the ground. Her thoughts faded back to the memories of her recent training sessions with the Magistrate.

"Concentrate." The order had come from a frustrated Magistrate.

They had been at it for hours. Paris had reached a level where she could block entry into her mind at a moment's notice, but now she was trying to break into the Magistrate's. He claimed he wasn't blocking her in any way, but she still felt the barrier.

"Relax, young Paris," he said, his voice softening. "You're on the right track. You must learn to focus, to ease in. You cannot, should not, bust through a mind's door with the stealth of a drunken rhino. You could permanently damage the recipient.

"Let yourself flow outward—don't push. Float. Seep. Slip in silently, without haste."

Paris willed herself calm once again, shook out her limbs, and refocused. Her thoughts slipped free of her own mind and drifted toward the Magistrate. There was a sense of hope, of frustration, of pride. Perhaps she was doing something right. She could see faint images of the Headmistress in a hallway. Then, with a jolt of recognition, she saw herself. Younger, looking up at herself. It was the meeting they had had before her graduation, the fight with Salem.

"Wow," she said.

"Nicely done," he said.

It was *Altweibersommer* in Germany. Indian summer. The last nice days before winter laid its icy hands on the land. Colder temperatures didn't bother Paris as much as when she had been a child on the streets of Bristol. Still, she had brought a light jacket, just in case. It was unnecessary as it turned out. The days were gloriously vibrant still. The nights, cool and breezy.

The sun had set an hour before they showed up at the cottage where Waltz was located. They met three local Valensi who had been assigned to guard the house until their arrival. They noted that he had been locked inside for over thirty-six hours, no further sign of him or attempt at leaving. Dawn waved them off, sending them on their way. She and Paris would be handling the situation from here on in.

"You take the back. Let's move quickly. If he knows we're out here, we don't want him trying to destroy the book before we can get to him." Dawn scanned the house and area, squinting in concentration.

"If he hasn't already," Paris said.

"Let's keep happy thoughts, shall we?"

Paris nodded and then sprinted to the back of the two-story cottage. It was in a decent neighborhood from what she could tell. Several houses along the *strasse* were very similar to Waltz's. She leaped a fence by the side of the house and kicked in the back door, never slowing.

She heard Dawn enter the front as she bolted through the rooms, searching for Waltz. She had to wonder why someone would turn on their own people the way this man had. It didn't make any sense to her.

Her review of his history was not so out of the ordinary except for one small detail. He had never chosen to become Valensi. His wife had been turned by a lover, but she wanted her husband to be with her forever. He refused. One day, he was thrown from a horse and had broken his back. Realizing he would never walk again, would probably die from his injuries much sooner than he should, his wife performed the Birthing against his will.

"Waltz!" Dawn called from the front of the house. "We know you are here. Do not make this any more difficult than it has to be."

Paris paused in the kitchen. She could make this search a hell of a lot easier. She relaxed, let her mind drift outward, searching for thought. She saw Dawn traipsing through the living room, moving the sofa to look behind it. No stone left unturned. Paris redirected her search upstairs. Room by room, she soared through the area, lightly open to hidden thoughts and emotions. She had found that thoughts could be hidden with practice, but emotions were ever so much more difficult to put a damper on.

Finding no one present upstairs, she refocused. Thinning herself out, she sensed a strange emotion drawing her down. She knew two things: Waltz was not afraid. He was angry. And he was in the basement.

Signaling Dawn, Paris motioned to the door in the kitchen, which she now knew led downstairs. Dawn nodded and led the way.

They found Waltz sitting in a chair in the middle of the basement, the glare on his face indicating contempt beyond compare.

"I suppose I knew it wouldn't be long before he sent someone like you." His voice was thick with the local accent, vowels punctuated by the harsh consonants surrounding them.

"We're here for the ledger," Dawn said, halting a few steps before the man. Paris couldn't take her attention from him, amazed at his belligerence before two of the High Guard. Did he know something they didn't? Why was he so calm? "Give us the book and we leave. Easy as that."

"*Scheiße!* You think I am a fool? The book is all that is keeping you at bay. I'm certain you will enjoy killing me as soon as you have it."

"Fair enough," Dawn said.

Waltz suddenly laughed—a harsh, bitter sound that echoed off the basement walls. "You think the book is the threat? You have no idea what's really coming."

Dawn's harrumphed. "Spare us your paranoid delusions."

"They're researching our weaknesses." Waltz leaned forward, his eyes bright with likely madness—or might have been clarity. "Human scientists. They're close to weaponizing them."

Paris stiffened. Something in his words triggered a memory—a classroom lesson from decades ago, dry facts delivered by an instructor who had seemed utterly unconcerned. *Organic compounds that disrupt cellular structure. Thankfully, humans lack knowledge to weaponize...*

"Who?" she asked, stepping closer despite herself.

"Does it matter? Wood, certain minerals, organic compounds—they're testing destabilization effects. Creating weapons that can kill us efficiently." Waltz's laugh was hollow. "You think we're the apex predators? We're prey that hasn't realized it yet."

Dawn scoffed. "Humans don't even know we exist."

"Some do. And they're preparing." Waltz's gaze shifted to Paris. "You feel it, don't you? That flicker of recognition. You've heard this before."

Paris exchanged a glance with Dawn. The older Guard's expression was dismissive, but Paris found herself wanting to ask more. Still, Dawn was probably right—this seemed like the desperate ramblings of a cornered traitor, trying to distract them with conspiracy theories.

"Mock me if you want," Waltz said, reading their expressions. "But it's coming. The question is whether your precious Magistrate is preparing for it—or causing it."

"Enough," Dawn said. "The book. Now."

Waltz settled back in his chair. "Kill me if you must. But without the book, you have nothing to bring back to your master. And I won't tell you where it is."

Dawn's smile was cold. "We'll see about that."

What followed was not pleasant. Dawn had brought tools, and she knew how to use them. Paris watched, her face carefully blank, as the interrogation progressed. She had seen worse—had done worse—but this was particularly distasteful. Waltz had been turned against his will, had never asked for this existence. Now he was being tortured for information he genuinely believed was worth protecting.

Not that his beliefs mattered. Orders were orders.

Waltz certainly did hate his fate. There was no doubt about that.

Paris saw the ledger in his mind. It was an old, leather-encased book, longer than tall, with thin rawhide strips as binding. She lost it for a moment or two as Gregor succumbed to another round of pain coinciding with one more lost digit. She slipped a little deeper into his thoughts and uncovered the memory of him placing the ledger in a secret nook. She had it.

Now, to uncover the secret without letting Dawn know how she got it.

Paris thought for a long moment, and then moved to kneel down in front of Gregor. He focused on her through his tears of pain and anger. Dawn hesitated in her torture.

"Gregor," Paris said, placing her hands on his knees. "Is this really necessary? Do you hate your fate so much that you would die for scraps of data that mean little or nothing to you?"

"They *mean* something!" His voice was hoarse, but still strong.

"You hid it, the ledger. Right? To keep it safe?" He grew silent. Paris found she also had Dawn's undivided attention. "But you would want to be prepared. You're always prepared, aren't you, Gregor?"

The man stared at her. She was being kind. She was seeing him as more than simply a doorway to the ledger, and he wasn't sure how to react. She saw him bite his lip and avert his eyes. She easily moved back into his field of vision and drew him back to her.

"You'd want to keep it safe. But you would also want to have it near. Close enough to destroy it if you had to. Right?"

She was leading him, and he nodded. Dawn caught the movement and moved around to see their faces better. Her focus darted between Paris and Gregor. The blood dripped from her instrument of torture, but none of them paid it any heed.

"Where would you be able to keep it safe, but close enough to destroy, eh? How to be able to destroy a book quickly?" He focused on her, and Paris smiled. "Ah. Thank you, Gregor. You may go now."

With that, she stood and yanked his head to one side with swift and immediate violence. His neck snapped and he crumpled. Paris walked over to the workbench in the corner, while Dawn nearly shook in rage. Paris nodded at her as she snapped the wooden handle off a garden rake and, in a quick and efficient motion, shoved it through Gregor's hearts.

"What? Why? We didn't get the book!" Dawn said, staring at her. Paris did not fail to notice that her hand tightened on the wire cutters. Still, she shook her head.

"You have to ask the right questions, look for the right answers. Follow me."

She led the way back upstairs. Paris walked over to the fireplace and felt along the sides until she found the bricks that were slightly loosened. She pulled them aside and retrieved the ledger from inside the hidden nook.

"Son of a bitch." Dawn stood staring at the book. She caught Paris' attention and then smiled. "That was fucking impressive, I admit."

Paris shrugged, tucking the ledger under her arm. "He wanted to keep it close enough to throw in the fire if we got too near. Simple logic."

Dawn's eyes lingered on her for a moment longer than necessary. "Right. Simple logic."

On the flight back, Paris stared out the small window at the darkness below, her fear of flying momentarily forgotten. Waltz's words kept circling in her mind like carrion birds.

Wood, certain minerals, organic compounds. They're testing destabilization effects.

She remembered the classroom lesson now, clear as day. The instructor's droning voice, the bored expressions of her fellow students. *Valensi cellular structure can be disrupted by certain organic compounds. Thankfully, humans lack the knowledge to weaponize these weaknesses.*

Thankfully.

But what if that was changing? What if humans were learning?

Paris glanced over at Dawn, who was already asleep, her beautiful face peaceful in repose. She could wake her, share her concerns. But what would be the point? Dawn had dismissed Waltz's warnings as paranoid ravings. And maybe they were. Maybe a bitter, unwilling Valensi had simply wanted to plant seeds of doubt before he died.

The question is whether your precious Magistrate is preparing for it— or causing it.

Paris filed the thought away, storing it alongside all the other small mysteries she had accumulated over the years. Someday, perhaps, the pieces would fit together. For now, she had a mission to complete and a ledger to deliver.

She closed her eyes and let the drone of the engines lull her into sleep.

But she didn't forget.

CHAPTER 27

1926 The Citadel Age 46

Garrett and Paris began to expand their friendship.

They sparred more whenever he was in the Citadel, and they began to notice similar tastes in books and music. It was nice having someone to talk to who had no apparent concern about what she said or how she acted. Being in the High Guard was a challenging role—the constant awareness of station, the careful management of relationships, the unspoken hierarchies within the hierarchy. Still, Paris loved it. She loved her steps into fiction, adventure, and romance as well. To discover that someone else loved to read as voraciously as she did was a complete joy.

Garrett was a Protector, not High Guard, which meant he came and went from the Citadel on assignments that could last weeks or months. But when he was home, he could often be found in the Abode, a book in his hands and a drink at his elbow. Paris had taken to seeking him out during the quiet hours before dawn, when the other Guards had retired and the stone corridors fell silent.

"Have you ever thought of going to America?" Paris asked him one night in the late autumn of 1926. "I mean, it seems like such a huge party over there now. At least, that's what I've heard."

"It does sound like fun," Garrett said, never taking his attention from *The Great Gatsby*. He'd read that book three times already—Paris had counted. She knew the thought of America intrigued him, could see it in the way he lingered on certain passages, the way he sometimes read aloud the descriptions of Gatsby's parties with apparent wistfulness. "Still, the world turns in cycles. For all of the lush living, there will soon come a downturn. It happens all the time."

"What do you mean?" Paris unfolded her legs from beneath her. They were sitting on the sofa in the Abode in the early morning, the gas lamps turned low, the teak furniture casting long shadows against the burgundy walls. Everyone else had gone to bed already, or was out on assignment.

Garrett finally laid the book on his leg, his focus on her. He was handsome in a weathered sort of way—strong jaw, dark hair silvered at the temples, eyes that had seen centuries pass and remained somehow kind despite it all. Paris had noticed these things before, catalogued them as she catalogued everything, but she had never let herself dwell on them. Garrett was a friend. That was all.

"There are a few signs," he said, "economic and such, that indicate that the fun will slow down. It shouldn't be all that bad, but it will certainly put a damper on all the flapper parties and unwarranted spending." He shrugged. "Cycles. Ups and downs. Every country, every society has them. America is no different."

"I still want to go. Sounds like fun." Paris felt a bit of a pout coming on and reeled it in before Garrett could comment. Nevertheless, she caught that sparkle in his eye as he lifted his novel back to view.

"Perhaps someday," he said. "When the timing is better."

Paris watched him read for a moment, marveling at his patience. She had known Garrett for decades now—had first met him when she was still a student at the School, a gangly almost-teenager who had looked up at this legendary Protector with awe. He had given her advice that day, about the importance of choosing one's battles. She had never forgotten it.

Now they were equals, or as equal as a High Guard and a Protector could be. Different branches of the same tree, serving the same master in different ways. She found she liked talking to him more than anyone else in the Citadel—more than Dawn, certainly, with her constant criticism and maternal disapproval. More than Dusk, whose silences could stretch into hours. Even more than London sometimes, though Paris would never admit that aloud.

With Garrett, she could simply *be*. No pretense, no careful management of words and expressions. He seemed to accept her exactly as she was—sardonic, curious, occasionally reckless—and never tried to smooth her rough edges into anything more palatable.

"Oh," Paris said, trying to be nonchalant in her tone, "do you happen to know Thorne very well?"

Garrett closed his book.

He stared at her for a long moment and then smiled—that knowing smile that made her want to throw something at his head. "Thorne, eh?"

"What? I'm asking."

"Yes, I can see that." He laid the book aside and faced her on the sofa. He pulled his hands together on his stomach, interlacing his fingers, eyes boring into her with undisguised amusement. "What do you want to know? If he has a *chica* in the hold?"

Paris was about to put on a look of denial, but why waste the time or the energy? "Yes. Is he involved with anyone?"

"No. Not that I am aware." Garrett tilted his head, considering her. "I suppose you both are about the same age now? Mid-forties or so?" He winked.

Paris huffed.

Although she looked to be seventeen or eighteen, she was starting to fill out better than she had expected. She was also feeling the urges that came along with that development—urges she had suppressed for decades, focused as she had been on training and advancement and proving herself worthy of the High Guard. But the body wanted what the body wanted, and lately her body had been wanting quite a lot.

Thorne was a new Protector, having only about fifteen years under his belt. Still, he'd been Birthed earlier than Paris had, so they were now about the same actual age. He appeared to be around twenty years old, physically—tall and lean, with dark hair and darker eyes, a smile that made something flutter in Paris's chest whenever he directed it her way.

"He has attracted my eye," she admitted. "I won't deny it."

"Good for you," Garrett said, performing a light golf clap. Paris smirked at him.

"So," she said. "Introduce us, damn it."

"Fine, fine. As you wish, Madame." He picked up his book again, but she could see the smile still playing at the corners of his mouth. "I'll arrange it. A dinner, possibly. Casual."

"Nothing too obvious."

"Of course not. Subtlety is my middle name."

Paris snorted. "Your middle name is probably something like 'Aloysius' or 'Bartholomew.'"

"It's actually 'James,'" Garrett said mildly. "But I appreciate the creativity."

They sat in comfortable silence for a while, Garrett returning to his Fitzgerald while Paris stared at the low flames flickering in the hearth. The Abode had changed since she and London had first proposed redecorating it—new rugs, new curtains, furniture that didn't look like it had been salvaged from a medieval dungeon. It felt like home now, in a way the Citadel never had when she was a student.

Home. Such a strange word for a place built on secrets and violence.

"Garrett," she said, breaking the silence.

"Hmm?"

"Why do you keep reading that book? You must have it memorized by now."

He lowered *The Great Gatsby* and considered the question with more seriousness than it probably deserved. "Because it's about longing," he said finally. "About reaching for something just out of grasp. About the green light at the end of the dock." He paused. "And because Fitzgerald understood something fundamental about the human condition—that we're all of us chasing something we can never quite catch. Even us, Paris. Even the immortal monsters hiding in the dark."

"That's rather melancholy."

"Possibly." He smiled, but there was sadness in it. "Or perhaps it's just honest."

Paris thought about that as she watched the fire burn low. She thought about Thorne, about the flutter in her chest, about the longing for connection that she had suppressed for so long. She thought about green lights and things out of reach.

All she knew, in that quiet moment before dawn, was that she was glad to have a friend.

"Read to me," she said. "From your book."

Garrett smiled and turned to a well-worn page. His voice was low and warm in the lamplight.

"'So we beat on, boats against the current, borne back ceaselessly into the past.'"

Paris closed her eyes and listened, and for a little while, the world felt peaceful.

CHAPTER 28

PRESENT

Paris's head swam as the nausea came and then faded quickly. She thanked all that was right in the world for her superior healing abilities.

She was still in the passenger seat of the Lincoln. Doug, the monster, was rummaging in the trunk for the tools he would need to enjoy his night with a fine little girl.

Whatever he drugged me with, Paris thought, it wasn't nearly enough.

She took the opportunity to quietly slip out of the car, trying to limit as much movement to the vehicle as possible. She didn't bother to shut the door—just slipped into the night.

They were parked in a secluded area, somewhere off Interstate 95. A quick glance back and a peek into Doug's mind let her know he'd used this spot before. Many times. The images she glimpsed there—fragments of screaming faces, bound limbs, the wet sounds of violence—only firmed her resolve. She kept out of the illumination provided by the headlamps of the car, which shone onto the ground surrounding a small but sturdy pine tree.

How poetic, she thought. He brought me to his killing ground. Now it, literally, becomes his.

She heard Doug's huff of exasperation upon seeing the passenger door open and his victim in the wind. In the light from the car she saw that he held a length of rope and a pair of handcuffs. He turned about, trying to determine where she might have gone.

"I'm sorry about that, young lady," he called, doing his best to soften his tone. "Come on out and we can talk about it. I didn't mean to hurt you."

Paris smirked at the ridiculousness of his statement. She darted to the left, making enough noise to draw his attention. "I bet!" she said. She wanted him to know she was still close by, let him try to come after her. She'd play the timing right and, hopefully, bring this to a close quickly.

"We can talk, figure things out." He was moving toward where he'd heard the sounds. As he did, Paris used all of her strength to leap over him, to the other side of the car. Her landing wasn't as graceful as she would have liked, but the move sufficed to confuse the monster. He stepped to the back of the car, peering out into the darkness.

Her movement was immediate and efficient. The force of her blow to his head may have been a bit of overkill, but she wasn't taking any chances.

The monster collapsed to the ground in a heap.

Doug spluttered and spat, shaking his head. The water Paris had doused him with wasn't cold—the bottle having sat in his car for a while—but it did the trick.

"What the fuck?" he said, trying to focus in the direct light from the car's headlamps. Paris moved to stand between him and the illumination. His expression darkened and he bit at the inside of his thick lip.

"Coo-coo-ca-choo, big guy."

"You little bitch." He tried to come at her, then realized that she had handcuffed him to the pine tree. "Goddammit!"

"Possibly," Paris remarked. She closed the bottle, keeping half of the liquid for later use. Then she knelt down in front of him, stared him in the eye. "You like the young ones, huh?"

"What?" His vehemence was admirable.

"Your targets. None of them were over twenty, as far as I can surmise."

"What are you talking about, you crazy bitch?"

The echo of her hand against his face rang out into the still night. A bird leapt into the air from the branches of the tree above them. The monster stared at her with the most evil of intent. She could see the flashes of his desires in his mind—the things he had done, the things he had planned to do to her. He was a nasty, sadistic bastard. That was for certain.

She leaned in a little, her eyes moving from the reddening jowl to the green of his own tormented orbs. "Don't ever call me that again."

"Who are you? What the fuck do you want?" Over his anger lay a carpet of curiosity and concern. Essentially, he was now her prisoner, and that put a damper on his motives for the moment.

"How old do you think I am, Doug?" Paris asked. She let him peer at her in silence for a few moments before she began to raise her hand once again.

"I don't know," he said. "Maybe nineteen. All that makeup makes you look older, but I can see through that."

"Of course you can. And, physically, you are about right. In fact, physically, I'm not quite eighteen." She watched him squirm as that information leaked into the deepest, darkest recesses of his twisted mind. "However, in actuality, I'm an old lady. I'm one hundred thirty-five years old. Can you believe that?"

"No." It was a simple and honest response.

"It's true, though," Paris said, letting the casual tone of her voice carry the veracity of it. "I remember World War I, the sinking of the Lusitania. I remember the influenza epidemic. I remember when Hitler went to prison. The first time I heard Gershwin's *Rhapsody in Blue*. Oh, it was so gorgeous.

"As a matter of fact, Doug, I was listening to the radio when news of Hiroshima seared across the world. I remember the birth of computer science. Hell, I even met Turing once, back in 1951. That was before his life went to hell, due in no small part to the small-minded England of the day."

She watched Doug as he tried to register whether she was insane or not.

"But you don't really care about any of this, do you, Doug? You only wanted me for my body—to ravage it, desecrate it, and then destroy it. Right?"

"Take these handcuffs off and you'll find out."

"Shame, shame, Doug. You seem like a smart man. I would've thought that by now you would have fully grasped the gravity of your situation."

"What are you talking about? What are you going to do?" It seemed to finally be sinking in.

"I'm going to ask you for a favor, Doug. The more willing you are to provide that favor, the less pain you shall endure. Fair enough?"

"You're insane."

"I've been called worse." Paris knelt before him, one hand bracing against his thick thigh. "You see, Doug, I've lived a long time and I've got a lot more time to go if I play my cards right. After a hundred or so years, I've come to the belief—the hope, if you will—that there is more to life than occupying this meat shell we call a body.

"Are you familiar with Biocentrism, Doug? No? How about quantum mechanics? You've heard of that, right? Any clue in that thick head of yours what quantum mechanics really is?"

He shook his head. Paris was fully aware that he was rapidly rattling off innumerable ways in which he might escape his predicament. She wanted to get her notions across to him, however. In her mind, his understanding might influence the outcome of this little experiment.

"Think of quantum mechanics as a theory of how, on a minute level, everything interacts with everything—past, present, and future. It's funny how you can say quantum mechanics and people take you seriously, since it is a defined and experimented-upon theory—although I tend to agree with Einstein in that no one really understands quantum mechanics. However, if you say parallel universes, people tend to think of comic books and science fiction novels. Funny thing is, they're both one and the same."

"If you're going to kill me, do it now," Doug said. "You're starting to give me a headache."

It was a good line, and Paris laughed out loud for a few seconds.

"Doug, I need you to understand what I expect from you. I want you to tell me everything you see, even as your vision will fade and you slip off this mortal coil. I want you to tell me if you're going to heaven or hell, or if you are simply falling into the abyss of nothingness, lost and separate from all of existence."

"I'll tell you what," he said, holding his chin up. "Why don't you go to hell instead? I'll be happy to watch. I'll relate that to your crazy ass. How's that?"

Paris lost her patience.

With a swift and exact motion, her tiny hand darted out. In the blink of an eye, she removed his left eyeball from its socket, leaving it dangling along the side of his heavy jowl. The optic nerve stretched along his cheek, blood and aqueous humor seeping down into his shirt. He howled in pain.

"What say we get this show on the road?" she said. She leaned in, placing the sharp fingernail of her index finger against his thick neck, punching into his jugular. The luscious red of his liquid life pulsed out onto the ground in time with the pounding of his heart—a strong, slow, steady stream.

"You bitch!"

"Under the circumstances, I will give you that one, Doug. But I did ask you not to call me that again. Do pay attention."

The big man went from defiant to defeated in a matter of seconds. He began to sob, the tears mingling with the blood and fluid from his dangling eyeball. Paris slipped into his mind, this time redoubling her efforts to remain unseen by his subconscious.

Doug's mind was all blank walls and dreary hallways. The thoughts dancing around inside the monster's mind were of everything from youthful memories to recent kills. His last victim appeared to have been in her early teens. What he had put that little girl through only served to solidify Paris's methods.

He deserved worse than she was going to give him.

"As you weaken, Doug, you'll find that time will slow to a crawl. You will feel every beat of your heart as it spits the life from your body. What is it that you see, Doug? Are you experiencing the whole life-flashing-before-your-eyes phenomenon?"

"I'll tell you what I see," he replied, his voice not quite as venomous as before. "I see a little girl who is just as fucked up as I am. You may take my life, believing me to be nothing more than a monster, but you are only the sum of your actions. You are monstrous and insane in your own right."

Paris nodded. Perceptive bastard, he was. "I can't disagree with you, Doug. It's just that, at the moment, I'm the bigger, badder monster. Looks can be deceiving, can they not?"

Doug's head lolled forward. It was time.

Paris slipped deeper into his mind as she commanded, "Tell me what you see, Doug."

She received the response she expected. He used the last bit of strength he had to lift his head, staring at her with his one remaining eye.

"Fuck you, you little bitch."

The cold grey walls of Doug's mind began to break apart, crumbling away to reveal a deep, palpable darkness.

In the distant black, Paris saw him appear, walking toward her with his head held high. She focused all of her ability on remaining unseen, cloaking her presence against his thoughts and perceptions.

All of her efforts in this were in vain.

"What do you see?" he asked as he approached her within the confines of his own mind.

"I see a man who has no regrets."

"Not true. But before I divulge my one regret, why don't you bend my ear with whatever notion you may have of why I should, indeed, have regrets?"

"You're a serial murderer and rapist. You served no purpose but to destroy. Do you feel nothing for the lives of the young women you stole? Of that man in Baton Rouge, the one you maimed with the jack handle?"

"I do not. I regret none of it. I am what I am. Did you ever stop to think that my purpose was that: to destroy?"

"You've got to be kidding me."

"Really? Have you ever thought of your own purpose? How many lives have you taken over your decades of death and destruction? And do not deny it. We're well past the petty lies of human nature, aren't we?"

Paris thought about what he was saying. Had her life really been nothing but death and destruction? It was certainly made up of quite a bit of that. Still, did she not serve a greater purpose? Did she even *have* a purpose? That question had nagged at her for decades. How was it that this monster saw into her as easily as she saw into him?

"I won't deny that I've doled out my share of death over the years," she said. "As much as it pains me to admit it, as you inferred—as you have yours, so do I have my own nature. I've found that it is nearly impossible to fight against one's own nature." She found her hands on her hips, staring him down as she added, "But it can be done."

"You're right," Doug said with a slight nod. "You can change your nature if it is what you truly wish. You must go after that change wholeheartedly, however. It's like smoking. It may be a bit of an addiction, but humans fail to realize the power they wield. You can change your habits as easily as turning the page of a book. You need only to truly want the change. Make up your mind, and do it."

"So you could have stopped your rampages. You could've stopped killing."

"I could have, yes. I just enjoyed it far too much. I didn't want to change."

"Yet you said that you have a regret," Paris said, lifting an eyebrow, wondering what he might have found sorrowful. What he might have been sorry he did, or did not do. "What is it, Doug? What is your one regret?"

The bastard smiled at her as the walls of darkness shook around them and cracks formed like lightning bolts against the deep surfaces. From the cracks, deep crimson began to ooze—bloody streams of promise. The bloody cracks separated more and more as Doug took a slow step toward her. Paris could feel the pull, like a strange vacuum pulling at the loose material of their clothes.

Doug made one more attempt at a step toward her, and she noted that the pull was stronger from behind him—the gashes in the darkness widening into bright red crevasses, valleys of threat that began to suck all of the thick crimson blood back into themselves. Doug was struggling to stand upright, his eyes focused on hers.

"My one regret?" he said, the strength of the vortex behind him dragging him now. "I only regret that I did not get the chance to flay the flesh from your sexy little body. I regret not having my chance with you. Someday."

With that, he stopped his struggle, and the bulk of him was lifted and drawn backward several meters into one of the growing, glowing red crevasses. He struck it with force, his arms and shoulder blades cracking from the brunt of it. Even as he was dragged into the cavernous maw of blood-red torment, his eyes never left hers.

In the moment he was gone, Paris's mind flashed back into her own body—just in time to feel the bullet rip into her back.

The bullet exited with a gush of blood from her upper chest, and she sat back on her haunches in shock. She tried to take a breath. It hurt like hell.

Determined, shocked, and pissed, she stood and turned to face her attacker.

Two large darts with metal tips buried themselves consecutively into her chest and stomach.

She managed only one step before the world around her pinwheeled from existence.

CHAPTER 29

1927-1935 The Citadel Ages 47-55

Paris had not planned on falling for Thorne.

She had planned on *using* him, if she was being honest with herself. After Garrett's teasing introduction, after the awkward first dinner where Thorne had been so charmingly nervous that Paris had wanted to simultaneously laugh and kiss him, she had told herself it was simply an exercise. Experience, as London had suggested. A way to learn the dance of romance without risking her heart.

She had been a fool.

1927

"I thought we might take a carriage ride, if that is acceptable to you," Thorne said. He'd knocked on her door at nine-thirty precisely.

"Please come in," Paris said, ushering him through the door and closing it behind him. She saw the look of anxiety on his face and emotions stirred deep inside her. She stared at him, looking him over, inspecting him from head to foot.

Thorne was a handsome bastard. At a little under six feet tall, he looked like he was carved from granite—all chiseled muscle and beautiful angles. Paris had felt the attraction the first time she had seen him, nearly a year prior. He was a Protector, a trained killer. Yet she saw a softer edge in his visage. He tried to hide it, but she had become rather perceptive over the last forty years.

"Is everything all right, Paris?" he asked, shifting awkwardly from one foot to another. It was adorably incongruous for someone in his line of work.

"Everything is fine, Thorne. I just wanted to... Well, I wanted..."

"Are you not feeling well?" It was an innocent question but, for folks of their fortitude, it was laughable in its naïveté.

"Oh, fine," Paris said with a huff, losing her patience both with herself as well as with his lack of action. "Let's get down to brass tacks, shall we?"

"What do you mean?"

"Let's get one thing straight, Thorne. I am not your property. I am not your servant. I am your equal. And if this... whatever this is... is going to work, you need to understand that from the very beginning."

He stared at her for a long moment. Then, slowly, a smile spread across his handsome face. "I wouldn't have it any other way."

Paris felt a loosening in her chest. "Good. Now—about that carriage ride."

1929

They had been together for two years when Paris first told him she loved him.

It was a quiet night in the Abode, the others long since retired to their quarters. They sat on the sofa where Paris had spent so many hours reading with Garrett, but now the books were forgotten, and there was only Thorne's arm around her shoulders, his heartbeat steady against her ear.

"I never thought I would have this," she said softly.

"Have what?"

"This. Someone who..." She struggled for the words. "Someone who sees me. Not the High Guard. Not the Magistrate's protégé. Just... me."

Thorne's arm tightened around her. "I see you, Paris. I've always seen you."

She tilted her head up to look at him, at those dark eyes that had become her favorite sight in all the world. "I love you," she said. The words felt strange on her tongue—foreign, dangerous. She had never spoken them to anyone before.

His expression faltered for a second, there and gone so quickly she almost missed it. Then he smiled, that beautiful smile that made her hearts stutter, and pressed his lips to her forehead.

"And I you," he murmured against her skin. "More than you know."

1932

"What do you think about the future?" Thorne asked one evening as they walked the moonlit gardens of the Citadel.

"The future?" Paris laughed. "We have rather a lot of it ahead of us, don't we?"

"I mean *our* future. Yours and mine."

Paris stopped walking. They had been together for five years now—five years of stolen moments and shared quarters, of missions that kept them apart for weeks at a time and reunions that made the separation worthwhile. She had never dared to think beyond the present, beyond the immediate reality of their connection.

"What did you have in mind?"

Thorne turned to face her, taking both her hands in his. "I've been thinking about asking the Magistrate for a permanent posting. Somewhere we could be together, properly. Not simply stolen hours between assignments."

Paris's breath caught. "You would do that? Give up being a Protector?"

"For you?" He raised her hands to his lips, pressing a kiss to her knuckles. "In a heartbeat. Both of them."

She laughed at the joke—the old Valensi humor about their oversized hearts—but tears threatened. "Thorne, I... I don't know what to say."

"Say yes. Say you want the same thing."

"I do." The words came out before she could stop them, before she could armor herself against the vulnerability of wanting this so badly. "God help me, I do."

He pulled her into his arms, and Paris let herself believe—truly believe—that she had found something worth keeping.

1935 — One Week Before Switzerland

"Spain?" Paris couldn't keep the disappointment from her voice. "But you just got back."

"I know." Thorne was packing his bag, his movements efficient and familiar. "It's a short assignment. Two weeks at most. I'll be back before you know it."

Paris sat on the edge of his bed, watching him. Something felt off—had felt off for months now, if she was honest. Small things. The way his smile sometimes didn't quite reach his eyes. The way he would sometimes stare at her when he thought she wasn't looking, with an expression she couldn't quite read.

"Is everything all right?" she asked. "You've seemed... distant lately."

Thorne paused in his packing. For a moment, he didn't move, didn't speak. Then he crossed to where she sat and knelt before her, taking her hands in his.

"Everything is fine," he said. "I've had a lot on my mind. This mission—it's complicated. But it will all be over soon, I promise."

"What do you mean, over?"

"I mean..." He hesitated, and she saw it. That same strange expression she had glimpsed years ago, the first time she told him she loved him. "I mean that after this, things will be different. Better. I promise."

Paris searched his face, trying to read the intent behind his expression. She could slip into his mind—could see for herself what he was hiding. But she had never done that, not with Thorne. It felt like a violation of the trust they had built.

Trust, she thought. That's what love is built on.

"I believe you," she said.

He leaned forward and kissed her—deeply, desperately, as if trying to memorize the taste of her. When he pulled back, his eyes were bright with tears.

"I love you, Paris," he said. "Whatever happens, remember that. I do love you. In my own way."

"What a strange thing to say." She laughed, but a coldness had settled in her stomach. "You're acting like you're going off to war."

"Perhaps I am." He stood, returning to his packing. "A war of sorts."

Paris watched him, that cold feeling spreading through her chest. *In my own way*, he had said. What did that mean? What kind of qualification was that?

But she pushed the thoughts aside. She was being paranoid. Thorne loved her—had loved her for years. They had plans. A future.

"Come back to me," she said as he shouldered his bag.

He paused at the door, looking back at her with an expression she would remember for decades—centuries—to come. Longing and regret and something that might have been guilt, all twisted together into a single, devastating glance.

"Goodbye, Paris," he said.

Not *I will*. Not *always*. Just—goodbye.

She should have known then. Should have seen it for what it was.

But love makes fools of us all.

One Week Later — St. Gallen

Paris had not gone more than three kilometers from the bank before she noticed she was being followed. From the pace and heaviness of the footsteps, the tracker was a man of medium size. It appeared her trip was not going to be as uneventful as she had hoped.

She was about to search out the mind of the person following her when the footsteps faded and then disappeared entirely. Perhaps she had been mistaken. She was not one to be paranoid, yet this whole assignment felt a bit off to her.

She continued on, making her way to the Abbey. As long as she was here, she was not going to miss the spectacle that was the Abbey of St. Gall. First built in 719, it had become its own principality in the thirteenth century. It was a piece of history worth visiting, she thought.

She strolled along Burggraben, onto Moosburggstrasse. She could see the cathedral to her right when she heard the stranger's approach—just in time to twirl about, protecting the intended target, her messenger bag. The metal lockbox was safe even as the leather strap was ripped from the bag with force.

Paris stepped onto the grass off the street and faced her attacker.

Her breath caught in her throat.

"Thorne? What the bloody—"

He stood before her in the moonlight, the man she had loved for eight years, the man who had promised her a future. His handsome face was a mask she no longer recognized.

"Just give me the box, Paris." His voice was calm, steady—the voice of a Protector doing a job. "Please. Don't make this worse than it has to be."

The world tilted beneath her feet. A million thoughts dashed through her mind, yet none of them made one ounce of sense.

Spain, she thought. He was supposed to be in Spain.

"What the fuck are you doing?"

"Please, Paris. I don't want to hurt you. I only need the box."

And there it was. The truth she had been too blind to see, laid bare in the Swiss moonlight.

Everything—every kiss, every promise, every whispered declaration of love—had been a lie.

CHAPTER 30

1935 St. Gallen, Switzerland Age 55

"I've got something special for you," Dusk said.

Paris had entered the Abode still nursing a headache from her training session with the Magistrate. The mental exercises were getting more intense, more demanding—pushing the boundaries of what she thought she could do. She'd spent the past hour trying to build walls in her mind that even the Magistrate couldn't breach. She had failed. Again.

London sat on the sofa, Vi leaned against the wall with her arms crossed, and Dawn stood near the bar with one hand on her slim hip, watching Paris with that perpetual expression of mild disapproval. They'd recently had the wet bar area built out and redecorated—a snazzy setup. Dusk and their newest member, Cairo, had taken it upon themselves to bring in a new solid walnut bar top and custom enhancements all around. Dusk currently stood on the opposite side of it, tapping a pencil on the surface.

The tapping halted. "You are to go to St. Gallen tomorrow. You will visit Wegelin & Co, where you will retrieve a package for the Magistrate."

"St. Gallen?" Paris said, trying to think of where that might be. Then the name of the bank rang a bell. "Wait. You're sending me to Switzerland?"

"Yes."

"Who's coming along?" They always traveled in pairs outside of the Citadel for both security and politics' sake. The High Guard was the most prestigious faction within the Valensi, aside from the Hierarchy and the Protectors.

"No one," Dusk said, his gaze locked to hers. "You're on your own."

Paris didn't know how to respond, or if she should. She held his focus and simply waited.

"The Magistrate trusts you to carry out this simple mission unaccompanied. Therefore, so do I."

She peered in silence over the bar at Dawn, who purposefully ignored her. This was odd, to say the least. It appeared Paris was about to go through another test of some sort.

"Fine," she said, strolling over and plunking herself down on the sofa. "Travel arrangements have already been made, I take it?"

"Yes."

Dusk then moved on to a number of other activities that the Guard was to handle over the next few days. Paris halfway listened as her mind raced over the situation in which she now found herself.

It was as simple a task as they came. A pony job. Still, she could not remember any task set outside the Citadel that did not warrant at least two of them at a time. Perhaps she was overthinking the matter. She pushed her thoughts aside and turned her attention back to Dusk's discourse in time to catch Dawn watching her intently. Dawn's attention moved on as she caught Paris's gaze. It seemed she must not agree with the trust that was being placed in Paris.

She would have to prove herself once again.

Summer was arriving in St. Gallen.

Since it was situated at close to seven hundred meters above sea level, it was one of Switzerland's highest cities. That translated to a decent amount of snow in the winter. Thankfully, Paris arrived to a much milder and more beautiful climate.

With Lake Constance to the northeast and the Appenzell Alps to the south, the city sat in a valley. Most of it was forested or used for agricultural purposes. What Paris was most fascinated about when researching the place was that, since the city was founded on less than stable ground, most of the buildings were built on piles. Once she arrived and debarked from the train, she made it a point to walk through the station and its plaza, as the whole thing had been built on hundreds of those piles. It was very interesting to see.

She made her way up St. Leonhard Strasse, past the Marktplatz, arriving at Wegelin & Co at precisely eleven o'clock at night. The building was a four-story box of an edifice. There was nothing interesting about its structure whatsoever. Paris waited in silence outside the front door, her schedule having been met exactly.

As she pondered the task at hand, the lights of the city lit the evening with a cozy feeling that permeated the world around her. She found herself quite relaxed.

That is, until the doors opened and out stepped a familiar face.

"Paris," he said with a slight smirk, motioning her inside.

"Elijah." Paris nodded and stepped briskly inside as he closed the doors behind them. "Haven't seen you in quite a while. All is well, I presume."

"Keep your presumptions to yourself, young lady. Follow me."

With that, he strode away inside to the left by the teller windows. Paris had not taken more than ten steps before they halted by a door and he ordered, "Wait here." He then disappeared behind the door.

Paris waited.

Throughout every single encounter she had had with Elijah, the one constant was his remarkable lack of interpersonal skills. The man couldn't care less whether someone liked him or not. He was a single-minded purpose machine, that one. Livia had spoken of him with such warmth, such pride—*the best of the best*, she'd called him. Paris had never quite understood what the Councilwoman saw in this arrogant bastard.

After two full minutes, Elijah reentered the lobby and handed her a small metal lockbox.

It was barely large enough to cover the palm of her small hand, yet it was surprisingly heavy for its size. Paris turned it over, examining the seamless construction, the lack of any visible latch or keyhole. Whatever was inside, it was meant to stay inside until the Magistrate himself decided otherwise.

What could be so important?

She looked up at Elijah and cocked her head. "This begs the question."

"What question?" he said, as he stared at her.

Paris smiled, if only to perturb the man. She had never much cared for Elijah. He was an arrogant ass most every time they had encountered one another.

"If you are already here, and you had the box, why not take it to the Magistrate yourself?"

Elijah's expression shifted, the hint of it there and gone in a flash. Defensiveness? Fear? His jaw tightened almost imperceptibly.

"I am no errand boy," he replied. But his tone had shifted slightly. Less dismissive now, more... careful.

"No?" Paris placed the box into her messenger bag, locking the clasp securely. The weight of it settled against her hip like a promise—or a threat. "A matter of semantics, I suppose," she muttered.

"Excuse me?" His irritation was evident. Paris shook her head, careful of the dangerous game she tended to play with him.

"Nothing. I suppose today it is I who is the errand boy." She politely curtsied and turned to leave.

"You will take utmost care in delivering that to the Magistrate."

Elijah's words came out as a specific order—more forceful than the situation seemed to warrant. Paris paused, glancing back at him. The legendary Protector, the best of the best, stood rigid in the empty bank lobby, watching her with an intensity that bordered on desperate.

What's in this box that has even Elijah on edge?

For a moment, Paris considered the weight against her hip, the seamless metal, the secrets it contained. She could open it. She had the skills—could probably figure out the mechanism given enough time. And what harm would a peek do? The Magistrate would never know.

But no. Duty required sealed delivery. Trust was earned through actions, not circumvented through curiosity. The Magistrate had sent her alone on this mission—a test of that very trust. She would not fail it.

"Of course, Elijah," she called over her shoulder. "Of course."

She stepped out into the Swiss night, the lockbox heavy in her bag, questions heavier in her mind. The city sprawled before her, ancient and beautiful, and somewhere in the back of her thoughts, a warning bell chimed softly.

Everything about this mission felt off.

Paris pushed the feeling aside and began making her way toward the train station. She had a long journey ahead of her, and a package to deliver.

She didn't know—couldn't possibly have known—that she would never make it back to the Citadel unchanged.

CHAPTER 31

PRESENT

"Wakey, wakey."

The voice was male, higher pitched but clear and strong. Paris opened her eyes against the splash of cold water that had been doused onto her face.

Her surroundings, dank and drab, were enough that she immediately realized the severity of her situation. Her hands were bound with metal wire behind her back and wrapped around the concrete post to which she was hung. Her hands were bound high enough to prevent any leverage, and the same thin strong wire encircled her neck, holding her head up as well. Her feet were manacled and bound by thick chains to the concrete post.

It took but a second to realize that she was going absolutely nowhere.

This was a professional binding.

It appeared she was well and truly fucked.

"Welcome back to the land of the living, so to speak," the man said. "I'm happy to see my research proved correct and the bullet and tranqs didn't actually kill you."

He appeared to be in his mid-twenties, athletic build, average looks. His black hair was slicked back over his head with copious amounts of product, and his eyes surveyed her with great interest. There was a familiar hunger in that gaze—not predatory in the way Paris understood predation, but covetous. Envious.

Ah, she thought. *One of those.*

"Where am I?" Paris asked. She noted that she had been here for many hours, since she could feel the ferocious itching in her chest where the bullet wound was already healing up rather well. One more scar to mark her years on this earth. The time had also been enough for this man to complete his elaborate binding job. Her mind began to work furiously on methods of possible escape.

"Somewhere quiet, safe from the prying peepers of the world." The man moved to stand directly in front of her. He was a good head taller than she was, and he stared down into her eyes with the strangest expression she had ever seen. "How old are you? Really, I mean."

It didn't take a genius to see what this one was. Paris had heard Garrett speak of them before—humans who wanted nothing more than to be Valensi. Or, rather, in their limited view of things, *vampires*. He was not afraid of her, although her binding spoke volumes to the contrary. She saw no reason not to be honest. For now.

"One hundred and thirty-five," she said.

"You look pretty good for your age."

"Thanks. Now, how about you tell me what the fuck I'm doing here?"

"Oh, I would've expected you to have figured that out by now. I take it you're pretty sharp, right? Or should I not give you the benefit of the doubt?"

"Wannabe. Right?"

"Excuse me?" His eyebrow lifted for a second, but then he smiled. "Ah. Gotcha. A wannabe. Right. Good one."

"Nailed it."

"Yes. You did."

"So can I ask my first question?" If there was one thing that was for certain, Paris wanted to draw this out as long as possible while she worked out her plan for escape. To be perfectly honest, however, she didn't have a clue where to begin.

"Sure," he said, dragging a stool away from the workbench along the wall. "We have all the time in the world."

He was a confident little prick. He sat on the stool and clasped his hands between his relaxed legs. As far as Paris could tell, they were in a basement of some sort, and since she had no gag there would be little hope in screaming or making any commotion. Those actions were ruled out.

"How did you find me?" she asked.

"The club," he said.

Paris remembered that there had been several people waiting near the exit as she and Greg the rapist had headed out that night. She hadn't paid much attention to the crowd, unfortunately. Lazy move.

Her mistake.

"My curiosity got the better of me," the wannabe continued. "Still, you stood out. So, I followed you. I kept my distance and watched. It wasn't long before I realized what you were." When he revealed this, Paris knew he had no clue about what had actually happened to Greg the rapist.

"I take it you've met my kind before." Paris spoke slowly, swallowing often. The wire around her neck was tight enough to prevent any excess movement without impeding her breathing or voice. This one had some experience in the kidnapping department.

"Oh, sure. I've been tracking your kind for years. Research, mostly. Library work. But I've had a few... encounters." He smiled, and there was ice beneath it. "None quite as cooperative as you're going to be, though."

"Is that right?"

"That's right." He stood from the stool and paced slowly in front of her, hands clasped behind his back like a professor preparing to lecture. "You see, I've spent my whole life preparing for this. Studying. Learning. I know more about vampires than most vampires know about themselves."

"First off, we don't call ourselves vampires. That's a human word."

"What do you call yourselves?"

"Wouldn't you like to know."

He smiled again—that cold, patient smile. "I would, actually. Very much. But we'll get to that."

Paris rolled her eyes. "Look, I hate to burst your bubble, sunshine, but this little interrogation of yours isn't going to go the way you think it is. I've been tortured by professionals. Ancient professionals. You're what—twenty-five? Twenty-six? I've got underwear older than you."

"Twenty-seven, actually."

"My condolences. Must be hard, being so inadequate."

The wannabe peered at her with the first crack in that confident facade. Good. Paris filed it away for later use.

"You know," he said, his voice dropping a register, "I was hoping we could do this the easy way. A civil exchange of information. But if you insist on being difficult..."

"Oh, I absolutely insist."

He nodded slowly, as if this was the answer he'd expected. "Very well."

Paris watched him turn and walk to the countertop that ran several feet along the wall of the room. He surveyed the tools laid out there with the casual deliberation of a chef selecting ingredients. Wire cutters. Pliers. A hammer. A blowtorch.

Lovely, Paris thought. A full service establishment.

He picked up the wire cutters—thick ones, similar to those Dawn had used on Gregor Waltz all those years ago—and turned them over in his hands, letting Paris see them clearly. Then, on second thought, he placed them back on the countertop.

Instead, he retrieved a set of thick brass knuckles and slipped them onto his right hand. The metal gleamed dully in the basement's fluorescent light.

"I want to know how to become a vampire," he said.

"Fuck you."

"As you wish."

He closed on her with surprising speed, sending an earth-shattering punch into the side of her face. Paris felt—and heard—her jawbone crack. Her head was wrenched to the right from the force of the blow, and the wire cut into her neck as well. Spewing blood and spit and a couple of teeth, she tried to curse at him, but the words came out as incomprehensible mush.

He followed through with more punches to her gut—one, two, three—each one driving the air from her lungs with explosive force. Then he stepped back to observe his handiwork.

"How long do you think it will take for that jaw to heal?" he said, running his bloodied fingers along his own jawline in question. "I should probably try and set it back in place, right? Otherwise, those stunning looks of yours will be ruined for sure."

The wannabe set the brass knuckles aside and then grasped her forehead in one hand, her jawbone in another. With a violent, sickening crunch, he reset the bones.

Paris whimpered reflexively.

She hated that he got that much out of her. She kept her eyes closed, trying desperately to control her breathing with the techniques she'd picked up from Master Asaro all those years ago.

It wasn't happening.

"I have to give it to you," he said, sitting back down on the stool. "You are one tough broad. You realize that this only firms my resolve, right? We can do this all week. If that is what it takes to get the information I need, then that's what I'll do." He leaned forward, elbows on his knees. "Why make this so difficult on yourself?"

When Paris spoke, it was in halting sets of words, painful and slobbery with blood and saliva. "Because... you do not deserve... to be what you aspire to be."

"Why not? What makes you so much better than me?"

"I earned it."

"Really?" he said, cocking his head to one side. "How's that?"

"I spent years... training, learning, and preparing."

"So have I."

"No." Paris forced herself to stare at him, to put every ounce of contempt she possessed into her gaze. "What you've spent your time on... is coercion, torture, and murder. My journey was honorable. Yours is little more than... desecration."

She could not control the tears that escaped her eyes as she spoke through the burning anguish that was her mouth. But they were tears of pain, not submission. Never submission.

"I understand your reticence," he said. "I really do. But you need to understand that this choice is not yours. You have no choice but to tell me what I want to know. I won't kill you. We'll dance this dance until you give in." He spread his hands, palms up, the gesture indicating no options. "You know that, right?"

The shock was evident in his face when Paris laughed out loud, sending blood in an arc that failed to reach his feet.

"What you fail to understand... you wannabe motherfucker... is that I am Paris of the High Guard... and you have no idea what I am capable of." She was grinning now, her broken teeth bared in some horrible tableau between a smile and a snarl. "So here's my last request... kiss my ass!"

Her tenuous grip on sanity seemed to slip away from her and she fell into uncontrollable laughter, ignoring the thin wire cutting into her throat. She repeated her request through her hysterics, and the wannabe sat there waiting for her to finish.

When she finally subsided into wet, painful chuckles, he stood from the stool and strolled back to the workbench.

"I know that the sun is your enemy," he said, reaching for what looked to be a small butane torch. "But what about fire?"

The wannabe turned back to face her, but Paris refrained from comment. He nodded his head, the corners of his mouth turning down in understanding.

He knew she was done talking.

It was all over but the screaming.

Paris realized she had passed out when the pain was what brought her back around.

He stood in front of her with the torch in his hand. The flame was off. From the searing agony on her belly, it appeared that he had been kind enough to cauterize the knife wound while testing out her pain threshold.

"How'd I do?" she asked through heavy breaths.

"Not bad. Let's try again, shall we?"

He brought the handheld torch back up, clicking the blue flame into life. The flame touched her chest where her bra came together in the front. When she saw what was next, the only thing she could do was close her eyes and try to shut her mind down.

She didn't have enough time.

Darkness overtook her to the sounds of her own screams.

She came back again to find him sitting on the stool, watching her with the patience of a man who had nowhere else to be.

"You know what fascinates me?" he said conversationally, as if they were old friends catching up over coffee. "Your kind's regenerative abilities. I've read about them, of course, but seeing it in person..." He shook his head in wonder. "Remarkable."

Paris looked down at herself. Her shirt was gone—cut away, leaving her in what remained of her bra. The burns on her chest and stomach were already beginning to heal, the blistered skin knitting itself back together in ways that would have been impossible for any human.

Her jaw, too, had mostly reset itself. It still ached like a bastard, but she could speak without slurring.

"Glad I could... be educational," she managed.

"Oh, you have been. Very much so." He stood and retrieved a notebook, thick with handwritten pages, from the workbench. "I've been documenting everything. Response times to various stimuli. Pain thresholds. Healing rates." He flipped through the pages with evident satisfaction. "This will be invaluable for my future research."

"Future research?"

"Of course. You're not my first vampire, and you won't be my last." He set the notebook aside and picked up the pliers. "But you might be the most stubborn. I'll give you that."

"High praise from a sociopath."

"Sociopath?" He seemed genuinely amused. "Is that what you think I am?"

"Well, let's see. You kidnap women, torture them for information, and keep detailed notes on their suffering. If the shoe fits, Cinderella."

"I prefer to think of myself as a... dedicated student. An enthusiast." He held up the pliers, opening and closing them with a metallic snick-snick. "Now, shall we continue your lesson? I have so many more questions."

"And I have so many more ways to tell you to fuck off."

"Yes," he said, moving closer. "I expected you might say that."

The pliers latched onto the fingernail of her pinky finger.

"Last chance," he said. "How does one become a vampire?"

Paris looked him dead in the eye.

"Eat me."

The slick, moist tearing was almost worse than the pain, there in the basement's silence. Paris screamed—she couldn't help it, couldn't control it—but even through the agony, even as her first fingernail dropped to the concrete floor, she found herself laughing again.

Because this stupid, arrogant, wannabe piece of shit had no idea.

He had no idea that somewhere out there, someone was looking for her.

And when that someone found her—*when*, not *if*—this basement was going to become a slaughterhouse.

All Paris had to do was survive until then.

She could do that.

She'd been surviving her whole goddamn life.

CHAPTER 32

1935 St. Gallen, Switzerland Age 55

"Why, Thorne? Why?"

The words tore themselves from Paris's throat before she could stop them. She stood in the moonlight near the Abbey of St. Gall, facing the man she had loved for eight years, the man who had tried to steal her mission—the man who had been ordered to *kill* her.

"You don't understand what he's capable of," Thorne said. His voice was calm, reasonable—the voice of a man explaining a complex situation in a simple way, as if to a child. "Few do. There's so much going on here that you're not privy to. Please. Trust me. I'm doing this for the right reason."

"No."

"What?"

"Any trust I once had in you evaporated the moment you attacked me."

"I didn't attack you! I tried to steal the case. Once I realized it was you that he'd sent, I changed my plans."

"Your plans?" Paris's hearts rate was slowing, her mind preparing for what was to come. The initial shock was fading, replaced by colder thoughts. Harder.

"My orders were to kill the messenger and retrieve the box. But I can say I managed to get the box without you knowing. You'll be safe. This will work."

Paris stared at him—this man she had held in her arms, whose body she had memorized with her hands and lips, whose voice had whispered promises of forever in the shelter of their shared bed. She had trusted him. *Loved* him.

And it had all been a lie.

"You think that because you didn't kill me I will surrender my mission and my duty?" Her voice was ice now; all the warmth she had ever felt for him freezing into something sharp and deadly. "Do you not have any notion of who I am and what I represent? You may have been a Protector by vocation, but you fucking threw that title and duty out the window, you bastard. But I *am* a member of the High Guard, not some lowly peasant girl returning from the market. You fool."

Her words hit him as she expected they would. His expression closed, his posture relaxing into a moment she recognized—the stance of a fighter preparing for battle. She had seen it a thousand times in sparring matches, in training exercises.

She had never expected to see it directed at her.

They moved as one.

Paris threw her torso to the side, bringing her knee directly up and into his chin. She let her anger focus the force of the blow and enjoyed the sound of bone giving way. His muffled cry began as pain and ended as anger.

She slipped down and to her right to avoid his counterattack, but he caught her arm and flung her around in a cartwheel motion, using her weight to her disadvantage. With only a split second to react, she spread her legs to increase her momentum and locked her opposing hand onto his wrist. Using that centrifugal force, she pulled him along with her as she planted her feet and jerked downward.

It wasn't much, but it was enough to get him off his feet for a moment—enough that she could recompose herself.

Then she saw the wooden knife in his hand.

Paris experienced a twinge of hesitation. This was new. She was facing off against her lover, who was now her enemy and prepared to kill her by driving a stake through her hearts.

Fan-fucking-tastic.

"I'm so sorry, Paris." His voice cracked on her name—or maybe she only imagined it did. "You've given me no choice."

For a moment, she almost believed him.

"Go to hell, lover," she said, reaching into his mind.

It was walled up pretty tight, but she could tell he was still new at the mind protection game. Instead of forcing her way in, she let her thoughts linger and divide and slide into the crevasses of his defenses. He made his move just as she saw it in his head—his momentum and speed formidable, and he might have succeeded if she had not foreseen the motion in time to react.

She wanted desperately to continue her excursion into his mind, to discover if he had ever loved her at all. But she couldn't afford the distraction. Not now. Not with a wooden stake aimed at her heart.

His hand lashed out, the wooden knife aimed square at her hearts. Paris let it come, waiting until the very last second to sidestep. Her hand came up beneath his, twisting the knife and therefore his wrist onto itself.

The bones in his wrist gave way.

The knife entered the skin under his chin.

Paris drove it straight up into his skull, using all the force she could muster.

He didn't utter even a sound, his mouth pinned closed by the wooden stake. His expression was one of shock, plastered to his face by the scrambling of his brain.

Thorne dropped to his knees.

Paris stood there for long seconds, her chest heaving, her mind refusing to process what she had done. His mind was gone now—the chemicals in the wood reacting with his biochemistry. If she left the stake there, it would be hours before the chemical reactions would lead to his final death.

She pondered doing just that.

The tears forced their way out despite everything she did to stop them. She didn't want to cry. She didn't want to let this man—her lover, her *betrayer*—see her breaking like this. It was unfair. He should not have the satisfaction of seeing what his treachery had done to her.

But his mind was gone. His eyes stared at nothing, vacant and empty.

And still she wept.

Eight years, she thought. Eight years of my life. Eight years of trust and hope and plans for a future that was never going to exist.

She had believed him when he said he loved her. Had believed every whispered promise, every tender touch, every plan they had made together. The permanent posting. The life they would build. A future.

All of it—every single moment—had been a performance. A long con. A lie designed to keep her close, keep her trusting, keep her *blind* to what he really was.

How did I not see it?

The question burned in her mind like acid.

How could I have been so fucking blind?

She stared into those vacant eyes—eyes she had gazed into on so many more intimate occasions, eyes that had looked at her with what she thought was love. Her vision blurred and she brushed the tears away with a quick swipe of her forearm.

"You never loved me at all, did you?" she whispered to the kneeling corpse. "Everything was a lie. Every moment, every touch, every word."

No answer came. No answer would ever come.

Maybe that's for the best, she thought. Maybe I don't want to know.

But she did know. Deep down, in the part of her heart that she had kept walled off since childhood, she had always known. Love didn't betray. Love didn't draw a weapon against the person it claimed to cherish. Love didn't accept orders to *kill* and then act surprised when the target refused to cooperate.

Whatever Thorne had felt for her—if he had felt anything at all—it had never been love.

And she had been too desperate, too lonely, too hungry for connection to see it.

I'm such a fool.

Paris gripped the end of the stake and ripped it free of his head. Blood and brain matter followed, spattering the grass of the Abbey grounds. With all the anger at being lied to for so many years, for being used and brushed aside as nothing more than an obstacle, she shoved the wooden knife deep into his chest.

His body folded to lie upon the cool grass in a heap.

"I wish I could say I'm sorry," Paris said, her voice raw and broken. "I wish I didn't have to be here. I wish this had never happened. But you are who you are, and I'm who I am." She knelt beside him, watching the deterioration begin in earnest—the skin graying, the flesh beginning to collapse. "Know this: I'm not sorry, asshole."

The tears came again—hot and relentless, pouring down her face as she watched him die. As she watched their future die. As she watched the woman she had been—the woman who had dared to hope, to trust, to love—die alongside him.

That woman was gone now.

She would never come back.

Paris made certain his remains were cleared of any evidence as to who he had been. It wouldn't take long before there was little left—certainly nothing recognizable as a man. Once the wood had reached and pierced his hearts, there was no coming back.

She had read some ridiculous novel once wherein a stake had been removed from a vampire's heart and he had come back to life.

Such bullshit.

Wiping the tears away, she quickly retrieved her messenger bag. The lockbox was still there, still heavy, still sealed. Whatever secrets it contained—whatever was so important that Thorne had been willing to kill her for it—remained intact.

You have no idea what's in there, he had said during their confrontation. Or had he? The words blurred together now, memory and imagination tangling into a memory she could no longer trust.

She couldn't trust anything anymore.

Paris paused a minute to take in the view from the rooftop. The Abbey spread below her, ancient and beautiful, utterly indifferent to the violence that had occurred on its grounds. Someone was walking along the street, nearing the area of their scuffle, and she waited to ensure it wasn't some sort of backup.

Although she was doubtful they would have thought a Protector would need any assistance to kill someone.

To kill me, she thought. To kill the woman he claimed to love.

She made her train with only minutes to spare, keeping alert for anything out of the ordinary. She encountered no one else who might be prepared to take her out for whatever the hell it was she was carrying.

Still, her senses were on high alert until she made it back to the Citadel the following night.

But the danger she felt most keenly wasn't external.

It was the knowledge that she would never—*never*—let anyone get that close again.

CHAPTER 33

1935 The Citadel Age 55

The Audience Chamber was full.

Paris stood with the rest of the High Guard along the wall to the right of the dais, her face a careful mask of composure. The Magistrate sat at the center of the raised platform, flanked by members of the Hierarchy—ancient figures whose faces betrayed nothing of their thoughts. As the elected leader of the Valensi, it was his duty to preside over—and lay down sentencing during—each and every Tribunal.

At the echoing sound of the gavel, the doors to the side of the Audience Room opened. Two Protectors—Elijah and Garrett—entered with a wire-cuffed Edward Frost shuffling between them. Frost had two thick ankle cuffs encircling each leg, a massive but short length of chain tying them together. His steps were but an inch or two at a time.

There were murmurs rising and falling in pitch as the accused was led to stand before the Magistrate. Once in place, the two Protectors took only one step back and waited.

"Edward Frost," the Magistrate began, his voice clear, his words enunciated even through his sometimes-predominant Spanish accent. "You have been charged by this Tribunal with the crimes of Sedition and Attempted Murder."

"Murder?" Frost asked, his tone one of surprise. Obviously, he was not as shocked by the charge of Sedition.

"Yes. It has been noted and proven that, in your efforts to destroy key evidence, you brainwashed and sent a former Protector of the Valensi—the one known as Thorne—to kill the member of the High Guard who was transporting said evidence."

At the Magistrate's words, Paris felt far too many eyes upon her.

She kept her calm, falling into her breathing techniques to relax her nerves. From the corner of her eye, she could see Frost's head swivel to look at her.

She refused to acknowledge him.

Brainwashed. The word echoed in her mind. Thorne had been brainwashed. He hadn't chosen to betray her—not entirely. Someone had gotten into his head, twisted his thoughts, turned him into a weapon.

Did that change anything?

Did it matter?

He had still drawn a weapon against her. Still tried to steal the lockbox. Still would have killed her if she hadn't killed him first.

Brainwashed or not, Paris thought, he made his choice when he pulled that wooden knife.

But some small, treacherous part of her wondered: What if he had loved me, before Frost got to him? What if it wasn't all a lie?

She crushed the thought ruthlessly. It didn't matter. It couldn't matter. The past was the past, and Thorne was dead, and nothing would change that.

"You bastard," Frost said, facing back to the Magistrate. "I only wanted to share this world between our peoples—us and the humans. You only want to destroy it all."

Paris found she could not resist herself.

She let her thoughts flow into Frost's mind. She wasn't sure why she was doing it—there was no valid reason she should be intruding into the mind of a traitor. Still, his vehemence, and the indelible faith that Thorne must have had in this man—whether through brainwashing or simple coinciding of beliefs—made her want to know.

Frost's mind was abuzz with thoughts of hatred for the Hierarchy and the Magistrate in particular, so Paris allowed that mélange of emotion to ease her passage into his thoughts. She caught but a glimpse of something—

Valensi in the sun. Standing in daylight. Shaking hands with what looked to be the current Prime Minister of England—

The gates came crashing down.

Someone had clamped down on Frost's mind. Paris remained stone-faced, yet out of the corner of her eye she could see a pained expression flit across the older man's face. His eyes swept the dais for any sign of who might have entered his head unbidden.

Paris closed her mind without hesitation, blanking her thoughts, relaxing into her breathing techniques once again.

What the hell was that? she thought. Valensi in the sun? That's impossible.

But she had seen it. Clear as day—if she could be forgiven the irony of that phrase. A vision of their kind walking in daylight, meeting with human leaders as equals.

Frost's vision of the future? Or something more?

"You can't do this," Frost yelled out. "I was doing what is right. I could have prevented it. You will destroy us all—"

His words were cut off by a swift punch to the back of the neck by Elijah. It was lightning fast, and Frost rocked from the blow yet remained standing. Within mere moments, he stood quiet, head hung in resignation.

"Edward Frost, as witnessed here today, you have been charged with Sedition—treason against your own people—and Attempted Murder. Your crimes are reprehensible and without remorse. For your crimes against the Valensi, you are hereby sentenced to Death by Chaining."

The crowd erupted in a multitudinous ruckus of quickly taken breaths, murmurs, and chatter. Paris could understand the commotion. The last Chaining had been, she believed, before she had even come to the Citadel.

She risked a quick glance at Frost. He had not reacted whatsoever to the sentencing. She assumed he had known this would be his fate.

Chaining was the worst possible sentence one could receive among the Valensi. The final death. The worst death sentence imaginable. Outside the Citadel, in the center of a glade surrounded by a hundred acres of protected Valensi property, stood a magnificent old yew tree. Like the hanging trees in the Old West of the United States, the Chaining Tree, as it was called, carried the same sense of dread.

Criminals who committed the most atrocious, unforgivable crimes were bound against the Chaining Tree at six o'clock in the morning. There they waited, facing their slow and terrible demise. Since the Valensi were basically allergic to ultraviolet light, being held there in the morning—facing the east and the rising sun—they were committed to the most painful death.

The time it took the condemned to die varied based upon age and previous exposure to the sun. If the person was young, having spent early years in the outdoors, death could be as long as a couple of hours in coming. If they were older, not having had much exposure over centuries—such as Edward Frost—death would be upon them within minutes.

The gavel came down hard, twice.

The Magistrate nodded at the two guarding Protectors, who then escorted Frost from the room. The members of the Hierarchy stood and exited through the side door at the back of the dais, followed by the Magistrate and the High Guard.

Paris saw Frost and the Protectors a little way down the hall as she left the Audience Room. Garrett caught her eye and gave a concerned nod. She returned the sentiment and escorted the Magistrate to his quarters along with the rest of the Guard.

He paused at his door and faced them all: Dusk, Dawn, Vienna, London, Cairo, and Paris.

"We must take care," he stated, his expression a blank mask. "It appears we are entering dangerous times. I can only hope that such traitorous activities have been ended with Frost, but we cannot lose our focus. Vigilance is of the utmost importance, yes."

"Yes, sir," they all said in unison.

"If only for propriety's sake, sir," Dusk said, "Dawn and I will station ourselves here until the sentence is to be carried out."

The Magistrate nodded and then disappeared into his quarters. Dusk turned to the rest of them.

"I will expect everyone to be at the ready in the Abode until we move the condemned in the morning." They all nodded in agreement. "Let's hope this is the last time we must attend such drastic measures."

In his words, Paris sensed the weight of that hope.

They were gathered by the northern entrance to the Citadel, the silence blanketing all in attendance.

Even Frost stood lips unmoving, staring at the outside world, biding his final moments. At ten minutes until six, the two Protectors—Elijah and Garrett—led Frost to the Chaining Tree, some hundred meters from the entrance.

In the eastern distance, Paris noted the fading false dawn. Frost would not have much time to further ponder his crimes against the people before the sun rose and he faced his fate. She watched with grim interest, as this was the first such sentencing she had experienced.

Do you doubt his guilt or that he deserves this fate?

The Magistrate's words were clear in her mind, as she had not made any effort to protect her thoughts.

I do not, Paris thought in response. When was the last incident that required such dire measures, sir?

It was the same year you became one of us, actually. One of our people lost his intellect. His age had driven him to his end, I'm afraid. There was a pause. Paris, do you remember the killings in Whitechapel?

She noted his continued lack of "young" when addressing her, but then what he said struck a chord.

Do you mean that one of our own was Jack the Ripper?

This bit of information took her aback. The murderer of eleven women had reportedly never been found. Here she was learning the truth.

Yes, I'm afraid so. Once we learned of it—far too late, I might add—we handled the situation. The man was unable and unwilling to be saved and, albeit somewhat less than agreed upon, the Hierarchy deemed him an example to be made.

He caught her eye for a brief moment and then turned back to the chaining of Frost.

This brings us to this man. We cannot allow ourselves to be discovered by the humans. Not yet. Perhaps never. What the future holds is forever uncertain, yet it is clear at this point that we could not protect ourselves should the humans decide to try and obliterate us. We hide for our safety, and that safety must remain inviolate.

Agreed, Paris thought.

And with that, their thoughts went silent as the Protectors returned to the Citadel.

Frost was now chained to the yew tree, facing eastward. Paris knew from Vi that the man was close to two thousand years old and had been Birthed into the Valensi at a very young age. Once the sun struck his skin, he would have only minutes of horrific pain before it was all over.

The attendees—the Hierarchy, the two Protectors, the High Guard, and the Magistrate—all waited until the last minute before closing the doors, thereby sealing off the screams that would soon follow.

Tonight, someone would be assigned to visit the tree, retrieve the chains, and verify the condemned's passing.

As the crowd dispersed, Garrett shuffled up beside Paris and asked if she would like to share breakfast. She nodded, and they headed to one of the four Citadel cafeterias.

Sitting down after selecting their food, Paris managed not to look him in the eye. He kept his commentary light and limited, giving her the time she needed.

Finally, she gave in—but kept her wall up regardless.

"I've had a bad week, my friend," she said as she began to chew on thick pieces of bacon and slug back her orange juice. Her appetite had not suffered, that was for certain.

"I know," Garrett replied.

"It seems impossible to know who to trust these days."

"Only time will tell." He winked at her, and she so appreciated how light he was keeping the conversation.

"Time is of little consequence," Paris said. "Hell, I was with Thorne for years. *Years*, Garrett." She shook her head. "And apparently I did not know him at all."

"People change, Paris. Perhaps the man you knew simply changed. Maybe he was brainwashed." He said it matter-of-factly, as if it were the most reasonable explanation in the world.

Paris smirked at him.

"It's rare, but it happens." He cut up his fried egg and shoved it in his mouth, bobbing his head side to side as he enjoyed his breakfast.

"I've known you for fifty years, Garrett. You have not changed one iota in all of that time."

"What's your point?"

"That some people are exactly who they present themselves to be. And others..." She trailed off, staring at her plate. "Others are nothing but masks all the way down."

"Perhaps." Garrett set down his fork and regarded her with those blue eyes—the ones with the tiny gold flakes around the irises that she had never noticed until recently. "Or, it's possible Thorne was simply weak. Weak enough to be turned, weak enough to be used. That's not your fault, Paris. That's his."

"I should have seen it."

"How? You're not omniscient. You loved him. Love makes us blind to the faults of those we care about. It's not a weakness—it's what makes us worth saving in the first place."

Paris looked up at him then, really looked, and saw the one thing in his expression that she had never noticed before. Patience. Understanding. A quiet, steady warmth that asked for nothing in return.

"Thank you, Garrett," she said softly.

"For what?"

"For not treating me like I'm broken."

"You're not broken, Paris." He picked up his fork again and gestured at her plate. "Now eat your breakfast. We've got a long road ahead of us, and I'd hate to see you waste away from hunger."

She almost smiled at that. Almost.

But the image from Frost's mind lingered—Valensi in the sun, shaking hands with human leaders—and she filed it away in the corner of her mind where she kept all the things she didn't yet understand.

Someday, perhaps, the pieces would fit together.

For now, she had bacon to eat and a heart to rebuild.

One day at a time.

CHAPTER 34

PRESENT

Paris opened her eyes to sunlight.

That alone should have killed her.

She lay in a hammock strung between two palm trees, the fabric swaying gently in a warm breeze that carried the salt-sweet smell of the ocean. Above her, the sky stretched in an impossible blue—not the deep indigo of twilight she had lived beneath for 135 years, but the brilliant azure of midday. The sun hung directly overhead, pouring golden light onto her skin.

Her skin, which should have been blistering. Burning. Deteriorating cell by cell into an agonizing death.

Instead, she felt... warm. Pleasant. *Alive.*

Paris sat up slowly, her mind struggling to process what her senses were telling her. She looked down at herself and froze.

She was wearing a bikini.

A bikini.

Her body—the body that had been stabbed and burned and broken by the wannabe's enthusiastic torture—was smooth and unmarked. The scar from when Dusk had broken her arm before she was Valensi: gone. The wounds that had been received during the duel in Paris: gone. The burn scars from the wannabe's blowtorch: gone.

She reached up to touch her face and discovered that her jaw was unmarred. It was then that she also noted that her brilliant red hair—the dye job she had maintained since arriving in Florida—was back to its natural light brown.

A strange bird called from somewhere in the distance. The beach stretched out forever in both directions, pristine white sand meeting turquoise water in a postcard-perfect curve. She had no idea where she was or why she was alive while clearly standing in sunlight.

"Hello!" she called, unable to determine what else to do.

As she stood from the hammock, noting—with some bemusement—how nice she looked in a bikini, she wondered what the hell was going on.

She had never once worn a bikini.

"Hello, Paris."

She whirled about at the sound of the voice, only to see Cassandra Dreys standing there in a bikini top and colorful flower-covered sarong. Her mouth fell open and no words would come.

"Paris of the High Guard is speechless?" Cassandra smiled that warm, knowing smile Paris remembered so well. "Someone call the Times."

"You're dead," Paris said. "At least, that's what they told me."

"Yes." Cassandra's expression softened. "Now that you mention it, I never got the chance to thank you for your friendship. I will always treasure it. Thank you for helping London, too."

"What the hell is going on? Where am I? This is a dream, right?"

"Have you ever dreamed of beaches before?"

Paris thought about that. She could not remember ever having had one single dream about a beach. Ever. She had been born in Bristol but had never been to the sea as a child. Once she entered the Citadel, it was rare that she ever came close to a beach. Beaches were for day people.

That was the one thing she had never been.

"Seriously, Cassie. What the fuck?"

"Think about it," Cassandra said, exuding patience beyond reproach. "Take your time."

Why would she be on a beach? Why would she be dreaming? Paris thought back, trying to mentally retrace her steps, and then she remembered the wannabe. The wire cutters. The pliers. The blowtorch. The brass knuckles shattering her jaw. The fire against her chest.

She stared at Cassie, and her breath caught in her throat.

"I'm dead?"

"Not quite," Cassandra replied. But it was clear from her expression that Paris was pretty close. "He really did a number on you, girl."

"But—" Paris spread her arms to indicate her entire body. "There aren't any scars."

"Silly girl. This isn't reality. This is so very far from reality."

"Okay, fine. So what the hell is it, then? If I'm not dead and this isn't real, what's going on?"

"You're at a crossroads." Cassandra began walking further onto the beach, motioning for Paris to follow. "You should really consider yourself one of the lucky ones. You know, I always admired you."

"Uh, what?"

"Sure," Cassandra said as Paris fell into step beside her. "You never let anyone else define you. Even when you became one of the High Guard, you were always your own person. That was one of the things that Dawn hated so much about you."

"Really?"

They sat together on the sand, beyond the reach of the water as it washed toward them. The waves were gentle, rhythmic—hypnotic in their consistency.

"Absolutely. Dusk admired you for it, too. At least, that's how I saw it."

"I'm sorry, Cassie, but I'm so confused right now. None of this makes sense. Why am I here?"

"You're here to welcome the darkness."

"What now?"

"You know who you are, Paris. Don't you?" Cassandra's dark eyes held hers with an intensity that felt almost physical. "You know yourself better than most people know themselves. You know what you are capable of. You know what you want out of life."

"Do I? I think you've got the wrong Paris."

Cassandra reached out and laid a gentle hand on Paris's bare knee. "You do know what you want, even if you refuse to admit it to yourself."

"Okay," Paris replied. "So what if I do? That doesn't explain why I'm here. Being here, this place—this is most definitely not who I am."

"True, but this is perfect neutral ground. An empty slate on which you can begin to rewrite your future. You do want a better future, do you not?"

"Anything is better than what I faced a few minutes ago." Paris stared out at the cresting waves, watching them rise and fall in endless repetition. "My life was pretty much over, wasn't it? One way or another."

"That doesn't have to be, you know. There are options that you've not foreseen."

"You've lost me again. No one can foresee their future."

"Well, that's true. But you can put yourself on the right path to a future that you hope to achieve. Right?"

Paris nodded, sort of understanding what she meant. The problem was that she was not your average person. She was not going to be able to flip her life over on a whim. It was simply not in her nature to be some do-gooder or heroine of any sort, if that was what Cassandra was driving at. She said as much.

"That's not what I mean." Cassandra's expression grew serious—more serious than Paris had ever seen it. "You're about to face some more challenges, Paris. You are going to be given choices. The choices you make will either send you down a short and dangerous path or a long and very dangerous path."

"Neither of those sounds very appetizing," Paris said.

Cassandra burst out laughing—that warm, effeminate giggle that Paris remembered so well. It left her smiling despite everything, wondering why this dream was so fucking weird.

"I suppose death is coming for me no matter what I do?" Paris asked.

"This fascination with death—where did it begin? I'm curious." Cassandra shifted in the sand to face her better, folding her legs beneath her. Looking at her now, Paris realized how much she had missed her. Besides London, Cassandra had been her best friend.

Paris thought about the question. "I guess it began the night I ran away from home. After seeing my mother murdered, watching the light leave her, I've always wondered where that light went. For some unknown reason, I've never believed that it faded away. Our light goes somewhere. I know it does." She paused, thinking of Rae. Of Doug. Of all the deaths she had witnessed in 135 years. "The last week has only gone to strengthen that belief."

"So your travels are far from over, aren't they?"

There was something about the way Cassandra said that. Paris peered at her. "Has that time come? Time to travel on?"

Cassandra laughed again. "No. As a matter of fact, it's time you got back on track. My time is done. Now it's up to you." Her expression grew grave. "But Paris—I need you to understand."

"What?"

"The war is coming. Whether you want it or not."

Paris felt the cold settle in her chest. "What war?"

"You'll have to choose." Cassandra's seemed to darken, to deepen, as if something ancient was looking out through them. "Your kind or theirs. The lines are being drawn even now, and you won't be able to stand in the middle forever."

"I don't understand—"

"You will. Soon enough." Cassandra stood, brushing sand from her sarong. "And Paris? London's path and yours will cross again. What you do when that happens... that will determine everything."

"London?" Paris scrambled to her feet. "What do you know about London? Cassie, wait—"

But Cassandra was already fading, her form growing translucent against the impossible blue sky. That warm smile remained, even as the rest of her dissolved into light and shadow.

"I hope you choose well, my friend," her voice whispered, seeming to come from everywhere and nowhere at once. "Welcome the darkness."

And then she was gone.

The bright light of midday fell with the sun, down and beyond the horizon, leaving Paris blind with only the constant sounds of the ocean to accompany her.

She welcomed the darkness.

Behind her eyelids, Paris saw blackness slip away into the dimmest shade of red.

Opening her eyes, she saw that she was lying on a bed. Her jaw ached. She ran her hand along her face, noting the healing was nearly complete. Still, she could feel the slightly raised line where the bone had been broken. She reached down to her stomach and ran her fingers over the scar tissue where the wannabe had stabbed and burned her.

Carefully, she lifted her head to look down at the wounds. They had healed nicely.

That was when panic set in.

She sat up too quickly and her world swam in a dizzying circle. Bracing her hands on the edge of the bed, she closed her eyes to allow herself some semblance of equilibrium. She was still dressed in her jeans, but her bra had been replaced—someone had put a fresh one on her while she was unconscious.

She remembered the final moments with the wannabe and pulled the cup away from her breast. The scarring would take years to fade completely, but it was fully healed.

As much damage as had been done by that little psychopath, she knew that this much healing could only mean one thing.

Valensi intervention.

Someone had found her. Someone had saved her. Someone had brought her here and fed her enough blood to accelerate her healing far beyond what her body could have managed on its own.

But who? And why?

"Good," a male voice said from the bathroom to her left. "You're awake."

Paris's blood ran cold.

She knew that voice.

CHAPTER 35

1935 The Citadel Age 55

The days following were horrible.

Paris's world shrank to exist only in her small, private quarters. No one dared disturb her. Even London kept her distance. She was alone. Truly alone.

The moments blurred together now, but at the time, they ricocheted from the sharp focus of her memories to the softer focus of the moments seen through her own weak-ass tears. She hated herself one minute and hated Thorne all the more the next.

She sat in silence on her bed, curled up and overwhelmed by the whole thing. She got up and splashed water on her face, willing herself to snap out of it, but the hot tears mixed with the icy water and she sank to the floor beside the sink and lost herself in the weight of the pain, the humiliation at being played, of being lied to for so long.

She had been blind to what was right in front of her.

He had betrayed her.

She knew it hadn't been love—not on his end—but still she had trusted him like no other. They had shared their lives, their bodies. They were lovers. The passion that they'd shared, the intimacy—it was nothing more than a façade for him. She meant nothing. Otherwise, how could he have turned on her so easily? For God's sake, no one knew her as intimately as Thorne had. No one knew him as she had.

Or so she'd thought.

How did she not see it coming? How could she have been so fucking blind?

Maybe she did not know him at all. It could be that it had all been an act. For *years*. How could he have played her so easily for years?

"Fuck you!" she cried out to Thorne, and to no one. She screamed out in agony as her fist crashed against the stone wall, the bones cracking, the pain only shifting from her heart to her hand. "You bastard," she whispered through the tears. "You bastard."

For nothing more than the continued shift in pain that she felt, she used her left hand to reset the bones in her right. She should go to the infirmary, but she was in no mood. Let them heal crooked. Let them remind her of her stupidity every time she looked at them.

Let them remind her never to trust again.

Three days later, Paris was ready when she heard the knock at her door.

It had taken London longer than she had expected before she came. Seeing Paris in the Abode earlier—she had forced herself to make an appearance, if only for propriety's sake—was sign enough for London that she could take her chances now.

"Enter," Paris called out. She was sitting up against the headboard of her bed, *The Good Earth* propped against her knees for ease of reading. London made her way in slower than her usual whirlwind appearances. She closed the door, never looking away from Paris.

"Is there something I can do for you, my friend?" Paris said. Her voice was flat. Hollow. The voice of someone who had scraped out her own insides and left nothing but the shell.

"Yes," London replied. "You can open up. Let me help."

"Sweetheart, there is nothing you can do for me, and you know that."

"You can talk to me. Confide in me. Maybe it'll do you some good." For a moment, watching her expression, Paris thought London might tear up. She shook her head.

"It is what it is, Sarah," Paris said, calling her by her birth name. "I thank you, from the bottom of my heart. But I need time. That's all."

"Damn it, Paris!" London's voice was louder than Paris was prepared for. "That man broke your heart and tried to fucking *kill* you. How can you not be a total wreck right now?"

"Who says I'm not?"

Paris put the novel aside and dropped her legs over the side of the bed, facing away from London's prying view.

"Who says I'm not broken? Completely broken and unable to think straight?"

For fifty-five years, she had built up this wall around her emotions. It was there for a reason. Thorne had managed to put some cracks in it, but she would be damned if she'd allow him to tear it down completely. She was better than that and she would show it to the world.

For London, though, Paris knew that her wall was one of the most frustrating things she'd ever encountered. She had even told Paris so on one occasion, years ago.

Paris would not be so stubborn as to deny that she was fucked up. But she would also not allow her own inner turmoil to ruin the reputation as a cast-iron bitch that she had worked so hard to build for the past half-century.

She stared into London's eyes and revealed the truth of what was going on inside of her, as any true friend would.

"Who says I am fit to go on sharing this world in the shape I'm in? Maybe I'm not."

Her voice cracked. She hadn't expected it to. Hadn't wanted it to.

"I loved him," she said. The words came out broken, fractured. "I *loved* him, London."

"I know."

"How did I not see it?" The tears were starting now, despite everything Paris did to hold them back. "How was I so blind?"

"Paris—"

"He never loved me." The words came faster now, tumbling over each other like stones in an avalanche. "It was always about the lockbox. Everything was a lie. Every moment, every touch, every word. Eight years of my life, and none of it was real."

"That's not your fault—"

"I'm such a *fool*." Paris's hands were shaking. She clenched them into fists, trying to stop it, but that only made the tremors worse. "I should have known. Should have seen the signs. I let my guard down. I *trusted* him."

"That's not weakness—"

"It *is* weakness!" Paris's voice rose to something dangerously close to a shout. "And it almost got me killed!"

She pulled back, wiping her eyes angrily. The tears kept coming anyway, traitors that they were.

"I can't... I can't make that mistake again."

London moved around the bed to sit beside her. She didn't touch Paris—not yet—just sat close enough that Paris could feel her warmth.

"Paris," she said quietly. "Look at me."

Paris didn't want to. Looking at London meant being seen. Being seen meant being vulnerable. And being vulnerable was what had gotten her into this mess in the first place.

But she looked anyway.

"Maybe I'm just... unlovable," she whispered.

"Don't say that—"

"No, listen. Really listen." Paris's voice was dead now, flat and empty. "My father killed my mother. I was seven years old, and I watched him push her down the stairs, and I couldn't save her. I couldn't do *anything*."

"Paris..."

"The Citadel took me in. Made me what I am. Made me kill to survive."
She stared at her hands—hands that had killed Thorne, that had killed so
many others. "Everyone I get close to either dies or betrays me. Maybe
it's me. It could be I'm the problem."

"That's not—"

"Maybe I'm lost in the consideration that I am unworthy of even a
traitor's love and affection." The words felt like broken glass in her throat.
"Maybe I'm less than deserving of anyone's love. How can I possibly go
on with that notion flitting around inside my brain like a drunken
butterfly?"

"Paris." London's voice was firm now, brooking no argument. She
came around to sit beside Paris, her arm encircling her shoulders. "Please
don't talk like that. Thorne is not worth a second thought from someone
of your caliber. He was lost well before he met you, I'm certain of it. His
lack of loyalty to anyone—even his own people, who, I might add, he had
sworn to protect with his own life—only goes to show that you are far
and away a better person and more worthy soul than he."

Paris turned to her, their faces only inches apart.

London was such a beautiful girl. Her almond eyes and sand-colored
skin were flawless, her jet-black hair long and straight and as shiny as
polished ebony. Yet her outer shell, beautiful as it was, could not hold a
candle to the gorgeous soul that inhabited it. She could be as cold and
calculating as anyone Paris had ever met, but in the end, she was simply
one of the nicest people Paris had ever known.

"How do you know?" Paris asked. "How do you know I won't drive
you away too?"

"Because I know you," London said. "The real you. Not the cast-iron
bitch you show the world. Not the High Guard warrior. *You.* And that
person—she's worth loving, Paris. She always has been."

Paris broke inside..

Not the wall—the wall stayed. The wall would *always* stay.

But, there, beneath it. Something she had been holding onto so tightly
that she hadn't realized how much it hurt until she finally let it go.

She threw her arms around London and hugged her for all of those myriad moments throughout their lives where London had been her sounding board, her confidante, her friend. She let it go. She broke down and let the moment be.

Her sobs were lost in the comfort of London's embrace.

They sat like that for a long time—Paris crying, London holding her, neither of them speaking. There was nothing to say. Words couldn't fix this. Only time could fix this.

If anything ever could.

Later, when Paris had cried herself empty and London had finally gone—with promises to check in tomorrow, and the day after that, and every day until Paris stopped looking like she wanted to die—Paris sat alone in the darkness of her quarters and made a vow.

Never again.

Never again would she let anyone get that close. Never again would she give someone the power to destroy her like this. She had survived the streets of Bristol. She had survived Dusk's cruelty and the Magistrate's tests and Dawn's constant antagonism. She had survived 135 years of being a monster in a world full of monsters.

She would survive this too.

But she would do it alone.

She would always be alone.

That was the price of survival. And Paris had learned a long time ago that survival was the only thing that mattered.

Never again.

CHAPTER 36

1962 The Citadel Age 82

Twenty-seven years.

Twenty-seven years of keeping everyone at arm's length. Twenty-seven years of building walls so high and so thick that even London—who knew her better than anyone—couldn't scale them. Twenty-seven years of convincing herself that she didn't need anyone, didn't want anyone, was better off alone.

And then Garrett turned the corner.

He was twenty feet away when their eyes locked. Paris's hearts thumped in her chest with the force of tribal drums—both of them pounding in furious synchronization, so loud she was certain he could hear them. Could smell the sudden spike of fear and want and something she hadn't felt in nearly three decades.

As if time had become overrun by amber, everything slowed. The corridor around her took on a hazy perspective, as if seen through a warped lens. The distant sounds of the Citadel—footsteps, voices, the ever-present hum of ancient stone—faded into white noise.

There was only Garrett.

As they drew closer, Paris realized she had never before encountered this sensation—this overload of sensory input. From an analytical perspective, it was quite fascinating. The way her pulse raced, the way her skin seemed to tingle with awareness, the way her breath came short and sharp despite no physical exertion.

From a personal perspective, she was scared shitless.

They stopped with only inches separating them.

Paris looked up at him as if seeing him for the first time. His brown hair was short but thick with waves that caught the torchlight. His eyes were the deepest of blue—almost navy in this light—with tiny gold flakes scattered around the edge of his irises like stars in a midnight sky. She had known him for nearly sixty years, had fought beside him, trained with him, shared countless meals and conversations and comfortable silences.

She had never really *seen* him until now.

"I needed time," she said after a few long moments. Her voice came out steadier than she'd expected, given that her insides were currently performing acrobatics.

"I understand." His voice was soft, with a husky edge that she did not remember hearing before. Or perhaps she had simply refused to hear it.

"You've the patience of Job."

"It wasn't easy."

Paris almost laughed at that. Twenty-seven years of him waiting—patient, constant, always there but never pushing. Twenty-seven years of her pretending she didn't see the way he looked at her, didn't feel the charge in the air whenever they were close. Twenty-seven years of using Thorne's betrayal as an excuse to never feel anything again.

"I have to be honest," she said, fighting back the tears that were suddenly, inexplicably welling up. "I'm unbelievably frightened of this."

"I understand," he said again.

With those two simple words, Paris realized that London was right. It had been right there in front of her the entire time, and she had been blind—completely ignorant of it. Or rather, she had refused to see it, because seeing it meant acknowledging it, and acknowledging it meant risking everything she had spent twenty-seven years protecting.

Garrett was the one.

He had always been the one.

"I'm an idiot," she said, finally breaking eye contact and hanging her head. The admission cost her something—some fragment of the armor she had worn for so long.

She felt his finger come gently up under her chin. She let him lift her face back into view.

"No." His voice was firm but tender. "You're amazing. You are who you are, and I love that about you." He broke into a wide grin and winked at her—that familiar, comfortable gesture she had seen a thousand times. "I always knew you'd come around."

"Why didn't you tell me?" she asked, wondering why he had waited in the wings for so very long. Why he had never pushed, never demanded, never given her an ultimatum.

"You weren't ready."

It was such a simple answer. Such a *Garrett* answer. He understood her in ways she barely understood herself. He had seen the walls she had built and recognized them for what they were—not rejection of him, but protection of herself. And he had waited, patient as stone, for her to tear them down on her own terms.

"I am now," she said, hearing the hoarse edge to her own voice.

For a moment, neither of them moved. The air between them was charged with some electric emotion Paris couldn't name—anticipation, perhaps, or the gravitational pull of two objects that had been circling each other for decades finally, *finally* colliding.

Then Garrett closed the distance between them, and his lips met hers.

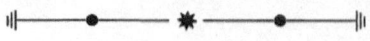

Later—much later—they lay tangled together in Garrett's quarters, the sheets a twisted mess around them and the false dawn beginning to lighten the sky somewhere outside the heavy-curtained windows. Paris's head rested on his chest, rising and falling with his steady breathing. His arm was wrapped around her, his fingers tracing lazy patterns on her bare shoulder.

"I should have done this years ago," Paris murmured.

"You weren't ready years ago."

"You keep saying that."

"Because it's true." His hand moved to her hair, threading through the light brown strands. "You needed to heal. To learn to trust yourself again before you could trust anyone else."

"And you waited."

"I would have waited forever."

Paris propped herself up on one elbow to look at him. In the dim light, his features were softened, boyish despite the centuries behind his face. "Why?" she asked. "Why me? There are dozens of women at the Citadel who would have been thrilled to—"

"Because it was always you." He said it simply, as if stating an obvious fact. The sky is blue. Water is wet. It was always you. "From the first time I saw you—this fierce little thing with fire in her eyes and a chip on her shoulder the size of Bristol—I knew."

"You're an idiot."

"Probably." He grinned. "But I'm your idiot now."

Paris laid her head back down on his chest, listening to the dual rhythm of his hearts. She had forgotten what this felt like—this warmth, this safety, this sense of belonging. She had spent so long convincing herself she didn't need it that she had almost believed her own lies.

"I'm terrified," she admitted quietly.

"Of what?"

"Of this. Of you. Of—" She paused, struggling to find the words. "The last time I let myself feel this way, he tried to kill me. He used me for eight years, and I never saw it coming. How do I know this isn't the same? How do I know you're not just—"

"Paris." Garrett's voice was gentle but firm. He shifted so they were facing each other, his hand coming up to cup her cheek. "Look at me."

She met his eyes—those blue depths with their scattered gold.

"I will never leave you," he said. "I will *never* betray you. Whatever comes, we face it together. Do you understand?"

Paris searched his face for any sign of deception, any hint of hidden agenda. She found nothing. Just truth. Just love. Just Garrett.

"I believe you," she whispered.

And the terrifying thing was—she did. For the first time in twenty-seven years, she trusted someone completely. She had let her walls crumble, had opened herself up to the possibility of pain.

But also to the possibility of joy.

"Make me a promise," she said.

"Anything."

"Promise me this isn't temporary. Promise me you won't leave. Won't betray. I couldn't survive that again."

Garrett took both her hands in his, his eyes never leaving hers. "Paris... Hear this and understand it. I am yours, now and forever. You are my priority. You will always be first in my mind. This is non-negotiable. Do you know why?"

She nodded slowly. The tears were back—happy tears this time, though she would die before admitting that to anyone.

My walls are completely down, she thought. And I don't care.

This was what love was supposed to be. Not the passionate intensity she had shared with Thorne, which had burned so bright and left nothing but ashes. This was something deeper. Something steadier. Something that felt less like fire and more like coming home.

"Come on," Garrett said, glancing at the window where the first hints of true dawn were beginning to show. "We should sleep. We have eternity for moments like this."

"Eternity," Paris repeated, testing the word. "I like the sound of that."

She settled back against him, letting his warmth surround her. For the first time in twenty-seven years, she felt at peace.

This is what it means to truly love someone, she thought as sleep began to claim her. Not the passion. Not the drama. Just this. Comfort. Safety. Joy.

I never thought I'd feel this way again.

But she did.

And she would spend the next fifty-two years grateful for every single moment of it.

CHAPTER 37

1962-1987   The   Golden   Years   Ages   82-107

1963

The Abode was full when Garrett appeared in the doorway.

Paris looked up from her book—she had graduated from *The Good Earth* to *To Kill a Mockingbird*, which Garrett had pressed into her hands with the insistence that she "needed to understand what the humans were grappling with"—and felt the now-familiar flutter in her chest at the sight of him. A year into their relationship, and the sensation hadn't faded. If anything, it had deepened.

"Ready?" he asked, that easy smile playing at the corners of his mouth.

"Give me a moment." Paris dog-eared her page—a habit that made Garrett wince every time—and stretched. Around her, the other Guards were engaged in their usual evening activities. London was sharpening her knives with methodical precision. Cairo had his nose buried in a newspaper, muttering about some news thing he called the "Cuban situation." Vienna and Dusk were playing chess in the corner, their game a silent battle of wills that had been ongoing for three days.

And Dawn was watching.

Not Paris—Dawn was watching Garrett. There was something in her expression that Paris had never seen directed at her: *respect*. Perhaps even a grudging warmth.

"Garrett," Dawn said, inclining her head slightly. "Taking our Paris out again?"

Our Paris. The possessive wasn't accusatory. It was almost... affectionate.

"If she'll have me," Garrett replied.

"She'd be a fool not to." Dawn's eyes flicked to Paris, and for a moment—just a moment—there was no hostility there. No competition. Simply one woman acknowledging another's good fortune. "Don't keep her out too late. We have training later."

"Wouldn't dream of it."

Paris rose, tucking her book under her arm, and crossed to Garrett's side. As they left, she glanced back and caught Dawn's expression—relaxed, content, in a way Paris had never seen when she was alone with the woman.

"She likes you," Paris said once they were in the corridor.

"Dawn? She tolerates me."

"No. She *respects* you. There's a difference." Paris threaded her arm through his. "I've never seen her like that around anyone else."

"We have history," Garrett said simply. "I trained her, centuries ago. Before she was High Guard."

"You never told me that."

"You never asked."

Paris filed the information away, adding it to the growing collection of things she was learning about the man she loved. Garrett had layers—centuries of them—and she was only beginning to peel them back.

"She's different when you're around," Paris continued. "Less... hostile. Toward me, I mean."

"Perhaps she sees you differently now."

"How so?"

Garrett stopped walking and turned to face her, his expression thoughtful. "Before, you were competition. A threat to her position, her standing, her sense of self. Now..." He shrugged. "Now you're settled. You belong to someone. In Dawn's worldview, that makes you less dangerous."

"I don't *belong* to anyone."

"I know that. You know that." He grinned. "But Dawn sees the world through a particular lens. Let her believe what she needs to believe, if it makes your life easier."

Paris considered this. It rankled, the idea that Dawn's acceptance of her was conditional on her relationship status. But Garrett was right—if it meant fewer hostile glares across the Abode, fewer cutting remarks during training, fewer moments of feeling like an outsider in her own home...

"Fine," she said. "But I'm not changing who I am for her approval."

"I wouldn't want you to." Garrett lifted her hand to his lips and pressed a kiss to her knuckles. "Now—dinner. I found a little place in Rome that does the most extraordinary carbonara."

"Rome? That's four hours by train."

"Then we'd better get moving."

1967

San Francisco was chaos.

Paris stood on a rooftop in the Haight-Ashbury district, watching the humans swarm through the streets below like colorful ants. The Summer of Love, they were calling it. Flowers in their hair, peace signs on their clothes, and enough marijuana smoke rising from the crowds to give even a Valensi a contact high.

"What do you think?" Garrett asked, settling beside her on the roof's edge.

"I think they're beautiful. And terrifying." Paris watched a young woman with daisies woven into her hair dance barefoot on the pavement, utterly lost in whatever music was playing in her head. "They have such capacity for joy. For connection. For—" She gestured vaguely at the scene below. "Whatever this is."

"Transcendence?"

"Maybe. But also self-destruction." She nodded toward a cluster of young men slumped against a building, clearly lost in something stronger than marijuana. "They burn so bright. And then they just... burn out."

"That's the human condition." Garrett's arm came around her shoulders. "They have such limited time. Perhaps that's why they feel everything so intensely."

"Do you ever miss it? Being human?"

It was a question she had never asked before—a question most Valensi considered rude. But with Garrett, she could ask anything.

"Sometimes," he admitted. "I miss the urgency. The sense that every moment mattered because there were so few of them." He was quiet for a moment, watching the crowds below. "But then I remember what I have now. The ability to see centuries of human history unfold. The privilege of watching them evolve—sometimes forward, sometimes backward, but always moving."

"And me?"

He turned to look at her, those blue eyes soft in the California twilight. "And you. Five years ago, I didn't have you. Now I do. That's worth a hundred human lifetimes."

Paris leaned into him, letting his warmth surround her. Below them, someone had started playing guitar—badly—and a group of humans had formed a circle, swaying and singing along to lyrics they were clearly making up as they went.

"What are we supposed to be doing here again?" she asked.

"Ensuring no Valensi exposure during the cultural upheaval."

"And have we seen any evidence of Valensi activity?"

"Not a trace."

"Then I suppose we could stay a little longer. For surveillance purposes."

Garrett chuckled and pulled her closer. "For surveillance purposes," he agreed.

They stayed until dawn threatened, watching the humans celebrate their brief, brilliant lives.

1969

The fear came back without warning.

Paris woke from a dead sleep, heart pounding, drenched in sweat. The nightmare was already fading—something about Thorne, about wooden stakes and betrayal and eyes she had once loved turned cold and murderous—but the terror remained, lodged in her chest like a splinter.

She reached for Garrett and found his side of the bed empty.

The fear spiked into panic.

Where is he where is he he's gone he left he was never real it was all a lie just like before—

She was out of bed and halfway to the door before rational thought caught up with her. She stopped, breathing hard, one hand braced against the wall.

Think, she told herself. Think, you idiot. Where would he be?

The bathroom door opened and Garrett emerged, toweling his hair dry. He took one look at her—wild-eyed, trembling, pressed against the wall like a cornered animal—and his expression shifted from confusion to understanding.

"Nightmare?" he asked quietly.

Paris nodded, not trusting her voice.

Garrett crossed to her slowly, the way one might approach a frightened horse. He didn't reach for her immediately—he waited, giving her time to settle, to recognize that he was here, that he was real, that he hadn't left.

"I woke up," she managed, "and you weren't there."

"I was in the shower."

"I know that. I know that *now*." She pressed the heels of her hands against her eyes, willing the panic to subside. "I'm sorry. I'm being ridiculous."

"You're not." He took her hands gently, pulling them away from her face. "Paris, look at me."

She did. His presence was steady, patient, full of nothing but love and concern.

"The fear doesn't go away," he said. "Not completely. Not after what happened to you. It will always be there, lurking in the corners, waiting for moments of vulnerability." He lifted one hand to her cheek, his thumb brushing away a tear she hadn't realized she'd shed. "But you don't have to face it alone anymore. When it comes—when the panic hits—I'll be here. Every time."

"What if you're not?"

"Then I'll find you." He said it with absolute certainty. "Wherever you are, whatever's happening, I will find you."

"You can't promise that."

"I just did."

Paris stared at him for a long moment. The fear was still there—it would always be there—but something else was there too. A feeling she wasn't sure she remembered.

Trust.

Not the naive, blind trust she had given Thorne. This was harder-won and more precious: trust built on seven years of evidence, seven years of Garrett being exactly who he said he was, seven years of him never once giving her reason to doubt.

"I believe you," she said.

And she did.

1973

They were on a rooftop in Prague when Paris realized she was happy.

Not content. Not satisfied. Not merely *okay*. Actually, genuinely, bone-deep *happy*.

The realization hit her like a physical blow. She was sitting with her back against an ancient chimney, watching Garrett read aloud from his battered copy of *The Great Gatsby*—his third copy; he kept wearing them out—and something in her chest simply... unlocked.

"'So we beat on,'" Garrett read, his voice soft in the pre-dawn darkness, "'boats against the current, borne back ceaselessly into the past.'"

He closed the book and looked up at the sky, where the first hints of false dawn were beginning to lighten the horizon.

"You really love that book," Paris said.

"It understands something most people don't. About longing. About chasing things that are always just out of reach." He turned to look at her, a smile playing at his lips. "Though I suppose I finally caught what I was chasing."

"Don't get sappy on me, old man."

"Old man? I'll show you old man."

He lunged for her, and Paris scrambled backward, laughing. They wrestled like children on the rooftop—all playful grapples and mock-serious holds—until Paris managed to pin him to the cold stone, both of them breathless and grinning like idiots.

"You let me win," she accused.

"Absolutely not. You're simply too skilled for me."

"Liar."

"Always." He reached up and tucked a strand of hair behind her ear. "But never about the things that matter."

Paris stared down at him—this man who had waited twenty-seven years for her to be ready, who had helped her rebuild herself piece by piece, who had never once asked her to be anything other than exactly who she was.

This is what love is supposed to be, she thought.

Not the wild passion she had felt for Thorne—that desperate, hungry need that had blinded her to everything else. This was calmer. Steadier. A fire that burned warm instead of hot, that gave light instead of consuming everything in its path.

"I never thought I'd feel this way again," she said quietly.

"What way?"

"Safe. Happy. Like I belong somewhere." She paused, then added: "Like I belong with someone."

Garrett's expression softened. He sat up, keeping her close, and took both her hands in his.

"You do belong," he said. "You belong with me."

She nodded, tears threatening to slip free.

"I do," she whispered.

My walls are completely down. Completely, utterly down.

And for the first time in her long, long life—she didn't care.

1979

They were in Moscow when the news came through: SALT II had been signed. The humans were trying, once again, to keep themselves from blowing up the world.

"Do you think they'll manage it?" Paris asked, watching Garrett scan the newspaper in their rented flat.

"Manage what?"

"Not destroying themselves."

Garrett set the paper aside and considered the question. "Honestly? I don't know. They've come close before—closer than most of them realize. But they keep pulling back from the edge at the last moment."

"Why?"

"Because for all their flaws, humans want to live. They want their children to live. And when it comes down to it, most of them will choose survival over ideology." He stretched out on the threadbare sofa, pulling her down with him. "The real question is whether they'll figure out the other ways they're destroying themselves before it's too late."

"Other ways?"

"The environment. Social inequality. The way they're burning through resources like there's no tomorrow." He shook his head. "For a species with such short lifespans, they're remarkably terrible at long-term planning."

"We're not much better."

"No," Garrett agreed. "But at least we have the excuse of having watched civilizations rise and fall before. We know that everything ends eventually. Humans haven't figured that out yet."

Paris nestled closer to him, listening to the steady rhythm of his hearts. Seventeen years they had been together now—seventeen years of moments like this, quiet and comfortable and utterly unremarkable. The kind of moments that didn't make stories but made a life.

"Do you ever think about ending?" she asked.

"You mean dying?"

"I mean... everything. The Valensi. The Citadel. This life we've built." She traced a pattern on his chest with her finger. "Do you ever think about what would happen if it all fell apart?"

"Sometimes." His arm tightened around her. "But then I remember that whatever comes, we face it together. That's what we promised each other."

"Together," Paris repeated.

"Always together."

1985

The mission went wrong in Berlin.

Intelligence had suggested a single rogue Valensi—young, recently turned, operating outside the established order. Easy extraction, they said. In and out.

Intelligence was wrong.

There were three of them, and they weren't rogues—they were soldiers. Trained, coordinated, and utterly ruthless. Paris realized this approximately half a second before one of them wrapped his hand around her throat and lifted her off the ground.

She clawed at his arm, kicked at his body, tried every technique she had learned in ninety years of combat training. Nothing worked. His grip only tightened, crushing her windpipe, cutting off her air supply.

Her vision began to tunnel.

This is how I die, she thought. In an abandoned warehouse in Berlin, killed by some nameless—

Garrett hit the rogue like a freight train.

Paris had seen Garrett fight many times over the past two decades. He was skilled, methodical, always thinking three moves ahead. He fought like a chess player—strategic, controlled, never wasting a movement.

This was different.

This was primal.

He tore the rogue off her with a roar that sounded nothing like the man she knew, hurling him across the warehouse with enough force to crack the concrete where he landed. Before the rogue could recover, Garrett was on him, raining down blows with a fury that was terrifying to witness.

Paris gasped for air, her throat healing, her vision slowly returning to normal. By the time she could stand, Garrett had already disabled the rogue—and turned to face the other two, who were circling warily.

"Paris." His voice was barely recognizable—rough, savage. "Can you fight?"

"Yes."

They moved together without needing to discuss strategy. Twenty-three years of partnership had made them more than teammates—they were extensions of each other, anticipating movements before they were made, covering weaknesses neither needed to articulate.

The fight was brutal and messy and far too close for comfort. But when it was over—when all three rogues lay neutralized and Paris and Garrett stood gasping in the wreckage—they were both still standing.

Garrett turned to her, his hands shaking as he reached for her throat. The bruises were already fading, but his fingers traced where they had been with desperate gentleness.

"I thought I lost you," he said. His voice cracked on the words.

"You didn't." Paris pulled him close, ignoring the blood and grime that covered them both. "I'm here. I'm alive."

"I can't lose you. I can't." He was holding her so tight it almost hurt, but she didn't pull away. "When I saw him choking you, I—I've never felt anything like that. This rage, this terror, this absolute certainty that if you died, I would—"

"I know." She pressed her forehead to his. "I know. I feel it too."

"You do?"

"Every time you're in danger. Every time I think I might lose you." She pulled back to look at him—this man who had torn through three trained Valensi fighters to save her, who was now trembling in her arms like a child. "We need each other, Garrett. I didn't understand that before. I thought love was about wanting someone. But it's not. It's about *needing* them. Needing them so completely that your survival becomes tangled up with theirs."

"Together," Garrett whispered.

"Always together." Paris kissed him—gently at first, then with increasing urgency. "Whatever comes, we survive it together."

"Whatever comes."

They stood in the ruins of the warehouse, holding each other as the false dawn began to lighten the sky outside. The mission was over, the rogues were neutralized, and they were both alive.

That was all that mattered.

1987

Twenty-five years.

Paris stood in the doorway of their shared quarters at the Citadel, watching Garrett pack for his next mission and she had already finished her own packing for the upcoming mission to Ghent. Cassandra would be joining her—one of Paris's closest friends besides London—and the assignment was relatively straightforward: investigate reports of unusual Valensi activity near the old belfry.

"You're staring," Garrett said without looking up.

"I'm appreciating."

"Appreciating what?"

"You. This. All of it." Paris crossed to him and wrapped her arms around his waist from behind, resting her chin on his shoulder. "Twenty-five years, Garrett."

"Twenty-five years," he agreed. He turned in her arms, pulling her close. "Any regrets?"

"Only that I wasted twenty-seven years being afraid before I let myself have this."

"You weren't ready."

"I know." She smiled up at him. "But I'm glad I got here eventually."

"So am I." He kissed her forehead, her nose, her lips. "So am I."

Outside their window, the eternal twilight of the Citadel stretched on as it always had, as it always would. But inside, in this room, with this man—Paris had found something she had never expected to find again.

Home.

Not a place. A person.

And she would spend the rest of her very long life grateful for every single moment of it.

CHAPTER 38

1988 Ghent, Belgium Age 108

"Haven't seen you in a while, girl," Cassie said as Paris met her in the hallway, headed to the cafeteria.

Paris smiled, unable to conceal her guilt for being incommunicado while Garrett was in the Citadel between assignments. He had only left again this evening.

"Sorry, Cassie," Paris replied.

They wrapped each other in a warm hug. Over the past couple of decades, they had grown closer—once or twice a month sharing a meal and conversation. Paris had found Cassandra to be a very interesting and worldly person. Funny and full of life. Still, there were times when Paris felt she was hiding something. Something dark. As she tended to do with friends, however, Paris decided to let her share that whenever she wanted to, if at all. Regardless of the abilities she now commanded, there was no reason to go delving into her friends' innermost thoughts and secrets.

"You have time for breakfast?" Cassie asked.

"Sure. I was headed that way." Paris hooked her arm in Cassie's and guided her toward the smell of food.

"So, how are things going?"

The question was left ambiguous, but Paris knew Cassie was asking about Garrett. She leaned into her friend a little. "It's going fine." She was shocked to find that she almost giggled like a schoolgirl.

"That's good to hear," Cassie said.

Again, Paris saw it. Behind the smile that didn't quite reach her hazel eyes. She forced herself to let it go.

They chatted about this and that, all the while wolfing down copious amounts of breakfast foods and fruit juices. Cassandra was heading out on a fact-finding mission for the Magistrate, so she was busy making sure all of her work ducks were lined up and ready to be without her for a little while. Paris knew she had a new assignment waiting for her back at the Abode, so they finished up and bid each other farewell with another warm hug.

As Paris watched her go, she noted how elegant Cassandra was. At least six inches taller than Paris, with long raven-black hair that was always beautifully straight and lustrous. She walked with the air of someone who had come from royalty—back straight, head high.

In Paris's estimation, her friend was quite a woman.

"Well, well," Vi commented upon Paris's arrival at the Abode. "Back from another honeymoon?"

Paris threw her a look but then decided it wasn't worth it. She had long accepted that Garrett was who she was with and would be with for as long as possible. No amount of ribbing could change her feelings now.

"Ready to rock and roll," Paris replied, blowing Vi a kiss, much to her dismay.

"What the hell happened to you?" Cairo asked, staring at her over a bottle of Jack Daniels. He was finally conversing with her in a civil and rather regular manner these days, and Paris didn't want to fuck that up.

"Nothing. Just in a good mood, I guess."

"That's perfect," Dawn chimed in. "Dusk, do we have something for little Miss Chipper here?"

"Why, we do indeed," he said in response.

"Anything not boring, I hope," Paris said as she leapt over the back of the sofa and landed with an elicited *whoosh* from the thick cushion.

"Oh, so boring," Dawn replied.

"The Magistrate has a special, easy-cheesy assignment for you," Dusk stated. "You get to play escort to none other than Miss Cassandra Dreys."

"Excuse me?" Paris said. After having seen Cassie, she remembered that she'd said she was going on a fact-finding mission. Still, this felt a bit odd.

"You know," Cairo said, "the Madge's squeeze?"

"Oh, for God's sake, stop calling him that." Paris frowned at Cairo, who only smiled and slugged back a rather large shot of whiskey.

"The man has specific instructions for you. Report to him at four o'clock today." Dusk then ignored her and ran through various other assignments with the others.

Paris sat pondering why Cassie would need an escort. *What kind of fact-finding mission was this to be?*

"Ghent?" Paris said, wondering why she was chosen for this rather mundane task. The Magistrate only nodded.

"Think of it as a short vacation," Cassie said, placing a hand on Paris's shoulder. "Ghent is a beautiful city. And one of the oldest in Belgium."

"I know it is a simple task, Paris. You are quite overqualified for such a task, admittedly. Yet, I value your service and talents, and Cassie could use the company. Consider it a personal favor from me." The Magistrate had never once in over a hundred years asked a favor of her. Paris found it ridiculous to even contemplate declining.

"Absolutely, sir." She turned to Cassie. "A little girl-time might not be a bad idea. I'll take good care of her, sir. I promise."

"I know you will, my dear. Thank you."

He turned away, and Paris struggled to keep the concern from her face when she heard his thought permeate her brain.

Stay alert.

The thought was not a request. Perhaps there was more going on than a simple meet and greet.

"I'm all packed and my people are set to handle things while I'm gone. We will leave tomorrow evening. We have a private plane set to go." Cassie began to guide Paris back out of the Magistrate's quarters.

"I'll be ready at six," Paris replied. She gave her a brief hug and made her way back to her room, all the while wondering what was going on.

Ghent was a gorgeous city. Old World. Very European.

They had arrived a day ahead of the meet, so they took the time to wander around the city center, taking in the sights. Paris had trouble keeping her thoughts free of distraction, and Cassie caught her lost in thought more than once. She apologized, blaming it on the beauty of their surroundings.

In truth, she couldn't shake the Magistrate's warning. *Stay alert.* What did he know that he wasn't telling them? What danger could possibly lurk in this peaceful, picturesque city?

The following evening, a little past sunset, they made their way to the Graslei. It was late summer and the weather was extraordinary. The buildings lined the waterway and people strolled along the edges and drank coffee outside the small shops. There was a feeling of warmth and freedom in the air, and it eased Paris's nervousness a little.

She did, however, keep alert for anything unusual.

"I've been here once before," Cassie said as they walked together toward the meeting place. The man they were to meet was a fellow Valensi and reportedly had some information that would serve the Hierarchy in some way. He was asking a price for the information, but it was not a hefty sum. Paris's understanding was that it was more to represent the value of the information than to set him up with riches.

"Really?"

"Yes. It was well over one hundred years ago. Before you joined us, I'm sure."

"What brought you here that time?" Paris asked, not sure if it was appropriate to pry. The question was innocent enough, yet Cassie hesitated.

"A man," she said finally.

"Ah."

"Ah, indeed," Cassie replied with a wink. "He was a mistake, but coming here was not. This city still holds the same charm as it did back then."

"Well, that says a lot for the city, doesn't it?" Paris said. Cassie nodded.

As they neared the meet site, Paris noticed the crowd had thinned out a little. Their contact was smoking a red pipe, as indicated he would. They approached slowly, but as soon as Paris saw the man, she relaxed.

Either he had been Birthed much later in his life than she would have guessed, or he was the oldest Valensi she had ever met. He looked to be in his early eighties—a little stooped at the shoulders and wrinkled as a raisin.

"I'm Franz," he said by way of introduction, reaching out to shake their hands. They each returned the old man's handshake. "You have what I asked for?"

"We do. And you, sir?" Cassandra asked.

Franz nodded and reached into his jacket pocket for a leather envelope, nondescript and relatively new.

"Inside is what I spoke to Livia about. Take care that it gets into the right hands."

The exchange was made. The man looked over at Paris.

"I probably should not ask, but how old are you, child?"

"Almost one hundred and ten. How about you, old timer?"

He laughed like a frog croaks, and it took Paris by surprise. "Older than you by far, my dear. But that is a tale for another time, perhaps."

He saluted them with his pipe and then turned and ambled away in the opposite direction.

"That was one seriously weird dude," Paris said.

She turned and found that Cassie was nowhere to be seen.

Paris's hand went instinctively to the knife at her hip. Her senses flared outward, scanning the crowd, the shadows, the darkened doorways—

"Looking for someone?"

Cassie's voice came from behind her, and Paris whirled to find her friend standing there with two cups of coffee, an amused expression on her face.

"Where the hell did you go?" Paris demanded, her heart still pounding.

"I saw a coffee vendor and thought you might want some." Cassie held out one of the cups. "You look like you could use it. You're wound tighter than a drum tonight."

Paris took the coffee, forcing her heartbeat to slow. "The Magistrate told me to stay alert. I'm staying alert."

"Did he?" Cassie's expression flickered—something passing behind her visage too quickly for Paris to read. "Well, I suppose it never hurts to be careful."

"Is there something you're not telling me, Cassie?"

The question hung between them. For a moment, Paris thought she saw in her friend's face... fear? Guilt? Something darker?

Then Cassie smiled, and the moment passed.

"Always so suspicious," she said, threading her arm through Paris's. "Come on. Let's enjoy the city before we have to go back to the Citadel and all its politics."

They walked along the Graslei, sipping their coffees and watching the humans enjoy the warm summer evening. Paris let herself relax slightly—but not completely. The Magistrate's warning still echoed in her mind, and the way Cassie had looked at her...

Something dark.

She had always sensed it. Always known that Cassie was hiding something. But Cassie was her friend—one of her closest friends. And friends didn't pry.

Besides, Paris told herself, everyone has secrets. That doesn't make them dangerous.

She would remember that thought later, when everything fell apart.

She would remember it, and she would wonder how she had been so blind.

CHAPTER 39

PRESENT

"Good," he said from the bathroom to her left. "You're awake."

Instinct kicked in.

Paris leaped to her feet, adrenaline flooding her system, the last of the fogginess slipping away like morning mist. She didn't think—couldn't afford to think. Thinking meant feeling, and feeling meant acknowledging who that voice belonged to, and acknowledging *that* would break her in ways the wannabe's torture never could.

So, she didn't think. She just moved.

The Protector emerged from the bathroom doorway, and Paris launched herself at him with everything she had—every ounce of training, every lesson from Master Asaro, every survival instinct honed over 135 years of existence. She was a whirlwind of fists and feet and fury, attacking with the desperation of a cornered animal.

Every blow she threw was deflected.

Every kick avoided.

She refused to look him in the eyes, knowing that if she did she might shut down completely. Nevertheless, she could feel his gaze upon her, and it was like someone had dropped an anchor on her chest. She found it hard to breathe.

Focus, she told herself. Breathe. Let the music swell.

Her dance began in earnest. She marked the first connection with his jaw—a solid blow, but far from enough to do any real damage. He rolled with it, absorbing the impact, and continued his retreat.

That was when she noticed it.

He hadn't thrown a single offensive strike. Not one punch. Not one kick. He was in a purely defensive mode—blocking, dodging, redirecting her attacks—but never, not once, actually trying to hurt her.

"Stop," he said, deflecting a cross to his temple. "Paris, stop."

She didn't stop. She couldn't stop. If she stopped, she would have to face the truth of who was standing in front of her—the man she had loved for over fifty years, the man who had promised to never leave her, the man who had apparently been sent to bring her back for execution.

He's not trying to hurt me.

The thought pierced through her battle-rage like a blade.

Why isn't he trying to hurt me?

She pressed her attack, driving him backward across the hotel room. A roundhouse kick that he ducked under. An elbow strike that he caught on his forearm. A knee to the midsection that he twisted away from at the last second.

And still he didn't strike back.

"Damn it, Paris—"

She caught him with a spinning backfist, snapping his head to the side. Blood bloomed from a cut above his eyebrow. He staggered, dropped to one knee—

And looked up at her. Those eyes with their tiny gold flakes around the irises. Those eyes that had looked at her with love for over half a century.

Paris's vision blurred.

No. No, not now. Not tears. Not fucking tears.

But they came anyway—hot and relentless, spilling down her cheeks despite everything she did to stop them. She stood over him, fists raised, body trembling, and watched through her tear-blurred vision as Garrett slowly rose to his feet.

He was propped on one elbow, staring at her with a truly pitiful expression. Her kick had cut him above his right eyebrow, and blood was trickling down the side of his face.

He didn't look like a Protector sent to kill her.

He looked like a man whose heart was breaking.

"You're here to kill me," she said. Her voice came out soft, broken. She wiped at the tears in her eyes, hating herself for the weakness.

"Then why did I save you, you idiot?" Garrett said. A smile formed on his bloodied face as he shook his head, looking at her with an expression that made her heart sink. She recognized that look. She had seen it a thousand times over fifty-two years—in moonlit bedrooms, on rooftops at false dawn, in the quiet moments between missions when they had nothing to do but hold each other.

Love. Pure, unconditional, unwavering love.

Paris fell to her knees.

"Why did they have to send *you*?" The words came out as barely more than a whisper. All the stress of the past week—past weeks, past *months*—crashed down around her like a wave. Rae's death. The vengeance. Dawn. London. The wannabe's torture. And now this—this final, cruel joke from a universe that had apparently decided she hadn't suffered enough.

Her shoulders slumped. Her throat burned with the emotion she fought so hard to hold back. Try as she might, she could not stop the tears, and that made her even more frustrated. She slammed her fist down on the carpet, if only for the momentary release.

"I volunteered," Garrett said. He was sitting up now, watching her with those heartbreaking eyes. "The Magistrate wanted you brought back alive. No one else could have done that, and they knew it."

"You think you're going to take me back alive?" Paris asked incredulously. "We're just getting started here, then."

"No." He held up a hand. "Paris. Damn it. Do you know nothing? After all of these years? A hundred fucking years and you act like you don't know me at all."

"What are you talking about? You're a Protector. I'm a fugitive. You've tracked me down. What the hell am I supposed to think?"

"You aren't supposed to think, girl. Don't you know that by now?"

"What?"

She was so confused. Here she was, saved from death by a man sent to bring her back to the gallows. Her thoughts circled in her head like vultures over a carcass. Nothing made sense. Why would he volunteer to bring her back? She thought he...

She sat back on her haunches and stared at him.

Garrett had always been the one consistency in her life. From the first time she'd met him, when she was but a child at the Citadel, to the decades she had spent in his arms. He was the one. He had always been the one.

Paris couldn't take her eyes from his. The pressure on her heart shifted, evolved—from fear and hate to the one emotion that represented this man, the one man in her life that made all others little more than pale imitations.

She didn't need to think. He was right.

She needed to feel.

Through her tear-blurred vision, she heard the words that saved her life.

"I love you, Paris. I always have. I always will."

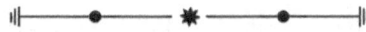

She leaped across the short space between them, falling into his arms, sobbing like a child.

She held him so tight that her arms began to ache. She refused to let go, and they lay there for nearly an hour—tangled together on the hotel room floor, breathing each other in, confirming with every touch that this was real, that he was here, that she wasn't alone anymore.

He stroked her hair and kissed her cheek, her forehead, her lips. He held her as she held him, as if they were trying to merge their souls once and for all.

"I thought I'd lost you," she whispered against his chest. "When I left France—when I had to run—I thought I'd never see you again."

"You couldn't lose me if you tried." His voice was rough with emotion. "Whatever comes, we face it together. Remember?"

"Together," she repeated. The word felt like a prayer. "Always together."

"Always."

They began to whisper in each other's ears—all the things they had been unable to say during the weeks of separation, all the fear and longing and desperate hope that had sustained them through the darkness. They spoke of what they each meant to the other. They spoke of their love.

Their hands and lips found their way to each other, and then they were on the bed, wrapped in the heat of love, of longing. Two people who had thought they might never touch again, rediscovering each other with desperate tenderness.

Time passed.

Later, lying tangled in the sheets, Paris traced lazy patterns on Garrett's chest. The cut above his eyebrow had already healed—Valensi regeneration working its quiet magic. Outside the window, the sky was beginning to lighten. They would need to find shelter soon.

But not yet. Not quite yet.

"What happens now?" she asked.

"Now we figure out how to keep you alive." His hand found hers, intertwining their fingers. "The Magistrate expects me to bring you back. When I don't..."

"He'll send someone else."

"Yes."

"Someone who won't be so gentle."

Garrett's jaw tightened. "Over my dead body."

"That's what I'm afraid of." Paris propped herself up on one elbow to look at him. "I won't let you die for me, Garrett. Not after everything we've survived."

"And I won't let you face this alone." He met her gaze—steady, certain. "We made a promise, Paris. Whatever comes, we face it together. I meant every word."

"Even if it means becoming a fugitive yourself?"

"Even if it means becoming a fugitive myself." He smiled—that familiar, warm smile that had been her anchor for over fifty years. "Besides, I've been meaning to take a vacation. The Citadel was getting boring."

Paris laughed—a wet, broken sound that was half sob and half genuine amusement. "You're an idiot."

"Your idiot," he corrected. "Now and always."

She laid her head back down on his chest, listening to the dual rhythm of his hearts. The world outside was dangerous—full of enemies who wanted her dead, a Magistrate she had betrayed, a future that looked increasingly bleak. But in this moment, in this bed, with this man...

She was home.

Whatever comes, she thought, we face it together.

It was the only truth that mattered.

CHAPTER 40

1995-2020 The Citadel & Various Locations
Ages 115-140

1995

The first time Paris noticed something different about London, she dismissed it as imagination.

They were in the Abode, sharing a bottle of wine after a long mission debrief. London had been quieter than usual during the meeting—not withdrawn, exactly, but distracted. Her attention kept drifting to the doorway, as if expecting someone.

"Everything all right?" Paris asked, refilling London's glass.

"Hmm?" London blinked, her attention snapping back to the present. "Oh. Yes. Fine. Just thinking."

"About?"

London was silent for a moment, swirling the wine in her glass. "Do you ever wonder if there's another way?"

"Another way to what?"

"To... this. All of this." London gestured vaguely at the Abode, the Citadel, everything. "The hiding. The secrecy. The constant fear of exposure."

"That's the life we chose," Paris said carefully. "Or rather, the life that was chosen for us."

"But what if it didn't have to be?" London's eyes met hers, and there was more in them Paris had never seen before—something feverish. "What if there was a way for our kind and humans to coexist? Openly?"

Paris laughed. "You've been reading too much science fiction. Humans would hunt us to extinction if they knew we existed."

"Would they?" London tilted her head. "All of them? Or just some? What if there were humans who understood? Who could help us integrate rather than—"

"Integrate?" Paris set down her glass, suddenly uneasy. "London, what's gotten into you?"

The fever in London's eyes dimmed. She smiled—that familiar, warm smile that Paris had known for over a century—and shook her head. "Nothing. Forget it. Just... philosophical musings. You know how I get after missions."

Paris did know. London had always been the thoughtful one, the one who questioned everything, who refused to accept easy answers. It was one of the things Paris loved about her.

So she let it go.

She shouldn't have.

2001

The world changed on September 11th.

Paris watched the towers fall on a television in a hotel room in Barcelona, where she and Garrett were on assignment. She watched the smoke and the fire and the tiny figures falling from windows, and she felt something she hadn't felt in decades.

Fear.

Not for herself—she was immortal, or near enough. But for her kind. For the Valensi. Because she knew what was coming.

"Increased surveillance," Garrett said, reading her thoughts without needing telepathy. "Security checkpoints. Biometric tracking. Facial recognition."

"The world is about to get a lot smaller for us."

"Yes." He put his arm around her shoulders, pulling her close. "It is."

When they returned to the Citadel, the atmosphere had shifted. The Hierarchy was meeting constantly, debating protocols and contingencies. The Magistrate looked older than Paris had ever seen him—worn down by the weight of what this new world might mean for his people.

And London was asking questions.

"How do we adapt?" she asked during a Guard meeting, her voice calm and measured. "The old methods won't work anymore. We can't just move from city to city, change identities every few decades. Everything is tracked now. Recorded. Stored."

"We do what we've always done," Dawn said coldly. "We survive. We adapt. We stay hidden."

"But for how long?" London pressed. "Technology isn't going backward. Every year, it gets harder. Every year, the margins get smaller. At some point, hiding won't be possible anymore."

"Then we'll deal with that when it comes."

"Or," London said, and her voice dropped, "we could start thinking about alternatives now. Before we're forced into them."

The room went quiet. Paris looked at her friend—her sister in all but blood—and felt that same unease she had felt six years ago in the Abode.

What alternatives? she wanted to ask.

But she didn't.

She should have.

2010

"Have you noticed anything strange about London lately?"

Garrett asked the question casually, as if it were of no particular importance. They were lying in bed after a mission—something routine, nothing dangerous—and his fingers were tracing lazy patterns on Paris's shoulder.

"Strange how?"

"The questions she's been asking. About High Guard protocols. About the locations of other Citadels. About our vulnerabilities."

Paris stiffened slightly. "She's always been curious. You know that."

"This is different." Garrett propped himself up on one elbow, looking down at her. "She asked me last week if we had contingency plans for widespread human awareness. What we would do if the humans developed weapons that could actually hurt us."

"That's not unreasonable. With all the technology they're developing—"

"She specifically mentioned 'organic compounds that could cause cellular destabilization.'" Garrett's voice was flat. "Paris, how would she even know to ask about that?"

Paris felt cold. She thought of Waltz, all those years ago in Germany. *They're researching our weaknesses. Wood, certain minerals, organic compounds—they're testing destabilization effects.*

She had dismissed it as paranoia then. Surely it was still paranoia now.

"London would never betray us," Paris said firmly. "She's my sister. In every way that matters."

"I'm not saying she would." Garrett's hand found hers, squeezed gently. "I'm saying... be careful. Pay attention. Something's not right."

Paris wanted to argue. Wanted to defend London with every fiber of her being. But deep down, in that quiet place where she kept the truths she didn't want to acknowledge, she knew Garrett was right.

Something wasn't right.

She just didn't want to see it.

2014

Paris followed London out of the Citadel one evening, telling herself it was concern. Not suspicion. Never suspicion.

London moved through the streets with purpose, her head down, her pace brisk. She wasn't being evasive exactly—she was moving like someone who didn't want to be stopped. Who had somewhere to be.

Paris kept her distance, using every surveillance technique she had learned in 120 years of service. She was good at this. One of the best. If London knew she was being followed, she gave no sign.

The park was small and unremarkable—a patch of green in a gray urban landscape. London sat on a bench and waited.

The man who joined her was human. Paris could tell immediately— the heartbeat, the scent, the way he moved. Middle-aged, well-dressed, carrying himself with the confidence of someone used to authority. A briefcase rested beside him.

They spoke for several minutes, too quietly for Paris to hear. Then the man handed London something—a flash drive, small and silver—and London handed him a manila envelope in return.

The exchange was professional. Practiced. This was not the first time they had done this.

Paris felt a piece of her crack inside her chest. She stayed hidden until the man left, then waited until London was alone again before stepping out of the shadows.

"Who was that?"

London didn't flinch. Didn't look surprised. She turned on the bench and looked at Paris with those caramel eyes that had been her anchor for over a century.

"An old friend," she said smoothly. "He helps with research."

"Research on what?"

"Patterns in human law enforcement. For protection." London smiled—but it didn't fully form. "You know how paranoid I've been about the surveillance state. I like to stay informed."

It was plausible. It was reasonable. It was exactly the kind of thing London would do.

And Paris didn't believe a word of it.

"London," she said quietly. "What's going on? Really?"

For a moment—just a moment—something flickered in London's expression. Fear? Guilt?

Then it was gone.

"Nothing's going on." London stood, brushing off her coat. "You're being paranoid, Paris. I thought Garrett was supposed to be the suspicious one."

She walked past Paris without another word, leaving her standing alone in the gathering dusk.

Paris should have pressed. Should have demanded answers. Should have reported what she'd seen to Dusk, to Dawn, to the Magistrate himself.

But she didn't.

Because London was her sister. And sisters didn't betray each other.

Did they?

2018

The questions came more frequently now.

"How would you respond if someone knew our weaknesses?" London asked one evening in the Abode. "Really knew them. Had studied them. Had developed countermeasures."

"I'd kill them," Paris said simply.

"And if there were too many? If it wasn't one person but an organization?"

"Then we'd kill the organization."

"And if the organization had resources? Reach? Positions of power?"

Paris looked up from her book. "London, what are you getting at?"

"Nothing." London's smile was brittle. "Just... thinking out loud. Academic interest."

But it wasn't academic. Paris could see that now—could see the careful way London phrased her questions, the specific information she was gathering. This wasn't idle curiosity. This was reconnaissance.

"There are people working on this," London said one night, and Paris's blood ran cold. "On the problem of Valensi-human relations. People with resources, reach, positions of power."

"What people?"

London caught herself. The mask slipped back into place. "Hypothetically. People *could* be working on it. Theoretically."

But the slip had been revealing. London knew something specific. Something real.

Paris didn't confront her. Didn't demand the truth.

She was too afraid of what the truth might be.

2020

"If anything ever happens to me," London said, "I need you to know something."

They were alone in Paris's quarters, sharing wine like they had a thousand times before. But something in London's voice made Paris set down her glass.

"What are you talking about?"

"Just... if something happens. If everything goes wrong." London looked as if she were about to cry. "Know that I thought I was helping. Everything I've done... I thought I was protecting us. Protecting all of us."

"London, you're scaring me."

"I know." London reached out, took Paris's hand. Her fingers were trembling. "I know I am. And I'm sorry. For everything. For what's coming."

"What's coming? London, what have you done?"

But London was already standing, already moving toward the door. "Nothing. Forget it. Just... remember what I said. Please."

She was gone before Paris could stop her.

Paris sat alone in the silence, her hand still warm where London had held it. She thought about following. About demanding answers. About dragging the truth out of her friend by force if necessary.

But she didn't.

Because deep down, she already knew. Had known for years. Had simply refused to see it.

London was involved in something. Something organized. Something dangerous.

And Paris had let it happen.

I'm as blind as I was with Thorne, she thought. I see what I want to see. I believe what I need to believe.

And it's going to destroy us all.

Looking back, after everything fell apart, Paris would recognize the patterns she had missed. The questions that were too specific. The meetings that were too professional. The rhetoric about "cooperation" and "alternatives" that had been building for decades.

London hadn't been curious.

She had been recruiting. Gathering intelligence. Building something.

The "human organization" wasn't some random group of paranoid conspiracy theorists. It was sophisticated. Resourced. Military-grade. It had been developing for years—possibly decades—and London had been part of it from early on.

HAWTHORN, they called themselves.

And Paris had been too blind—too loyal, too trusting, too desperate to believe the best about someone she loved—to see it coming.

Just like with Thorne.

Some lessons, it seemed, she would never learn.

CHAPTER 41

TEN DAYS AGO The Citadel Age 135

The summons came at sunset.

Paris was in her quarters, preparing for a routine patrol, when the knock came. Not Garrett's familiar pattern, nor London's casual rap. This was formal. Official.

She opened the door to find one of the Magistrate's attendants—a young Valensi named Foster, barely a century old, with the earnest expression of someone who took his duties very seriously.

"The Magistrate requests your presence in his chambers," Foster said. "Immediately."

"What's this about?"

"I wasn't told." But understanding flickered across Foster's face. And something that looked uncomfortably like pity. "Dawn is already there."

That was unusual enough to set Paris's nerves on edge. She and Dawn were rarely summoned together unless a significant event had happened. The last time had been the assignment to track Waltz in Germany, over a century ago.

"Let's get going, then."

She followed Foster through the winding corridors of the Citadel, her mind racing through possibilities. A mission. A crisis. A threat to the Hierarchy. None of those explained the strange tension in Foster's shoulders, the way he kept glancing back at her as if he expected her to bolt.

The Magistrate's chambers were deep in the heart of the Citadel, protected by layers of security both physical and psychic. Paris had been here many times over the decades—to receive assignments, to report on missions, to seek counsel from the man who had been something like a father to her since she was eight years old.

Tonight, the atmosphere was different.

Dawn was already seated when Paris entered, her posture rigid, her expression carefully blank. The Magistrate stood by the window, his back to them, staring out at nothing. He looked... diminished. Older than Paris had ever seen him, despite the centuries that should have made age meaningless.

"Sir?" Paris said carefully. "You sent for me?"

"Sit down, Paris." His voice was rough, scraped raw by whatever situation had dictated this meeting. "There's something you need to know."

She sat in the chair beside Dawn, acutely aware of the tension radiating from her partner. Dawn's jaw was set, her hands folded in her lap with white-knuckled precision. Whatever this was, Dawn already knew—and she was furious about it.

The Magistrate turned from the window. His steel gray eyes found Paris's, and she saw in them what she had never seen before.

Heartbreak.

"Here is what we know for certain," he said, his voice heavy with an exhaustion that went beyond the physical. "London has been working with Cassandra Dreys against the Valensi for some time."

The words hit Paris like a physical blow.

She felt her breath catch, her hearts stutter in their rhythm. *London. Cassandra. Working against us.* The two women she trusted most in the world outside of Garrett—conspirators. Traitors.

Beside her, Dawn made a small sound—not quite satisfaction, but close. Vindication, perhaps, for suspicions Paris had never wanted to acknowledge.

"As the director of vendor relations," the Magistrate continued, "Cassandra had access to multiple avenues of human civil services. Government contacts. Law enforcement connections. Intelligence networks. If anyone was in a position to use such external influence against us, it was her."

Paris's mind flashed to Ghent. To Cassie's smile that didn't reach her eyes. To the "something dark" she had always sensed but never pursued.

How did I not see it?

"From what we have gathered, Cassandra recruited London to her purposes some time back. Years, perhaps decades." The Magistrate's jaw tightened, and Paris saw the personal cost of those words written in every line of his face. Cassandra had been his lover. His confidante. His companion for longer than Paris had been alive. "They were working with a human organization. We don't yet know its full scope, but it appears to be sophisticated. Well-funded. Dangerous."

The questions, Paris thought. London's questions about resources, reach, positions of power. She wasn't theorizing. She was describing something real.

"London discovered, as we did, that their secret was going to come out," the Magistrate said. "It seems that for decades, Cassandra had been working against us—derailing our efforts, leaking information, positioning human allies in places of influence. We aren't certain for how long she had involved London in her activities."

Paris found her voice, though it came out barely above a whisper. "You don't think she could turn traitor, do you?"

The Magistrate fixed his gaze to hers. She knew he hadn't read her mind—her walls were up, locked down tight—but it didn't take telepathy to read her expression. The shock. The denial. The desperate hope that this was all some terrible mistake.

"I do find it difficult to believe, sir," Paris managed. "Cassie doesn't seem the type. Not to mention London, who has been a valued member of the Guard for as long as I have."

"It doesn't matter," Dawn stated, turning a cautioning eye to Paris. Her voice was cold, clinical—the voice of someone who had already made peace with what needed to be done. "We do as we're told. We will track them both down."

The Magistrate cleared his throat, catching Dawn's eye. Something passed between them—a warning, perhaps—and Dawn sat back, falling silent.

"Cassandra is dead."

The words hung in the air like smoke.

"The two of them attempted to escape the Citadel a few hours ago. I had Foster watching them." That explained the guilt in the young Valensi's eyes—he had been the one to end Cassandra's centuries-long existence. "He was able to intercept Cassandra. In the ensuing struggle, she was killed."

Cassie. Dead. The woman Paris had shared breakfast with, traveled to Ghent with, trusted without question. Gone.

Paris thought of Cassandra's elegance, her raven-black hair, the way she walked like royalty. She thought of the beach—the vision she had experienced while the wannabe tortured her—Cassandra's spirit warning her that the war was coming.

"London managed to escape."

Paris sat in stunned silence, trying to process what she was hearing. Where had all of this come from? How had she not known that her best friend was a traitor?

But she had known, hadn't she? Some part of her had seen the signs and chosen to look away. The meetings with humans. The specific questions. The cryptic warning: *If something ever happens to me, know that I thought I was helping.*

I thought I was helping.

"Paris." The Magistrate's voice drew her back to the present. He had moved closer, and now he placed a large hand on her knee, drawing her to look directly at him. "I have absolute faith in you. You have proven yourself unwaveringly loyal on far too many occasions to mention. However, knowing your relationship with London, I have to ask."

She knew what was coming. Knew it and dreaded it.

"Are you capable of putting aside your own personal emotions and beliefs in order to apprehend this fugitive?"

Paris understood why he phrased the request in that manner. It was to separate his personal beliefs and emotions, which must have been so much deeper and more confused than her own. He had loved Cassandra. Had shared his bed and his life with her for longer than Paris could comprehend. And now he was asking Paris to hunt down her own sister of the heart.

She sympathized with him. Remembered her own experience with Thorne—the betrayal that had nearly destroyed her.

Is this my curse? she wondered. To love people who betray me?

She nodded.

"Yes, sir. We will bring her back. Absolutely."

She could not contain all of the hurt in her voice, and both the Magistrate and Dawn easily picked up on it. Dawn's expression flickered—something that might have been sympathy, quickly suppressed.

"I'm sorry it has come to this," the Magistrate said. "I chose you for this mission due to your intimate knowledge of and friendship with London. You and Dawn have proven to be quite an effective team. I expect nothing but the best from the both of you, especially in this instance."

He sat back, crossing his long arms over his chest. His steel gray eyes looked them over—assessing, weighing, perhaps wondering if he was making the right choice.

"Just before she managed to slip out, I had someone watching her. They were smart enough to slip a tracker on her person. I don't know if she has changed her appearance or clothes, so the GPS may only get you so far. Regardless, it will be a start if nothing else."

He paused, and when he spoke again, his voice had hardened into something cold and official.

"Now, go. You have your orders."

They walked in silence through the corridors, Dawn slightly ahead, her stride purposeful and sure. Paris followed, her thoughts churning like storm clouds.

London. A traitor. How is this possible?

But even as she asked the question, she knew the answer. London had told her, in a hundred different ways, over decades of conversations. *What if there's another way? What if cooperation is better than hiding? What if we don't have to be enemies?*

Paris had dismissed it as philosophy. As intellectual curiosity. As the harmless musings of a friend who thought too much.

She had been wrong.

"Don't," Dawn said without turning around.

"Don't what?"

"Don't start second-guessing. Don't start making excuses for her." Dawn stopped and turned to face Paris, her expression hard. "I've watched you rationalize London's behavior for years. The questions. The meetings. The strange absences. You saw the signs and you chose not to see them."

"You don't know that."

"I know you, Paris. Better than you think." Dawn's voice softened, slightly. "You're loyal. It's one of your best qualities. But it's also your greatest weakness. You refuse to believe the worst about people you love, even when the evidence is staring you in the face."

Paris wanted to argue. Wanted to defend herself, defend London, defend the friendship that had sustained her for over a century. But she couldn't find the words.

Because Dawn was right.

"This mission isn't going to be easy," Dawn continued. "London knows you. Knows how you think, how you fight, how you feel. She's going to use that against you. She's going to appeal to your emotions, try to make you doubt yourself, try to convince you that she had good reasons for what she did."

"What if she did?"

Dawn's expression hardened. "There are no good reasons for betraying your own kind. No justification for working with humans against us. Whatever she tells you, whatever excuses she makes—remember that."

Paris nodded slowly. "And if she won't come quietly?"

"Then we do what we have to do." Dawn's hand moved to the knife at her hip—an unconscious gesture, but telling. "We do as we're told. We protect our own."

Our own. Paris thought of London's face, her smile, the way she had held Paris through the darkest nights after Thorne's betrayal. Was London no longer one of their own? Had she ever been?

"The tracker shows her moving toward Paris," Dawn said, pulling out a small device. "She's heading for France."

"Why France?"

"I don't know. But we're going to find out."

Dawn started walking again, and Paris followed.

She didn't know what she would find when they caught up with London. Didn't know if she could do what duty demanded. Didn't know if anything London said could possibly justify the betrayal.

But she knew one thing with absolute certainty:

Whatever happened next, nothing would ever be the same.

CHAPTER 42

EIGHT DAYS AGO
Paris, France Bassins du Champ de Mars Age 135

The Eiffel Tower loomed against the Paris sky like a sentinel of iron and light, its golden glow reflected in the still waters of the Bassins du Champ de Mars. At three in the morning, the park was empty save for a single figure sitting on a bench near the water's edge.

London.

Paris spotted her from two hundred meters away, her heart clenching at the familiar silhouette—the jet-black hair, the elegant posture, the quiet stillness that had always made London seem like she belonged to a different, more refined world.

"You take this side," Dawn instructed, her voice a cold whisper in the darkness. "I'll approach from the opposite. Let's see if we can make this as painless as possible."

Paris nodded and watched Dawn disappear into the shadows. She took a breath, steadying herself, and began her approach.

London didn't move as Paris drew near. Didn't flinch. Didn't make any attempt to run. She simply sat there, hands folded in her lap, watching the water with an expression of profound exhaustion.

Paris sat down beside her on the bench. For a long moment, neither of them spoke.

"I got farther than I expected," London said finally.

"What the hell is going on, Sarah?" Paris asked, using London's birth name—the name that only she was allowed to use. "We're supposed to take you back to face trial for treason."

London's expression flickered—surprise first, then something that looked like understanding. Without a word, she reached up with one hand, stared Paris in the eye, and pointed to her temple.

I got it.

Paris's mind slipped quickly and easily into London's. They had done this a thousand times over the decades—sharing thoughts, memories, secrets that words couldn't capture. This time was different. This time, London was showing her everything.

In a quick series of flashes, Paris saw it all.

The Magistrate's plans—not just for maintaining Valensi secrecy, but for something far more ambitious. Research into eliminating their vulnerability to sunlight. Infiltration of human power structures at the highest levels. A long-term strategy that would give the Valensi dominance over humanity, not through cooperation but through control.

She saw the organization London had been working with—HAWTHORN, they called themselves. Not a ragtag group of paranoid humans, but a sophisticated network with resources, structure and powerful members and leaders. People on both sides who wanted peaceful coexistence. People who believed there was another way.

She saw why London had joined them. Not out of hatred for her own kind, but out of love for what they could become. Out of hope for a future where Valensi and humans didn't have to be enemies.

There are so many who want peace, London's thoughts whispered through the connection. And so many who want war. The Magistrate is planning something terrible. Something that will destroy any chance of coexistence forever.

"Is that all true?" Paris said aloud, noting Dawn's approach from across the park.

London nodded, her caramel eyes bright with unshed tears.

Dawn arrived at that moment, settling onto the bench on London's other side. Her gaze swept over the scene—Paris's hand on London's knee, the intimate closeness of two friends who had been sisters for over a century.

"I figured someone would come for me pretty quickly," London said. "He didn't waste much time sending his best, did he?"

"So, you admit it?" Dawn's voice was ice.

"I admit nothing." London's shoulders slumped, her hands wringing in her lap. "I knew he couldn't let the truth get out. You're supposed to take me back? I'm surprised he didn't just send a Protector to kill me outright."

"I don't understand," Paris said, although she did. She understood everything.

"What is there to understand?" Dawn said. "We were assigned to come and get her, bring her back to the Citadel to face trial. That is what we will do. Simple as that."

"Dawn, do you not see what I see here? You don't even know the truth."

"What truth? I see a woman who is resigned to the fate set before her. That makes things simple." Dawn's eyes narrowed, her gaze shifting to Paris. "And I see you, sitting here holding her hand like she hasn't betrayed everything we stand for."

Paris felt London tense beside her. Felt the silent communication pass between them—*Run. When it starts, run.*

"London," Dawn continued, her voice dropping to a dangerous tone, "if you make things difficult for us, I might ensure you get back alive. But you might not be so sound. Do I make myself clear?"

"Dawn!" Paris said.

London only nodded. "It's okay, Paris. Today will be as good a day as any."

"A good day for what?" Paris asked, though she already knew the answer.

London turned her stunning face toward her, brushing back a strand of jet-black hair behind her ear. "Dying."

Paris focused on London, sending a thought into her mind: When I move, run. Don't look back. Don't stop for anything.

London nodded almost imperceptibly.

Dawn was more observant than most.

Her hand struck out with lightning speed—claw-like fingernails slashing into London's cheek as she twisted and followed with a vicious punch. The impact was devastating. London's head snapped back, bones cracking against the bench. She slumped sideways, unconscious.

"I always hoped I was wrong," Dawn said, standing and wiping the blood from her hands onto her pants. Her blue eyes bored into Paris with undeniable hate. "Still, I never trusted you. I always knew that your loyalty was only a mask. A survival instinct." She stepped over London's crumpled form, positioning herself between Paris and escape. "But you've just made a grievous error. One that will cost you your precious survival."

Paris was on her feet in the blink of an eye, falling into a fighting stance. "You don't understand. The Magistrate is the bad guy here."

"The Magistrate is our leader. Our protector. The one who has guided our people for millennia." Dawn's lip curled. "And you're nothing but a traitor who's been playing us all along."

"I can't let you take her back there," Paris said, the words were spit through her gritted teeth."

"And yet, you will," Dawn replied, waving her crimson-stained hand over London's unconscious body. "I have no orders to bring *you* back alive. I will be doing everyone a favor by eliminating one traitor and capturing another." A smile spread across her beautiful face—and Paris realized, with a chill, that the expression actually detracted from her beauty. She'd always thought Dawn was beautiful on the outside. Such a shame that wasn't the case for the inside as well. "You've accomplished nothing but your own destruction. A task at which I will take great pleasure in completing."

"Please don't do this."

The words came out before Paris could stop them. Not begging—she would never beg—but a final attempt to reach whatever humanity might still exist in the woman she had known for over a century. The woman who had trained beside her, fought beside her, served the Citadel beside her.

The woman who had once saved her life.

The memory surfaced unbidden—forty years ago, a mission gone wrong in Prague.

Paris had been cornered by a rogue Valensi twice her size, his hands around her throat, crushing the life out of her. She had been seconds from death when Dawn had appeared like an avenging angel, tearing the rogue away with a fury Paris had never seen before.

Afterward, as Paris gasped for breath on the cobblestone street, Dawn had stood over her with an expression Paris couldn't read.

"Why?" Paris had asked. "You hate me."

"We protect our own," Dawn had said simply. And then, so quietly Paris almost missed it: "I lost someone once. I won't make that mistake again."

It was the closest thing to vulnerability Dawn had ever shown her. The only glimpse Paris had ever gotten of the person behind the ice.

Now, watching Dawn's face twist with hatred, Paris understood that whatever had existed between them—whatever grudging respect, whatever reluctant kinship—was gone. Destroyed by the choice Paris had made when she looked into London's mind and saw the truth.

"You know," Dawn said, circling slowly, "I thought you'd finally turned a corner. All those years being so lovey-dovey with Garrett. I thought maybe you'd grown up. Settled down. Found your place." She cocked her head to one side like a confused bird. "But that was just cover, wasn't it? You've been a traitor all along."

"I've been loyal to the Citadel for over a century. I've bled for us. Killed for us. Given everything I had." Paris's voice cracked. "I *admired* you, Dawn. For all your cruelty, I admired your strength. Your dedication. This shouldn't be how it ends."

"It shouldn't," Dawn agreed. "But you made your choice." She settled into her fighting stance—the same stance they had practiced together a thousand times. "And now I'll make mine."

They launched themselves at each other.

Dawn was a dastardly fighter.

On more than one occasion over the decades, she'd put Paris on her ass, broken a bone, or flat-out knocked her unconscious during sparring. But this was nothing like sparring. This was life and death, with the Eiffel Tower as their witness and the dark waters of the Bassins reflecting their violence.

Their hands and feet flew in unerring combinations, both taking hits and returning the favor. It didn't take a genius to see that Dawn was faster. She wasn't quite as graceful, but she had a couple of inches on Paris and about ten pounds. She used it all to her advantage, the force of her blows causing Paris to retreat more often than she advanced.

From the corner of her eye, Paris saw London stir. Saw her rise unsteadily to her feet, blood streaming from her ruined cheek. Their eyes met for an instant—a lifetime of friendship compressed into a single heartbeat.

Then London was gone, disappearing into the Paris night like smoke on the wind.

Good. Run, Sarah. Run and don't look back.

Dawn noticed the escape but didn't pursue. Her focus was entirely on Paris now, blazing with decades of accumulated resentment.

"So tell me," Paris said, circling, trying to buy time for her screaming lungs to recover, "what did I ever do to you?"

"I spent so much time building my reputation. I was always his favorite before *you* showed up." Dawn's voice dripped with venom. "Then it was Paris this and Paris that. My God, how I've come to loathe the very sound of your name. I can't even bear being in this city anymore."

"You're jealous of me?" The exclamation took them both by surprise.

"Don't flatter yourself, asshole. I'm better than you. Always have been. You were just different. All shiny and new." Dawn's lip curled in disgust. "Well, today all of that changes. Things will go back to normal. Even better, probably. Today, I take my rightful place once again. After I finish you once and for all."

Dawn came at her with a flurry of punches and kicks.

Paris let the music rise in her mind—that internal rhythm that had guided her through every fight of her long life. Her body took hold of the beat, and the dance began in earnest.

Her hands snaked out, twice ripping into Dawn's face, tearing skin and splitting her lip. Her body twisted and turned, lifting and falling to avoid the majority of Dawn's attacks. She misjudged the timing once, and Dawn's nails ripped through her right ear, blood sluicing down the side of her neck.

They backed off and circled, both breathing heavier now. Paris could see the damage she had dealt—and vice versa. Her left eye was beginning to swell, and Dawn was taking advantage, attacking more from Paris's blind side.

Paris scanned the environment. Open ground surrounded them, with only a few steel benches bolted to the concrete. The Eiffel Tower glittered mockingly in the distance.

"You have no idea how long I've wanted to see which one of us would come out on top if we stopped holding back," Dawn said. That terrible smile spread across her face again.

"You mean you were holding back?" Paris teased, even as her mind raced to form a plan.

Dawn bolted toward her, shifting right, leaping up to use a bench as a launching point. The push-off from the metal seating accelerated her momentum. Paris heard the music swell in her head and responded—a deft turn, folding her body hands to toes, performing a graceful doubled-over pirouette that narrowly avoided the attack.

They faced each other again, both trying to determine their next moves. Paris's hearts were pounding, and she noted with cold clarity that Dawn appeared barely winded. For one split second, the thought crossed her mind that she might not survive this confrontation.

Then that deep-seated survival instinct kicked in. Her mind cleared. Focused.

"I always admired you, Dawn," Paris said, and even as she spoke, she knew it was true. For all of Dawn's ridiculous hatred, she had been a decent leader to all of them. "I'm sorry it has to end this way."

"I'm not," Dawn replied. "Let's get this shit over with."

Paris knew she had to time it perfectly. Even if it was perfect, the result might not be successful. Nevertheless, she stood up straight, allowing her thoughts to finish focusing, her breathing serving that effort.

Dawn saw the pause and took advantage.

She was only feet away when Paris let loose.

In their practice sessions, the Magistrate had taught Paris a skill she wasn't certain he had meant to—a laser-pointed mental attack, direct and devastating. She had never used it in combat before. Had never had cause to.

Until now.

With everything she had, Paris sent the attack directly into Dawn's mind.

The effect was immediate.

The scream erupted from Dawn with the force of a sonic boom. Her body was thrown backward, hands grasping at her head in desperation and pain. Those piercing blue eyes squeezed shut so tight her eyelashes disappeared, her mouth curled down in agony.

Paris kept the attack going, focusing her mental intrusion as much as possible. She knew it wouldn't last long—but with luck, long enough.

She moved in toward Dawn, ready to deal the killing blow.

Without warning, Dawn's eyes flew open. The scream transformed from anguished to furious. She was on Paris before she could react, slashing and punching with the desperation of a wounded animal. Her weight dragged Paris to the ground, and her fingernails—like the claws of an enraged bear—dug into the flesh of Paris's stomach.

Paris gasped in agony but maintained the mental attack, watching it continue to deteriorate Dawn's mind even as Dawn's body fought on pure instinct.

End this. End it now.

Paris reached up with both hands and drove her thumbs deeply, directly into Dawn's eyes.

Dawn screamed—a different sound now, higher and more horrified—and flew to the side, slapping at her ruined eye sockets. Blood streamed between her fingers as she thrashed on the ground.

Paris struggled to her feet. Blood seeped from the wounds in her stomach. It hurt to breathe—Dawn had managed to break several ribs with her final fury. Her left eye was swollen completely shut now.

But she was alive.

And Dawn was blind.

With her one good eye fixed on Dawn's terrifying rage, Paris circled around behind her. The benches. She needed the benches.

"I'll kill you!" Dawn screamed, swiping blindly at the air. "I'll kill you!"

Paris planted her feet against the bolted-down bench, using the stability to brace herself. Then she lunged forward, grasping Dawn's head in both hands.

"I'll kill you! I'll—"

The words cut off as Paris twisted with all of her might.

The snapping of Dawn's neck was the loudest sound Paris had ever heard.

Dawn crumpled.

But Paris knew—had seen it happen before—that even a broken neck might heal. Valensi were resilient beyond measure. If she left Dawn like this, there was a chance—small but real—that she would survive.

And if she survived, she would hunt Paris to the ends of the earth.

Tears streamed down Paris's face as she knelt beside the woman who had been her rival, her tormentor, her sister-in-arms for over a century. The woman who had once saved her life. The woman who had just tried to end it.

"I'm sorry," Paris whispered.

Then she grasped Dawn's head and wrenched it from her body.

The disintegration began immediately.

Paris had seen Valensi die before, but never like this—never someone she had known so well, for so long. Dawn's body crumbled in on itself, cells breaking down at an accelerated rate, flesh and bone and muscle collapsing into a greasy pile of ash.

Within seconds, there was nothing left but a stain on the concrete. As was Paris' life.

One hundred and thirty-five years of existence. Centuries of service to the Citadel. A lifetime of triumphs and failures and petty jealousies and hidden vulnerabilities.

Gone.

Paris stood over the remains, her body screaming with pain, her vision blurred with blood and tears. The Eiffel Tower sparkled in the distance, indifferent to the violence that had occurred in its shadow.

I can never go home. I no longer have a home.

She was a refugee now. A fugitive. Everything she had built over more than a century—her reputation, her relationships, her place in the world—had just disintegrated along with Dawn's body.

And for what?

For a friend who had already disappeared into the night. For a truth that might not change anything. For a choice she could never take back.

Paris drew herself up straight, ignoring the agony in her ribs and stomach and face. She looked down at the smear that had been Dawn—the woman who had hated her, envied her, saved her, tried to kill her.

Slowly, deliberately, she raised her hand to her brow in a final salute.

"Goodbye, Dawn," she said quietly. "We protect our own. I wish you'd understood that."

Then Paris turned and disappeared into the French night, leaving nothing behind but ash and shadows.

CHAPTER 43

PRESENT
Charleston Safe House Age 135

Paris stared at her reflection in the bathroom mirror, brushing away the tears that refused to stop falling. The young woman's face that stared back at her—eternally seventeen, frozen in time—seemed absurd given the weight of what she had lived through. What she was about to endure.

She imagined what she should truly look like at close to one hundred and forty years old. The thought was perverse enough to make her laugh out loud.

"You see something amusing?" Garrett asked, poking his head into the bathroom.

"An old woman," she said.

"Strange. That is not at all what I see." He threw her a brief wink, and then all happiness fled his face. "You ready?"

"No."

She couldn't stop herself from wrapping him in her arms one last time. They had made love earlier—slowly, desperately, memorizing each other's bodies as if they might never touch again. Because they might not. After tonight, everything would change.

"No matter what, Paris," Garrett murmured into her hair. "Please remember that I will always love you. Nothing will ever stand in the way of that. Even what I'm about to do."

She nodded against his chest, feeling the steady rhythm of his dual hearts beneath her cheek. He would be risking everything in this—his position, his reputation, his very sanity—while she would be running away. It felt wrong. She knew it was the only way, but it still felt as if she was betraying the one person in the world who would die for her.

And he just might, at that.

"How is this going to work?" She still hadn't let go of him.

"Well, first," he said, "you're going to have to leave."

"I don't like it." She loved the warmth of his breath in her hair as he laughed at that.

"Neither do I, my love. Neither do I."

"Seriously." She took a step back to look him in the eyes—those blue depths with their scattered gold flakes. The eyes she had trusted for over fifty years. "Are you sure this is going to work? What if he sees through it?"

"Don't worry. I've had to do it once before." Garrett's voice was steady, reassuring. "The old Yogi from whom I learned these techniques was not one for failure. He was one of the few who adapted the self-trance practices of the Yogi with the Reiki."

"Reiki?" Paris had heard the word before but was unclear of its meaning.

"Reiki is the Japanese technique for relaxation and stress reduction. It's used to promote healing. The Yogi had combined the two forms to produce an irrefutable method of self-hypnosis and self-healing. The auto-suggestion part is where I will be placing my emphasis."

"So you're going to convince yourself that you've killed me?"

"More than that." Garrett's expression grew somber. "I'm going to create and place an entire experience—finding you, trying to capture you, bringing you back to the Citadel for trial. You will have nothing of it, and we will fight. In the end, you will leave me no choice but to kill you."

Paris realized she was clutching the front of her shirt, the horror of such a scene cutting into her heart like a dull stone blade. Garrett came close and placed his forehead against hers.

"It will only be a self-induced memory. It won't be real."

"It will be real to you." Her voice cracked. "It'll be real enough that the Magistrate will see it and believe that I am dead. In your mind, I *will* be." She paused, her breath coming faster. "I'm not sure I can accept that— your believing that you've taken my life. It will be horrible for you, won't it?"

"You have no idea," he said, and she felt his body tremble for a second or two. "But I see no other way that you can be free and I can return to give you that opportunity."

Paris pulled back, a thought striking her. "Wait. I've heard of hypnotists giving their subjects an out—a word or phrase that, when spoken, can bring them out of the trance. Can't you incorporate something like that?"

Garrett was silent for a long moment, his brow furrowed in concentration. Finally, he began to nod. "It will have to be unique to you and me. Something I can remain blind to within the suggestion. It has to be something the Magistrate won't pick out if he searches my memories."

"Something mundane, but unique to us?"

They both stood there, thinking. Minutes seemed to pass. The weight of the silence pressed down on Paris as a physical thing—the knowledge that they were planning the erasure of everything they had built together.

"Tell me about the first moment you trusted me completely," Garrett said suddenly. "Not when you loved me—when you *trusted* me. Absolutely. Without reservation."

Paris quieted herself, letting the memories wash over her. So many moments. So many years. But one stood out above all others.

"The morning in Prague," she said softly. "On the rooftop. You were reading *Gatsby* at false dawn, and we were playing like children, and I realized..." She opened her eyes, meeting his gaze. "I realized my walls were completely down. For the first time since Thorne. And I didn't care."

"What did I say to you that night?"

Paris remembered. The words had burned themselves into her memory, branded there by the weight of what they meant.

"You said I belonged with you."

Garrett smiled—that familiar, warm smile that had been her anchor for over half a century. "That's it. That's the trigger."

"Just those words? 'You belong with me'?"

"Those exact words, spoken by you. When *you* say them, the compulsion will break. The false memory will dissolve, and I'll remember everything." He took her hands in his, his grip warm and steady. "The simplest things are often the strongest."

Paris felt tears burning again. "What if it doesn't work? What if the false memory is permanent?"

"Then we improvise." Garrett's voice was gentle but firm. "But this is our best chance. Our only chance, really."

She knew he was right. The Magistrate would probe Garrett's mind the moment he returned. If there was any deception, any hint that Paris still lived, they would both be executed. The false memory had to be perfect. Unassailable. Real.

"When you emerge from the trance," she whispered, "you won't know me. Won't love me. Won't remember any of this."

"No."

"You'll believe you killed me. The guilt will be crushing."

"Yes."

"Garrett, I'm so sorry. I'm so sorry that I—"

"Don't." He cupped her face in his hands, forcing her to meet his eyes. "Don't be sorry. This is my choice. I'd do anything to protect you, Paris. *Anything.* Including things you'd hate me for."

She remembered him saying those words years ago, after a mission where he had demonstrated the terrifying depths of his strategic mind. She hadn't fully understood then. She did now.

"I love you," she said. "I love you so much it hurts."

"I love you too. Even when I don't remember—even when I believe I've killed you—I will love you." He kissed her forehead, her cheeks, her lips. "That's the one thing the hypnosis can't touch. Love doesn't live in memory. It lives deeper than that."

They stood in the center of the bedroom, the curtains drawn against the coming dawn. Garrett had explained the process—the meditation, the trance state, the careful construction of the false memory. Paris would watch. Would witness the man she loved erasing her from his mind.

"I need to show you first," he said. "A test run. So you know what to expect."

He sat cross-legged on the floor, his back straight, his hands resting on his knees. Paris watched from the edge of the bed as his breathing deepened, slowed.

For several minutes, nothing seemed to happen. Then his face began to change—subtle shifts of expression, micro-movements that spoke of some internal process she couldn't see. His breathing became almost imperceptible.

Then his eyes opened, and he looked at her with an expression that stopped her heart.

Blankness. No recognition. No love. No memory of who she was or what they meant to each other.

"Garrett?" Her voice came out as a whisper.

For an eternal second, he simply stared at her.

Then he smiled. "Just testing. I'm still here."

Paris let out a breath she hadn't realized she'd been holding. But the test had shaken her to her core. For that one moment, she had seen what was coming—the emptiness where love used to live.

This could be permanent, she thought. *I could lose him forever.*

"Are you sure about this?" she asked, hating the tremor in her voice. "There has to be another way. There has to be—"

"There isn't." Garrett rose smoothly to his feet and crossed to her. "The Magistrate is too powerful. Too paranoid. If I return without proof of your death, he'll know. He'll search my mind, and he'll find the truth, and then we'll both die." He took her hands again. "This is the only way, Paris. Trust me."

"I do trust you." And she did. With everything she had. "I just... I can't bear the thought of you suffering. Believing you killed me. Living with that guilt."

"It won't be forever. Someday—maybe soon, maybe years from now—you'll find me. You'll say the words. And I'll remember." His voice softened. "I'll remember everything. And I'll spend the rest of eternity making it up to you."

Paris laughed despite herself—a wet, broken sound. "Promise?"

"Promise."

She kissed him then—long and deep and desperate, pouring everything she felt into that one point of contact. All the love. All the fear. All the hope and grief and terrible certainty that this was goodbye.

When they finally broke apart, Garrett pressed his forehead to hers.

"It's time," he said.

"I know."

He returned to his position on the floor. Cross-legged. Back straight. Hands on knees. Paris watched from the bed, her arms wrapped around herself as if she could physically hold herself together.

"When I enter the final trance," he said, "don't speak. Don't touch me. No matter what you see on my face. If you interrupt the process, it could... complicate things."

"I understand."

He nodded once. Then he closed his eyes.

Paris watched his breathing slow. Watched the tension drain from his shoulders. Watched the man she loved slip away into some internal space where she couldn't follow.

His face went peaceful first—serene, beatific. Then it began to change.

Pain flickered across his features. His brow furrowed. His jaw clenched. He was creating the memory now, she realized. Living through the false experience of hunting her, fighting her, *killing* her.

His hands clenched into fists.

His breathing became ragged.

A single tear escaped from beneath his closed eyelids and traced a path down his cheek.

Paris pressed her hand over her mouth to keep from crying out. Every instinct screamed at her to stop this—to shake him awake, to tell him it wasn't worth it, to find some other way.

But there was no other way.

This was love. Real love. Not the passionate intensity she had shared with Thorne, which had burned bright and left nothing but ashes. This was sacrifice. This was one person willingly walking into hell to keep another safe.

Garrett's face twisted with grief—the grief of a man who had killed the woman he loved. Paris watched him live through the worst moment of his life, a moment that had never happened and never would happen, and she wept silently for what they were both losing.

"I'm sorry," she whispered, so quietly she could barely hear herself. "I'm so sorry, my love."

After what felt like hours but was probably only minutes, Garrett went still. Completely, utterly still—like a statue, like a corpse, like something that had never been alive at all.

Then his eyes opened.

He looked at her, and Paris saw it—the absence. The emptiness where recognition should be. He was looking at a stranger.

"You should go," he said. His voice was flat. Professional. The voice of a Protector addressing an unknown fugitive. "The Magistrate will want confirmation of your death. I need to return to the Citadel."

Paris rose on trembling legs. This was it. The moment of separation. She would walk out that door and leave behind the man she loved, knowing that in his mind, she was already dead.

She crossed to him—slowly, carefully, as if approaching a wild animal. He watched her with wary confusion, clearly wondering why this stranger was moving toward him.

She stopped inches away. Close enough to touch. Close enough to kiss.

"You belong with me," she whispered.

For one terrible moment, nothing happened.

Then Garrett blinked. His eyes cleared. Recognition flooded back into his face, followed immediately by overwhelming relief.

"It works," he breathed. "Thank God, it works."

Paris threw herself into his arms, sobbing. He held her tight, his own body shaking with emotion.

"I had to test it," she gasped. "I had to know—before I left—I had to know you could come back to me."

"I can." He pulled back to look at her, his eyes bright with unshed tears. "Whenever you say those words, wherever we are, I'll come back to you. I promise."

"Then do it again." She stepped away from him, wiping her tears. "Do it for real this time. And I'll go."

Garrett nodded slowly. He returned to his position on the floor. Cross-legged. Back straight.

"When I wake," he said, "I won't know you. I'll return to the Citadel believing you're dead. The Magistrate will search my memories and find exactly what he expects to find." He met her gaze one last time. "But I will love you, Paris. Even when I don't remember. I will always love you."

"I love you too," she whispered. "Forever."

He closed his eyes.

And Paris watched the man she loved disappear into a false memory of her death.

When it was done—when his face had gone through all the terrible stages of grief and guilt and settled into that awful blankness—she rose from the bed. She walked to the door. She paused with her hand on the knob.

"Goodbye, Garrett," she said, knowing he couldn't hear her. Knowing that in his mind, she was already gone.

Then she opened the door and stepped out into the night, leaving everything she had ever loved behind her.

EPILOGUE

Fall was in the air, soon to arrive here in the south. The leaves had not yet begun to turn, but it would not be long—perhaps only days until the first colors began to show. I parked the car about a mile away from my destination, deciding that an approach on foot was a better plan.

The street was dark, only the light atop the pine post in the yard providing any illumination this late in the night. After several reconnaissance passes, I came to the conclusion that there was no one home.

Taking a chance, I walked up onto the front porch and knocked on the door. No answer. I was startled by a sound to my right and turned to find a gorgeous cat with luminous orange eyes staring at me. I recognized the breed—a French Chartreux, the eyes gave her away along with the rich blue-gray fur. It made sense, I supposed, since her owner was French as well.

"Hello, there," I said. "Are you the property owner here?"

I was amused at my own remark, but discovered a strange feeling upon seeing the cat sit down upon its haunches and look at me with a cock of its head. Out of nothing but sheer curiosity, I slipped into the cat's thoughts, trying to see if there might be a way we could communicate.

"Hello," it thought to me.

My eyes widened. This was no ordinary cat.

"Hi," I thought back. "What's your name?"

"Mimi."

"That's a nice name. So, where's your friend, Mimi?"

"You're welcome to wait. But I don't think she will be back before dawn."

A more interesting situation than I had thought. I walked over and sat down in the rocking chair next to the divan upon which Mimi sat. If there were anyone who might sympathize with my tale, it would be Brianna Van Demir.

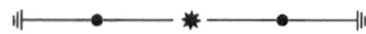

"You killed her?"

Brianna Van Demir's voice carried a weight I recognized—the careful cadence of someone who had learned long ago to measure every word. Her face appeared no older than forty, though something in her bearing suggested that was a generous underestimate by centuries. She sat with perfect stillness in the wingback chair, one hand resting on an antique pendant at her throat. A locket, worn smooth by decades of absent touches.

"That wasn't the plan," I said.

The woman beside Brianna—Daphne, she'd introduced herself as—shifted in her seat. Young, mid-twenties at most in appearance, with an anxious energy that seemed at odds with her surroundings. She couldn't quite hold my gaze, her eyes darting to Brianna every few moments. There was something unfinished about her, like a painting still drying. A fledgling, I suspected. Recently Birthed.

"I should think not," Brianna said. Her thoughts were closed to me completely—which raised questions I dared not ask aloud. In my experience, only the very old or the very trained could achieve such mental silence.

The third member of my audience sat apart from the others, positioned where he could see both the door and the windows. Ross. A man in his thirties, with the kind of face that might have been handsome before life hollowed it out. His hands trembled slightly as he held a pen over a leather notebook, though he'd written nothing yet. When I'd described my flight from the Citadel, he'd flinched. When I'd mentioned the violence, his jaw had tightened and his gaze had gone somewhere far away.

A hunter's eyes. I'd seen them before. This one had seen things he couldn't unsee.

"It's a rather convoluted tale, I'm afraid," I said. My audience sat in continued silence, urging me on with their attention. I noticed I was wringing my hands and forced myself to place them flat on my knees. The chair in which I sat was uncomfortable, but it seemed appropriate for the story I was about to share.

Mimi had settled herself on the arm of Brianna's chair. Those luminous orange orbs watched me with the intelligence I'd sensed when we'd first spoken mind-to-mind.

"I know I have to share this with you," I continued, "but you'll have to accept that some of it isn't going to be easy. I'm sure you can understand that."

Nods from Brianna and Daphne. Ross remained motionless, his pen hovering.

"I will say this." I drew a breath, steadying myself. "I regret nothing. All that I've done was what I had to do to survive. Whatever comes from this—whatever the future holds—I accept the consequences fully and without hesitation."

Brianna's fingers moved against her pendant. Daphne leaned forward slightly, and I caught a glint in her expression. Hunger—though not the kind I was most familiar with. A hunger to understand.

Ross finally wrote something in his notebook. His hand shook as he did it.

"I'm not quite sure where to start," I admitted. "So please, bear with me."

I took one last look at the three of them—the ancient one hiding in plain sight, the fledgling still finding her footing, and the broken man who knew too much about monsters. They wanted my story. They would have it. All of it.

I took a deep breath and launched into my tale.

I don't know how many hours passed. Time had lost meaning somewhere between my mother's murder and Garrett's final trance. When I finished speaking, I felt hollowed out, emptied of everything except the bone-deep exhaustion of confession.

Mimi had migrated during the telling from Brianna's chair to my lap. Her weight was warm and grounding, her rumbling purr a counterpoint to the heavy silence.

For a long moment, no one spoke.

Then Brianna leaned forward.

"In your position," she said quietly, "I might have done the same."

Something loosened in my chest. I hadn't realized how much I needed to hear those words until they were spoken.

"I killed a member of the High Guard," I said. "I chose a traitor over my duty. I—"

"You chose to see the truth." Her fingers moved against her pendant— the gesture I'd noticed throughout the telling, as if the locket held its own memories. "Those are not the choices of a traitor."

Ross stirred in his chair. "Thank you," he said. His voice was rougher than I remembered—scraped raw by whatever demons my story had awakened. "For telling us." He'd filled half his notebook with cramped, hurried writing. Now it sat closed on his knee. "It helps. Knowing others have faced impossible choices."

I nodded, sensing the weight behind his words without needing to probe his thoughts. This man had seen things. Done things. Carried guilt that had nothing to do with me and everything to do with whatever had put that haunted look in his eyes.

"You're not what you think you are."

The words came from Daphne—so quietly I almost missed them. She was looking at me with fierce conviction.

"I've met monsters," she continued. "Real ones. The kind that enjoy causing pain." She shook her head. "You're not that."

After 135 years as a Valensi, after everything I had done and seen and survived, this newly-made creature was offering me grace I hadn't asked for. The kindness of it brought tears to my eyes that I was too tired to fight.

"What happens now?" I asked.

The question hung in the air. The future stretched out ahead, uncertain and terrifying—a war brewing between my kind and the humans who had finally begun to fight back, a lover who believed I was dead, a mentor who wanted me destroyed, a best friend who had vanished into the night carrying secrets that could change everything.

Brianna rose from her chair with a fluid grace that belied her apparent age. She crossed to me, and for a moment simply stood there, looking down at me with that ancient, knowing expression. Then she extended her hand.

"Now we decide what comes next. Together."

I stared at the offered hand. Such a simple gesture. Such an impossible promise.

"Together?" The word came out as barely more than a whisper.

"Whatever is coming—and something *is* coming—you don't have to face it alone."

I thought of Garrett, living with the false memory of my death. Of London, somewhere out there in the world, still fighting for whatever she believed in. Of the Magistrate's plans, the sun-immune army, the political infiltration that would reshape the balance of power between Valensi and humans forever.

I thought of Cassandra's warning on the beach: *The war is coming. You'll have to choose. Your kind or theirs.*

Maybe there was a third option. Maybe there were others—like the people in this room—who refused to accept that war was inevitable. Who believed that coexistence wasn't just a dream.

Maybe I didn't have to choose.

I took Brianna's hand and rose to my feet. Mimi leapt gracefully from my lap, landing with a soft thump on the carpet. Ross closed his notebook and stood. Daphne moved to stand beside Brianna—the woman who had clearly become something to her that I couldn't quite name. Mother, perhaps. Or something more complicated.

We stood together in the fading light—a 1200-year-old exile, a traumatized hunter, a newly-born Valensi still learning to control her hungers, and a waif who had clawed her way up from the streets of Bristol to become one of the most wanted fugitives in the supernatural world.

An unlikely alliance.

Outside the windows, the first light of false dawn was beginning to brighten the sky. I would need to find shelter soon—the sun that had been my enemy for 135 years would not spare me simply because I had found allies.

But for now, in this moment, standing in a stranger's living room with my hand in hers and a telepathic cat at my feet, I allowed myself to feel something I had almost forgotten existed.

The story of the waif was far from over.

In many ways, it was only beginning.

A MOMENT

If Paris's story resonated with you, a review helps other readers find their way here. Every one matters more than you might think.

Thank you for reading.

THE VALENSI CHRONICLES CONTINUE IN

WIDOW

Spring 2026

She has hidden among humans for over a thousand years. Built a life. A career. A careful, quiet existence far from the violence of her past.

But the past doesn't stay buried. And when an old enemy resurfaces with obsession in his eyes and blood on his hands, she'll discover that the war between worlds has already begun—and neutrality is no longer an option.

The Magistrate is building an army. The humans are learning to fight back. And caught between them, a small group of survivors must decide what they're willing to sacrifice for a future worth living.

Paris's story was just the beginning.

STAY IN THE SHADOWS

Join the Studio Valensi mailing list for release dates, exclusive short fiction from the world of the Valensi, and the occasional dispatch from the darkness.

www.CLStegall.com/subscribe

Your email stays as secret as the Citadel.

MORE BY THE AUTHOR
THE VALENSI CHRONICLES

Novels

WAIF

WIDOW (Spring 2026)

WITCH (Summer 2026)

Short Fiction

"One Night in Hollywood"

"Blood and Amber"

For release updates and exclusive content, visit

www.CLStegall.com

ABOUT THE AUTHOR

C.L. Stegall spent a decade in U.S. Army Military Intelligence, a career that bestowed two gifts essential to fiction writing: an appreciation for secrets worth keeping and a finely honed ability to make things up convincingly. After ten years of service, he traded one set of classified documents for another—manuscripts—and hasn't looked back.

Now working under the Studio Valensi banner, CL writes across modern fantasy, contemporary thrillers, and horror, often blending genres in ways that keep readers guessing and slightly unsettled. His work explores the strange territories where myth bleeds into the mundane, where monsters wear familiar faces, and where the supernatural has paperwork and office politics just like everyone else.

Before fully committing to the writing life, CL served as President and Senior Editor at Dark Red Press, sharpening an editorial eye that now torments his own drafts through countless revisions. Because one creative pursuit is never quite enough, Studio Valensi also serves as home for original music demos—soundtracks for stories that don't exist yet and a few that do.

CL lives in Plano, Texas, with his wife Mona and a black cat named Shoyu who has never offered a single note on any manuscript but maintains an air of devastating literary judgment nonetheless.

When not writing, CL is likely deep in a research rabbit hole about mythology, obscure history, or something unsettling enough that his browser history could raise eyebrows. He maintains that all of it is "for a book," and this is technically true at least sixty percent of the time.

ACKNOWLEDGMENTS

It's rare that a novel is ever the work of one single person. We need eyes on. We need feedback to see if what we are trying to accomplish even makes sense.

Luckily, I've had an insane amount of luck for years with those who really connected with my characters in this tale.

This is set to be a trilogy, and the story has grown to unbelievable portions given the wonderful conversations I've had with so many people. Too many to name.

However, I would like to call out all my Army buddies from Panama who read the initial tale back in the early 90s. (Oh, my!)

Also, my lovely, irrepressible Wife, Mona, has been my sounding board for almost 30 years. Love you, babe!

Thank you, sincerely, to all who've had a hand in shaping Paris' story.

I hope you really love what plays out and how it plays out.

This is for you all!

www.ingramcontent.com/pod-product-compliance
Lightning Source LLC
Chambersburg PA
CBHW030514120726
47904CB00005B/1450